LITTLE TOWN,
GREAT BIG LIFE

CURTISS ANN MATLOCK

LITTLE TOWN,
GREAT BIG LIFE

Recycling programs for this product may not exist in your area.

ISBN-13: 978-0-7783-2788-2

LITTLE TOWN, GREAT BIG LIFE

For questions and comments about the quality of this book please contact us at Customer_eCare@Harlequin.ca.

www.MIRABooks.com

Printed in U.S.A.

First Printing: June 2010
10 9 8 7 6 5 4 3 2 1

This book is dedicated to all my readers—
to each one of you who has over the years bought and
enjoyed the Valentine series of books. For those of you
who have written me: your letters have touched me, inspired me,
given me smiles. Thank you from the bottom of my heart
for sharing my Valentine people and their stories.

I am grateful to my agent, Margaret Ruley, and to sisters-in-heart
Dee Nash and Deborah Chester for their guidance and support.

With this book, I say goodbye to writing my beloved Valentine.
It has been a fine, adventuresome ride, but now it is time to change
horses. It is, however, goodbye to the writing only. My characters are
so real to me—Winston, Vella, Belinda, Corrine, Willie Lee
and all the others—that I see them going on still in that small,
sometimes dusty town somewhere in southwest Oklahoma.
On quiet early mornings, I hear Winston's voice
over the radio..."Goood Mornin', Valentinites!"

PART ONE

Everybody's Dreaming Big

CHAPTER 1

Winston Wakes Up the World

IN THE EARLY DARK HOUR JUST BEFORE DAWN, a lone figure—a man in slacks and wool sport coat, lapels pulled against the cold, carrying a duffel bag—walked along the black-topped ribbon of highway toward a town with a water tower lit up like a beacon.

Just then a sound brought him looking around behind him. Headlights approached.

The man hurried into the tall weeds and brush of the ditch. Crouching, he gazed at the darkness where his loafers were planted and hoped he did not get bit by something. A delivery truck of some sort went blowing past. As the red taillights grew small, the man returned to the highway. He brushed himself off and headed on toward the town.

Another fifteen minutes of walking and he could make out writing on the water tower: the word *Valentine,* with a bright red heart. Farther along, he came to a welcome sign, all neatly landscaped and also lit with lights. He stopped, staring at the sign for some minutes.

Welcome to Valentine, a Darn Good Place to Live!

Underneath this was:

Flag Town, U.S.A., Population 5,510 Friendly People and One Old Grump, 1995 Girls State Softball Championship, and Home of Brother Winston's *Home Folks* Show at 1550 on the Radio Dial

Looking ahead, the man walked on with a bit of hope in his step.

The man would not be disappointed. The welcome sign pretty much said it all. Like a thousand other small towns across the country, Valentine was a friendly town that was right proud of itself and had reason to be. It was a place where the red-white-and-blue flew on many a home all year through and not just on the Fourth of July (as well as lots of University of Oklahoma flags and Oklahoma State flags, the Confederate flag, the Oklahoma flag and various seasonal flags). Prayer continued to be offered up at the beginning of rodeos, high-school football games and commencements, and nobody had yet brought a lawsuit, nor feared one, either. Mail could still be delivered with simply a name, city and state on the envelope. It was a place where people knew one another, many since birth, and everyone helped his neighbor. Even most of those who might fuss and fight with one another could be counted on in an emergency. The few poor souls who could not be counted on eventually ended up moving away. It was safe to say that most of the real crime was committed by people passing through. This exempted crimes of passion, which did happen on a more or less infrequent basis and seemed connected with the hot-weather months.

In the main, Valentine was the sort of small town about which a lot of sentimental stories are written and about which a lot of people who live in big cities dream, having the fantasy that once you moved there, all of your problems disappeared. This was not true, of course. As Winston Valentine, the self-appointed town oracle, often said, the problems of life—all the fear, greed, lust and jealousy, sickness and poverty—are connected to people, and are part of life on earth the world over.

It was true, however, that in a place like Valentine getting *through* life's problems often was a little easier.

In Valentine, a person could walk most everywhere he needed to go, or find someone willing to drive him, or have things come to him. The IGA grocery, Blaine's Drugstore, the Pizza Hut, the Main Street Café and even the Burger Barn provided delivery service, and for free to seniors or anyone with impaired health. Feeling blue could be counted as impaired health. When you needed to leave your car at the Texaco to have the oil changed or new tires put on, the manager, Larry Joe Darnell, or one of his helpers, would drive you home, or to work, and would even stop for you to pick up breakfast, lunch or your sister. When Margaret Wyatt's husband ran off and left her the sole support of her teenage son, people made certain to go to her for alterations, whether they needed them or not, and for a number of years every bride in town had Miss Margaret make her wedding and bridesmaids' dresses. It was a

normal course of events in Valentine for neighbors to drop gro-
ceries on the front steps of those on hard times, and for extra
to go into the church collection plates for certain families;
small-town people knew about tax deductions. Yards got
mowed, repairs made and overdue bills paid, often by that
fellow Anonymous.

And in Valentine, when an elderly man no longer had legs
strong enough to walk the sidewalk, and got his driver's license
revoked and his car taken away because of impudent daughters and meddlesome friends, he could still drive a riding lawn
mower to get where he wanted to go.

This good idea came to Winston Valentine after a fitful
night's sleep in which he had dreamed of his long-dead wife,
Coweta, and been left both yearning for her and relieved that
her presence had only been a dream. Their marriage had been
such a contrast, too.

Now in his tenth decade, Winston was a man with enough
experience to understand that life itself was constant contrasts.
He lay with his head cradled in his hands on the pillow, studying
this matter as he stared at the faint pattern caused by the shine
of the streetlight on the wall, while from the other side of it
came muffled sounds—creak of the bed, a laugh and then a
moan.

In the next room, the couple with whom he shared his
house—Tate and Marilee Holloway—were doing what Winston
had once enjoyed with his Coweta early of a morning.

Remembering, Winston's spirits did a nosedive. He was
long washed-up in that department. In fact, he was just about
washed-up, period, as Coweta had put forth in the dream. He
was ninety-two years old, and each morning he was a little sur-

prised to wake up. That was his entire future: being surprised each morning to wake up.

It was at that particular moment, when his spirits were so low as to be in the bottom of the rut, an idea came upon him with such delightful force that his eyes popped wide. A grin swept his face.

"I'll show 'em. I ain't dead yet."

His feet hit the cold floor with purpose. Holding to the bedpost, he straightened and stepped out quietly. Then, moving more quickly, he washed up and dressed smartly, as was his habit, in starched jeans and shirt, and an Irish sweater. Winston Valentine did not go around dressed "old," as he called it.

After a minute's rest in the chair beside the bedroom door, he picked up his polished boots, stepped into the hall in sock feet and soundlessly closed the door behind him.

He had forgotten his cane but would not turn back.

The hallway was dimly lit by a small light. The only bedroom door open was that of Willie Lee. Winston automatically glanced inside, saw that the boy had thrown off the blankets.

The little dog who lay at the foot of the bed lifted his head as Winston tiptoed into the room and gently pulled the blankets over the child, who slept the deep sleep of the pure in heart. When Winston left the room, the dog jumped down and followed soundlessly.

Gnarled hand holding tight to the handrail, Winston descended the stairs, knowing where to step to avoid the worst creaks. He located the small key that hung on the old rolltop desk in the alcove.

Then he went to the bench in the hall and tugged on his boots. Seeing the dog watching, he whispered, "Go on back up."

The dog remained sitting, regarding him with a definite air of disapproval.

"Mr. Munro, you just keep your opinions to yourself." Winston slipped into his coat and settled his felt Resistol on his head.

The dog still sat looking at him.

Winston went out into the crisp morning, closing the door on the dog, who turned and raced back down the hall and up the stairs, hopped onto the boy's bed and over to peer through the window. His wet canine nose smeared fog on the glass. The old man came into view on the walkway, then disappeared through the small door of the garage.

Munro's amber eyes remained fastened on the garage. His ears pricked at the faint sound of an engine. The small collie who lived next door came racing to the fence, barking his head off. Munro regarded such stupid action with disdain.

Moments later, a familiar green-and-yellow lawn mower came into view on the street, with the old man in the seat. Munro watched until machine and old man passed out of sight behind the big cedar tree in the neighbor's yard. The sound faded, the stupid collie lay down and Munro reluctantly lay down on the bed. All was quiet.

Winston headed the lawn tractor along the street. The cold wind stung his nostrils, bit his bare hands, but his spirits soared. He imagined people in the houses hearing the mower engine and coming to their windows to look out.

Halfway along the street, it came to him, as he noted the limbs of a redbud tree that had just begun to sprout, that only the calendar said spring. The morning was yet cold and everyone's house shut up tight. No one was going to hear him racing along the street.

Crossing the intersection with Porter Street, he hit a bump and had to grasp the steering wheel to keep from bouncing off the seat. He saw the newspaper headlines: *Elderly Man Ends Life Plowing Mower into Telephone Pole.*

But he was not about to downshift like some old candy-ass.

He kept his foot on the pedal and tightened his grip on the steering wheel. He wished he had thought of gloves.

He did slow when he came alongside the sheriff's office at the corner of Church and Main streets. Maybe Sheriff Oakes was in this morning.

No one came to the door, though.

Driving down the middle of the empty highway, he was forced to slow a little. His hands were growing weak on the wheel, the old arthritis getting the best of him. He turned onto graveled Radio Lane and bounced along until he finally came to a stop outside the door of the concrete-block building beside Jim Rainwater's black lowrider Chevrolet.

He had made it. And in all the distance traveled, nearly two miles, he had encountered no other person or vehicle. It was a deep disappointment.

He got himself off the mower, and was glad to have no witnesses. He moved like the rusted-up Tin Man. Inside the building, he might have leaned back against the door, but just then Jim Rainwater, coffee mug in hand, appeared from the sound booth. Winston brought himself up straight.

Jim Rainwater's eyes widened. "Well, hey, Mr. Winston. Whatta ya' doin' here so early?" Jim Rainwater was a tall, slim young man in his twenties, a full-blood Chickasaw, and of a solemn nature. In a worried manner, as if he had missed something important, he checked his watch. "You know it isn't even six?"

"Hey, yourself. I may be old, but I can still tell time. I got up early…what's your excuse?" He sailed his hat toward the rack, but it missed.

Jim Rainwater picked up the hat, saying, "I always get here by now."

"You need a life, young man." Winston shrugged out of his heavy coat. "I thought I'd start us an early-mornin' wake-up show."

"Now, Mr. Winston, no one has said anything to me about that. Have you worked it out with Everett or Tate?"

Winston's response to this was, "Why do you always call me mister?"

"Uh…I don't know."

"You don't call any of those other fellas mister."

Jim Rainwater gave a resigned sigh. "Mr.…Winston, what is it you want to do?"

"Aw, boy, don't get your shorts in a wad. I'm not gonna step on Everett's toes. He can have his show at seven, but we need somethin' before that. A lot of those city stations start mornin' shows at five. We're losin' audience share."

"This is Valentine, Mr. Winston."

"So it is, and it is time for a change. There's folks here that need wakin' up. I'll thank you kindly for a cup of coffee," he added as he made his way stiffly into the sound studio and dropped with some relief into his large swivel chair.

Jim Rainwater returned with the coffee. Winston sipped from the steaming mug that bore his name, stared at the microphone hanging over his desk and felt himself warm and his heart settle down.

"We'll start up on the hour," he told the young man.

★ ★ ★

Jim Rainwater shoved the weather forecast and a playlist in front of Winston. Slipping on his headphones, Winston positioned himself and adjusted the height of the microphone. He spoke in a moderate tone. "Testing…one, three, six, pick up sticks." Retaining his own front teeth helped Winston to come over clear, and Jim Rainwater corrected a lot of the graveling of his voice with electronics.

The hour hand hit straight up. The young man pointed a finger at him.

Winston put his lips to the microphone and came out with, "GET UP, GET UP, YOU SLEE-PY-HEAD. GET UP AND GET YOUR BOD-Y FED!"

Jim Rainwater jumped and grabbed his earphones. Dumbfounded, he stared at Winston.

For his part, Winston, imagining his voice going out over the airwaves and entering radios in thousands of homes of people just waiting breathlessly for him, continued happily: "It's six o'clock, 'n' day is knockin'. GET UP, GET UP, YOU SLEE-PY-HEAD! GET UP AND GET YOUR BOD-Y FED!"

CHAPTER 2

1550 on the Radio Dial
Joy in the Morning!

IN ACTUALITY, WINSTON'S ASSUMPTION AS TO THE number of listeners was quite overblown. There were perhaps only two-dozen people with their radios tuned to the small local station. In the main, these were those whose cheap radios could not pick up the far-off stations, and mothers and school-teachers who listened while they drank strong coffee and waited for Jim Rainwater to provide the weather forecast and school lunch menu, followed by an hour of uninterrupted guitar in-strumentals and alternative folk tunes of the sort that hardly any radio station played at any time, but which made a pleasant change from their little ones' Disney radio or teenagers' MTV.

At Winston's shout, at least two people raced to turn off their radios, and three to turn up the volume, wondering if they had heard correctly. More than one person had been in the act of something they would not want anyone to know about and were jarred out of it.

One normally dour wife and mother, Rosalba Garcia, smiled a very rare smile, stamped out her cigarette and proceeded to the beds of her husband and three teenage sons, leaning over each head and shouting the singsong tune, *"GET UP, GET UP, YOU SLEE-PY-HEAD!"*

Inez Cooper, an early riser who was working on an agenda for the next meeting of the Methodist Ladies' Circle, of which she was president, spewed her first sip of coffee all over her notes on that week's scripture lesson about seeking peace. She jumped up to go tell her husband what Winston had done. Norman was also an early riser and out in his workshop. Inez got another shock when she caught Norman smoking a cigarette, which he was supposed to have given up three years ago, when the doctor told him that he had borderline emphysema and high enough cholesterol for an instant stroke. Winston had just ruined Inez's morning all the way around. Norman wasn't happy with him, either.

Julia Jenkins-Tinsley, early forties and an ardent jogger, had just settled her headset radio over her ears as she headed for the front door. Her overweight and much older husband, G. Juice Tinsley, was sprawled in his Fruit of the Looms on the couch where he usually slept these days, snoring like a freight train, and she was sick of hearing it. Winston's voice hit Julia's ears as she stepped out the door. She had the headset volume turned up and was about struck deaf.

Winston hollered out his reveille again at six-fifteen, like the chime on Big Ben.

Just after that, the phone rang back at his own house, where

Corrine Pendley was already up and trying on her new, and first ever, Wonderbra, which she had bought, in secret, at a J. C. Penney sale, and viewing her sixteen-year-old breasts in the bra in front of her full-length mirror. At the ringing of the phone, she jumped, grabbed her robe and threw it around her as she raced to answer. In her mind, she imagined Aunt Marilee coming in and finding her in the bra. Aunt Marilee had ideas about what was age-proper, and she had been known to see through doors, too.

The caller was old Mr. Northrupt from across the street. "I want to talk to Tate!"

"Yes, sir," was the only reply to that.

Checking to make certain her robe was securely tied, Corrine stepped out into the hall and almost ran into Papa Tate heading into the nursery, looking all tired and with his hair standing on end, as he often did in the morning. Handing him the phone, Corrine went to take care of her tiny niece, who was climbing over the toddler bed rails. She could hear Mr. Northrupt's voice coming out of the phone. "Did you cancel my show? I think you could at least have told me. I didn't have to find out by hearin' Winston on there. Did you know he's on there? Well, he is. He's doin' a reveille."

Papa Tate calmed Mr. Northrupt down. "Winston's just playin' a prank. You still go on at seven." He had to repeat this several times in different ways. Then Papa Tate hung up and told Corrine that he had changed his mind about the fun of owning a radio station.

Across the street, Everett Northrupt was not appeased. He stomped around, mad as a wet hen. He was the host of the 7:00 a.m. *Everett in the Morning* show. He liked that his show came right after Jim Rainwater playing a solid block of instrumental music, of a respectable nature. It was a perfect intro to Everett's two hours of easy listening and intelligent commentary on the news and world at large. He considered his show an equal with NPR, and one of the rare venues in town for raising the consciousness of his listeners. Why, he had even interviewed by phone half a dozen state congressmen, one U.S. senator and a Pulitzer nominee (who happened to be station owner Tate Holloway).

Now old Winston was going to ruin all that. Winston stirred everything up with his rowdiness and wild musical leanings.

Emitting a few curses and condemnations as he pulled clothes from his neatly arranged drawers and closet, he woke his wife, Doris, who wanted to know what in the world was happening.

"It's Winston…that's who it is!" shouted Everett, jerking up his trousers. "Big windbag."

His wife said, "Well, for heaven's sake, shut up about it!" and threw a pillow at him.

Out at the edge of town, John Cole Berry was tiptoeing around his kitchen, attempting to slip out to a crucial early-morning business meeting without waking his light-sleeping wife, Emma, who was sure to want to make him breakfast. Emma thought food solved all problems. John Cole had just lifted the pot from the fancy stainless coffeemaker that Emma had recently bought, when some voice started yelling to get up and get his body fed.

Surprised, John Cole sloshed hot coffee all over his hand and the counter. He stared at the coffeemaker, a brand-new modern contraption that Emma had bought just the previous week, which did everything in the world, except make good coffee. It apparently had a radio in it. He went to punching buttons to shut it off. Why did a coffeemaker have a radio? Had Emma programmed it to say *get fed?* It would be just like her.

The radio, now playing music, shut off just as Emma called sleepily from the bedroom, "Honey…"

Grabbing his travel mug and sport coat, he slipped out the back door, leaving the telltale coffee spilled all over. He would tell her that he had missed cleaning it all. He could no longer see crap without his glasses. Somehow having the world by the tail at twenty-two had turned into the world having him by the tail at fifty-two.

Down in the ragged neighborhood behind the IGA grocery, seventeen-year-old Paris Miller, sleeping in the front seat of her old Chevy Impala because her grandfather had been on a drunken rampage the night before, had just turned on the car radio and snuggled back down into her sleeping bag. Her life was such that it was prudent to keep a sleeping bag in her car. All of a sudden a voice was shouting out.

Paris came up and hit her head on the steering wheel. Seeing stars, she fell back onto the seat, until, at last and with some relief, she figured out it was not her grandfather hollering at her. She thought maybe she had dreamed the yelling voice, because now Martina McBride was singing.

She snuggled back down into the warmth of the sleeping bag, dozing, until fifteen minutes later, when the yelling came out of the radio again. This time she recognized it as Mr. Winston's voice. She started laughing and about peed her pants. Mr. Winston was always doing something funny.

She had to get up then, and the cold made her really have to hurry. She raced across the crunchy grass, into the musky-smelling kitchen, hopped over an empty vodka bottle and on to the bathroom. Glancing in the medicine-cabinet mirror, she was dismayed to see a bruise, good and purple, high up on her cheek, where she had not been able to duck fast enough the previous evening.

Down at the Main Street Café, owner Fayrene Gardner, tired and bleary-eyed after a lonely night kept company by a romance novel, a Xanax and two sleeping pills, was just coming down late from her apartment. Her foot was stretching for the bottom stair when Winston's shout came crystal clear out of the portable radio sitting on the shelf above the sink, which happened to be level with her ear.

Fayrene popped out with "Jesus!" stumbled and would have plowed headlong into the ovens had not someone grabbed her.

Over at the grill, Woody Beauchamp, the cook, said, "Miss Fayrene, I'm gonna assume you's prayin'. We wouldn't want to give this visitor a poor impression, would we?"

Fayrene assured him that she had truly been praying. She was now, anyway, as she found herself gazing into the dark eyes of a handsome stranger, who had hold of her arm. *Dear God, don't let me make any more of a fool of myself in front of this handsome man.*

The dark-eyed stranger grinned a wonderful grin, and Fayrene wondered if she might still be dreaming. Those sleeping pills were awfully strong.

Across the street, at Blaine's Drugstore, which was on winter hours and not set to open for another hour, Belinda Blaine, who was not a morning person and not feeling well, either, was in the restroom peeing on a pregnancy-test strip. Somehow the radio on her desk just a few feet beyond the door, which she had not bothered to close, had been left on. (Probably by her cousin Arlo, when he had cleaned up the previous afternoon—she was going to smack him.) Hearing Winston's familiar voice within two feet got her so discombobulated that she dropped the test strip in the toilet.

"Well, shoot." She bent over and gazed into the toilet, trying to figure out the exact color of the test strip.

"Belinda? You in here?" It was her husband, Lyle, coming in the back door of the store.

She yanked up her reluctant panties and panty hose, while Lyle's footsteps headed off to the front of the store. The panties and hose got all wadded together. Her mother swore no one should wear panties with panty hose, that that was the purpose of panty hose. As much as she hated to ever agree with her mother, this experience was about to convert Belinda to the no-panty practice.

Snatching up the test-kit box, she looked frantically around but found no satisfactory place to hide it. She ended up stuffing it into the waistband of her still-twisted panty hose.

"Of course I'm here. I was in the bathroom, Lyle," she said as she strode out to the soda fountain.

Lyle was on his way back, and Belinda almost bumped into him.

She asked him where he thought she had been.

"Well, honey," he said, with a bit of anxiety, "I saw your car out back, but didn't see any lights turned on in front here, so I just wanted to check things out."

Lyle was a deputy with the sheriff's office next door. He had just gotten off night duty, and wanted coffee and to chat with her before he went home. Lyle listened to a lot of late-night radio when he was on patrol, which seemed to be encouraging morbid thoughts. Late-night talk shows were filled with a lot of conversation about scary things, such as UFO invaders, terrorist cells and, last night, the report of murderers who broke into the house of an innocent family up north and ended up killing them all.

Belinda, who made it a point to never listen to the news and really could have done without her husband telling her, ended up walking around with the test-kit box rubbing her skin while she got Lyle a cup of fresh coffee and tried to look interested in his report of world affairs and the idea of installing a security system at their home. Since she was already at the drugstore and had coffee made, she ended up opening early and got half a dozen customers coming in. At least Lyle had someone else to talk to, letting her off the hook.

All around a radius of the radio signal, roosters came out to crow, and skunks, armadillos and other annoying critters headed back to their dens, while early risers got up to let out the dog, let in the cat and look hopefully for the newspaper, which was often late. Word of Winston Valentine's wake-up reveille spread, and Jim Rainwater began to take call after call, and to keep a running total of for or against.

Out front of the small cement-block radio station, Tate Holloway, who had received a number of telephone calls, and Everett Northrupt arrived at the same time. Everett, a short, rather bent man, was in such a state as to forget that Tate was the owner of the station and therefore his boss, and to jostle him for going first through the door. A man with a good sense of humor, Tate stood back and waved the older man on.

They reached the sound studio doorway just as Winston put his mouth to the microphone for his final reveille.

"Gooood Mornin', Valentinites! This is your last call. GET UP, GET UP, YOU SLEE-PY-HEAD. GET UP AND GET YOUR BOD-Y FED!"

This time Jim Rainwater over at the controls played a symbol and drum sound, and he and Winston grinned at each other. Jim had more fun working with Winston than he did any of the other volunteer disc jockeys.

Winston saw Everett Northrupt glaring in the doorway. His response was to lean into the microphone to say, "Well, folks, we're leavin' you now that we've gotcha woke up. Stay tuned for my good friend Everett, who will ease you into the day. Join me again for the *Home Folks* show at ten, and until then, remember Psalm 30, verse 5—For His anger is but for a moment, His favor is for life; Weeping may endure for a night, but a shout of *joy* comes in the mornin'."

The men, all except Everett, chuckled.

CHAPTER 3

Belinda Blaine of Blaine's Drugstore and Soda Fountain

THE MORNING RUSH STARTED. TING-A-LING WENT the bell over the door. *Brrring* went the cash register.

"Mornin', Belinda. Hey, Arlo. Get up, get up, you sleeepy-heads! I'll take three lattes and two Little Debbies to go. Hurry up, I'm already supposed to be in Duncan."

"Just a large coffee this mornin'. Black. Get up, get up, you sleepyhead. Get up and get your body fed! Uhmmm…second thought—I'll take a honey bun, too."

"Hey, y'all. Get up, get up, you sleeeepyheads! Oran, you got my wife's prescription? I'll be back in a minute…wanna get a coffee."

"Two large Coca-Colas to go, and here, four packages of peanuts, too. I'm gettin' my body fed. You know, it'd be great if y'all would serve sausage biscuits."

"Whoo-hoo! Everybody get up, get up…and get your bod-y fed!"

"What is this all about?"

"Didn't you hear ol' Winston this mornin'? Well, he…"

Whatever happened in town, and of any interest anywhere, would be told and discussed first, or at least second, down at Blaine's Drugstore and Soda Fountain. Built in 1909, it had escaped two tornadoes, a small fire and been in continuous operation by the same family since its beginning in a tent during the land run. It had been written up in every insurance magazine in the state, been filmed for two travel shows, included as a backdrop in one movie and featured in *Oklahoma Today* magazine. The previous year Belinda Blaine had succeeded in getting the store on the state register of historic buildings. Now the building bore a bronze plaque that Belinda polished once a week.

The original black fans turned slowly from the tin-lined ceiling winter and summer, lemonade and cold sweet tea were still made from scratch and sundaes were still served in vintage glass fountain dishes at the original granite counter. Old Coke, Dr. Pepper, headache powder and tonic signs graced the walls, along with a number of autographed pictures of notable people who reportedly had dropped in, such as Governor "Alfalfa Bill" Murray and Mifaunwy Dolores Shunatona, Miss Oklahoma 1941 and the country-music stars the Carter Sisters, Hoyt Axton and Patsy Cline.

The Patsy Cline one was a fake. Fenster Blaine, who had been working all alone one day in 1962, decided to tear the photograph from a country-music magazine and sign it himself, and tell everyone that Patsy had come in. A number of people at the time had recognized his handwriting, but as the years had passed, the photograph remained on the wall and the truth was lost.

The store was a favorite hangout for teens after school and the first place that parents allowed their young daughters to go when beginning to date. It hosted Boy Scouts and Brownies, the Methodist Ladies' Circle and Baptist Women on a regular basis. Romances had begun, marriages had ended, business and political deals, large and small, had been struck, at least three holdups had happened, along with several heart attacks, fist-fights and two deaths.

Pharmacist Perry Blaine, Belinda's father, had been gone several years now, but a good replacement had at last been found in Oran Lackey, who could not only dispense modern medicines, like Viagra and Cialis, on an up-to-the-minute computerized system, but he also knew the ages-old art of compounding medicinals such as cough-suppressant lollipops and natural hormone creams, just as Perry had done. Because of this ability, the store was growing an ever-enlarging mail-order business and even made some veterinary medicines. They also carried vitamins, herbs and homeopathic remedies, all of which were coming back around in popularity.

Vella Blaine had installed Oran in the apartment above the drugstore, enabling him to be available day and night. Some people wondered why in the world Oran would take on such a job, when he could have gone with Walgreens over in Lawton and not had to work nearly so hard. Oran, who had been a medic in the army and gone through some tough times in Somalia and Afghanistan—fights hardly anyone back home knew about but which had left him with chronic fatigue and a bad limp—was a shy, solitary man who did not like the bustle of a large pharmacy. He came from Kansas City and had abso-lutely no family. He had found one when he came to Blaine's Drugstore. Not only the Blaines but the entire town needed and wanted him. He knew all of his customers by name, and was privy to many intimate details of their lives. He had on

numerous occasions saved people money and possibly from
death by his careful monitoring of their medications. He had
embarrassed quite a few doctors and made them hopping mad
because he found their mistakes. He had, very quietly and as only
Belinda knew, put one unscrupulous doctor out of business.

Most people had pretty much forgotten that Vella and Perry
had *two* daughters. Their eldest, Margaret, who had grown up
the favored and really beautiful one, had left town some
twenty-three years ago in the Ford Mustang her parents had
given her as a high-school-graduation present. She had gone
all the way to Atlanta, which she apparently considered far
enough away and where she had built a good career as a travel
specialist. Margaret had come home only three times. The last
time had been when Perry Blaine had died. She attended the
funeral and the reading of the will, got her inheritance in cash
and picked up a few mementoes her mother thought she
should have and left again, this time going all the way to a new
home in Miami.

Belinda was the daughter who had stayed. Except for a year
and a half away in college—she had quit during her sophomore
year—she had lived all her life in Valentine. This was not something she had planned, although she did say, and without apology,
that she never had desired to live anywhere else. She had begun
working in the store at nine years old. She thought it silly to go
out and struggle to find a job when she had a perfectly good one
handed to her. Belinda had never possessed much ambition, and
she was not ashamed of this. She considered herself a smart
woman, and found ambition highly overrated.

Belinda's keen intellect—she had surprised everyone by
being valedictorian of her graduating class and the second
highest in academics for the entire state that year—combined

with a blunt nature, had tended in her early years to discourage male attention. She had seen the unhappiness in her parents' marriage and calculated that her chances of following in their footsteps were high, so she felt she would do best to avoid such a union. Also, she did not care to change herself to accommodate a man, and this, as far as she could see, was the foolish thing that women kept doing.

Then one fall evening, as she was driving home, Lyle Midgette came by in his brand-new police car and pulled her over for speeding, and actually gave her a ticket. None of the other officers, not even the sheriff, ever gave her a ticket. Lyle was such a pleasant, even-tempered man that no insult she threw at him affected him. And even further, after that he went to following after her like a puppy dog.

Lyle had moved up from Wichita Falls to take the deputy position in the sheriff's office. He was a man dedicated to law enforcement, something of the complete opposite of Belinda, who lived by her own rules. He was also a Greek god in his tan deputy sheriff's uniform. The instant Belinda saw him, against all of her good sense, she had fallen into such lust as she had never known. For Lyle's part, he often said that the minute he laid eyes on Belinda, he fell in love.

Belinda asked him if he did not mind that she was of a womanly shape. He said straight out, "Oh, that's what I like. You remind me of my mother."

Another woman might have been offended. Belinda was practical. She asked to be introduced to his mother, who lived all the way down in Wichita Falls—another really good thing, as far as Belinda was concerned.

As it happened, Lyle was the only boy after four older sisters, who all spoiled him so much that he had not had to walk a step before the age of three. And his sisters, as well as his mother, were all full-figured like Belinda, which proved to her that humans were given to liking what they knew, just as she liked the drugstore.

At the time of their meeting, Belinda, having existed primarily within her mind, had little idea of her sensual, womanly side. That changed with Lyle's abundant attentions. She quickly came into full bloom. One day she found the Home Shopping Network, Delta Burke lingerie for womanly figures and Nina dyeable pumps, and her life changed forever. Valentine was fifty miles from a mall, but everything that you could want—and that you might not want others to know you bought—came right to Belinda via Buddy, the UPS driver.

As it turned out, having known and served most of her customers for all of her life, Belinda already knew their most intimate likes and dislikes. She began buying for them as well as for herself, and pretty soon she not only had a good personal shopping business going but was supplying the drugstore with all manner of unique specialty and gift items. She installed an entire perfume counter with locally hard-to-find scents such as Coco, Interlude and Evening in Paris. She stocked the favored brand and color dye for every woman in town who did her own hair, and every preferred shade of cosmetic and fingernail polish. The store's profits soared. Belinda discovered yet another talent—making money hand over fist, and with little effort at all.

Three years ago, Belinda had finally allowed Lyle to talk her into marriage. They had a small but lovely church ceremony, and in the end Belinda was secretly thrilled. But she insisted on keeping her own name. She felt to change would cause all manner of complications at this late stage of her life. Everyone

LITTLE TOWN, GREAT BIG LIFE   33

knew her as Belinda Blaine of Blaine's Drugstore and Soda
Fountain, not to mention that she was of a size to wear a DD
cup bra. The name of Midgette just did not fit her at all. It
didn't even fit Lyle, who was six-two, but one could not change
what one had been born with. One could only seek to make
the best of it.

When Winston came into the drugstore, everyone went to
clapping and cheering him.

Winston made a courtly bow. "Thank you...thank you. I
commend your good taste."

At his voice, Belinda laughed right out loud, so rare a happening that she received a number of curious looks.

Winston said, "I guess I accomplished somethin' this
mornin'. I got a full laugh out of Miss Belinda Blaine."

"Oh, yeah, you made me laugh," she said, with the image
in her mind of dropping the pregnancy-test kit in the toilet.

As Winston held court at his usual table, surrounded by a
knot of other gossipy old farts, Belinda brought him a cup of
coffee and a sweet roll.

When her mother had left on her European vacation, she
had said to Belinda, "The store and Winston are in your hands.
Don't let either of them die on me while I'm gone."

Her mother had meant it as a joke, but they both knew there
was a kernel of truth in the sentiment. The store and all who
came in it made up their lives.

The day became quite dreary, and the midmorning lull
started early. She had sent Arlo to the storeroom to unpack
boxes. All was silent from there. The low drone of the television sounded from the rear of the pharmacy.

Taking a feather duster, Belinda strolled along the health and intimate products section, whacking here and there, until she came to the pregnancy-test kits. She scratched the back of her head.

They had three different brands. It had been the $6.99 one that she had dropped into the toilet. The $9.99 product guaranteed to give easy-to-read results.

Could she read it in the toilet, should she drop it? She really hated flushing money away.

Just as she reached for the box, the bell rang out over the front door. She snatched back her hand as if from a flame and went to whacking the duster. At the end of the aisle, a familiar figure passed.

"Emma! Hey, girlfriend! What are you doin' out this mornin'?"

"I've got to get my hair color." Emma pointed at her head as if for evidence.

"Well, come on over and get a cup of coffee on the house," Belinda called, and headed for the soda fountain counter.

What a treat! Emma Berry was her best friend, although somehow the two of them had not seen much of each other the past winter. Emma was deeply into her art—she designed greeting cards and stationery that sold in the drugstore—and into her family, which had increased with a new daughter-in-law the past fall.

And things had just sort of changed, as things often did…but in that instant of seeing her friend, Belinda thought: *I will tell her.*

Emma brought the box of L'Oréal light ash blond to the cash register and dug money out of her purse with pretty manicured hands.

Belinda handed back change, saying, "Latte or coffee? On the house."

"Oooh, latte." Emma scooted her small frame up onto a stool at the counter. "I only like yours."

Belinda stuck a large cup beneath the aromatic, steaming machine, while Emma chattered on about needing caffeine because she had been up that morning since half past six, when, over the radio alarm in the new coffeemaker, she heard Winston shouting and then found out that John Cole was already heading off to work.

"Don't put any whipped cream on it. Did you hear Winston this mornin'?"

Belinda, who had paused with the whipped cream can pointed, said, "Oh, yes, I heard." She brought the steaming cup to Emma at the counter. Her thoughts were in something of a tangle, wondering why anyone would want a coffeemaker with a radio in it at the same time that she tried to figure out how to bring up the subject of her worries.

"I'm afraid he's gonna have a heart attack," Emma said. "Can I have a spoon?"

Belinda handed her one. "Winston? Well, we all are. He *is* ninety-two."

"No. John Cole. Really? I didn't know he was that old. He's workin' twelve- and fourteen-hour days…again," Emma added with pointed annoyance.

Belinda thought, John Cole…Winston…John Cole again. Conversation with Emma was apt to be a little convoluted.

"I've learned by now, though, that I cannot control him," Emma said, aiming for resignation, although she did not quite reach her mark.

Belinda agreed, and the two women tossed around comments about how everyone had their own lives to lead, the sort of practical statements that everyone knows but forgets when trying to help other people live their lives.

Then Belinda leaned forward on the counter. "I've been goin' to call you."

"You have?"

Belinda nodded, then found herself averting her gaze. "Uh-huh. I…" It was just silly. She should not speak of it.

Just then the bell over the door rang out. Both women looked over. If Belinda had not already stopped talking, she would have then, because the person who came in was Gracie Berry, Emma's daughter-in-law.

Emma waved and called out, "Hi, honey!"

Belinda felt her spirit dipping as she watched the women hug.

"We're drivin' down to Dallas," Emma told Belinda. "Gracie has a meetin', and afterward we're goin' shoppin'."

"Ah-huh," said Belinda, her gaze moving back and forth between the two women.

It was somewhat astonishing how much the women, not at all blood kin, favored each other. Emma was fair and Gracie dark, but they were of the same petite size, and possessed of the same sort of innocence and liveliness.

Belinda offered to put Emma's latte in a foam cup to go and asked if Gracie would like something to drink.

"Thank you. I think I would like a latte, too." Gracie had a very polite and precise way of speaking. She was from "up north," as everyone said, a beautiful, very stylish young woman.

Belinda turned to the rear counter and focused on carefully filling the foam cups and putting on the lids.

She waved away Emma's offer of payment. "You two have a great day."

"We will…thanks!"

Standing there with her hands flat on the counter, Belinda watched through the glass as the two women disappeared down the sidewalk. Then she gave a great sigh. She felt like a tiny speck on the great big planet.

Fayrene Gardner came blowing in the door, then paused to shake her plastic rain cape.

"Hi, Fay. Wet out there?"

As expected, the woman shot Belinda a frown. She hated the short version of her name.

"Hello, Belinda." Spine straight, she looked forward and flounced—there was no other way to describe Fayrene's walk—her skinny frame directly to the pharmacy counter, calling in a faint and wavering voice, "Oran?"

The lanky pharmacist came shooting out from the back. "Good mornin', Miss Fayrene. What can I do for you today?" he asked with such a tender and delighted expression that Belinda had to turn away, rolling her eyes.

Shy Oran loved bold Fayrene, who was way too dense to see it. Or if she did, she discounted the man's feelings. She never was interested in a quality man. Thank goodness, was Belinda's opinion. Occupying herself straightening the nearby perfume counter, she listened without any shame nor reaction to Fayrene's annoyed glances.

"I think I need…" Fayrene looked at Belinda and dropped her tone lower, causing Oran to lean over close. Belinda heard about every other word. "…to…off…sleepin' pills…some natural…I could…"

"Well, yes," Oran said soothingly and with some eagerness. Since he had come to work at the drugstore, he had been trying to help Fayrene, who kept getting dependent on one prescription drug after another.

Finding the sight of the two together annoying, Belinda left the perfume counter and went to the soda fountain register, opened it and began counting the cash, something she often did to settle herself.

Going out the door, Fayrene called out to Belinda, "When you speak to your mama, you be sure and tell her how much we *all* miss her."

"I'll do that." There were some people you just wanted to smack.

Only seconds on the heel of that thought came the sound of squealing tires and a scream.

Belinda hurried toward the door, but Oran was already ahead of her and sprinting outside with his paramedic bag swinging from his hand.

Belinda saw Fayrene's legs on the wet pavement and people coming from everywhere. She ducked back into the drugstore, got an umbrella and hurried out again to hold the umbrella over Fayrene and Oran and a man she did not recognize, who came from the café.

Talk about never a dull minute.

The phrase was repeated half a dozen times during the lunch hour. The conversation was now divided between Winston's morning reveille, the rain, which had entered the picture, and Fayrene getting hit by a car. Between making three chicken-salad sandwich lunches, four hot barbecues and a number of jalapeño-cheese nachos, Belinda downed two extra-strength aspirin for a headache that had reached pounding proportions. Glancing over at Oran, who was still sitting at a table drinking his second hot coffee, she shook two more aspirin into her palm, grabbed a small glass of ice water and took both to him.

"Doctor, tend thyself."

He had really been shook up. Luckily there had only been a tiny bit of blood on Fayrene's skinned knee, and Oran had been able to press a bandage over it almost without looking. Belinda thought the torn fabric of Fayrene's pants had shook him up the most. That and the handsome stranger who had come to lift Fayrene and carry her back to the café, leaving Oran staring after them.

Oran gazed at the pills in her hand as if he didn't know what they were, but then he took them. Handing her back the glass of water, he gave her a crooked grin.

As Belinda returned behind the soda fountain counter, a voice hollered out for service over at the pharmacy. She was relieved to see Oran's lanky body rise and hear him answer in an exaggerated drawl, "Keep your shirt on. This ain't New York City."

"Was Fayrene hurt bad?" asked Iris MacCoy, who was waiting on an order of half a dozen barbecue sandwiches and the same number of fountain drinks to take back to MacCoy Feed and Grain.

"No, ma'am," said Arlo, passing over two sizable cardboard carry containers. "I put in extra bags of potato chips."

Arlo's gaze lingered on Iris's chest, which was where most men's eyes lingered. Iris was a stunning woman. Belinda knew that Iris was over fifty years of age, and had more refurbishment on her than a 1960 Corvette.

"Well, I saw the whole thing," said Julia Jenkins-Tinsley, scooting her small frame up on a stool, sitting half on and half

off. Julia was postmistress and a woman who lived life in per-
petual motion.

"I had just come out of the P.O. on my way down here. The
car didn't hit her—Fayrene hit it. She ran right out in the street.
She had her hood up to protect her hairdo—you know how
she is about her hair. She was no more lookin' where she was
goin' than the man in the moon. She never is, and is always
crossin' in the middle of the block. Maybe this will teach her
a lesson. We have crosswalks for a reason. Here's your mail."

Julia passed a wad of mail held by a rubber band across the
counter to Belinda. "I saw you hadn't come by your box yet
today. I know you are just swamped here with your mother on
vacation. Thought you might want to see you got another
postcard from her, but she didn't really say anything. Just that
she's havin' a good time, and what she writes every time—*Love
to Valentine*."

Iris said, "That pavement is really slick from the rain. We
haven't had any all winter, and now it's just dangerous out there.
I about slipped comin' in here. And, Belinda, I just love your
reports from your mother. Please tell her I'm missin' her."

At this, Belinda gave a polite nod.

Iris gave her and then everyone else at the soda fountain a
feminine little wave as she left. The eyes of the three men
followed her, and old Norman Cooper, of all people, jumped
up and ran after her, saying, "Let me help you get all that to
your car, Iris."

Belinda found the postcard. It was an aerial photograph of
Paris, France. She took it over and stuck it on the bulletin
board, below the previous two, one from New York City,
another from London.

Julia, looking up at the menu on the wall as if she had not

seen it every day of her adult life, finally said, "I guess I'll have a chicken salad on lettuce, no bread, and a sweet tea with lemon—two slices. I can do the sugar. I jogged an extra mile this mornin'. Make it to go. I need to get back. Norris didn't come in today."

As Belinda turned to get the order, she noted that Julia's gaze dropped to her hips with a distinctive disapproving look. Julia went at keeping in shape as if it would give her a ticket to heaven.

Belinda knew that she had something Julia would never have: six years of youth, womanly breasts and total guilt-free eating of anything she wanted.

"Did you see that guy who picked up Fayrene and carried her back to the café?" Julia asked.

"I saw him, but I haven't heard who he is. Jaydee said he thought maybe the guy missed the bus to Dallas…that he saw him earlier in the café. Lucky for Fayrene." She glanced over to the pharmacy, where Oran was waiting on Imperia Brown, who had all three of her children down with the flu.

Julia said, "No…he's some guy Woody brought into the café this mornin'. Where Woody met him, nobody seems to know, and Woody won't say. You know how he can be—that in-scrutable old wise black man routine."

Belinda, closing the plastic container of chicken salad and resisting licking her finger, asked if the stranger had a name.

Julia eagerly filled in with all she knew. The man's name was Andy Smith, and he had a very cool British-type accent but was from Australia. Bingo Yardell had asked him. Bingo had also asked what had brought him to town, but he had been distracted working the counter and had not answered. "He knows how to brew a proper cup of tea. Bingo Yardell was in there havin' breakfast this mornin', when this woman came in off the Dallas bus and ordered a cup of hot tea. She made a big deal out of the café needin' to have china teapots, not those little metal deals. I have thought that, too, ever since Juice and I went to New York for his grocers' convention and stayed on the *concierge* floor. Every mornin' the hotel served a layout, and they had tea in china pots. It really does make all the difference. And this Andy fella was able to make the woman a *proper* cup of tea."

Belinda set the woman's foam cup of cold tea on the counter. "I doubt there's a large call for hot tea over at the café."

"That's what Fayrene said, but Carly said she serves it right often to customers over there in the cold months—mornin's like this one was, a cup of hot tea is nice. Tea has a lot of anti-oxidants." The postmistress put her mouth to the straw and sucked deeply, as if eager to get antioxidants that very moment.

"It's got somethin' everyone likes." Belinda cast an eye to the cold-tea pitcher. All the talk was making her want some.

"Well…" Julia laid the exact change on the counter and picked up her lunch. "I gotta get back. I'll be listenin' to your report this afternoon. I like to hear about your mother's trip. Be sure to tell her to keep writin' home…and tell her to write somethin' interestin' on the postcards."

"Wait a minute, and I'll give you her e-mail address so you can write her yourself."

"Oh, Lordy, I don't mess with that e-mail. I work for the U.S. Postal Service. You just tell her for me, 'kay?" The woman went out the door.

Belinda said under her breath, "I don't have another blessed thing better to do than send messages from ever'body and their cousin to my mother."

★ ★ ★

Nadine called with an excuse again. Her voice, as usual, came so faintly over the telephone that Belinda strained to hear.

"I'm sorry I missed the lunch hour, Miz Belinda. I had a flat tire."

"I really need you tomorrow, Nadine," Belinda said with a sternness that she hoped would motivate. She could fire the young woman, but a replacement was likely to be worse.

As she wiped up the counters and appliances, she heard in memory her mother's voice: *I am so tired of this store, you can just shoot me now.*

Belinda had never believed her mother when she said this. It had always seemed that the store was her mother's life. Both her parents had seemed happier at the store than anywhere else. It had been at home with family that all the problems went on.

Belinda, too, loved the store, and had for the past couple of years wanted her mother to turn over the full running of it to her. *Be careful what you ask for.*

She would have bitten her tongue off before admitting it, but after ten days of running it alone, she was thinking, *I am so tired of this store, you can just shoot me now.*

Belinda tossed her apron on the stool and headed for the storage room, where she found Arlo sitting, as she had known he would be, on a box, reading a comic book. He didn't bother to jump up, simply cast her a questioning expression. She told him to go take care of the soda fountain and that he needed to slice another lemon. Then she called him back and gave him the comic book he had laid aside.

Following him out of the storage room, she went to her office, which was nothing more than a partitioned area sandwiched between the back door and the restrooms. She had it fixed up nicely, though, framed art on the walls, and the most stylish in desks and computer setups—although the very day her mother had left for Europe, she'd had Arlo exchange her modern desk for her mother's old heavy one. This was the desk that had belonged to Belinda's father, and, before that, the two uncles who had founded the drugstore.

Now the desk belonged to her, Belinda thought, sitting herself behind it. At least until her mother returned.

The radio was already on from that morning. She turned the volume up slightly and pulled her carefully typed notes in front of her.

Each Wednesday, Belinda did a radio advertising spot for Blaine's Drugstore called *About Town and Beyond,* in which she told all the social news and light gossip, and ended with a health or fashion tip. The following Sunday, the same piece she gave over the radio would appear in print in the *Valentine Voice.*

Even Belinda, who was not easily surprised, was amazed at the things people would tell out of the great desire to hear their name on the radio or see it in the newspaper. It was curious that these same people would readily talk about the intimate details of a relationship to all and sundry, but would not for love nor money mention trouble with constipation. Speaking publically of sex was acceptable and speaking of constipation considered dirty. What a world.

Jim Rainwater's voice announcing her upcoming spot came over the airwaves, followed by an advertisement for the Ford dealership out on the highway. Belinda opened the desk drawer to get a piece of gum.

Her eye fell on her mother's package of cigarillos.

She hated it when her mother smoked them. But now

Belinda quite deliberately pulled out one of the narrow little cigars. She searched back in the drawer, finding a box of matches. She put the cigarillo between her lips, struck the match on the box and lit the tobacco, puffing expertly.

Belinda had smoked for a couple of years in her early twenties. She was one of those few very fortunate souls who did not get addicted. One time a cousin had done a study of the family and found that not one Blaine woman could ever be said to have had an addiction of any sort, excepting having the last word.

The cigarillo's pungent taste caused a few coughs, but she took another puff and blew out a good stream of smoke. She could see what her mother saw in smoking one of these.

Just then the telephone on her desk rang. Jim Rainwater said, "Ten seconds."

She brought her notes in front of her, turned off the radio and took one more good puff. Through the telephone receiver came the drugstore's theme music and Jim Rainwater's voice. "This week's *About Town and Beyond,* with Belinda Blaine of Blaine's Drugstore and Soda Fountain, your hometown store."

"Good afternoon, ever'one." Her voice was a little husky from the cigarillo. She liked it.

"This week over here at Blaine's hometown drugstore we have fifteen percent off all Ecco Bella natural cosmetics, a buy-one-get-one-free special on vitamin C for those late-winter colds and a superspecial of buy two little travel packets of aspirin and get a third free. Many of you may remember—my daddy used to say that there was no better a remedy than aspirin.

"Now, for our *Around Town* news. Willie Lee Holloway and his dog, Munro, took the title of Best in Show the past Saturday at the Women's Auxiliary Annual Community Dog Show, for the fourth straight year! I won't say who said it, but there was at least one jealous whiner who said Munro should step down.

"Munro, honey, you just go on competing as long as you are able. Don't let people who are jealous hinder you.

"And now, I'm sorry to give the news to the ladies, but our favorite UPS man, Buddy Wyatt, has become engaged. The fiancée's name is Krystal Lynn Howard, and she is manager at McDonald's on the turnpike and also attends junior college as a business major. The wedding is tentatively planned for late September.

"Ummmm…" For a moment, she found herself distracted by the cigarillo, for which she had no ashtray. "I want to assure everyone that Fayrene Gardner, who ran into a car this morning while crossin' Main Street in the middle of the block, only got a scraped knee, praise God. She was well tended by Blaine's own druggist and paramedic, Oran Lackey.

"Now, for *Beyond*. For those of you who may have been dead and escaped hearing, my mother is vacationin' in Europe, along with Lillian Jennings. Here is her latest letter home:

"Bonjour, mes amis,"

(A number of listeners were a little awed at Belinda's fluid pronunciation of the French; Belinda frequently watched a foreign language show on PBS.)

"We arrived yesterday afternoon at our destination at last. Things are different over here. I saw armed military at the airport. I'm talking machine guns…or whatever they are called these days. I could not decide if I felt more secure or worried that I might at any moment be gunned down. People are very friendly, though.

"My daughter Margaret did us proud—this place is as beautiful as she had promised. We are about fifteen minutes from Nice. That is Neece for those of you who may not know. It is on the Riviera, playground for the rich and famous. Oh, at the airport, Lillian thought she saw Frank Sinatra, but I kind of doubt it. How would we even recognize him at his age? Is he dead yet?

"The weather is real nice in Nice, slept under blankets but already getting warm today.

"*Au revoir,*

"Love, Vella Blaine, who does not wish anyone was here.

"That's it from Mama…. Now, I want to speak a plain word about constipation. Don't turn the dial. Ladies, regular eliminations of body waste is the best beautifier for complexion, hair and attitude. Increase your energy and your sexual stamina, too, by getting yourself regular. Come see me down here at Blaine's Drugstore, and I'll fix you up with some natural remedies. There is just no need to suffer.

"That's it from Blaine's Drugstore, providing the best of the old and the new, and we will always beat the big discount drugstores on price. Back to you, Jim."

"Thank you, Miss Belinda," she heard him say just as she clicked off, and in a tone that made her think he was red as a beet.

She saw she had dropped ash on the desk and remembered why she disliked smoking. It was just dirty. With relief, she found an ashtray in the rear of the center drawer, then relaxed back in the chair for a couple more puffs, since she did have it lit.

"You look like Aunt Vella, sittin' there." Arlo's head poked around the partition.

"I presume you didn't abandon the cash register just to make that observation." She vigorously tamped the cigarillo into the ashtray.

"Huh?" He looked confused.

"What did you want?"

"Oh. Yeah…Inez Cooper is out here at the herbs and vitamins. She wants to know if there's somethin' she could slip her husband to make him stop smokin'."

"Tell her I'll be right there." She tossed the package of cigarillos into the trash can, followed by the ashtray.

Passing the soda fountain counter, she told Arlo, "Soon as you get a chance, I want you to switch the desks back around. Put Mama's desk back in her place, and move mine back into my office."

She could tell she had confused him again.

CHAPTER 4

The Great Compromise

AFTER TWO DAYS OF TATE GOING BACK AND FORTH across the street between the houses of the two old neighbors and using all his negotiating skills, the matter was settled. Winston and Everett would share hosting of the new *Wake Up* show for an hour each morning. This could be managed mostly because Willie Lee would join them. Willie Lee's presence always encouraged people to be on their best behavior.

Corrine stood with her aunt Marilee in the yellow light on the front porch. Each with a baby on the hip, and each disgusted about the early hour.

"You all come right back after the show and get a proper breakfast," said Aunt Marilee. "And don't go eatin' a bunch of doughnuts. Remember your cholesterol, Tate…your sugar, Winston. Don't you make Willie Lee late for school."

Corrine, ever vigilant over her younger cousin, put in, "Somebody tie Willie Lee's shoestring."

To which Willie Lee hollered back, "I ca-n do it!"

Willie Lee and Winston exchanged looks. Winston well understood the boy. Willie Lee was mentally handicapped but not a baby, and not deaf, either—as so many tended to treat *him* in his old age.

Corrine and her aunt Marilee continued to stand and watch as the men and boy and dog got into the Bronco that Papa Tate already had warming up. Doors slammed. The Bronco went backing out, and then Aunt Marilee hollered, "Watch out!"

Although Papa Tate no doubt could not hear her with the windows rolled up, he had already slammed on his brakes, avoiding hitting Mr. Everett's Honda Accord backing out of his driveway so fast that the rear end bounced two feet when the tires hit the street. Then the Honda roared off ahead of the Bronco.

Aunt Marilee looked at Corrine, and Corrine looked back at her. With sighs, they went back in the warm house, turning out the porch light.

At the radio station, Everett had gotten into the sound studio and sat himself in the executive chair at the microphone. He cast a wave to Tate, who bid him good-morning.

Winston took note of the situation. There were two more rolling chairs, both smaller and against the wall. Winston had never sat in either. He was a big man, and required a big chair.

He turned and went to get a cup of coffee, then returned to stand in the studio doorway, sipping it. Everett studiously kept his gaze on some papers in front of him. Tate was leaning over and having a discussion with Jim Rainwater at the controls. Willie Lee had taken one of the chairs against the wall, as he usually did, with his dog's chin on his still-untied shoe. He grinned with some excitement at Winston, who shot him a wink.

A check of the clock. Two minutes to on-air.

"Tate…could I speak to you and Everett a moment?"

Tate turned. Everett sat there, blinking behind his glasses.

Winston said sweetly, "Just a minute before airtime, Ev." Tate turned his gaze to the other man, causing him to reluctantly get up and come out of the room.

"I just want to say thanks for the opportunity, Tate, and thanks for joinin' us, Everett. I know we're gonna have us a time." As Winston spoke, he eased himself around the men and slipped through the studio door, and headed directly for the big armchair at the microphone. In one movement, he plopped down and put the headphone to his ear with one hand, reaching for the microphone with the other.

"You dang…" Everett was beside himself.

"Thirty seconds," said Jim Rainwater.

Everett pulled one of the smaller chairs over and took hold of the microphone. Winston did not let go. The two glared at each other. Tate threw up his hands and walked out.

Jim Rainwater counted, "Five…four…three…two…you're… *on.*" His finger pointed.

Winston jerked the microphone toward him. "Goooood mornin', Valentinites! Rise and shine. GET UP, GET UP, YOU SLEE-PY-HEAD. GET UP AND GET YOUR BOD-Y FED!"

For the last part, Everett joined in, his face jutted so close to Winston that they about rubbed whiskers. The result was the call coming out sort of like an echo: "GET-et YOUR-or BOD-od-Y-ee FED-ed!"

"You're listenin' to the *Wake Up* call with Winston…"

"And Everett!"

"And Willie Lee and Munro!" Willie Lee had squeezed in between the two old men. Munro let out a bark.

"Wa-ake UP, ev-ery-bod-y!" said Willie Lee happily, followed by another bark from Munro and Jim Rainwater's sound track of a trumpet playing reveille.

The audience share had increased tenfold over the past two days as word had spread about the reveille and the feud. People all over town tuned in just to hear the amazing *Wake Up* call from one—now four—of their own. Truckers picked up the radio out on the highway, and there were even a few listeners from as far away as Kansas and West Texas, people who experienced the early-morning show out of Valentine via skips in the signal.

Many listeners had their radio volumes turned up in order to join in with the reveille. The Dallas route bus driver, Cleon Salazar, was one of these. He sang out, helping to wake himself up and jarring a number of his dozing passengers.

Deputy Lyle Midgette, a perpetually cheerful soul, also joined in, repeating the words at the top of his voice as he drove home, windows wide and cold air snatching his breath.

Woody Beauchamp, an equally cheerful soul, reached over the pan of hot biscuits just in time to turn up the volume on the radio and holler out. His new friend, Andy Smith, jumped and almost fell back out the door, while upstairs in her bathroom, Fayrene Gardner stamped on the floor.

Rosalba Garcia stood ready with a pot lid and wooden spoon. At the yell from her radio, she went calling out and banging over the beds in her all-male household. At the discovery of the empty bed of her youngest, she was alarmed, until she looked under the bed and found that, after two mornings, he had anticipated her actions and gone to sleep underneath, with pillows and quilts as insulation. Not to be thwarted—this was the son born in America and she meant him to go to college—Rosalba dragged him out by his ankle.

On the opposite end of the spectrum, there were a number of listeners who deliberately tuned out, or at least down. These people wanted to hear the pertinent information of the weather and road conditions, school lunch menu and sales at the IGA, but they did not want to be jarred out of their skins, nor did they want anyone else in their household to be awakened.

Having gotten Aunt Marilee back to bed with both tiny tots, Corrine went all over the house, making certain every radio was turned off. Then she fell gratefully back into her own bed for another half hour's sleep before getting up for school. One needed sleep when one lived in a nuthouse.

Across the street, Doris Northrupt sighed peacefully, giving thanks that her husband was gone, and that she could sleep to midmorning, when he would return. Retired life was good.

Julia Jenkins-Tinsley used the new iPod she had purchased the previous day; however, she couldn't get it to work, so she had to jog listening to her own breathing in the cold morning air.

Inez Cooper turned her kitchen radio off in midreveille. "Idiots," she said, as she counted her husband's morning pills into the little medicine cup. She stuck in one of the quit-smoking herbal pills Belinda had given her. Norman would never notice an extra pill. She had gone all over his workshop and found two packages of hidden cigarettes, which she had torn up into the trash. Now, with firm determination, she set a small pamphlet about quitting smoking next to the coffeemaker.

Out at the edge of town, John Cole Berry was filling a travel mug of coffee and remembered just in time to punch the button that silenced the radio on the coffee machine. Standing there, sipping his coffee with both relief that Emma still slept and anxiousness about the busy day ahead, he felt a tightness come across his chest. He did not have time for Emma's worries to transfer to him, he thought, taking up his jacket and slipping from the house. He was able to catch the reveille fifteen minutes later on his truck radio and have a good laugh.

Having slept a peaceful night in her own bedroom, Paris Miller was putting on her eye makeup while listening to her boom box set to low volume. She smiled at the *Wake Up* call. She loved sweet Willie Lee and Munro, and Mr. Winston, too, who had always been so kind to her. Sometimes she imagined her grandfather was like Mr. Winston; he could be, if only he would stop drinking. Turning off the radio, she tiptoed to the kitchen, carefully closing the door to her grandfather's room as she passed. She prepared the coffeemaker, and set out an orange and a packaged sausage biscuit, all in readiness for her grandfather when he got up. If she could just love him enough, he would quit drinking.

Two miles away in her king-size bed with the leather headboard, Belinda slept soundly beneath fine Egyptian 1200-count cotton sheets and down comforter, head cradled on a soft pillow, with earplugs and a violet satin eye mask. A few feet away to the right, on the night table near her head, was a small decorative plaque, which she had purposely placed there the previous night. It read: *Today I will be handling all of your problems. I do not need your help.* —God.

Belinda had found the plaque stuffed in the back of a cabinet while searching for a bottle of aspirin. She had thought that she was only too glad to dump all of her problems on anyone who would take them. And with that, she rejected all responsibility if Arlo did not open the store on time, and she herself would get there when she got there.

She was still asleep past all three reveilles and did not hear the telephone ringing.

Lyle did, though, as he came in the back door. The caller was Arlo, saying that he had overslept and was sorry. Lyle went in and saw his beautiful Belinda sleeping peacefully, and was a little hesitant about awakening her. While fearless in the face of armed robbers, dangerous illegal-alien smugglers and desperate crack dealers, the deputy was definitely wary of waking his wife. After gazing at her a moment, he solved his problem by turning around and going down to the drugstore himself. Any mistake he could make behind the soda fountain counter could not be as great as waking a soundly sleeping Belinda Blaine.

Despite all the years he had been with Belinda, he had never in his life worked the soda fountain counter. Belinda never would let him do anything. But opening the door was easy, and he had help from a few customers to get the coffee and latte makers going.

Andy Smith, who needed shaving supplies and who had heard that Blaine's Soda Fountain had the only latte in town, and that it was good, hopped over there to get a cup. He was a little disconcerted to find a deputy sheriff, with a gun protruding on his hip beneath the white apron, waiting on him.

"Hi, man. I'm Lyle Midgette." The tall man with boyish eyes offered his hand with a friendly grin. "What can I get for ya'?"

"Uh, nice to meet you. I'm Andy…Smith." He shook the man's hand. "I'll have a latte, if you please."

CHAPTER 5

Growing Up

"WEAR A COAT!" CALLED AUNT MARILEE FROM the kitchen.

"O-kaay!" returned Corrine, who was in the foyer and had no intention of complying. She leaned into the hall mirror, put on lipstick. Aunt Marilee was not likely to approve of either the lipstick or the Wonderbra underneath Corrine's blue sweater. Her aunt was bound and determined that Corrine was not going to follow in the footsteps of her mother, who, as Aunt Marilee put it, "has lived a life more difficult than she had to."

Aunt Marilee was Corrine's mother's older sister. Corrine had come at a young age to live with her aunt because her own mother had had "difficulties"—those being men, drinking and destitution. Aunt Marilee had been known to say, "Put men and drinking together and you get the third without a doubt." Corrine had never known a father, until Papa Tate.

While her own mother had been for some time "on her

feet," as it was said, had a solid job and a stable relationship with a prominent, well-to-do man, and she and Corrine got on well, Corrine chose to remain with Aunt Marilee and Papa Tate. For one thing, that Corrine's mother had still not married but lived with her boyfriend drove Aunt Marilee nuts. The main reason, however, was that Corrine could not bear to leave her aunt. Her own mother said that Corrine and Aunt Marilee were two peas in a pod. Corrine supposed this was true, and oftentimes did not like it. But she knew that Aunt Marilee needed her in a way that her own mother never had.

"Love you," she called out to Aunt Marilee as she grabbed up her backpack and raced out the front door in her blue sweater.

"Good morning," said Rosalba, coming up the steps.

"Good morning," Corrine answered, halting her racing and walking more sedately. Her gaze surreptitiously went to the side, down Rosalba's legs to her feet, watching her movements. Corrine tried to move the same. Rosalba was a sexy woman. And she was probably the only nanny-housekeeper who wore fishnet stockings and high-heeled pumps. No one could figure out how she could go all day in those shoes.

A big gleaming blue tow truck waited in the driveway. The door flew open, and her friend Jojo extended her hand. Corrine grabbed it, put her foot on the chrome step and hauled herself up into the tall vehicle. It was not easy to remain a graceful lady doing that.

Over behind the wheel, her friend's elder brother, Larry Joe, said, "How you this mornin', Miss Corrine?" and winked at her.

"Just fine," she said. Stupid. *Couldn't she think of something more clever?*

The big truck backed out and started off for the school.

Corrine, her gaze on Larry Joe's hands on the steering wheel, tried to think of something to say.

"Did you hear Granddaddy and Everett this mornin'?" Jojo asked.

"No. After we told them goodbye, me and Aunt Marilee went back to bed."

"You must be the only ones in town. They were really funny. Willie was good, too," she added loyally. "He's speakin' more clear."

Jojo Darnell was Winston's real granddaughter and Corrine's best friend. They shared a love of horses.

Larry Joe Darnell, who had been driving them to school most mornings that year, was Winston's oldest grandson, manager of the Texaco, a hunk, twenty-four and the love of Corrine's life.

Corrine said, "Yeah, I know. It's that new speech teacher they hired at the first of the year. Aunt Marilee says she's a miracle worker."

"You mean Monica Huggins?" Larry Joe said.

"Uh-huh," Corrine replied, wondering at the left turn Larry Joe took onto Porter. That was not the way to school. She saw him looking over at her with a curious sparkle in his eyes. Larry Joe had these blue eyes that just shone out from his face. "Do you know her?"

"Well, that's who we're pickin' up this mornin'," put in Jojo.

Corrine looked at her, saw a pointed expression on her face.

"I've known Ms. Huggins for a few years," said Larry Joe as he drove on down the street and pulled into the driveway of a small bungalow. "I went to junior college with her brother. I got her car in my shop...." He shoved the shifter into Park and hopped out. The truck rumbled.

The teacher came out the red front door. Larry Joe met her

on the walkway and gave her a quick kiss. Corrine felt Jojo elbow her, but she kept her gaze straight ahead. She didn't want Jojo to see her face.

Larry Joe escorted Ms. Huggins over to the driver's side of the truck and helped her get in to sit right next to him.

"Good mornin', Ms. Huggins," Jojo said.

Corrine didn't say anything. The lapse did not appear to be noticed. Jojo and Larry Joe were busy talking to the teacher.

"I don't know," Jojo said, in answer to Corrine's question about how long Larry Joe had been seeing Ms. Huggins. "We just found out about her last night, when he brought her home to supper."

Corrine quickly stuck her burning face into her locker in a search for books. She could not bear to reveal herself to Jojo, who knew that Corrine had a crush on her older brother, but her friend had no idea as to the depth and breadth of it. Jojo was several years younger than Corrine. She had not yet been in love.

Jojo, a loyal friend, said, "I don't think Mama likes her. I heard her tell Daddy that she does not think Ms. Huggins is Larry Joe's type."

"What type would that be?"

"Well…I don't know. But Mama said that Ms. Huggins does not seem like the type to like a pot of beans…whatever that means." She frowned in puzzlement.

Corrine understood and agreed, although what she said was, "I think Ms. Huggins is older than Larry Joe."

"Two years—I asked her—and you're only sixteen."

The comment stabbed. *So?*

"Well, Mama also said it was about time that Larry Joe was finally interested enough in a woman to bring her home for supper. It looks sort of serious. And, well, he can't wait around for you to grow up."

"So who's wantin' him to?" Corrine slammed her locker closed. "I gotta see Ricky Dale before class. Catch ya' later."

Thankfully, her on-again-off-again boyfriend, Ricky Dale, was standing right across the hall.

It was just bizarre.

She could hardly remember ever seeing the woman, and then suddenly, on this day, every time she turned around, there was Ms. Huggins. *What was up with that?*

Then—as Corrine was finishing lunch late, because she had stayed longer cleaning up in art class—she saw Ms. Huggins on the far side of the lunchroom with Mrs. Yoder. Seeing the two teachers rise and carry their trays to deposit at the counter nearby, Corrine remained seated, waiting for them to pass behind her.

A napkin came flying off Ms. Huggins's tray and skittered on the floor beneath the tables.

"They pay people to pick that stuff up," said Ms. Huggins, and went on out of the room.

Corrine got up to deposit her tray and trash, and ended up going around to pick up not only Ms. Huggins's napkin but a couple of others. She knew that Mrs. Pryne, the cleaning lady, had bad arthritis, but indelibly written in her mind was Aunt Marilee's voice saying: "Clean up messes wherever you can. Let it begin with you."

At times that voice was just the ruination of her life.

Aunt Marilee picked her up from school. Willie Lee had left earlier, with his girlfriend, Gabby.

"Can I drive?"

"Well, sure, honey." Aunt Marilee scooted over rather than get out.

"Hey, shortcake." Corrine grinned at little Emily, who giggled at her from the car seat in the back. "Is Victoria home with Rosalba?"

"Yes. That woman is a pure answer to prayer." Aunt Marilee's face lit with delight, then she sighed a long sigh. "But I cannot imagine how she does it all day in those heels. I really can't. Oh, I need you to go by Blaine's on the way home. I've got to consult with Belinda."

"Okay," said Corrine, quite thrilled with the prospect of more driving and the opportunity to say, "I might as well go on by the Texaco, since we're goin' that way."

"We need gas?"

"We're down to half a tank." Almost.

Corrine glanced at herself in the rearview mirror. She had not dared to put on fresh lipstick. Thankfully Aunt Marilee did not seem to notice any difference in her chest, which really was not so reassuring.

"Aunt Marilee?"

"Hmm?" Her aunt dug around in her purse.

"How much older than you is Papa Tate?" She was pretty certain she already knew the answer.

"Ten years. Why?"

"Oh, I just thought of it today," said Corrine, sitting up a little straighter and shaking back her dark hair. Her hair and her eyes were her best features; even Aunt Marilee, who was knowledgeable about such things, said so.

"Well, I cannot find my credit card," said her aunt, with her head nearly into her purse. It was a large tote-bag size and had everything in there in case of emergency—moist wipes, tissues, first-aid kit, crackers, tea bags, collapsible cup. Corrine had even seen a pair of panties in there. Aunt Marilee pretty much believed in emergencies, and counted being ready for them on the same scale as righteousness.

"We can just charge the gas to the account," Corrine told her.

"Well, yes. We can do that." Aunt Marilee brushed her hair out of her face and sat back with a deep breath.

What did age have to do with maturity? Corrine wondered. That was an enormous, unanswerable question.

As Corrine pulled up to the gas pumps, she looked over to see Larry Joe coming out from the garage, wiping his hands on a rag. She felt this silly grin come over her face, and she dared not look at her aunt, but she did catch sight of herself in the side mirror. She wet her lips.

Larry Joe almost never waited on cars anymore. Usually Dusty or Rick did that. They even washed the windshields. The Valentine Texaco was one of the few gas stations that still provided such service. Lots of men who went there all the time pumped their own gas, but ladies always waited. Corrine had heard Larry Joe talking with Papa Tate and saying that women made the majority of purchasing decisions. It was well-known that he had been the saving of the Texaco when he took over managing it from old man Stidham. Aunt Marilee had said it was due to both service and cleanliness. The women's restroom was now spotless.

In fact, Corrine was delighted that Aunt Marilee got out to go use it (and check it out to see if it was holding up), leaving her alone with Larry Joe. He set the gas running into the tank and then stood there, talking through the driver's window. He spoke first to Emily in the backseat, getting her to grin and show him her bottom teeth. Then he asked Corrine how old

Emily was now, and she told him a bunch of things about her baby cousin. At least it was a topic that she knew, and he seemed interested. Larry Joe was something of a kid magnet, Jojo said. The idea, in that moment, was a little uncomfortable.

Aunt Marilee came back and complimented Larry Joe all over the place for the good shape of his ladies' restroom. She went on at great length about it, so that Corrine wanted to crawl under the seat. As Aunt Marilee slipped into the car, she said under her breath, "You just can't encourage a man too much."

When the tank was full, Corrine followed Larry Joe inside, while he wrote out the ticket, and while she stood there, Rick came in. He grinned at Corrine and let out a low whistle. "Whoa, chicky, lookin' fine today!"

Corrine was both thrilled and embarrassed.

"That's her aunt Marilee out there in the car," said Larry Joe, pointing with the pen. "You'd best watch yourself."

Rick winked and went on through to the garage.

"Here you are, Miss Corrine." Larry Joe handed her a yellow slip of paper, then touched the brim of his ball cap. "Thank you for your business. See you in the mornin'."

"See you."

She wondered if he watched her walk back out to the car. She was able to casually glance back as she opened the car door. Larry Joe was not looking. He was over in the garage beneath a car with Rick, deep in conversation.

Disappointment and frustration caused Corrine to press harder on the accelerator than she otherwise might have.

"Watch out when you pull into the street!"

"I *am* watchin', Aunt Marilee. I've been drivin' for a year now—and I am not the one who has had a wreck and a ticket."

To this, Aunt Marilee responded in a dozen different ways, and all the way to the drugstore, including how it was her car and when Corrine got her own car (which they would not let her do until starting the next school year), she could drive any way she wanted. She also had to instruct Corrine on how to pull into the head-in parking place.

Corrine was thinking, *Let me in the convent now, just to get away from an overprotective mother.* Would they let a Methodist in?

Help Wanted.

The sign was in the drugstore window. Corrine looked at it, and then again at the back of it when she got inside the store.

"Hi, sugars."

Miss Belinda sounded more like her mother every day, something that Aunt Marilee often commented on, but then she would say, "Don't say it to Belinda. She won't appreciate it."

Belinda did not look at all like she was related to her mother. Aunt Vella was dark eyed, tall and statuesque, and Belinda was light eyed, short and voluptuous. One day Corrine had said that Belinda was a voluptuary, like Elizabeth Taylor. Belinda had been so thrilled with this description that she had forever after seemed to favor Corrine.

Belinda told her now, "Sugar, you go on over to the soda fountain and get yourself a Coca-Cola or anything you want… and can Emily have a peppermint stick? Just get her anything she won't choke on."

As Corrine headed away with her baby cousin, Aunt Marilee said, "I tell you, Belinda, I am fixin' to spontaneously combust with these hot flashes, or else slap somebody, and the doctor I saw today was no more help than the man in the moon...."

The current bane of Aunt Marilee's existence was meno-pause, with doctors coming in a close second.

Between her mother, who Corrine had more or less taken care of instead of the other way around, and then living with Aunt Marilee and helping with her mentally handicapped cousin, Willie Lee, and then with the babies, and adding in Aunt Vella and Miss Belinda, Corrine knew far more than the average teenage girl about the intimate details of womanhood. She was able to assist in instruction in health class at school. Many times the girls at school, even those in senior class, sought her out for answers that their mothers were too embarrassed to tell them about boyfriends and sex. With Aunt Marilee's latest trials, Corrine knew more about menopause than any other young woman of her age should be burdened with knowing.

And that she was in love with a young man of twenty-four would be considered surprising? What could be considered sur-prising was that she had loved Larry Joe since the age of thirteen and knew that she always would.

Corrine thought all of this as she made herself a Coca-Cola vanilla float, at the same time keeping Emily's quick hands out of everything within her one-year-old reach. While she was going about this, a man came in and wanted a sweet tea and an order of nachos to go.

Corrine instantly seized the opportunity. "I'll get it, Miss Belinda," she called out.

Miss Belinda's hand came up above the shelves, waving. "Okay, sugar. Thanks. We'll be there in a minute."

Corrine made the man his order and even took the money, which she placed at the cash register.

When she sat down at a table with her float and Emily, she thought about the sign in the window.

Help Wanted.

It was time she quit working for free.

Corrine caught sight of her own and Aunt Marilee's reflections in the dark dining room windows as they got supper on the table. Gathering courage, she told her aunt about her idea to work at the drugstore.

Aunt Marilee looked at her with wide eyes. "You want to go to work?"

You would have thought she had said she wanted to fly to Mars.

"Yes." She had all the arguments ready. "You have Rosalba to help you now. I need to be responsible and earn my own car insurance. And Blaine's will be perfect for me. I already know how to do everything. And Miss Belinda *is* your cousin. And she could use my help with Aunt Vella away."

"You want to go to work?" Aunt Marilee repeated and dropped into a chair.

"I'm sixteen. Lots of the girls are already workin'. Paris has worked since she was fourteen."

Papa Tate walked in and snitched tomatoes out of the salad.

Aunt Marilee said, "She wants to go to work."

"I heard." His eyes met Corrine's. He was caught in a tight spot.

Later that evening, Aunt Marilee came into Corrine's bedroom and put her arms around her and said, "You are growin' up," and cried a little, as if Corrine had caught some rare disease.

Corrine, patting her aunt, wondered which one of them was growing up. Or if, indeed, anyone ever really did grow up.

CHAPTER 6

Ahead of Her Time

WHEN THE TELEPHONE RANG, BELINDA WAS curled on the end of her couch, half a glass of wine at hand, fire in the fireplace and Rod Stewart on the stereo. She was reading about menopause in *Prescription for Nutritional Healing*. It was the same book that she had consulted to help Marilee that afternoon. The book was continually kept open on a stand at the pharmacy for the convenience of customers. After reading in it and talking with Marilee, Belinda had about convinced herself that she was not pregnant but into early menopause. She had experienced hot flashes for two years. This was not at all surprising to her. She always had been a woman ahead of her time.

"Hello, Belinda? This is Corrine."

"Well, hello, sugar. How are you this evenin'?"

"Fine."

Belinda stopped in the middle of a sip of wine. *Oh, Lord, don't let the girl be in trouble.*

Her mother had for years taken many an after-hours call from teenage girls, and a couple of boys, wanting to know how to get rid of some nasty infection or a surprise pregnancy. It was amazing how young women today were as ignorant of their bodies as young women had been some hundred or even fifty years ago. Parents, supposedly modern in thought and accepting of all manner of "alternate lifestyles," still did not speak plainly to their children at an early age about normal sexual behavior. They let their children learn the way everyone had learned for generations: from movies, television and the stupid kid up the block—and none of it accurate, healthy information. Basically, modern young women were not modern in regard to any of it. They could smoke weed and get a tattoo and let a boy do all sorts of things to them, but by heaven, they didn't want to know about their own vaginas and uteruses. They were too busy paying attention to boys during health class to pay attention to what they needed to learn, until they got a crash course. It was said that experience was the best teacher.

In cases of pregnancy, Vella Blaine had a rule about referring the girl to a good counselor that she knew, who would help navigate the decision-making process. (Belinda had the urge to jump up and look for the woman's card, which her mother had given her for this express purpose.) For any nasty infections, Vella gave private instructions for remedies, or a referral to a good physician.

Three times in the past few years, Belinda had received similar inquiries. She had referred them to her mother, but now, with her mother's absence, she saw plainly that she would be the one to have to step up to the plate. She did not care for the idea. It was all just awkward and annoying. She had the wild thought to give out the phone number of her mother in France.

Thankfully Corrine ended Belinda's worry in the next instant with, "I was callin' about the help wanted sign I saw in the drugstore window."

"Oh." Belinda brightened and took a fresh breath.

"Is that for full-time or part-time?"

"Well, sugar, at this point I will take any good help I can get. Are you interested?"

"Yes, ma'am."

"Honey, you are hired!" Belinda raised her glass with joy.

"Well, I first need to know the hours and what you are payin'." Politely but firmly said.

"Of course you do," replied Belinda instantly. She'd always liked Corrine, and the girl's statement just increased her opinion, which was that the girl was highly intelligent and a go-getter.

On the spot, Belinda quoted a salary twenty-five cents an hour more than she had planned to offer.

The headlights of Lyle's patrol car pulled in the drive right at 8:55 p.m.

When on night duty, Lyle liked to take a break around nine and come home for a snack, either a health drink or for a more intimate snack of a different sort. Any of his nightly stopping in, however, had to come before Belinda settled herself in her beautiful bed, with her reading, everything from the Bible and Bible commentary to the *Wall Street Journal* and the day's financial reports printed from the computer to the biography of some highly successful person, either current or from history. Sometimes Belinda had all of that in the bed with her. One thing was certain—she disliked, for any reason, to be disturbed from what she called her nightly reading, meditating and consciousness raising.

She would tell him, "Sugar, you have your health routines, and I have mine."

Lyle's consisted of lean meats, vegetables and fruits, special protein drinks, lifting weights and running.

Clearly one focused on the mind and one on the body. Belinda thought them a perfect pair.

Already showered and wearing her favorite Delta Burke rose-print satin gown, Belinda met Lyle in the kitchen, anxious to tell him the good news about Corrine. She had just gotten started when she found herself scooped up into his arms and carried so quickly into the bedroom that her head spun.

"You haven't started readin' yet, have you?" he asked.

"No, sugar," Belinda said, just as he entered the bedroom, where the bedside lamps and candles were lit but the books were still stacked on the night chest.

In inspiring movie-scene fashion, Lyle smiled a delighted, sensuous, promising smile and laid her as carefully as a fine jewel upon the bed.

Belinda found herself once more grateful and amazed by the gift she had been given in her man. Truly, as the scriptures said, a woman was made for a man, a fact Lyle proceeded to prove.

Twenty minutes later, Lyle, his shirt still off, made a protein drink in the blender on the kitchen counter. Belinda, all soothed and happy, gazed at his broad, muscular back while she enjoyed a cheese Danish and remembered to tell him about the good fortune of hiring Corrine Pendley.

"She's goin' to work each afternoon after school, and close

the store twice a week." She licked her fingers happily. "Now all I need to do is find someone to open the store a couple times a week and work mornings. At least three days. That will sure take a load off."

"Honey, I'll be glad to help," said Lyle, glancing over his shoulder. "I really liked openin' the other mornin'. I did."

Belinda, who thought, *Ohmyheaven,* said, "Sweetie, you have a job. You do not need to stretch yourself by workin' in the drugstore. You are the head sheriff's deputy. That is demanding enough."

"When I'm on nights, I'm never tired when I come home, anyway. I have to unwind, and I just sit around for a couple of hours watchin' TV. I'd just as soon open the store for you. When I go on days, I can still open, *and* I can close, since the store's open later." As he spoke, he got out his carry mug and poured his drink into it, snapping on the lid.

"I appreciate the offer, sugar—" she sidled up to him, rubbing her hands over his back "—but we can surely get by the two months until Mama comes home. And you are a *sheriff's deputy,* and that's important. You know you don't work firm hours, either. What if you're caught up arrestin' somebody right when the store needs to open or close? You can't just tell them to wait."

"I can cuff 'em to a pole and come on to the drugstore," he said.

Belinda tried to judge the seriousness of this statement. He looked serious. She replied, "Well, maybe you *could* do that, but we are not goin' to jeopardize what we just enjoyed—I'm not lettin' you waste energy on a second job workin' in the drugstore." She smiled seductively.

He looked away as he put on his shirt.

Belinda started clearing the counter, remembering the previous morning, after Lyle had opened the store and worked the soda fountain counter with Arlo for an hour. She had come in to find coffee and latte splashes and spills all over, the barbecue pot set on high, a half-eaten banana set aside, and could not walk across the floor without sticking to it. The receipts did not add up to what was in the cash drawer. Lyle never could count change, and he had simply piled a lot of money to the side of the cash register.

"You just think I can't do anything," Lyle said.

"What?" She looked over to see him near the door, hat in hand. "I do not think that."

"Yes, you do. You don't let me do anything for you."

"I do so. Who does the mowin' around here? And...the grilling. And keepin' me safe." There, that last one was important.

"I mean that you don't let me do anything for *you,* Belinda. You could hire a guy to do everything I do for you."

"I am hirin' people to work in the store."

"It's not the same. You just don't let me help you in a special way. And you and that store have your own marriage."

He actually pointed with his hat, then plopped it on his head and left.

She hurried to the door and called after his shadowy figure, "Well, who was it just in the bedroom with me, then?"

He did not reply.

She stood there and watched his patrol car leave, wondering what had just happened. It was not like Lyle at all to have a complaint or cross word. She had never seen him so perturbed.

Belinda carried her purse into the master bathroom and plopped it on the long counter.

Pausing, she turned back to lock the door, just in case. Then she dug down into the bottom of her purse and pulled out a new pregnancy-test kit—another $6.99 one. She hiked up her thigh-high gown, positioned herself over the toilet and took careful aim at the test strip. It might have been easier for a smaller-breasted woman. And, darn it, she should have drunk a whole glass of water with the sweet roll.

Brrrnnnggg!

The telephone on the wall right beside her ear rang. The test strip slipped out of her fingers.

It could not be. She could not have done it again!

The phone rang again.

She gazed at the test strip floating in the water.

The phone rang yet again. She snatched up the receiver. "Hell-o!"

"Belinda? Sugar, is that you? It's your mama. Over in France," her mother added, as if Belinda might have forgotten where she had gone.

"Yes, it is me, Mama. What other woman would be answerin' my home phone at ten o'clock at night?"

Her mother, who had at the age of seventy quit living by anyone's normal hours, said, "Oh, is it ten o'clock there? I must have miscalculated."

Belinda knew her mother had not bothered to calculate whatsoever.

Her mother continued, "*However,* is that any way for a daughter to speak to her mother?"

Her mother launched into a lengthy lecture on Belinda's less-than-cordial attitude, for which Belinda immediately apologized, because her eye had fallen on the pregnancy-test box and she imagined her mother seeing all the way from

Europe. She did not think it a stretch of the imagination that her mother had such power.

Her mother then wanted to know how everything was going at the drugstore, and had Belinda been listening to Winston's new early-morning radio show? Her mother's awareness of Winston's escapades was the perfect example of her mother knowing everything, even over in France.

Just then, with her mother's voice in her ear, Belinda tucked the telephone in the crook of her neck and snatched up the pregnancy-kit box, folded it into a small shape and stuffed it down in the bottom of the wastebasket.

After hanging up with her mother, she went to the kitchen and drank a full glass of water. Returning again to the master bathroom, she shut and locked the door and turned off the phone.

Digging down again into her purse, she pulled out yet another home pregnancy-test kit. After all, Belinda was both the owner of a drugstore and a practical woman who anticipated contingencies.

Opening the box, she removed the test strip and set it on the counter. Then she brought a plastic bedpan from the closet, along with a set of medical collection cups. A drugstore owner had plenty of equipment. She expertly pulled off one collection cup, put it in the bedpan and set the bedpan atop the closed toilet.

She looked at everything with satisfaction.

Then she positioned herself and filled the little collection cup.

She dipped the test strip into the warm liquid.

It *was* easy to read.

She was pregnant.

A chill swept her. With a precise motion, she rose, set the test strip on the marble counter and got her robe off the hook on the back of the door. She tied the robe snugly, then leaned toward the mirror, studying her face.

Suddenly her head spun and her legs turned to water. She sank down on the side of the large tub, where she put her head in her hands and cried.

CHAPTER 7

1550 on the Radio Dial
The Hank Williams Sunday Morning Gospel Hour

IN FRONT OF THE BATHROOM MIRROR, WINSTON ran an electric razor over his craggy cheeks. From a small black portable radio on the nearby glass shelf came his own voice.

"Good mornin', folks, and welcome to the Hank Williams Sunday Mornin' Gospel Hour."

He mouthed along with the words. He thought he sounded mighty fine.

"And, yes, Hank Williams, Sr., is still dead, but we're resurrectin' some of his gospel tunes for this special show. This program is recorded, meanin' when you hear this, we're all doin' something else, but right this minute our own Felton Ballard is here in the studio to sing for you. Many of you know Felton from the Saturday evenin' singings over at the First Baptist. He plays these tunes in the original style, just like ol'

Hank sang 'em. We're mighty proud of Felt. He starts off here with 'I Saw the Light....'"

Winston hummed along with the tune. Felt sang it well. They had recorded the show back last winter. Miracle of modern life, the way music and voices could be recorded, and then all manner of changes made. Had not been like that back in his day, no, sir. Hank Williams, Johnny Cash, Loretta Lynn— they all went to the station and sang into the microphone before getting recorded.

Winston was not a fan of recording. It hindered him from adding in the clever things that came to his mind when he was listening on a Sunday morning in the bathroom.

"Well, folks, I want to tell you that our Sunday gospel hour today is brought to you thanks to Tinsley's IGA, the All Church Pastors Association of Valentine and the Burger Barn. And you can hear Felton Ballard playing Hank Williams's gospel live at the First Methodist Church this Sunday, where a special nine-thirty service is an entire singing service. Everyone's invited.

"Up next we got 'Are You Walking and a-Talking with the Lord?' What a lot of people don't know is that in his short career the original Hank Williams wrote some fifty gospel songs. Isn't that right, Felt? You're somethin' of an expert on this, I understand."

Felton answered, "Yes, sir. My wife sometimes sings with me, like Audrey sang with Hank...and Hank recorded a series of gospel albums as Luke the Drifter. I guess they thought it wouldn't fly with his real name, with all his drinkin' and carryin' on."

"Well, I can recall that he always sang one or more gospel tunes with Little Jimmy Dickens in his Grand Ole Opry appearances. This one is for all of my friends out there who remember the Grand Ole Opry in the old days. Go ahead, Felt."

The music started, and Winston could sing along with this song, too. He remembered that this one had been a favorite of Coweta's.

Suddenly he looked around and saw Coweta racing toward him in the garage, where he was tuning up the Ford. Her little black shoes flew over the ground. "Oh, Win! Look at this. Birdy sent it. Can we go? Oh, let's! Won't cost us nothin' to stay with Birdy. Just you and me. Mama can take care of Freddie."

The yellow playbill floated up before his eyes. Blurry. He had to squint, and then it came in plain: *April 1, 1951, Robinson Memorial Auditorium, Little Rock…Star! Hank Williams! and His Drifting Cowboys…also Lefty Frizzell…*

Coweta's dark eyes shone like they could, pulling him in. He and she had just come out of a big fight, and he was in that place where he would lasso the moon for her. She knew it, too. That's how it played out for them again and again. Took them thirty years to see it, and some more to start doing anything to break the cycle.

Somehow, just as she could always work a miracle, she had made the phone call and gotten them tickets. "Yes, I did. Row five. Don't ask what they cost." She laughed, and the skirt of her dress swirled as she raced up the stairs to pack.

He shook his head. He never had been one to worry over money. It was her who worried over it.

"Not that time," she said now, grinning at him right there in their bedroom. "I loved that Hank Williams."

He never could understand it. "That Hank was so scrawny, he'd blow away in a good wind."

Coweta smiled. There was a pink glow around her, pretty as could be. She said, "We had us a good time. Remember?"

"Yeah. I remember…we had to drive through five hours of sleet and rain and the windshield wipers actin' up."

"Oh, Winston. You never remember the important things. Like you held my hand, and we danced after, all alone. Why don't you remember that?"

"That was near fifty years ago," he defended. "I was born before ol' Hank, and have lived far after him, and I got a lot clutterin' my brain." He pointed at the playbill in her hand. "I've outlived ever'body on that poster."

"No, honey, you haven't."

"No kiddin'—really?"

"Now, why would I kid about such a thing? Don Helms was in the Drifting Cowboys then, and he is still alive—and playin', even. He's younger than you."

"Isn't ever'body?" Winston said, a little sadly. Then, "I've outlived so many, Coweta. Just so much has happened in my life. I can't piece it all together half the time."

"I know, honey." Her hand came over his, so pale and soft against his leathery skin.

Then he heard her humming. It took him a second to recognize the tune—Hank's "I'm Going Home."

"Mis-ter Wins-ton…Mis-ter Wins-ton."

It was Willie Lee, standing right in front of him.

Why, he was now sitting on his bed. He didn't remember sitting on the bed.

Willie Lee's eyes blinked behind his thick glasses. Looking downward, Winston saw Willie Lee's smaller hand, soft and white, lying on his own.

"I'm okay, buddy. Just caught in some memories."

"Yes. You are o-kay," the boy said confidently.

Willie Lee knew these things, so Winston felt reassured.

"Moth-er says we need to go to church ear-ly. It is rain-ning. I will get you-r coat."

The boy fetched Winston's blue sport coat from the butler chair and held it up for Winston to slip into. Winston checked himself in the dressing mirror before following the boy from the room. As he went out the door, he paused and glanced around, looking for signs of Coweta.

There were none. She had been gone a long, long time now. As were so many who had made up his life.

Over at her small house, Paris Miller peered out her bedroom window through hard rain pouring from the roof and washing over the glass. It ran in the ditch that divided the yards. Behind her on her boom box, a voice sang out an old country tune. "Please make up your miinnd…"

She was actually contemplating going to the Methodist Church. That was the only church she had ever been able to go into alone. She had gone to the Good Shepherd with a friend, and she liked that they were real friendly, but the thought of being there on her own with them jumping up and running around made her nervous. The Methodists were a quiet bunch. She could slip in, sit in the back and hardly be noticed. She had done that before, enough so that the usher— Leon Purvis, who slicked back his gray hair—no longer tried to get her to fill out a visitation form. When the final closing hymn was sung, she would slip out again.

She wondered what she hoped to get out of it. She usually did feel a lot better afterward, but then she would come home, and her whole life started all over again, not a thing changed, no matter how hard she prayed.

She heard a plunk and looked up. A wet stain was spread-

ing on her ceiling, where many had been before. She needed
to get a pan to catch the leak.

"What in the hell are you listenin' to?" Her granddaddy had
come in his wheelchair to her door.

"It's a special Hank Williams gospel show today." She did
not know that she hunched her shoulders and sort of winced.

"Hank Williams? What in the hell you want to listen to
that old stuff for? Turn that mess off...." He rolled himself
away, mumbling.

She turned off the radio, stood there a moment, then
hurried to get boots, purse and coat. No one had to dress up
to go to the First Methodist, especially this special singing, as
they called it. Lots of women came in jeans. There were
farmers who came from the field in their overalls.

Pausing to glance around, she saw everything in a blur of
drab brown-gray. She had a sense of desperation, and felt that
if she did not get out and around color and sound and people,
she was going to choke to death.

"Where you goin'?" her granddaddy asked.

She hesitated, her eyes moving to the bottle on the table. "I'm
runnin' over to a girl's house for a few minutes." And she was
out the door, ducking in case the bottle came flying after her.

What flew after her was him hollering, "Bring me back a
six-pack of—"

The back door closed, and she raced away to her car,
hopping over the puddles.

As she backed out, a car pulled up in front. One of her
granddaddy's drinking buddies. The tightness in her throat
grew so great she had to gasp for breath.

She pulled into the Quick Stop for five dollars' worth of
gas and ended up helping LuAnn wait on a flood of custom-

ers driven in there by the rain. Everyone was talking about it, and depending on circumstances and temperaments, people moaned about the dreariness and inconvenience, or gave happy praise for coming green lawns and May flowers.

Over at the First Methodist Church, a few of the smokers, who usually had a quick cigarette on the front lawn before service, snatched a couple of puffs in the shelter of a large cedar tree. From here they watched the men with umbrellas, who ran to meet those arriving and hold cover over the women and girls.

Jaydee Mayhall, feeling guilty, stamped out his butt, and hurried to get the umbrella out of his own car and help. He began right then planning to put up an awning over the church walkway.

Parking was directed by men in slickers and ball caps. There was an unusually large crowd—many who only came on Easter and Christmas, as well as Baptists and Assemblies of God and the Good Shepherds from out on the highway who loved to sing, and a couple of brave Episcopalians. Vehicles filled the church parking lot, the grassy yard where the church played baseball and up and down both sides of the street.

Bobby Goode, who lived just south of the church, had the idea to make some money by charging three bucks a car to park in his circle driveway and spacious front yard. His wife's response to this idea was to have a fit and tell him that if she saw one rut on her front lawn, his funeral would be the next event at the Methodist Church. She said that he could let people park in the driveway—for free.

She said nothing about not taking what people offered, though, so when Rick Garcia parked his big-wheel mud truck in Bobby's driveway and waved a five at him, Bobby took it quick, and directly after the truck, Bobby waved in two little foreign jobs that he got parked bumper to bumper. He held out his hand and received eight more dollars.

Across the street, Inez Cooper punched off her radio right in the middle of "Wait for the Light to Shine."

"If we wait for the light, we'll miss the singin'," she said to the radio. The cloud cover had kept it so dark that at nine-thirty in the morning the streetlights still glowed.

She called for her husband, Norman, to hurry up. Unfortunately, she immediately caught the scent of cigarette smoke on him. "I cannot believe you. Go wash your hands, at least, so's maybe not everybody will smell it. And hurry up. You're gonna make us late."

Norman did as he was told, while Inez put on rain boots and carefully color-matched a green umbrella to her suit. When he reappeared, she stepped onto the porch, opened the umbrella and was halfway down the walkway when she realized that Norman was lagging behind, like he always did. She hated that, and of course it was because smoking cigarettes was cutting down his wind, which she told him. He did not answer, nor did he speed his steps. She had to pause again at the curb and wait for him. "Would you get under this umbrella? You are gettin' all wet…you're gonna catch your death."

At that moment, Juice Tinsley's car stopped. The car window on the passenger side came down, and Julia called out, "Can we park in your driveway, Inez?"

"Well, no…no, that's not a good idea."

"Why not?"

"It's just not. I don't want people parkin' up and down my drive—we may need to get out later. Come *on,* Norman."

Bobby Goode popped out into the street and directed Juice into his driveway. He said, "I'm takin' donations for parkin'."

Juice pulled a couple of dollars out of his pants pocket, then hurried after Julia, who had removed her shoes and was already halfway across the churchyard, running barefoot with her Bible held over her head. Juice idly wondered if maybe rain would not hit the Bible, a holy book. His gaze slid over to Norman Cooper.

The men's eyes met for a second of understanding neither could ever put into words, and then each looked straight ahead, heading for the church steps. Iris MacCoy was just going up, and Norman hurried to walk beside her.

Woody Beauchamp's old black Plymouth came slowly down the street. It was so old that it had the great rear fender fins, and so well cared-for that the rain made tiny beads on the shiny finish. Seeing two cars pulling into a curved driveway, Woody followed. At first he wondered if he had made a mistake, but he recognized a couple of his customers from the café getting out of the cars ahead. Then Bobby Goode was there, waving him up a couple more inches. "Bring her on out of the street."

As Woody got himself out from behind the wheel, Bobby had his hand out. Woody shook it and said, "Thank you, brother."

Andy Smith got out of the passenger side and, in his lanky walk, came around the front of the Plymouth. Woody wore a good felt hat, but Andy's head was bare.

"You got to get you a hat, boy," said Woody.

Woody had not told anyone about picking Andy up in the alley behind the café, the younger man so hungry that his belly thought his throat had been cut. Woody was a man who kept his business to himself, and he liked to let people wonder. He felt it had become his nearest duty to help this white boy, who had not yet confided in him, but who Woody knew needed more than simple food and shelter.

"Yoo-hoo! Y'all wait up!" It was Fayrene running down the street in a plum-red coat and high heels, and holding a purse over her head. She was as unsteady as ever a woman was who rarely wore such shoes, and her ankle turned and she almost fell.

"Law, woman…"

Woody sprinted forward, opening his suit coat, and Andy came quickly behind. Woody's generously cut coat nearly covered Fayrene completely, while Andy on the other side took hold of her elbow.

Fayrene, in heaven between the two men, felt as if she fairly glided up the church steps. When she got up into the foyer, she stopped at the wall mirror and tried to help her wet hairdo. Then, with Woody gallantly gesturing her ahead of him, she found herself staring into the sanctuary and at the enormous stained-glass window at the far end. She had not been in a church in some time. Her steps faltered. In a furtive manner, she bent her head and crossed herself. She didn't know if that was the thing to do, but she felt the need to do something. Then she happily sat next to Andy in the pew and artfully crossed her legs.

By the time Tate Holloway and his carload got to the church, there were only two hearty souls with umbrellas standing ready. Stopping in the street beside a little Subaru that had parked at the curb, blocking the front walkway, Tate complained that they were so late that he might just have to drive back and park on Main Street.

Winston's reply to this was, "I'd just leave the car right here." As he got out of the front seat, he was immediately met by an umbrella, which he grabbed into his own hand, leaning on his cane with the other. Willie Lee and Munro walked close beside him.

Corrine opened the rear passenger door and was also met by an umbrella. She looked up into the beautiful blue eyes of Larry Joe Darnell. He had two umbrellas, one for her and one for Aunt Marilee. He held the umbrellas over the women, each of them with a baby on her hip, all the way along the walk, up the steps and into the church foyer. Corrine was thrilled. She had gotten Aunt Marilee to let her wear her new two-and-a-half-inch heels, lip gloss and Aunt Marilee's dangling silver earrings.

Then they ended up sitting on the pew right behind the Darnell family, where Jojo had saved the space for them by lying down. Corrine thought, There is a God, after all.

And then, wouldn't you know it—when Larry Joe came to sit beside his mother, he brought Ms. Huggins with him. Corrine had a view of the teacher's head. She had dark roots in the back.

Belinda was late to the church because she had stopped to open the drugstore for an emergency. Janice Oakes had required a bottle of Imodium for her ex-mother-in-law, Miss Minnie Oakes. Miss Minnie enjoyed her poor health and liked her medications, with the result that she was always needing either Imodium or Milk of Magnesia.

Janice went out of the store saying, "I may have been able to divorce Neville, but I got custody of his mother." The truth was closer to Janice being both loving and controlling.

Arriving at church, Belinda pulled into the already full parking lot, stopping behind Jaydee Mayhall. Most assuredly she would leave before he did, and if not, he could just wait for her. She opened her violet umbrella out the door, raised it overhead and walked without hurrying across the parking lot and up the church steps.

Stepping into the foyer, she heard music beginning to play on the other side of the sanctuary doors. Lila Hicks at the piano. There was no mistaking Lila's robust playing. Felton Ballard and his gang had not started yet. Belinda propped her umbrella away from the others, which were all pretty much falling in a pile. She checked herself in the mirror, then slipped through the sanctuary doors just as voices began to sing, "'What a fellow-ship…'"

The place was packed full. Belinda experienced a sinking feeling and the sudden wish not to have come. If she wanted to get in touch with God in her difficult hour, she should have waited for the regular service. The crowd unnerved her. She looked down the center aisle, recognizing most everyone at the ends of the jam-packed pews. There was Jaydee, crammed at the end of his regular pew, his arm poking out. She looked right and then left, where the overflow had been placed at the very back in folding chairs.

Just then she spied Emma Berry at the back on the far right. Instantly brightening, she edged in front of people. "Excuse me… Hi, how are you? Excuse me…"

Just as Belinda reached Emma, who welcomed her with a smile, she saw Gracie was there, too.

Gracie smiled.

Of course, thought Belinda, returning a polite smile.

Young Ricky Dale Oakes, wearing his older brother's sport coat as usual, came from the hallway with a hymnal and a folding chair that he opened for her. Taking her place in front of the chair, she joined in the singing from memory: "'Leaning on the everlasting arms…'"

The song ended, everyone sat and the lay leader got up to do the welcome.

Emma leaned forward and put out a hand to summon Belinda, who leaned forward so that they could speak around Gracie, who shrank back.

"Where's Lyle?" Emma asked in a hushed voice.

"Called in for a double shift. The highway patrol stopped a carload of illegals. Where's John Cole?"

"Workin', too." Emma made a face. "Have you spoken to your mama?"

"Yes, early this mornin'. I guess she and your mother are not hardly talkin'."

"That's what I hear, too."

Their eyes silently agreed that it had been bound to happen. They had an unspoken agreement not to discuss their mothers' relationship.

Then the distinctive voice of Felton Ballard came out over the speakers. Both women sat back in their chairs.

Belinda looked around at everyone, then at Gracie's lap and gracefully arranged legs. She imagined bending forward and saying to Emma, *I am pregnant.*

With the thought, she took a deep breath. Her gaze slid to the side, to Emma's burgundy skirt, and then Gracie's black wool, and then her own deep blue paisley print and her hands in her lap. Their seating was a perfect reflection of their relationship these days. Gracie squeezed in between.

Facing forward, she saw that there was actually a good view from the rear, which she had not before experienced. Generally she sat with her mother in the third pew from the front, where her family had sat since she had been a child, when her mother had decided going to church would save them all. Belinda had not known what her father had thought—no one ever knew what her daddy thought—but he had started coming with them. When he had died a few years ago, her mother had presented Belinda with his Bible. It had been well-worn and written in, with passages underlined. That had somehow been a surprise. She had thought that only saints would show such signs of reading the Bible. She had more thoroughly realized that she had never known him and doubted that anyone could ever know anyone.

Her gaze drifted over the heads in front of her. Some she knew vaguely, by sight if not name, and others she had known nearly her entire life. Inez Cooper, who could get on her last nerve…and Julia, who could do the same. There was Fayrene's Clairol-red head, a surprise. Again the last nerve. It occurred to her that quite a few people could get on her nerves, which indicated the truth: she was not a people person.

That unfamiliar head beside Fayrene must be that Andy fellow, whom she had seen only briefly the day of Fayrene's run-in with the car. Belinda's eyes lingered on the man's hair, judging his haircut and finding it quite suited to the man.

Her gaze moved along to her cousin Marilee, elegant as always, with her baby grinning and spitting over her shoulder. She did so much appreciate, even love, Marilee.

And she liked Lila Hicks, she was glad to say. Sweet Lila, who played the piano, and had done so since Belinda was a teen. Lila bought her blond hair color, home permanents and prescription for a lifelong disease caused by a wild youth, at Blaine's. Now Lila had become the perfect Southern lady and a beloved grandmother figure to many of the children, handing out home-baked cookies and candy all the time.

Winston stood to say something in honor of Felton Ballard, and her gaze passed over his white head, aglow in the shine of one of the recessed spotlights.

Her attention was drawn to Felton Ballard as he began to sing. Felton was like one of those Elvis impersonators in the way he did himself up to look like Hank Williams, fringed coat and all. He was equally as skinny as the famous singer, too. His wife was more normal and modern-looking, although not by much. Her name was, fittingly, Melody. She and their daughter mostly sang backup for Felton, but together mother and daughter did sing the old standard "I'll Fly Away," which got a lot of people joining in, singing and clapping. The teenage son, who played fiddle in a shy, half-turned stance, was actually named Hank, and the daughter was Audrey, which Belinda thought was a poor thing to do to two young people. A very round cousin played an electric keyboard, and the group put on an old-time, energetic, gospel-preaching show from an era long gone by and did not disappoint the number of older folks in the audience. A few in the congregation had not known exactly what to expect and were somewhat stunned. They were not used to such loudly played music, nor the vocal and emotional display of faith. They thought they had come to a Methodist Church, and here they were getting some sort of old-time Pentecostal-like revival. Felton did, at one point in his own testimony, look up to the ceiling and hold a conversation with God, then went right into singing "The Prodigal Son."

Belinda thought how her mother would have gotten a kick out of the entire service. Her mother was a lively woman, and she would have enjoyed the frowns on the faces of the Peele sisters and a few others.

But then Belinda realized that she rather enjoyed a lot of it, too. This realization perturbed her. After all, she was way too young for such old-time music.

Running her gaze again over the congregation, Belinda came to a realization, which seemed a little sorrowful, considering the term "church family," that there was not one person, with the possible exception of Emma, in all that crowd whom she would call a close friend. Marilee was family, not one in whom to confide. In fact, there was not one person anywhere in the world she could claim as a close enough friend in whom to confide her situation.

She was not certain what this fact illustrated about herself, but she could see what it illustrated about her life.

The one person to whom she was the closest was Lyle, and he was the last person in the world she could tell about her situation.

With that thought, her gaze dropped to her hands, which clutched each other in her lap.

The next instant that she became aware of anything, she was outside the church, going down the steps. She even had her umbrella held over her head, thank goodness, because it was still raining. She got into her car and closed the door. She sat there a moment to collect herself before backing up and turning for the exit.

Gazing out the windshield, beyond the rhythmic swish of the wipers, she pressed the accelerator. One mile, and she was clear of most of town. She punched the button of the CD player, and the bluesy sound of Mark Knopfler filled the car, which sped over the blacktop. She saw little on the road. She was looking inside at her own perplexity and fear and confusion.

It was in the back of her mind. Little Creek Cemetery. Her father was buried there. And there came the barest whisper: *Artamincy Tice…mystic, herbalist… Her house is there, just on the other side.*

Belinda bit her bottom lip and let up on the accelerator. Then she pressed it again.

Through the wet windshield, she saw the sign for Little Creek Cemetery up ahead. It leaned toward the ditch that was filling with water.

Then…there was a car pulled to the side. It was Paris Miller's beat-up Impala, with the hood up. As Belinda passed, she saw Paris leaning in toward the engine.

Instantly Belinda let up on the gas pedal and expertly made a U-turn, her tires spinning and sinking as she drove off the road. She returned to the Impala, stopped and lowered her window, blinking in the sprinkles hitting her face.

"Sugar…get over in here out of the rain."

Paris looked up. The poor girl resembled a wet puppy dog. "Sometimes the carburetor just takes spells…. I usually can get it goin' again."

Belinda raised her window against the rain but sat there. Then she lowered the window again and told the girl firmly, "Come on…I'll take you home." The rain coming in was very annoying.

Thankfully, the girl shut the hood, reached inside the car and got her purse and hurried around to the passenger side of Belinda's Chrysler. She hesitated. "I'm soaked, Miz Belinda."

"Oh, sugar…just get in. These seats'll dry." She punched a button, turning the heater fan on high.

The girl slipped inside and sat compressed, as if not to spread her dampness. Belinda asked her where she had been going, to which she replied, "I just needed a drive."

They passed the mailbox with Artamincy Tice painted on it. Belinda glanced over to see Paris looking down the driveway. Could she have been coming to see Artamincy? She found the idea disturbing. What Belinda had thought of doing, the girl was way too young to think about. If she were in trouble, she needed to get reliable help. Belinda wrestled with knowing what to say.

She asked the girl if she wanted to go home, and Paris said she did. Belinda attempted a few comments to encourage conversation, but all she got from the girl in return were short sentences and a lot of silence. It was as if she were trying not to take up too much space or words in the world. Not only did Belinda have the urge to say, *Let me wash that mess off your face and get those earrings out of your eyebrows,* but she wanted to scream, *Sugar, take a deep breath, or you're gonna die!*

What she finally did say was that she would phone Lyle and have him take care of getting the car to Paris's home.

"Oh, but…" Paris began.

"It won't be any trouble. It's part of his job, you know." Belinda often gave Lyle jobs; she already had her cell phone to her ear.

She reached him at the sheriff's office, and, like he always did to any of her requests, he said he would handle it.

Belinda knew where Paris lived; she had some time ago delivered medicine to the grandfather, Joe Miller, a decorated Vietnam veteran. But still, the sight of that wreck of a house struck her hard as she stopped in front.

Paris thanked her, and then, "Miz Belinda?"

"Yes, sugar?"

"Do you know anything that my granddaddy could take to make him stop drinkin'?"

Ah…that explained the proximity to Artamincy Tice's place.

"Well, there are some medicines that people have used to help battle the addiction, but they do not cure. It would take a lot of cooperation from your grandfather, too. A lot of help emotionally and physically."

The girl looked downward.

"Has he ever been to Alcoholics Anonymous?"

"He won't go. Thanks again." The girl opened the door.

Belinda put a hand on her arm. "Sugar…you can get some help. I have a friend…I don't have the phone number right now, but I have it at the drugstore. There's a flyer on the bulletin board for a group called Al-Anon, and my friend's number. She's really nice, and I think talkin' to her would help you. Next time you are in there, you get the number. Okay?"

The girl gave a slight nod, ducking her head. She started to get out again, but Belinda said, "Listen…if you need help—money, a place to stay, anything—you come to me. I mean it. You can always get me through the drugstore number, and you know where I live."

Paris's gaze passed quickly over hers, and then she was out of the car with a mumbled thanks.

Belinda, somewhat startled at the offer she had made, watched the girl jump over puddles in the driveway and then enter through a side door. Her gaze went again over the small house. The sight of it through the rain was somewhat alarming. It was hard to believe that people actually lived there.

Driving off, Belinda thought of the young woman, living with her handicapped grandfather. Paris's mother had run off and left her as a baby.

The thought stabbed. The weight of the very world lay on a mother's shoulders. Belinda just did not think she could hold up.

CHAPTER 8

Steak Night at the Main Street Café

FAYRENE WAS MAKING FRESH COFFEE WHEN SHE
saw Belinda and Lyle come into the café. It was steak special
night, which generally brought Lyle in. At least twice a week
Belinda stopped in for takeout. Belinda did not like to cook,
and as much as Fayrene wanted to be catty about this, she could
not, because Fayrene herself suffered that same malady. It
seemed an odd trait for a woman who owned a restaurant. Look
at that Paula Deen—she blew her love of cooking into a restaurant, and then a hit television show and bestselling books.

People were all the time asking Fayrene about the café's
recipe for potato salad or guacamole. She could not tell them
that both came premade from a restaurant supply company, and
she swore her cooks to secrecy.

Belinda and Lyle, while chatting with other customers as
they crossed the café, headed for their usual rear booth. Fayrene

glanced over to see if the booth was empty. She was somewhat disappointed to see that it was. It seemed in that moment to be further evidence of Belinda Blaine's charmed life. And Belinda was one to go after what she wanted. At least one time when the booth had not been empty, Belinda had asked the occupant to move—but it had just been Arlo with a girlfriend.

Bringing the couple the tall glasses of cold sweet tea, with lemon, that she knew they wanted, Fayrene went to the table. She prided herself on remembering the preferences of her regulars and on giving prompt service.

"How are y'all tonight?" she said, setting the beverages on the table and even getting napkins to put under them. She would never give Belinda an opportunity to point out a lapse, no, ma'am.

"Hi, Fayrene." Belinda was always friendly as could be, and totally to annoy her, Fayrene knew. "Where's Denise tonight?"

"Over to Altus. Her sister's sick. We've got real good prime T-bones tonight, Lyle." Fayrene cut her gaze to the deputy. She knew he would get the steak no matter what. Belinda, she could not guess. Belinda chose something different all the time. That's the sort of woman she was. Fayrene, if she stopped to think about it, which she rarely did, could tell a lot about her customers by their ordering patterns.

Lyle ordered the T-bone, and Belinda chose the grilled honey-chicken with rice and steamed green beans.

"And bring me a dish of applesauce and two slices of corn bread—if it's what Woody made," Belinda added, raising an eyebrow that Fayrene noticed was a perfect feminine shape.

"It is," said Fayrene, making the note. Belinda was never shy about eating a lot.

It was just so annoying how Belinda was a fat woman but managed to go around looking so good. Her skin was alabaster—women would die for her skin—and she knew how to dress to advantage. It was amazing, but whenever Belinda walked into the café, men's heads turned to watch her. Fayrene had seen it, and she just could not understand it.

The thing that annoyed her most was Belinda's attitude. She was just so sure of herself. While Fayrene, tall and wearing the same size eight that she wore at twenty-one, and with good hair and talents of her own, had never in her life felt sure of herself more than a few fleeting hours at a time, and that usually when alone or when starting a new antidepressant medication. She was fifty-six years old now, and she had thought that she would be confident of everything by this age. She owned her own business and ran it well—yes, ma'am, she did—and had taken care of her own self for years, and supported her mother, too. She had just tried so hard for years to grow up, and she really wanted to do so now that she had somehow been blessed, and Andy had dropped into her life.

Just then, she looked over and saw Andy come through the kitchen door, as if summoned by her very thoughts.

He smiled. "What do you think?" With arms out, he showed off his new shirt, denim sport coat and jeans. He had left work earlier, going off with Woody to buy some new clothes.

Then he thrilled her by leaning over to kiss her cheek.

The next instant he had turned and disappeared back into the kitchen so fast that she was left staring at the swinging door.

"Hey, Fay…how about a bit more coffee over here?" It was Morley Lund down at the end of the counter. As she refilled his cup, Luwanna came around behind her, saying, "Two men just came in for table five, and I'm about to pee my pants, I've waited so long. Can you take care of 'em? I'll be right back."

Fayrene got the new customers—a couple of strangers who asked if there was a motel in town, so she told them about the Goodnight—set up with waters and coffee, and gave them the lowdown on the special. Then she had to get a round of refills of coffee before she could get back into the kitchen, hoping to catch Andy before he left again.

When she went through the swinging door, she saw the totally unexpected sight of Belinda Blaine standing there. Carrying on a conversation with Andy. Right there, yes, ma'am, Belinda had come right into her kitchen to chat with her own boyfriend.

Fayrene flushed. She would have died had anyone been able to read her mind, and she always felt like Belinda could do that. She quickly busied herself checking the orders on the wheel, but she called over her shoulder, "This kitchen is way too small for visitors. There's Board of Health rules, you know."

Belinda replied, "I had just heard so much about your new waiter that I wanted to meet him. Oh, are those our plates?"

Nearby, Carlos was loading Belinda's and Lyle's orders onto a tray to carry out.

"Yes, they are," said Fayrene.

Belinda said a breezy goodbye to Andy and went out, stopping to hold open the door for Carlos to carry the heavy tray.

Fayrene made a to-do of checking the stock of clean dishes, keeping her face from Andy. It was too much, Belinda coming right in like that, to a place that was all Fayrene's. Suddenly Fayrene saw everything so differently. The worn face of the kitchen, and the worn face of herself, and that Andy was younger and so sophisticated.

Then behind her Andy said, "How about we take some steak dinners over to Woody's house? And I'll buy, seeing as how I'm earning now. Can you get away, darl'?"

"Oh." His movie-star accent crept down her spine. She looked around over her shoulder and searched his eyes.

He actually appeared hopeful. Earnest.

"Well…okay…I can…if you can wait another fifteen minutes. Gail should be here to replace Denise then."

He smiled and gave a wink. "I'll give Woody a call and tell him we're on."

Happily she told the cook to put on three steaks, then headed up the stairs to get out of her waitress uniform and fix her face.

She was tearing her dress over her head when she remembered that she had not waited for Gail, and likely Luwanna and Carlos were running their feet off downstairs.

It was Belinda running her feet off, although in an unhurried manner. When Fayrene did not come back out from the kitchen, and Belinda wanted a refill on her cold tea, she got up and got it herself.

When Luwanna saw Belinda with the tea pitcher, she called, "Will you go round the room?"

Belinda refilled cold-tea glasses and visited with those she knew and those she did not, which were two men who appeared to be traveling salesmen or something like that. They were nicely dressed. Maybe real-estate investors. Valentine was getting a lot of that sort these days. The men ended up giving her their orders, because they had been overlooked and were not happy about it, either. Belinda went to the window and told the orders to the cook. While doing that, she rose up on tiptoe and tried to see around the kitchen. Neither Andy nor Fayrene was in sight.

"Can I have two more pieces of corn bread as payment for

my work?" she asked the cook, then carried them back to the table, to finish her own half-eaten meal.

Belinda asked, "What do you know about this Andy Smith?"

Lyle replied, "Well...he came in with Woody one mornin'. Seems like a nice guy. He's just jumped in to help Fayrene. She had a refrigerator go on the blink that first mornin' he was here, and he fixed it. He needed a job, and Fayrene gave him one."

"That's all? Didn't you run a check on him?"

"No. He hasn't broken any law."

She frowned at that. "Well, he does not seem like the type who would be hitchhiking across America or somethin'. Don't you think it is strange that he just showed up here in Valentine?"

Lyle shrugged. "Everybody has to be somewhere. And unless he was to break a law, it is none of my business. If we ran a check on people for no reason, we'd be at it night and day...."

"Lyle, sugar, would you please not point with your knife?"

He put the knife down. "Sorry, honey. But I am duty bound not to go runnin' makes on people just because of curiosity. I signed an oath, you know. It's invasion of privacy...and runnin' background checks costs money, and it comes from us taxpayers. Even if we did run a check, we could come up empty, which doesn't mean anything...."

He went on, and Belinda did her best to pay attention. Her eyes kept moving to the kitchen door, but Fayrene never did come back.

Later, as they drove home, perhaps watching the coral setting sun made her melancholy, but Belinda said, "Lyle, I'm just a little worried about Fayrene, that's all. We do not know anything about this Andy guy. He could be a con man, who goes around lookin' for women that he can bamboozle out of money, or even their businesses. Maybe he marries women and kills them."

The idea that the man might be after the café seemed a little far-fetched. Yet it was also a little far-fetched that Belinda could be so worried about Fayrene, but she actually was.

"Fayrene is a woman on her own, and she is our neighbor. I think you should see what you can find out about this Andy fella."

Belinda spoke in such a way that Lyle nodded and said, "Yeah, I guess you're right." And the rest of the drive home he told her the ways and means that he would do the checking.

When they entered the house, the phone was ringing. It was Belinda's mother.

"It's your mother in France," her mother said.

Belinda replied to this, "Oh, I was expectin' my mother in China."

"What time is it there?" her mother asked, as if Belinda had not said a word.

The time and weather were discussed, and then the special that evening at the café, at which time Belinda found herself talking of the stranger who had showed up and with whom Fayrene seemed in love. She told all about Andy and her concerns, and that Lyle was going to run a check.

When Belinda got off the phone, she thought back over the conversation. She realized that she had talked for twenty minutes with her mother about Fayrene's life, and together they had attempted to figure out what could be done for the woman's welfare. They had even discussed the café and how well Fayrene had done with it, and what else still could be done with it. Yet Belinda could not tell her own mother about her own difficulty that so desperately needed straightening out.

Most of the time it was far easier to straighten out the lives of other people than to work on one's own.

Woody lived on the street behind the café. It was a street of older two-story homes, with porches front and back, and narrow but deep yards. Fayrene had been known to holler out a rear window of her apartment above the café to Woody in his yard.

"Thank you much for my good supper, Miss Fayrene," Woody told her as she got ready to leave. He stood in the kitchen door, with the light behind him. "But you tell Selena she needs to learn how to sear those steaks a bit more."

"You know I am not goin' to tell her any such thing and risk her quittin'," Fayrene said. Laughing and feeling very much a young woman, she bid him goodbye and went lightly down the steps into the dark yard, with Andy right behind her.

Andy took her arm in the shadowed and unfamiliar yard. He had been living with Woody for more than a week now and had helped the older man with his extensive gardening. He knew the yard was clear to the rear concrete wall that separated it from the alley behind the café.

There was no gate in the wall, but a stile to climb over.

"I can get home from here," she told him. "You go on back—it's cold."

"Oooh, nooo, darl'. I'll see you properly to your door."

It sounded like he called her *doll,* and his tone caused warmth to wash over her.

Andy stopped just outside the pool of light at the rear of the café. Fayrene looked at him, and he bent his head, avoiding her mouth and kissing her cheek. "In you go…" He opened the door, told her to sleep well, then turned and hurried away into the shadows, jogging to the stile. He felt her gaze, and as he went over the concrete wall, he saw her standing at the door watching him.

When he came through the back door, he saw the glowing red hands of the kitchen wall clock. It was nearly eleven-thirty. The kitchen was dark, but warm lamplight shone from the living room.

Woody sat there, filling an old gooseneck rocker with his sizable girth, an enormous mug of coffee near at hand. The older man drank coffee seemingly nonstop, either black or laced thick with sugar, and slept only about four hours a night.

Andy started to tell the man good-night, but Woody said, "Sit with me a few minutes, if you would?"

There was nothing to do but go over to the opposite well-worn chair and sit. He rubbed his hands down his thighs, waiting for the question he knew was to come and attempting to form an answer.

"I think it might be best if you tell me what you're runnin' from, boy…and why you think it necessary to put on that phony accent."

Andy swallowed. He had not expected the bit about his accent.

"The accent is only half-phony," he said, without a trace of it. "I was born in Australia. My father was, *is,* Australian."

"Uh-huh." Woody regarded him expectantly.

"I don't know where to start."

"Why not start with your real name?"

"Ansel…Ansel Sullivan. But when I was a kid, I was often called Andy."

Woody nodded.

Andy tried to read the older man's face but couldn't. He pressed his palms on his thighs and shifted in his seat. Finally he said, "Back almost two years ago, I got involved with an organized group of cargo thieves. Semitruck cargo theft."

Woody did that nodding thing.

"Well, it was a nationwide operation, and not the sort to let a guy out once he's in with them."

Now that he had begun, he was finding it easier. Woody had spoken of a rough life himself—a wild twenty-year career playing piano in "juke joints" all over the South and up to Chicago, even, with Otis Spann and Louis Armstrong. The big man nodded his dark head as Andy went on to tell how he had been a junior partner in a large trucking company that operated mostly along the Southern corridors. They had been based in Dallas but then opened a terminal in Los Angeles.

"I know I was stupid. I'm not even certain how I got into it—my wife left me, and I had so much debt…and I was so mad at everyone and everything. I guess I just didn't care about anything," he said, rubbing his forehead.

Woody asked exactly what he had done.

Andy explained that his part had been to provide the information of what was in the trucks and the best times to intercept them. He knew all the schedules. At first it was done easily, guards bribed. But then things expanded, and there were guards who wanted a lot more money, or who would not take bribes. Two guards got beat up, and one shot. Not killed, but hospitalized. That was when Andy wanted out but was told that wasn't possible.

He had started out on a vacation up in Colorado, stopping in Oklahoma City for a few days for business meetings. Their trucking company was expanding again with a new terminal there. While he was in Oklahoma City, a couple of men from the theft ring paid him a visit, wanting to be let in on the details. "It was like this great, growing spiderweb," he said in anguish.

After his meetings, while walking back to his hotel, he decided to just walk out of his life. He had had the idea in the back of his mind for weeks, had brought extra money with him for his vacation. And no one would miss him. The only thing his ex-wife would miss was the alimony checks. He had no kids, no siblings; his mother was dead, and he was estranged from his father, who lived in Australia. He had no close friends, had gradually lost them all. He had hit rock bottom.

He called his secretary to tell her that he was off for Colorado for two weeks of vacation. No one was likely to start looking for him until those two weeks had passed. Then he packed all that he could in the one duffel bag, dropped his other suitcases and belongings at a local homeless shelter and sold his car to one of those small car dealers, receiving cash. He took a cab to the nearest truck stop, where he hitched a ride.

He waited a few moments for a response from Woody, who did no more than nod thoughtfully.

Andy then said, "Two of the men from the organization came into the café this evening."

"Ah-huh." This time Woody's eyes flickered with sharp interest.

"They must be checking around in the towns along the highway I took. I didn't think about them doin' that. I didn't count on anyone lookin' for me already. I guess they tried to reach me in Colorado."

Woody pulled on his ear.

Andy said, "But those guys aren't likely to stay and look

around. They'll check the motel, not find me and move on. I think most people would assume I've headed down to Mexico."

Woody nodded, closing one eye in thought. "I guess you'd better not work the breakfast shift tomorrow mornin', just in case."

Andy breathed a little more easily. The old man seemed to be on his side.

Then Woody said, "You watch yourself with Miss Fayrene. She's got a tender heart."

"Yes, sir."

"Now, I guess you'd better get on up and get some sleep."

The big man had a voice to be obeyed.

"Yeah…thanks, Woody."

Woody nodded and watched the younger man disappear up the stairs. He wondered how much of Andy's story was true. Sometimes people lied to themselves so much that they completely lost track of the truth.

The streetlights and the large Blaine's Drugstore sign illuminated Fayrene's apartment over the café, all the way through the living room and into the bedroom. It was an exceedingly romantic room, with lots of floral print and lace. She had made it up from several magazine covers.

She came out of her bathroom after her extensive ablutions, in which she attempted to hold back time, and had plenty of light to see to get into bed. She sighed as she sank onto her three down-filled pillows. Her hair was pinned back from her face, and she had Frownies taped on her brow and at the corners of her eyes and mouth, but in her mind's eye she saw herself as a womanly beauty, lying romantically in the speckled light, enjoying dreams of *the* man in her life. Finally, her prince had come.

I do so know a lot about him, she mentally answered a voice that sounded vaguely like a cross between her mother and Belinda Blaine.

"Nothing?" Belinda said. They were in her small office in the back of the store.

"Nothin' on any Andy Smith matchin' this guy's description. There's no priors and no warrants of any kind. Not even any traffic violations, at least not in Oklahoma. In fact, there's not an Oklahoma driver's license for any Andy Smith matchin' his description."

"Can you check other states?"

"He could have a license from another country, but, honey, unless he breaks some law, I just don't like pryin' into the guy's life. That's abusin' the office."

It was always difficult for Lyle to deny Belinda anything, much less stand up to her. She might have been a lot shorter than he was, but she was tougher. Only his regard for what was right about the law enabled him to take a stand now.

"I don't think Andy Smith is his name," she said.

"Probably not, but usin' an alias is not against the law. People have private lives and a right to live them."

He noticed her look at him for a long minute with an expression that raised his curiosity, but then he decided not to take a chance, and distracted her by grabbing her and kissing her. She responded quickly, before pushing him aside, as the bell rang out above the drugstore door as people entered.

She said, "Go on home and make one of your sleepin' drinks with yogurt. I bought you a fresh quart."

"Okay, honey." He kissed her cheek. "I sure love you."

She watched him leave and pass in front of the plate-glass

window. Her hand went to her belly. She was going to have to tell him. She was going to have to tell him all of it.

But not yet. She had time. She would wait and see.

CHAPTER 9

Girls to Women

TEACHER MEETINGS! SCHOOL LET OUT AN HOUR early. Corrine and Paris came running out, and threw themselves and their backpacks into Paris's car. Paris turned the key, and the car chugged in a manner that made them hold their breath. Then it caught. They grinned at each other.

Belinda Blaine's voice—it was the *About Town and Beyond* report—came out of the radio as Paris headed the car out of the parking lot. "…incident of burning leaves gettin' away. A cedar tree in Leon Purvis's yard went up like a torch, while Leon stood there tryin' to dribble it to death. I saw this myself, because I was makin' a delivery to Margaret Wyatt across the street, when I heard this big whoosh and turned and saw the tree, and Leon standing there with his hose. Leon said that he had not checked, and the hose turned out to have so many leaks from being left out during the winter that only a small stream came out the end.

"Now, for *Beyond,* here is the latest letter from my mother in France...."

The girls looked at each other and giggled.

Corrine said, "Belinda says stuff just like that all the time, real serious, but it just comes out funny. The other day I heard her talkin' to a customer on the phone, and she said, 'Sugar, I don't know what to tell you. I guess just get better or die.'" Corrine's imitation caused both girls to laugh out loud.

"How's your aunt Marilee takin' you workin'?" Paris asked. "You not bein' around all the time?"

"Oh, okay. She has Rosalba, who's really good help." Corrine turned her gaze out the windshield. That Aunt Marilee was okay with it was not exactly true. Aunt Marilee had asked several times if Corrine liked her job, and when Corrine said she did, Aunt Marilee had all but cried. Corrine still felt that she had abandoned her aunt, no matter that she also knew perfectly well that she had to grow up and live her own life.

"So you like workin' for Miss Belinda?" Paris shot her a raised eyebrow.

"Yeah...it's pretty cool. She's particular, but she's okay. I meant to tell you that if you want any makeup or anything, I can get it for you at ten percent discount."

"Hey, cool. I'll take a look."

After a minute of thinking and deciding it was okay because she wasn't mentioning names, Corrine said, "Some people come to the back door of the drugstore, and Belinda gives them stuff. One time I saw her give a barbecue lunch, and another time I saw her take cash out of the drawer and give it to this guy."

"Really?" Paris looked ahead. She herself had done the

same while clerking at the Quick Stop. Usually kids that she knew who didn't have a lot of snacks to eat. They might steal it, if she did not simply give it, and the Berrys, who owned the Quick Stop, told her to give if she thought it necessary. She couldn't tell this to Corrine, though.

Corrine was saying, "Uh-huh. It was to that old guy you see pickin' up pop cans all the time. I just never expected that to go on—people to come to the rear door of the drugstore."

Paris thought of how Corrine lived, in Mr. Winston's big house, and with a beautiful bedroom and just about anything she could want—and *two* mothers, her aunt Marilee and her own mother down in Louisiana.

Corrine was saying, "Well, Belinda acts pretty tough, but she isn't. She gives people free stuff all the time. She gives Willie Lee and Munro free ice cream—the drugstore is the only store in town where Munro can come. And she doesn't bill anything that old Minnie Oakes steals."

Just then, squinting in the bright light, Corrine saw Willie Lee pushing Mr. Winston in his wheelchair along the sidewalk. Munro trotted along behind them. They appeared to have just come out of the IGA.

She rolled down her window. "Hey, Mr. Winston… Hey, Willie Lee!"

Paris slowed and waved, too.

Mr. Winston had gotten a motorized wheelchair at a yard sale, and sometimes Willie Lee simply walked along beside; however, very often the motor failed. Mr. Winston refused to buy a new one. He said, "I'm dead set on seein' which of us goes first, the chair or me."

"You know what Belinda says to this?" Corrine told Paris. "She says, 'I'll get my gun and satisfy your curiosity.' Mr.

Winston and Belinda act like they don't like each other, but she waits on him hand and foot."

The two girls decided they had time to cruise the length of Main Street before Corrine had to get to work. Windows rolled down, they waved and hollered at everyone they knew. There were a number of other cruising teens doing the same thing, giving evidence of the full arrival of spring at last.

It seemed to have come overnight. The previous day, the new digital sign in front of city hall, Mayor Upchurch's pride and joy, had a temperature reading of forty-five degrees. Paris pointed to the sign now; it read sixty-eight.

Up and down Main Street, the decorative flags of the spring season had been attached to the light poles, and signs in plate-glass windows announced all manner of spring specials. Grace Florist had their green awning unfurled and a display of assorted flowers in buckets of water out front. They always sold double the amount of bouquets all through summer with this technique.

Across the street, the Main Street Café advertised new healthy salads made with organic spring greens, and Fayrene had even been overheard once again giving voice to the idea of setting up tables on the sidewalk out front. She had been thinking about it for three years. What held her back was the thought of the winds. As Winston kept telling her, "Darlin', this is not New York City. Your tables could end up in Kansas."

Several doors down from the café, the window of Molly Hayes, Accounting, promoted last-minute income tax filing, with a countdown of days until the deadline, and opposite, the Sweetie Cakes Bakery advertised a special on Easter cupcakes and ladies' club sweet rolls. On the corner, the Community Bank's digital sign advertised special spring CD rates.

The girls cruised on past the intersection of First and Main, and turned around in the large area beside the fire station, heading back again. Paris stopped in the street in front of the drugstore, causing traffic to pile up behind her. Corrine grabbed her backpack, hopped out and raced away with a wave.

The bell over the door gave out its friendly ring as Corrine entered the store, and she heard, "Hey, sugar!"

Turning, she saw Belinda at the wide window on the pharmacy side of the store.

"Come on over here, girl, and help me make up a spring display."

Belinda was absurdly happy to see Corrine, and to experience doing a window display with someone other than her mother. She and her mother always ended up in arguments, but she and Corrine seemed to have the same train of thought about how things should be done. Belinda liked simplicity, and so did Corrine. Belinda liked keeping to the point, and so did Corrine. Belinda liked traditional spring colors, and Corrine knew what those were.

The girl was absolutely the best worker Belinda had ever had. In the total of ten days that she had been working, she had learned to handle a busy counter all by herself, remember three and four orders at a time, and who had paid and who needed to be reminded to pay, and she was not shy about reminding people, either.

"Hi, there, beautiful." Larry Joe Darnell slipped onto a vacant stool at the end of the counter.

"Hello. Root-beer float today?" asked Corrine, cocking her head.

"Yep, think I will."

"Comin' right up!"

Belinda watched this exchange from over at the cash register, where she stood counting the day's money and stuffing it into the bank bag. Corrine was lit up like a Christmas tree, and Larry Joe's eyes remained on her as she bent into the freezer to dig out the ice cream. He asked her about school that day, and she asked him about work.

Since the first day the girl had started working, Larry Joe had not once missed stopping in around four o'clock. The school crowd still filled the drugstore, so Corrine was kept busy getting soft drinks, nachos and ice-cream dishes. In between customers, mostly rowdy teen boys and smart-alecky teen girls, she would pause in front of Larry Joe and chat with him. Anybody with the least perception could see what went on between them when they came together, except Larry Joe himself.

Young men could be so thick, Belinda thought.

After Larry Joe left, when Corrine was clearing away his float dish, Belinda said, "You're crazy about that guy, aren't you?"

Corrine's response to this was to duck her head and shrug. "He's cute." Then her chin came up. "I like him."

"Oh, I can see that." Belinda watched Corrine put dishes in the small dishwasher.

"I'm not even eight years younger than he is," Corrine said, raising her chin higher. She had the neck of a swan and the eyes of a woman already.

"That's not anythin'," replied Belinda.

Corrine then said, "But he thinks I'm just a kid."

"Oh, sugar, his lips may say that, but his eyes do not."

"Do you think so?"

"Oh, yeah. And time flies. You'll be catchin' him in two years. Eighteen and then twenty comes pretty fast. You are a young woman gettin' older all the time."

"I just hope he waits." The girl's eyes looked at some distant point.

"Oh, he'll wait, or he'll be goin' through a divorce," said Belinda in a manner so certain that Corrine took it as a pronouncement of her good future to come.

The next instant Belinda grabbed her rather large purse. "Now, I'm off early to the bank, and then I gotta run up to Lawton for an appointment. I'm leavin' you to close up tonight. You have any trouble, you just call on Oran, or you can call my cell phone, but you may have to leave a message."

"I can handle it, Miss Belinda."

"I know you can, sugar."

Again the woman spoke with such breezy confidence that Corrine felt fully capable of anything that might come her way. In fact, she went around to the magazine shelves and told the tough senior-class boys there to stop their loitering and made them pay for the magazines they had crumpled, then she moved on to the makeup rack and told the girls to stop shoplifting and made them pay for packages they had pried open. All the teens complied quite readily, and at least two said, "Yes, ma'am."

Returning behind the soda fountain counter, Corrine made herself a cherry Coca-Cola, with two real cocktail cherries. She then scooted her little fanny up on Miss Belinda's stool to sip her drink through a straw while dreaming of how she and Larry Joe were going to get engaged. In the ten days that she had worked for Belinda Blaine, she had learned that the woman had eyes in the back of her head, as Aunt Marilee would have said, and was rarely wrong about anything.

Belinda would have laughed at that description of herself. Right then, as she drove, with eyes shielded by large dark sunglasses, she felt wrong all the way around. In fact, she was so preoccupied by feeling wrong that she did not see anything. She drove completely on automatic pilot, and by the time she arrived at her destination, her head was about to explode.

When she pulled into a parking space in the lot of a small but modern building and found herself gazing at the sign— Women's Health Care—she could not remember making the trip. How long she gazed at the sign, she did not know, but suddenly she blinked, looked at her watch and got out of her car, straightened her suit in a nervous manner, then walked slowly into the building.

Dr. Desirée Zwolle, Gynecologist, was the last of the three names printed on the glass door. Belinda took a deep breath and entered.

The receptionist handed over a clipboard with about a million forms that Belinda filled out in a less than diligent manner, then returned the forms to the receptionist, who took them without looking up.

Belinda sat back down, this time choosing what appeared to be a more comfortable large wingback chair. She looked around the room and found herself impressed. It was very tastefully, femininely decorated.

There were only four other occupants in the waiting area. A very tired-looking mother with a rambunctious toddler sat on the couch. The woman closed her eyes intermittently.

Belinda thought she looked the sort who probably had at least five more children at home.

A young couple sat in adjoining chairs. The girl had long straight blond hair and cheerleader makeup. The boy looked like a toothpaste advertisement. They were going through a book of baby names and speaking the names aloud to try them out. Their last name was apparently Oxley. "Aiden Oxley… Bethany Oxley… Caleb Oxley…" Listening to them wore Belinda out.

When the tired-looking mother was called back to the exam rooms, she passed the young couple and said, "You might want to make sure you pick a name now. After you've been in labor for thirty-six hours, you come up with something like Cyrano…Cyrano Schultz. That's what I named my third one."

The younger woman's eyes widened and swung anxiously to her husband. *Thirty-six hours,* she mouthed.

The young man looked totally helpless; then he took to the baby name book like a life raft and began reading more names aloud.

Belinda's cell phone rang. She pulled it out of her purse and looked at the small screen. *Unknown Caller.* But Belinda knew, in that way that is without doubt, that the caller was her mother. That was how things worked between them.

She turned the phone off and tucked it back into her purse, and attempted to make her mind a blank so that her mother could not read it all the way from France.

Finally Belinda was escorted back to an exam room. The nurse, who introduced herself as Betty, was an older woman with a competent manner. She looked over Belinda's chart, saying things like, "So you are pregnant…well, mostly those home tests are accurate… First time? I see you are thirty-eight…get a lot of older mothers these days…" She was quite friendly, until, "You have not seen a doctor in over seven years."

Her gaze shot over the top of her glasses, demanding an explanation.

"I rarely get sick," Belinda offered. She felt absurdly lacking.

"Well, honey, how do you *know?* Pap smears and mammograms are to catch things early."

Nurse Betty took Belinda's blood pressure and shook her head. Belinda, who had been feeling more wrong and more alarmed by the minute, watched the woman pull items out of a drawer and plop them onto the tray near the examination table that Belinda had been trying not to look at.

"Dr. Zwolle will be in here in a few minutes," the nurse said, the words sounding like something of a threat. Then she gestured toward the wall. "There are some pamphlets with information for mothers over thirty-five…and on *why we have regular exams*. You might want to give those a look."

She breezed out. The door closed.

Belinda gazed at the door for a moment, then slowly turned to the rack of pamphlets. They were very disorderly. She went over and automatically began straightening them. "*We* need to keep more order," she said aloud.

She spied *Pregnancy After 35*. This one she slowly took down and began to read.

Women over the age of 35 may have trouble conceiving… Ha! Then next: *They also have a greater chance of having twins.*

Barely realizing that she did so, Belinda sank into a straight-backed chair.

Her eyes returned to the pamphlet in the vague hope that she had misread and then continued in some sort of frantic manner: *Increased risk of miscarriage…Down syndrome…gestational diabetes…high blood pressure…*

Well, even if she didn't have any of those things, she was in danger of being scared to death.

"Ms. Blaine?"

"Yes?"

"Did you hear me? I said you can get dressed, and I'll be back to talk with you."

"Oh. Yes. Thank you."

Belinda realized that she was sitting up on the exam table. She slowly stepped down to the floor. As she began to dress, she became aware of having no memory of the exam.

She remembered meeting Dr. Zwolle, who proved to be a surprisingly youthful and beautiful woman, with very good taste in clothes. The doctor was also competent and cordial, and she did not say one word of censure about Belinda not having regular checkups. Obviously the woman had good sense, and kept to what was important and her own business. Belinda had felt reassured. And she had made a point of telling the doctor how much she liked the pleasant waiting room and that the exam room had hooks on the wall for her clothes. She didn't say anything about the disorderly pamphlets.

Belinda remembered being left alone to undress, and then the doctor returning and helping her onto the examination table. After that was all a blank. Except—

She looked upward over the exam table. Yes, there was a poster of a debonair George Clooney fastened onto the ceiling.

The doctor returned again and took the rolling stool. Belinda sat in the straight-backed chair, clutching her purse and her senses. She watched the woman's face and listened as carefully as possible, although there seemed to be a sort of roaring in her head after the doctor said, "Yes, I agree with that little stick that you are pregnant."

There was more about necessary blood tests and keeping a watch on her blood pressure, which was a little high. The doctor suggested Belinda get a blood pressure home tester. She also wanted her to watch her sugar and carbohydrate intake, and to get moderate exercise. She gave Belinda several pages of instruction on these matters.

"Do you have any questions?" the doctor asked when she had finished.

"Yes," said Belinda. She then shifted in her seat and gazed at the doctor so long that the woman leaned forward with a questioning expression.

Finally Belinda forced out the words. "I had an abortion. Twenty…well, nineteen years ago. I've read that there can be a higher rate of miscarriage."

"Ah-huh." The doctor sat back.

Belinda watched the woman's face, finding no clue as to her thoughts.

"Well, yes." The doctor nodded. "A number of studies have indicated higher rates of miscarriage in women who've had abortions. And miscarriage rates for women over thirty-five begin to climb, too. What this means for you is that we will monitor you very carefully. We will need to have the results of your blood tests to get a more complete picture. However, I see no problem at this point. You appear a very healthy woman, Ms. Blaine, and you do not indicate any other risk factors. You don't smoke…drink…take drugs?"

"No!" The thought pricked. "I have sometimes had a glass of wine at dinner or at night…or on special occasions."

"That small amount is fine, but cut it out for now. You're in good shape, and we're going to take good care of you." The doctor looked intently but not unkindly at Belinda. "You do want this baby, then?"

"Yes, yes, I *do*."

She had said it now. Aloud. Her ugly secret was out. She had told someone for the first time in nineteen years that she had had an abortion.

She drove along the boulevard. The sun sank in glorious gold to the west. She turned on the headlights and raked a hand through her hair in a careless manner that she normally did not do.

Nineteen years old, she had been at the time. Her second year in college. The first time she had dared to fall in love. Madison Ferguson. It had started by her tutoring him in English. She had not been pretty or popular, but she had been necessary. She could hardly believe when Madison had stayed late with her. It wasn't until later that she realized they had never been on a date. He had never gone anywhere they might be seen together.

"Stupid fat cow, why weren't you on the pill?" he said when she told him. Then, "It was just for fun…for laughs…and it might not even be mine."

She had thought she would die of the pain, shame and humiliation. "Fat cow," she would hear over and over in memory.

She did not go to her parents, because she had never gone to her parents. She could not remember clearly, but it might have been during one of her parents' flares of not talking to each other. She had no close friends. She had always done everything on her own. There had been plenty of information about abortion around the university campus. It had seemed the only way.

Since that time she had avoided regular gynecological checkups and doctors in general. She could hardly stand for a doctor to touch her. She avoided children in the same way. She told herself, and rightly so, that she would not make a good mother. And after all, was not Lyle enough of a child for her?

She wanted this baby. She had said that aloud now, too.

How much she wanted it was a surprise to her.

Wanting the baby was not a question. Being *deserving* of a baby *was*.

Her hand went to her belly.

She was certain the baby was going to be taken from her, as punishment for what she had done. Who she was. Who she would never be.

That sounded crazy. Didn't she believe in a loving God?

She supposed she did, except for this one point. Maybe she believed God loved everyone else, but that she was a particularly hard and bad case, so He could not love her. What sort of mother would she make? She did not know how to be a mother. Everything she had learned was from her own mother, who had never been exceptionally good at the job. Her mother even admitted this. No women in their family should have children. They messed up the job.

Just then she became aware of something uncomfortable on her arm. It was the bandage on her inner elbow, where she'd had the blood test done. She reached up her sleeve, yanked off the bandage and tossed it out the window. She did not want to risk any questions from Lyle or anyone else.

What if she ended up having a miscarriage? What if God took the baby from her like that? Lyle would be crushed. She would fail him terribly. It was better to wait and see, at least for a time.

She tried not to get herself attached to the idea of being pregnant. That way she would not be too hurt if things went wrong.

When she got home, she poured herself a glass of wine and took it to the bathroom, where she ran hot water for a bath. She was immersed in the water and had drunk half the glass before remembering that the doctor had told her not to have alcohol, and wondering if she should be in the hot water. She hopped out of the tub and poured the wine down the sink. For some reason, afterward she felt compelled to drink a full glass of water as an antidote.

PART TWO

It Takes Faith, Not Expectations

CHAPTER 10

1550 on the Radio Dial
Riding Along on a Carousel

THE EARLY-MORNING *WAKE UP* HOUR AND WHAT was now the signature reveille were a success.

By the end of the first week, Jim Rainwater had made a recording of Winston, Everett and Willie Lee yelling, "Get up! Get up, you sleepyhead!" complete with the sound effect of the bugle call. All Jim had to do was flip a switch, and the yell went out, first to open the show at 6:00 a.m., then at the half hour, and to close at 7:00 a.m. Once in a while Winston would yell out the refrain at an unexpected moment, just to keep everyone on their toes and to amuse himself.

The second week of the program, a radio station over in Ardmore called and wanted to purchase rights to use the tape. This request resulted in Tate, Everett and attorney Jaydee Mayhall getting in a deep discussion about all manner of property rights and values. Winston listened to the men for a few minutes, and then slipped away to Jim Rainwater's crowded little office, picked up the telephone on the crowded little desk and called the manager of the Ardmore station. After a brief, friendly discussion, Winston privately conferred with Jim Rainwater and had the young man send over the recording. He informed the others after the fact.

"Got to strike while the fire is hot," Winston said, and told the men they could now work out their legalities.

This proved to be a fortuitous path of action, because by the end of the week, two more radio stations contacted them. Winston happened to take the second call, which was from a major station in the Oklahoma City market. Winston doubled the asking price and received it readily.

That Winston pretty much called the shots on everything aggravated Everett Northrup to death. On the air, Winston continued to just spout out anything he wanted to say, while Everett felt that was a poor way to conduct a radio show. He tried writing script after script for them to follow, but Winston never went along.

What bothered Everett the most was that no matter how hard he tried, he was not able to think up clever, witty things like Winston did right on the spot. Sometimes Everett was awake half the night, attempting to think up witty things to say. He would come up with a few that sounded good in those dark hours, but when he tried to say them in the light of day, they came out all twisted.

Further annoying was that Winston told him, "Everett, you just got to loosen up, buddy," or "Don't take it so serious, you won't get off the earth alive."

Those comments, and many others, drove Everett crazy. He

did try to loosen up, but the more he tried, the worse every-thing seemed to turn out for him and the tighter he got.

Another frustration was that everyone persisted in calling the show *Waking Up with Winston*. Sometimes people might say *Waking Up with Winston and Willie Lee,* but no one ever went to the trouble to add Everett's name. Worse yet, a lot of people just called it *Winston's Early Morning Hour,* which would throw Everett into a tizzy. Once Everett had gotten so worked up as to yank off his hat, throw it down and stomp on it, yelling, "It is the *Wake Up* show—PERIOD! That's the name, if you want to say it right!"

Yet still and all, as the weeks went on, Everett began to have more success than ever in his relatively short life as a radio-show host. Maybe than ever in his life, period. The call-ins to his *Everett in the Morning* show doubled, and people actually stopped him on the street and complimented him (or com-plained, but that counted) on something he had said on the air. He began to see that being second banana, or in some cases third, as he and Willie Lee ran neck and neck, was a lot better than being no banana at all.

Then one day Winston came in with one of those grand ideas of his, and Everett realized something.

"I was cleanin' out old newspapers," Winston said into the microphone, "and I found this news item from the *Valentine Voice*—that's our hometown newspaper and actual owner of this station, so we should give them a plug, don't you think?" Winston raised an eyebrow at Everett.

"Yes, we should," said Everett, conscious of filling airtime. "And what is the news item?"

"Well, it is about another Oklahoma town, Elk City. Y'all know where Elk City is, don't you?" Raised eyebrow again.

"Yes," Everett said, then added, so as to not sound stupid, "It's out west on Interstate 40." The question reminded him that he was not a native Oklahoman.

Then Willie Lee chimed in, "Al-most to Tex-as, on what was his-tor-ic Rouu-te 66."

Winston's obvious rehearsal with Willie Lee made Everett jealous. He tried to get a look at the newspaper item, but Winston kept it turned from him.

Everett said, "Well, what about the news item? Are you goin' to tell us today?"

Winston drawled, "Yes, I am. This item is about Elk City havin' their centennial celebration last year. That's quite a feat, you know."

"Cen-ten-nial is one hun-dred years," put in Willie Lee.

"That's correct. And you all know this is Valentine's centennial year."

"Yes, sir," said Everett importantly. "The library already has special education programs on the first Saturday of every month, and we got plans for a grand celebration the first weekend of November, the very month that Valentine was first incorporated. We've got a grand parade, a bluegrass festival, and the famous Red Earth dancers comin', too. We'll be havin' more on all of that as it develops," he added into the microphone.

"Well, bein' around for a hundred years is quite an accomplishment. I've been around for over ninety myself, so I know. A bang-up celebration is definitely in order."

Winston could sure milk it, Everett thought. There was no way he could equal Winston and all those years. Everett was just old, but Winston was an *institution*.

"Well, sir," continued Winston, "for their centennial, the Elk Citians raised money and put in a real wooden carousel.

I'm talkin' hand-carved horses…all Western themed. And they built a building, too, just to house it. Now, that's celebratin', wouldn't you say, Everett?"

"Yes…yes, it is."

At last Winston passed over the newspaper clipping. Everett tried to focus through his bifocals.

Winston was saying, "I remember carousels from when I was a kid. Lots of towns had them in city parks. And I recall seein' big ones up in Oklahoma City and down in Dallas. Do you recall those, Everett?"

"I remember one at the state fair up in Michigan," said Everett, which was the best he could think of.

"Well, in the early 1900s even small towns might have a carousel. They were just real popular, but durin' the Depression things like carousels were let go. There just wasn't the money to keep 'em up. When things started gettin' prosperous again, the move was to cheap and modern on everything, and everyone got cars and drove around and didn't go so much to city parks. Pinball machines and pool parlors came in. Do you remember those, Everett?"

"Oh, yes," said Everett, although he really did not. He had not had the wide life that Winston had led.

"Well, this carousel Elk City put in is the real deal. A small town like that has got them a real prize. And the idea that came to me this mornin' was that we in Valentine should think about doin' the same. We might not be near as big as Elk City, but we sure do have gumption. I think in celebration of Valentine's hundred years, we should see about improvin' our city park with a carousel. What do you all think?"

Everett saw Winston speaking directly into the microphone, and he realized then that Winston was speaking as if all those people out there were right in front of him, and he was talking directly to each one. Winston's eyes behind his glasses were looking far off and intent.

Then those eyes swung over to Everett. "What do you think of that idea, Ev?"

"Well…it would be a grand gesture." Everett pushed his brain to work fast. What he was thinking of was the cost, and that there was a city road system in dire need of repairs, and the newly built library requiring shelving and computers, and the city pool was far too small and old. He opened his mouth to give voice to this, but Winston jumped in.

"Yes, sir, it would be *grand,*" said Winston. "My thoughts exactly. Why, durin' rodeo weekend, we wouldn't need that little carnival merry-go-round if we had the real thing. I think we need to get the city council goin' on this idea. How 'bout you all out there call in with what you think of the grand idea of a carousel for our town."

Everett stared at Winston a moment, then reached out his hand and grabbed the microphone. "What I *had* been going to say is that a carousel like this would be a grand gesture, but it would require a mammoth amount of *money,* not to mention *time.* You can't just pick up a carousel at the Wal-Mart, you know. We have roads that need repair, and the swimming pool needs attention, and the library had its funding cut last year. The tax base is not here for it. Before we go pursuin' a thing like a carousel, we need careful examination of our income, and the best use of our money and energy for the community."

He was pleased to find that he did not stumble over the words. He may not have been as eloquent as Winston, but he spoke his convictions.

The next instant, Winston slapped him on the back, hard

enough to push Everett forward. "You got it, buddy," said Winston with enthusiasm. "We do need careful examination, and we don't want to be mired down with the city government and any new taxes. The citizens of Valentine can raise the money for a carousel themselves. Keep the government out of it, and we can get things done.

"Now, let's have some callers. What do you all out there think? We'll start a vote—for or against a carousel for our town."

Everett stared at him.

In that minute, while watching Winston's animation, Everett saw clearly that Winston came off looking so witty because he stole words out of other people's mouths and twisted them around to suit him. Winston paid no attention to facts. He made his own world.

"Put me down as a vote in favor of the carousel," said Rosalba Garcia, calling and adjusting her stockings at the same time. "We need a merry-go-round for the kids."

"I'm a vote against a carousel. We have plenty of other things that need money, and we can't hardly get those done. This is Inez Cooper. If you are gonna take any sort of real survey on this thing, you will need to keep track of the names with the vote, or we'll have people votin' twice."

Inez knew this, because she had voted several times on the panty-hose issue a couple of years ago. She had thought it all in fun, but people had sure gotten upset when Belinda Blaine had found out about Inez's multiple votes and told it all over.

"Miss Inez makes a good point," Winston said into the microphone. "We might want to consider drawin' up a petition. You could do that, Everett. You're good at such details."

"Ah, well…"

"Let's play a little Alan Jackson for the folks, and y'all keep those calls comin' in."

The phone rang again. Jim Rainwater recorded: "This is Rosalba Garcia. I called the first time. I want to vote *for* a carousel. Some people in this town are what you call stick-in-the-muds and do not want fun. And I want you to put what I said on the radio…air."

"This is Julia Jenkins-Tinsley, and I vote for a carousel, if it's one adults can ride. I tried to get on the one at the county fair, and they told me it was just for kids."

"This is Lyle Midgette…heck, yeah for a carousel. That's a merry-go-round, right?"

"This is Gabby Smith. Hi, Willie Lee. I will see you later at school. I vote for the carousel, and my brother Fisk says to put him down, too. Bye."

"Hi back, Gab-by," said Willie Lee, shyness in his voice.

The calls trickled in all through the hour and continued right on into the *Everett in the Morning* show.

At first Everett was annoyed. He had planned to discuss the serious subject of illegal immigration. He even had a telephone interview scheduled with Senator James Inhofe, but now he was kept busy with listeners calling in and talking about the carousel. It turned out that when he did get to speak with Senator Inhofe, the senator had been informed about the carousel discussion and said, "I want to be put down as a vote in favor of the carousel, and our office will donate to the fund." The interview ended up focusing more on the senator's childhood experiences with carousels than it did on political matters.

Everett was torn in his emotions. He was aggravated that the discussion revolved around the carousel, but he was thrilled to receive call-ins to his program like he'd never had before.

By that evening, after being questioned about the facts by several people he met during the day, he finally realized that his entire purpose was to be the opposite of Winston. He was the straight man to Winston's foolishness. The more he went against Winston's viewpoint, the more controversy he stirred, and the more publicity he got.

He could do it!

Down at Blaine's Drugstore, Belinda put out a yellow tablet with the heading *Carousel,* and below that *For* and *Against.* Everett came in and suggested that she needed a third column headed: *How Much Will You Give?*

"Oh, people would just lie about it," said Belinda.

Quite quickly Fayrene over at the Main Street Café followed suit with a petition. At Andy's suggestion, she decided to be first at fundraising and set out a widemouth old Tom's Crackers jar, with a note that read: *Contribute to a Fund for Carousel, Park and Library.* She thought she would touch all the bases. Apportioning of the money could be decided later.

Then Tate Holloway, as editor and publisher of the *Valentine Voice,* made the carousel idea the subject of his Sunday editorial. He said he was not ready to commit the newspaper to a certain stance yet, and he invited people to drop by his office to chat with him about it. He loved for people to come by and talk with him about things. "The coffee's always hot," he always ended his editorial.

The first person to drop by the *Voice* and talk with Tate was John Cole Berry. The two men were good friends and both on the chamber of commerce. One thing Tate admired about

John Cole was that the man had built one small convenience store up into a chain of five thriving stores, and three of those were large truck stops. John Cole knew how to make money, and what only a few knew was that the Berry Corporation also gave away a lot of money through a charitable trust run by Emma Berry. When Emma heard about the carousel idea, she told John Cole that she wanted to involve the entire company in the fundraising efforts.

"The Berry Corporation will start the fund drive off with a five-thousand-dollar donation," John Cole told Tate, "and we'll match dollar for dollar the first ten thousand raised around town."

Tate announced this in his Wednesday editorial, when he officially brought the newspaper out in full support of the centennial carousel, as he named it.

After that, the Community Bank put up the question on their digital sign: *Do You Want a Carousel? Fund Open Here.* And the bank, not to be outdone by the Berry Corporation, put in ten thousand dollars.

The Cut & Curl put out a jar to collect money, and MacCoy's Feed and Grain said they would match the Berry Corporation's donation. Iris MacCoy jumped right in with this announcement on Winston's *Home Folks* show.

Vella Blaine, all the way over in France, read Tate's editorial on the *Valentine Voice* Web site, and telephoned to the radio station during the *Wake Up* hour.

"Am I on live now? Is that what Jim said?"

Jim went to adjusting sound levels.

"Yes, Miss Vella. You're on the air. This is Winston. How are you this mornin'?"

"Hello, everybody! This is Vella Blaine callin' from over in

France. Can you hear me okay? Jim told me not to shout." She still raised her voice because she was on a cell phone.

"Yes, darlin', you're comin' in just fine. How are you this mornin'?"

"It's afternoon over here. I can't get over how clearly I can hear you…well, I could, but now this guy over here started playin' a guitar and singin'." She moved the cell phone, but everyone could still hear her say, "Pardon…*pardon,* sir? *S'il vous plaît!* English…*s'il vous plaît,* move on. I'm tryin' to talk on the phone. *Oui…merci.* Now, where was I?"

"You're over in Nice, France," Winston said, being funny.

To which Vella said blithely, "No, actually, I'm not."

"You're not?"

"No. Lillian and I came up here to Monte Carlo for a couple of days. Lillian wanted to see some museum or somethin' old and educational. She never misses that stuff. I came to go to the casino. We parted company while we're here. She likes to stay in those old hotels to get the flavor of the area and keep her pocketbook closed. I say I've come on vacation to have what I do not have at home. I'm stayin' at the Monte Carlo Beach Hotel. I'm on a lounge chair in the shade, and enjoyin' free drinks and surrounded by gorgeous young men just happy to wait on lonely ladies with money. "

"Sounds like a time, Miss Vella."

"You bet it is. And just last night I was over at Le Sun Casino. I won over a thousand dollars. There's a part of that place decorated like a circus, and they have these slot machines all arranged like a carousel. Had a beautiful top over them and ever'thing. Carousels are big over here. Just about every town I've been in, I've seen a carousel. Double-deckers, even."

"Double-decker carousels?" One of the few things that Winston had never heard of.

"Yes. Now, the point of my call is that I want to be put down as a vote *for* gettin' a carousel for Valentine. And I've decided that if Valentine puts in a carousel—and I don't mean some little slipshod job, I want a *real* carousel—I will donate the money for the building to house it."

It was a rare moment, when Winston could think of nothing to say.

Over at the drugstore, Belinda had been listening to her mother on the small radio behind the soda fountain counter. At her mother's statement, Belinda choked on her coffee so hard that she had to grab a napkin to put over her mouth.

"Hey…that's nice of Mother Blaine," said Lyle, who had dropped in after his night shift to hang around and help at opening the store. Thus far he had not found anything to do, though, but refill the foam cup dispenser and drink coffee.

Jaydee Mayhall, who had been let in early, was halfway onto a stool at the counter. He froze, his eyes meeting Belinda's and his dark eyebrows rising. He listened as Vella and Winston made a few more comments on the radio. When music came on, he pulled out his cell phone and dialed the radio station.

Winston greeted him. "Hi, there, Jaydee… Folks, this is Jaydee Mayhall on the line. He's a local attorney and current member of the city council. Whatcha got for us, Jaydee?"

"I'm callin' strictly as a citizen," said Jaydee. "I own the twenty acres adjoining the city park. It even has a small pond. I've been goin' to put in a little housing development, but I would like to donate that property to the town for the express purpose of putting in a carousel park, with a pond for ducks and other activities, and gardens, and maybe a children's train."

The last part just came falling out of his mouth in his effort to match Vella's gesture and show her that he could be as generous and free-spirited as she could.

"Whoo-weee!" Winston said. "We're ridin' along on a carousel now!"

CHAPTER 11

Best Laid Plans

MAY WAS WELL UNDER WAY. TEMPERATURES ROSE more quickly than normal, bringing the sound of lawn mowers and hum of air conditioners to rival the chirping of birds. Blaine's Drugstore and Soda Fountain and MacCoy's Feed and Grain went on extended summer hours. Children began to get impatient and rambunctious, having less than a week left in school.

Little Gabby Smith, who never gave anyone a moment's trouble, had one day last week skipped school with Willie Lee. They had gone to the Quick Stop and bought Häagen Dazs chocolate ice-cream bars and eaten them as they walked back to school.

While they were walking, Gabby's father, the Reverend Stanley Smith, came driving by. "I've been lookin' for you, young lady," he said sternly. He had to work on this. There was not much stern within him.

The two children got readily into the car, where Reverend

Smith scolded and pointed out it was illegal to skip school, and that the Bible instructed us all to obey people in positions of authority. He said this as he passed out napkins. He rather wished he had waited for the children to finish their ice cream before ordering them into the car.

Gabby was nearing twelve years old now. She remained petite and with a halo of childish curls, but this minute she drew herself up and responded, "Daddy, I am a straight-A-plus student. I have skipped one full grade and would be in a special advanced class, if our school had one, but they do *not*. Today I had my lessons all done, so I took it upon myself to go on a field trip."

Reverend Smith had no words to answer her perfect logic, much less his daughter's reasonable tone. His Gabby, like her sisters and their mother, was a being quite beyond him. He shifted his eyes to Willie Lee. "And you?"

"I want-ed to go out-side. It is a nice day to be with Gabby."

Reverend Smith sighed. There was no beating *that* logic, either.

When the good reverend faced the elementary-school principal, he said, "The children went on a field trip. They practiced using initiative and how to count change."

He drove away from the school a little hunched over after receiving a scolding from the principal, and also thinking about how fast the years passed and that surely only yesterday his little girl had been six years old. He thought about how Gabby had said since that age that she loved Willie Lee. He had expected her childish infatuation to fade. Especially as she matured and proved to have a genius-level IQ, and Willie Lee, well, stayed just where he was. But the pastor-father's expectations were not being met.

Reverend Smith found himself explaining his dilemma to

Belinda Blaine across the soda fountain counter, while he drank a latte.

"I'm not really complaining, but she will need to grow up and go to college. They're already talkin' with her class about preparing for college. She's already provin' that she will likely get good scholarships. She's likely to have schools like Rice and Vanderbilt after her. Her mother suggests Duke, but I don't want her that far away."

He thought a moment, then asked with a frown, "Why is it that she is drawn to a boy like Willie Lee?"

"What you're describin' sounds like a normal relationship between boys and girls…and men and women," Belinda said, then added philosophically, "There is no figurin' it out."

He blinked, then said, "I guess you're right, there. But Willie Lee is not quite normal."

"Well, I'm not certain I know what normal is." Belinda thought about this for a moment, then added, "And I think you could do a lot worse. Willie Lee cares for Gabby, and he is more loyal and kind than anyone I've ever known."

She had experienced the urge to stick up for Willie Lee, and from there she became very aware of the child she carried in her womb. In fact, she moved to sit on her mother's high stool. She really needed not to stand for long periods. She had to do her best by this child, especially considering all that could go wrong. She really wished she had not read as much as she had.

All of a sudden, Reverend Smith smacked the counter with his palm, causing Belinda to jump.

"You're right!" he said with vigor, and then fell into his preaching voice. "'For I know the plans that I have for you, declares the Lord! Plans for welfare and not for calamity…to give you a future and a hope.' Jeremiah 29:11. I don't know what God has planned for Gabby, nor for Willie Lee...and I don't need to try to put this thing into the box of my limited thinking. All I need to do is believe that it is good."

He was on his feet and bringing change out of his pants pocket to toss on the counter. "I sure thank you, Miss Belinda, for makin' me think."

"Uh...you're welcome." She hopped from the stool and picked up the money to put in the cash register.

She gazed after the pastor as he went fairly blowing out the door. She could not imagine how she had made the pastor think what he did, but now *she* was thinking—of Willie Lee and Gabby, which made her think of herself and Lyle, and how no one could ever see herself and Lyle as a match.

Certainly she and Lyle were not quite as extreme a case as the children, but it was true that Belinda had great intellect and Lyle did not, and Lyle knew it and never worried over it, just like Willie Lee.

Willie Lee and Lyle had something else, something not so easily measured, but Belinda would define it as pureness of heart. True goodness.

In that moment, she got so grateful for Lyle and so sentimental that she had to call him up and tell him how much she loved him.

He answered in a sleepy voice, and she remembered that he was on night duty again and sleeping days.

"Oh, sugar, I'm so sorry to wake you. I just wanted to tell you that I love you."

"That's okay, honey...I love you, too." That said, Lyle promptly hung up. He had the innocent sort of mind that never

wondered if Belinda loved him. His love for her was unconditional and quite enough.

Punching the off button on the phone, Belinda started to
get back on the tall stool, then stopped. She eyed it with a raised
brow, as if it were personally responsible for luring her. She'd
had no business jumping down from that thing. It was her
mother's stool. The stool Belinda normally used was a lot
shorter. Since her mother had left, Belinda had shoved the
shorter stool on the other side of the small freezer. Now she
dragged it out and put the tall stool away in its place.

As she settled herself carefully on the shorter stool, she had tears
in her eyes. She could not imagine why. She never got teary.

Help me, God, she thought in a prayer that she could not
quite admit to making. She had no right to pray, but she said
in a whisper she did not know she spoke, "Help me to carry
this baby, and it to be all right."

The drugstore soda fountain business was brisk. Repeatedly,
the bell over the door and the one in the cash register drawer
rang out, metal spoons clinked against glass, the soda machine
whooshed and voices rose over it all. Whenever the weather
got nicer, people came out more—especially the senior
citizens, who predominated at the moment.

Winston was at his normal table, along with his domino-
playing buddies. They had a game going, while carrying on
conversation with the men and women at an adjoining table,
as well as a couple at the counter and whoever came through
the drugstore door.

The discussion centered around the prospect of the carousel
park, as it had quickly become known, much to Everett
Northrupt's annoyance. Everett kept putting forth that they all

needed to attend the city council meeting to be held that night. "We got to get a committee formed to handle this project before it gets any more out of hand."

He went on at length about all the points that he saw needed addressing, although it seemed to Belinda that he kept repeating himself. In his defense, some of this was necessary because of the people coming through the door and asking, "What are y'all talkin' about?" Everett would then launch into his explanation and urge the person to come to the city council meeting.

After this had gone on for some time, Belinda had the disconcerting realization that Winston was being unusually quiet, and that he was more or less allowing Everett to hold court.

Shoving the cash register door closed, she walked to the magazines and peered around to the opposite side of the rack.

There, as she had suspected, was Willie Lee sitting on the windowsill, with Munro at his feet. Munro lifted his head, causing Willie Lee to look her way.

"Aren't you supposed to be in school?" she asked, folding her arms.

Willie Lee blinked his baby blues behind his thick glasses, guileless as always. "Yes. I left."

"Obviously." She shook her head and turned back to the counter. Then she stopped and went to the boy. She stretched her hand to touch his soft blond hair. "You need a haircut," she said, because something seemed required. She did not know what had taken hold of her, acting like this. She jerked her hand back and again folded her arms.

Willie Lee tilted his head at her, then bent back over the magazine on his lap. Belinda looked at the magazine, too, the pages filled with colorful photographs of nimble boys on skateboards. Boys doing what Willie Lee could never do. How Willie Lee longed to be normal.

Belinda's hand went to her belly. She thought about the child she had never had, and about the child she carried now. She thought how Marilee had never known what had gone wrong to cause Willie Lee to be brain damaged.

"Your ba-by is o-kay."

Belinda looked downward to see Willie Lee gazing up at her. His face so sweet.

"It is?" Breathless.

Willie Lee nodded. "She is a *gir-l*."

Belinda swallowed. "Will she be okay when she is born?"

Willie Lee tilted his head. "I do not know. I cannot fore-*tell* the fu-ture," he said pointedly.

"Please don't say anything, Willie Lee…don't tell anyone about her."

"I will not," he replied simply, his gaze returning to the magazine.

She continued to hover, finally saying, "You want an ice-cream cone?"

"Yes, ma-am. I would like a van-illa one." He smiled brightly, jumped to his feet and carefully replaced the magazine, as she herself had taught him to do.

As she made the boy a double-dip cone and fixed a small dish for the dog, she thought, *A girl*.

She might possibly have done better to have a boy. A boy would have ended the long line of poor mothers.

Would her darling girl make it through? That was the fear that now haunted Belinda—the worry that she would miscarry. She had begun to feel as if she were walking on eggshells, waiting for the horrible and inevitable. What if she told everyone about her pregnancy, and began hoping and planning, and she ended up losing the baby? Lyle would be crushed. And Belinda did not think *she* could stand it, either.

The entire time she thought all this, she gazed at Willie Lee. She had no doubt whatsoever that he was correct in that she carried a girl child. Belinda was one of the few in town who knew of his talents. She had seen with her very own eyes a baby horse hurt in a storm, and Willie Lee had healed it with his hands. All of them who knew about Willie Lee kept his secret, in order to protect him. And he protected many another person's secret, she would imagine.

All of a sudden she asked, "Is Winston okay, Willie Lee?"

Willie Lee carefully licked his ice-cream cone. "Yes. He is o-kay." Then, uncharacteristically, he added, "But he is ti-red."

Belinda looked over at Winston and saw this truth with fresh, hard awareness.

And just then she saw Marilee walking past the front window. "Come on, Mr. Willie Lee," she said, taking hold of the boy. "Bring your cone, and we'll get you back to school. Don't worry about Winston…I'll see he gets home."

She and Willie Lee, with Munro scurrying along behind, hurried out the back and to Belinda's car, while Marilee came marching in the front, asking immediately, "Have any of you seen Willie Lee?"

The phone only got out half a ring before Belinda yanked it up, saying, "I'm ready."

"For what?" said a female voice.

"*Mother?* I was expectin' you to be Jim Rainwater. It's time for my radio spot." Belinda adjusted the pages of her notes in front of her on the desk.

"Oh. Well, what are you goin' to say on the spot today?"

"I cannot give you an entire reading right now. Jim is goin' to call any minute. I'll need to hang up from you. Oh, there's a beep now."

"Oh…well, then, I'll call you back afterward. Bye, now."

There was something in her mother's voice.

"Mama—wait! Why don't you call me back on my cell phone. I'll leave it open for you to hear me do the radio spot on the landline."

Panicked at hearing the second call-waiting beep, Belinda did not hear her mother's answer but pushed the flash button. "I'm ready!" she said again, before making certain it was Jim.

Thankfully, Jim's voice came over the line. "Ten seconds."

Her cell phone rang. She shoved the landline phone against her neck and pulled the cell phone from her purse. "Mama…I got you."

"It's me. Jim," he said in a perplexed voice.

"Hi, again, sugar," came her mother's voice.

She had Valentine on her left and France on her right.

"Are you there, Belinda?" asked Jim.

"Yes, I'm here."

"I hear you, sugar."

"Be quiet, Mama. You'll get me confused."

Blaine's Drugstore theme music played in her left ear, with Jim's recorded voice. "This week's *About Town*…"

"Whew!" she said to the radio audience. "How many of you ever have had a regular phone on one ear and a cell phone on the other? Well, that was me just now. My mother is listening in from France on the cell phone as I speak to you."

From the cell phone sitting on the desk, she heard her mother yelling, "Tell everyone hello for me!"

"My mother, Vella Blaine, says hello from France." How did she get herself into these predicaments?

"In case you are confused, this is Belinda Blaine with *About Town and Beyond* from Blaine's Drugstore and Soda Fountain, where this week we are runnin' a special on all greeting cards at five percent off. Spring is such a good time to stock up for your resolution to send more cards. We also are having a special on the Reacher at thirty percent off. The Reacher is a handy-dandy gadget to reach those things on high shelves, or on the floor, for those of you who have a hard time bending over. I think they also make an unusual kid's toy. I had to hang them out of the way of the kids who kept coming in here and playin' with 'em.

"For the *About Town* news, we know—for those of you, like my mother, who have been elsewhere and may not have heard—Everett Northrupt was appointed chairman of the Carousel Park Centennial Celebration Committee at Monday's city council meeting. The meeting had a good crowd, who turned out to participate in confirming the decision to construct a carousel and carousel building to celebrate Valentine's hundredth anniversary. What I have to say to that is, people, get busy! There's a long way to go and a short time to get there!

"And here is a news flash, heard first here from your hometown drugstore—Tate Holloway told me only an hour ago that he personally spoke with Reba McEntire, and she has agreed to appear at the dedication of our carousel park."

Her mother's voice squawked from the cell phone. Belinda reached over and turned down the speaker volume. She was tickled and thought it was too bad that she could not do that in person to more people.

★ ★ ★

Dr. Zwolle perused Belinda's chart. "Your blood pressure is in the high-normal range, but it's okay."

"Your nurse causes it."

"She does mine, too."

Belinda watched the doctor's face as the woman continued to read the chart.

"Your weight gain is right on track, but your sugar is climbing, and we do not want that. Are you exercising… walking?" The doctor raised an eyebrow at her.

"I'm tryin'. It's not somethin' I've ever been especially good at. And I guess I sort of worry about the jarring."

The doctor's eyebrow rose again.

"You know, when I walk. I get afraid I will shake the baby loose."

She knew it was silly, but she could not seem to help herself. She had taken to practically walking on tiptoe. Once Oran Lackey had noticed and said, "Belinda, do you have blisters on your feet? We got in some new Dr. Scholl's…those new gel pads."

The doctor said, "No, you will not shake that baby loose. At this point walking is the best thing you can do—for you and the baby."

"Okay." She tried to believe it.

The doctor's eyes returned to Belinda's chart. "Well, I want you to watch your sugar and carbohydrate intake more carefully. You're doing okay now, and we want to keep you that way."

"Oh," Belinda said.

"You can look up on the Net about a good diet. The simplest thing is to cut out most of the commercial breads and baked goods, and empty sugars. Stick mainly to lean meats, fresh fruits and vegetables—all you want. And cheeses…but not too much cream cheese," the doctor ended as she closed the chart.

Belinda wondered what she was to eat cream cheese on.

"Get your husband to join you on the diet—tell him I said so," the doctor said with a grin as she and Belinda both left the examination room.

"I haven't told him yet, about the baby." The words popped out before she thought, and then she saw the doctor's expression. "I…I want to make sure that I don't…lose her. He'll be very hurt if I do."

Dr. Zwolle looked at her as if she had lost her mind. "Mrs. Blaine, I strongly urge you to tell your husband. You are both in this together, you know."

Just then Nurse Betty called out, and the doctor excused herself.

Belinda gazed at the two women at the desk, then abruptly turned and headed quickly away down the hallway. With relief she turned the corner and spied the sign for the laboratory. She dashed inside, like a sneak thief looking for a place to hide, and hoped the doctor would not come after her.

"Where've you been?" Lyle asked. He was at the counter making one of his blender health drinks when she came into the kitchen. She had forgotten it was his day off.

"Oh, up to Lawton, shoppin'."

She removed her jacket, wrapped her arms around him and leaned against his strong back for a moment. Then she opened the refrigerator. Her eye fell on the container of strawberry cream cheese. She closed the door and took a banana from the basket of fruit.

"What's that?"

"A banana." She gave a puzzled frown at the question.

"No, not that—that bandage on your arm."

"Oh…it was time for my hormone check," she said, pulling off the bandage and throwing it in the trash. A sure way to stop Lyle's questions was to give mention to women's hormones.

She was turning into a liar.

She stopped in the doorway of the room Lyle had converted to his workout space.

The room that would be the nursery.

"Sugar, I'm gonna work on some accounts for a bit."

"O-kay." He pressed the bar over his head as he spoke. His muscles bulged beneath his T-shirt.

It was on her tongue. *You're going to be a daddy.*

The words evaporated somewhere downward.

In the living room, she sat at her small desk and opened the lid of her notebook computer. She glanced in the direction of the workout room, hearing the clink of weights.

She straightened her spine and firmly punched the button. The computer sprang to life.

Fingers on the keys, she typed. A listing popped up, and she began to click and read screen after screen. *After the age of thirty-five, birth defects rise…miscarriage in first trimester…second trimester… diabetes…refined sugar…glycemic index…gluten ataxia…blood pressure…mercury poisoning, peptides, contaminated* this and *contaminated* that. One page led to another. She wanted to stop reading but kept on, as compelled as any addict.

Some ten minutes later, Lyle came in the room. "Honey, you want somethin' to drink?"

Belinda closed the computer lid with a snap. "Yes…that would be lovely. I'll come find somethin' with you."

She was sure her blood pressure was up. After all she had read, it had to be. The recommendation on one page for pregnant women over thirty-five was to get a blood pressure monitor. She had the great urge that minute to race down to the store and get one off the shelf.

Well, that was the end of her reading. As far as she was concerned, she did not need to look up any more information about her health, pregnancy or diet. It was all just scaring her to death.

"I'll have one of your health drinks," she said to Lyle.

He stared at her with wide eyes, then said with delight, "I'll put an apple in it for you…and how about—"

"No." She held up a hand and turned her head. "Don't tell me what you put in it. I don't want to know."

Lyle…sugar, I have somethin' to tell you. It seems that we are goin' to have a baby.

She gazed in the bathroom mirror. She did not have to tell him about the abortion. Why did she think she had to do that?

Well, now the doctor knew it and might say something.

Of course the doctor won't say anything. What are you waiting for? Just tell him. Let yourself be happy and let Lyle be happy.

We're goin' to have a little girl. Willie Lee said so.

All right…all right, I *will* tell him. We *are* in this together. And if I miscarry, he will find out, and that certainly won't be a good time.

A slight breeze from the open window fluttered her peignoir as she stepped into the bedroom. The breeze held the sublime scent of early summer and caused Belinda to sneeze. Without realizing, she instantly held her belly in the protective manner that she had now adopted.

Lyle was in the bed, turned on his side.

She slipped between the soft sheets, whispering, "Lyle, honey…"

He was asleep. His long lashes lay nearly on his cheeks. She gazed at him for a minute. He was so beautiful.

Well, she was not going to wake him.

Pastor Smith's words had half stuck in her mind. *I have plans for you, says the Lord…*or something like that.

She found her Bible under a pile of *Money* magazines, which did not seem to reflect well on her. Where had the pastor said that verse was from? The Bible had a concordance in the back.

There it was…Jeremiah… "Twenty-nine, eleven…twenty-niiine, e-leven…" she whispered. Then, "'For I know the thoughts and plans that I have for you, says the Lord, thoughts and plans for welfare and peace and not for evil, to give you hope in your final outcome.'"

Well.

She scratched her head and slowly lowered herself to the couch. Hope flickered, and the picture of a nursery floated into her mind. Disney forest animals came to life on the wall.

The next minute the memory of what she had done came flooding back, pushing out the Disney forest animals.

If God had ever entertained good plans for her, how was it that she had ended up with an abortion?

Buddy Wyatt, the UPS man, brought her order of two walking outfits and two pairs of shoes to match. One set was pink and white, and the other gray and yellow. Belinda was pleased to find the shades did not clash with her hair. She believed in dressing correctly for every endeavor. Dressing correctly gave a person fortitude. Tennis shoes sure had changed since her teenage years. These had a wide tread for walking but resembled cute Mary Janes.

Arlo and Oran Lackey, the only occupants of the drugstore at that moment, both stared at her.

"I'm takin' up walkin'. It's healthy."

Oran hurried to open the door for her.

Whatever got into people? It wasn't such a big deal.

She found that she still walked rather gingerly. The doctor may have said that she could not jar loose the child, but all that warning information on the pamphlets and Web sites was simply not reassuring.

In the first minute, she remembered why she did not much like walking in Oklahoma—windy days.

Peggy Sue Langston, the home economics teacher, brought a group of her female students into the soda fountain after school. She bought a round of ice-creams cones.

"Oh, that's one too many," she said, looking from the waffle cone Belinda handed over the counter to the girls scattered behind her. "Yes…I'm sorry. I guess I must have counted wrong. I'll pay for it."

Belinda waved her away. "No problem. I probably counted wrong." She settled on her stool and began to lick the ice cream. Vanilla, her favorite. Except as she ate, she felt a little nauseous.

All of a sudden, she caught sight of her image in the mirror on the wall behind the sundae dishes. *You can't have that!* It was Dr. Zwolle's voice.

She had three more quick licks, then offered the cone to Corrine, who held one hand to her stomach and the other up like a stop sign. "No, way. You are sure smart to say we can have anything we want in the soda fountain. I probably won't ever be able to eat ice cream again."

Neither will I, Belinda thought dismally as she threw the cone in the trash.

CHAPTER 12

Phone Calls

SUMMER VACATION HAD ARRIVED, AND CORRINE was at her first full day of work at the drugstore alone. It was just after nine, the early-morning rush over, and not one customer for the past twenty minutes. Corrine had cleaned everything there was to clean and replenished everything there was to replenish. Just then the phone delighted her by ringing.

"Blaine's Drugstore and Soda Fountain," said Corrine, with a snap in her voice. "Your hometown store serving your needs."

"Who is this?"

"Corrine. Who is this?" She frowned into the phone.

"Sugar, this is your aunt Vella," said the voice, all warm and amused.

"Hey, Aunt Vella!" said Corrine in the same manner, quite delighted. Vella Blaine was her mother's and Aunt Marilee's aunt, and one of Corrine's favorite people. Aunt Vella was always doing and saying something interesting.

"What are you doin' answerin' the drugstore phone, honey?"

Corrine explained about her new job. She was a little disappointed that Belinda had not relayed the important information to her aunt.

"Well, I know the store will benefit from your work," Aunt Vella said. "Can you hear me okay? I'm still all the way over in France."

"You were a little fuzzy, but it's better now."

"It's the cell phone, but I guess we're expectin' a lot, given the distance. Is Belinda there?"

"No, ma'am, she's out. She went to get her hair done and some other things. You might call her cell phone."

"Well, sugar, that is the problem. My cell phone gave up the ghost and took all the phone numbers with it." She went on about this predicament at length, telling of her many frustrations at either getting the phone fixed or getting another one. She was at that moment using Miss Lillian's cell phone, and said, "Lillian is not a habitually generous person."

Corrine knew Belinda's number from memory. She was able to provide step-by-step directions for the older woman to store the number in Miss Lillian's cell phone. Then Corrine ended up going through the phone book and giving the older women the numbers for six people. Twice during this exercise, customers came in and Corrine handed them the phone to talk to Aunt Vella while she made their soda fountain orders. Before Aunt Vella hung up, she requested to speak to Oran Lackey. Corrine walked the phone over to the pharmacy storeroom, where Oran was sitting in the recliner and watching the Discovery Channel.

Miss Julia Jenkins-Tinsley came in. She wore her summer U.S.P.S. uniform of shorts with bobby socks and walked as if she thought she was really cute. She passed the mail across the soda fountain counter and ordered a Coca-Cola to go. "Put a lemon in it. I want to try how Vella said they serve Cokes over there in Europe."

"Did Miss Vella call you?" Corrine asked.

"Uh-huh. Right before I came down here. It was real nice talkin' to her. I can't imagine who would think to put a lemon in a Coca-Cola, but keep an open mind, I say."

Corrine prepared the fountain Coke with a fresh lemon slice, then turned to find Miss Julia had gone off to the pharmacy shelves. The petite woman returned with a box she surreptitiously slipped across the counter.

"I know Oran's back with the TV, but…" Just then there was a strange buzzing, and Miss Julia quickly unsnapped a case on her belt and jerked out a cell phone. "Postmaster here."

Corrine picked up the box to ring up the woman's purchases. It was a package of Enzyte.

Focusing on the cash register, Corrine punched the buttons, then slipped the box into a small Blaine's Drugstore bag, managing not to laugh her head off.

Miss Julia snapped her phone shut, paid and said, "I count on your discretion, Corrine."

Well, shoot. She had been imagining telling Belinda right off.

"Yes, ma'am," she said firmly, looking the woman in the eye. The drugstore had a sacred duty to its customers. Miss Belinda had impressed that on them all.

There were a couple of lists kept between the cash register and the telephone. One was a list of people who had a charge account with the drugstore, and the other was a list of people who were never charged at all. Three of those people came in that day. Two were children from one family, who got ice-cream cones, and the third was old Miss Minnie Oakes.

Miss Minnie appeared in her right mind at that moment, because she got a bottle of body lotion and actually paid Oran for it at the rear counter. Corrine saw this, and then watched Miss Minnie go to the magazine rack and take a magazine and put it under her sweater. Then the elderly woman waved and called to Corrine, "Tell Vella I said hello, when she calls. I hear she is callin' everyone."

Obviously Miss Minnie knew what she was doing, and that she could do it.

Mr. Winston and Willie Lee and Munro were not on any list, but Belinda said she never did charge them for anything. Winston sometimes paid; other times he would say, "I'm family."

The man who picked up pop cans around town showed up. Corrine saw him through the screen when she propped open the rear door. She hesitated, not quite knowing what would be polite. Belinda had not said anything specific about him.

Then she went to the soda fountain and put together a barbecue sandwich basket, without saying anything to Arlo, who had come in to help with the lunch crowd. She took the basket quickly to the back door. "Uh…would you like a barbecue sandwich?"

"Thank you, missy," said the man very politely as he walked across the alleyway and took the basket. He was not as old as she had thought.

Corrine saw that he had a small paperback book sticking out of his jacket pocket. *Walking Across Egypt*. Mr. Winston owned the book, and Corrine had read it. It was good. Mr. Winston laughed out loud every time he read it.

★ ★ ★

Corrine could tell right off that Miss Belinda was upset about something. She came blowing in the door, said, "Hey, Oran…Mr. Murphy," to the pharmacist and a customer at the health-aids shelf, but continued straight toward the soda fountain, where she threw her large purse underneath the counter so hard it about bounced.

"Fayrene has gone and done it again," Miss Belinda said in a hushed sort of voice that only Corrine could hear. She stuck a foam cup under the latte machine spout. "You would think that after all her failures with men, she would not be so silly…although why I would think that, I do not know."

"What's she done?" Corrine asked, speaking in a hushed voice, too.

"Oh, she's gone and turned over all her accounting to that Andy fellow she's got over there. I mean, he's got online access to the café bank account, is handlin' all of it. I was just down at the bank, and ran into him and Fayrene. She has lost any shred of sense that she ever possessed over him. She doesn't know anything about him—*no one* knows anything about him. And her record with men is just dismal."

Miss Belinda sat herself on her stool and sipped her latte, and spoke about Miss Fayrene's former husbands and boyfriends. "It is genetic," said Belinda. "She got it from her mother. Her mother moved all over West Texas with wildcatters, and was married and divorced four times, and never found one of them to take care of her."

Miss Belinda's purse began ringing. "Oh, gosh, I'll bet that's my mother. She called me earlier, and I didn't pick up. Will you hand me my cell phone, sugar?"

Corrine retrieved the phone and handed it over, then turned

away and focused on counting and straightening the money in the cash register. Her thoughts were full with *her* mother, whose record with men could also be counted as dismal. What did that say about her own future?

She was deciding her future, Corrine thought firmly.

"I need four cold sweet teas and three milk shakes to go… Is Belinda in?" Inez Cooper barely slowed down on her way to Miss Belinda's office.

"Yes, ma'am." The woman had long legs and was already going through the storage room doorway.

A few minutes later, as Corrine served two teenage girls and Mr. Fred Grace, who sat and talked to Corrine in a most boring fashion, the two women emerged, with Miss Belinda leading the way to the herb and vitamin shelves. She packaged something up for Miz Cooper, and came to the soda fountain cash register, where Miz Cooper paid and picked up her drinks to go.

"You know what's the savin' grace?" Belinda said in a low voice to Corrine.

"What?"

"People come in here to get free advice, but they always cover themselves by purchasing food."

The phone rang, and Corrine answered it. "Blaine's Drugstore." Having said the spiel a thousand times, she was no longer thrilled with it. She stuck the receiver into her neck while she gave two junior-high boys their milk shakes and took payment.

"Corrine…it's Jojo."

"Oh, hi. You want somethin'? I'm kinda busy, and my feet feel like they've been run over." A man gazed at her impatiently and tapped a five-dollar bill on the counter.

"No. I just wanted to tell you before you heard it from somebody else. We all just found out—Larry Joe and Miss Huggins got engaged last night."

"What?"

"They got engaged. I just found out that Larry Joe told Mama at lunch."

"I'm in a hurry, kid. I got to make my shift," said the man across the counter.

"There isn't anything else to tell you, 'Rin," said Jojo in her ear. "That's all there is."

Not ten minutes later, three chattering women entered the drugstore. It was Monica Huggins, with two other teachers— Miz Fields, the Spanish teacher, and Miz Langston, who was the most scatterbrained home economics teacher in the history of the world.

The women took a table at the rear of the soda fountain.

Corrine finished serving a barbecue basket and ice-cream sundae, and went to wait on the women, and to see this engagement ring for herself. Her eyes sought out Miss Huggins's hand, but the woman kept it under the table.

It had to be a mistake.

Miz Langston said she thought she wanted a chocolate milk shake, and Miz Fields said she *knew* she wanted a banana split, with extra nuts. Miz Huggins said she thought she would just get a Coke. She still didn't bring that hand out from beneath the table.

"Monica…this is a celebration, and I'm payin'," said Miz Langston. "Get somethin' celebratory."

"I *am* celebratin'," said Miss Huggins. "I'm celebratin' and watching my figure, too. I don't want to be a fat bride."

At that moment, just like a trumpet had sounded, she brought her hand out and displayed the ring on her finger. The diamond caught the light.

The next instant Corrine was looking into Miss Huggins's eyes, which were straight on her like two pinpoints. Miss Huggins said, "We are celebratin' my engagement to Larry Joe Darnell. I want a large Coke, please."

Corrine turned and went back to the soda fountain and began putting together the orders, while in her mind she saw the look in Miss Huggins's eyes.

There were lemon slices sitting there on the cutting board. She plopped two into the middle of the ice in Miss Huggins's Coca-Cola. This apparently ended up going unnoticed. The woman never said a word about it.

Belinda was snuggled on the couch in her pajamas, watching the late movie on television and eating plain organic goat yogurt over blueberries, when the telephone rang. She checked the caller ID and saw Corrine Pendley's name.

But across the line came, "Miss Belinda…this is Paris…"

Belinda set aside her bowl. "Yes, sugar."

"My car broke down…and we—Corrine's with me—and we need some help, Miss Belinda."

"Where are you?" Belinda was already off the couch.

The girls were all the way up in Lawton. Half an hour's drive with her foot pushing the accelerator over the speed limit. A spring storm had come in. Lightning flashed, rain pelted and the windshield wipers thumped as Belinda peered hard through the glass and the glare of oncoming lights.

There was Paris's car next to the curb of a side street.

Belinda directed her own car over in front of the battered Impala. As she gathered her breath to get out in the rain, she saw the dark figures approaching in her side-view mirror. She just knew it, and when they threw themselves inside, drips going everywhere, she could smell it.

"Hey, Miss Belinda," Corrine said from the backseat. "Thank you for comin'."

"I'm sorry, Miss Belinda, but I thought it best not to call Miz Holloway." Paris did not look at her. The girl's newly bleached spiky hair gleamed in the interior light just before she closed the door.

As Belinda shifted into gear, she remembered that it had been raining the last time she had picked Paris up from her broken-down car. Was there something about the girl that rain followed her?

Without a word, Belinda headed to her house. Apparently the girls knew enough not to question her. Then she looked in the rearview mirror to see Corrine's head back against the seat.

"It's sure bright in here," said Corrine, blinking in an unfocused sort of way.

Belinda sat them at her kitchen table and served them hot coffee.

"I don' drink coffee," Corrine said, looking down at the cup.

"You do right now. Drink it."

Paris picked up her cup and went to sipping.

"Okay, tell me where you were that served you alcohol."

Two pairs of eyes looked at her. Corrine's drifted.

Paris did the explaining, while Corrine reached for a banana.

They had been to a party held by college boys. At this information, Belinda's blood alternately boiled and went cold.

She knew the scenario only too well. She was amazed that Corrine, of all people, had done something so stupid, but then she learned that the apparent escapade had been prompted by Larry Joe Darnell's engagement to Monica Huggins, a fact that came as some surprise to Belinda. Mostly she was surprised at being behind in gossip.

Corrine, her tongue quite loosened by the alcohol, told of the incident with Monica Huggins at the drugstore that afternoon, complete with affecting the accent and manner of the woman. Belinda could imagine it clearly. The teacher was obviously aware of Larry Joe's fondness for Corrine and was jealous.

"He's gonna marry her, Miss Belinda. And I love him," Corrine said with banana in her mouth.

"I know you do."

Paris put an arm around Corrine. The girl's fierce protectiveness touched Belinda deeply.

The next instant, Corrine put her hand over her mouth, hopped up and ran for the bathroom. Belinda jumped up and followed, directing, "To the right, sugar!"

With a sigh, she returned to the table. "She'll be a little better after she throws up."

Paris looked at her, then dropped her gaze.

Belinda said, "You know, I am surprised at Corrine, but I am really flabbergasted that you would be so pure-D stupid!"

They sat there a moment with Paris still looking downward.

"But I'm glad you called me. You did the right thing."

Paris's eyes came up, met Belinda's, and the girl sat up straighter.

Then Belinda told her to go check on Corrine and for both of them to use the new toothbrushes in the bathroom drawer to brush their teeth really well.

★ ★ ★

"Okay. You two girls watch my lips." Belinda stood, arms folded over her ample bosom. "There is not a man on earth worth losin' your good sense and dignity over. Not one. Men— and family and friends, too—are goin' to break your heart sometimes. That is just how it is. It is the way of life. You can go on and hurt yourself further by doin' stupid stuff that could cause you to completely lose your good future…or you can pick yourself up, dust yourself off and make the best of things.

"So think about that the next time you two want to go to some stupid wild drinkin' party."

"We—" Corrine began.

"Are you interrupting me?"

Corrine shut her mouth and dropped her gaze. Belinda stood silent until both girls again looked at her.

She could practically read the question going through their minds. "No, I am not goin' to tell Marilee. Mostly for her sake— she might have a breakdown. You think about that, Corrine."

Belinda found herself wagging her finger in the same manner as her mother had done. She instantly dropped her hand. "I guess we all do stupid things that we would rather others not know about."

It was a commentary on Paris's life with her grandfather that Belinda never even thought about telling him.

While driving to the Holloway home, they hatched their story as to how Belinda had just happened along right after Paris's car had broken down. She even gave them each a piece of gum when she let them out at the curb.

But as she drove herself back home, she worried about her actions in hiding the truth. Perpetuating a lie did not seem like the thing a mother should do. She could hardly sleep for worrying over this, and was awake in the early hours when Lyle came in. She ended up telling him all about it, and he said he thought she'd done right. He said the girls could choose to tell the truth in their own time. And he also said he would get Paris's car the following day, and have it fixed, too.

Belinda lay back in the shelter of his arm and said, "Thank you, sweetheart."

Warm gratitude for this man flooded her. She felt she was leaning on him in a way that she had never before done. She decided to tell him about the baby right then...but she did not. She fell comfortably asleep instead.

She was awakened by the phone ringing. She sat up, and Lyle conked her in the head with the receiver as he passed it to her. Falling back against the pillows, she squinted against the bright sunlight pouring through the windows and reached for the receiver hovering over her head.

"Belinda?"

"Yes?"

She had expected it to be Marilee's voice, blessing her out for not telling the truth about the girls. But it was an unfamiliar voice. She struggled to sit up and think. Was something wrong at the store? Wasn't that new girl, Barbara Jean, supposed to open today? Was this her? What time was it? The digital clock read 7:50.

"Belinda, this is Gracie Berry."

"Oh." Instantly wide-awake. "Gracie...what is it?"

"I'm sorry if I woke you. Emma said you are always up to open the drugstore, but I called there and the girl said you were home."

"It's fine. What *is* it, Gracie?" She was already getting out of bed, ready to meet whatever was coming.

"Papa—John Cole—had a heart attack. I think Emma could use you, if you can come."

Good heavens!

As she dressed, she wondered if anything else could be heading her way, and maybe that she needed to quit answering her phone.

CHAPTER 13

Cinnamon, Lies and Sweet Green Grass
Grasse, France

"A CRUDE ESSENTIAL OIL IS PRODUCED BY distillation, and this is then refined by rectification. This is a procedure in which…" The young woman guide spoke flawless English.

Vella felt ashamed of her small ability with the French language. When she realized how many people in the world could speak English, and she could not speak one other language, she felt she fell far short.

She also fell far short in her interest in museums. While the International Perfume Museum was one of the few that she did find interesting—she especially enjoyed seeing their roses—she was a woman who liked to take in things and move on. In fifteen minutes of perusing the museum, she had seen all she needed to see.

"Now, if you will follow me…" the guide said and led the way from the room.

Vella watched the tour party flow out of the room, taking along her traveling companion, Lillian Jennings, who was an avid museum goer. At that moment Lillian was chatting happily with another member of the tour. Vella could imagine what Lillian was saying. She was probably going into every detail of the perfume-making process, things the guides likely did not even know but that were very accurate. Lillian was a walking encyclopedia, and she had something to say on every subject. Vella found the behavior highly annoying, although she was not unmindful that likely at least some of her annoyance came because she, too, possessed a similar intellect and habit. Lillian was enough to make Vella change her ways.

Doing just that, Vella turned and walked back to the museum entry.

A clerk who sat beside the door jumped to his feet. "Is something wrong, *madame?*"

"No…*non*…*merci*…*magnifique*…" She smiled and waved at the perplexed man as she went out the door.

She strode quickly away from the museum, having the very absurd feeling that Lillian might be coming after her to drag her back.

At a low wall, she sat and pulled out the cell phone that she had borrowed that morning from Lillian, and had managed to keep. Lillian barely used the thing, anyway. In all their weeks away, Lillian had, to Vella's knowledge, only telephoned home three times, and for absurd reasons, such as to make certain her daughter, Emma, picked up her mail and that her air-conditioning was not coming on in her apartment.

Vella, on the other hand, and as incredible as it sounded, was homesick. Here she had what she had always wanted—to travel the world—and she had called someone back in Valentine nearly every day. She called Belinda several times a week. When her cell phone had conked out, Lillian had said Vella wore it out.

While Vella would not have admitted it, she did wonder at her need to have to continually speak to someone back home. Her level of attachment rather flabbergasted her. She actually would have called Belinda every day, if not hampered by embarrassment and knowing her daughter would react poorly. She had called her eldest daughter, Margaret, several times, which was the most she had spoken to Margaret in years. And Margaret had not answered the last two calls, so obviously she had had enough.

Her call that moment to Belinda went unanswered. Flipping the phone closed, she considered who else she might call back in Valentine. Then she gave a large sigh and dropped the phone back into her purse.

Sticking on her sunglasses, she got to her feet and started off leisurely along the sidewalk that took her downhill.

This town, as so many they toured, was built on a hillside, and the streets wound up and down. Impossibly narrow, some of them, and not really bordered by yards but terraces of fragrant bushes and flowers—roses, lavender, bougainvillea and what she would call Spanish sword, but maybe in France it would be French sword. All of the flowers and small gardens everywhere were lovely, although she had a sense of being cramped and hemmed in. She had an absurd longing for a wide expanse of green lawn, something apparently not cultivated in this part of the world.

Just then the delicious, and quite familiar, sweet aroma of sugar and cinnamon came from a building—a bakery, with a window of delightful-looking sweet cakes. For a moment, she was reminded of walking past Sweetie Cakes Bakery on Main Street.

She went inside, where a stocky—and *handsome*—man in the vicinity of her own age stood behind the glass cases. Instantly he gave her a wide, quite engaging smile.

"Bonjour…American, madame?"

It was as if she had a sign on her. "Yes…I would like two of those *pomm*…two of those."

"Ah…" He kissed his fingertips. "An apple slipper. Puff pastry filled with apples and cinnamon. You will love it. You like cinnamon?"

She said that she did, and he said that he had judged her a cinnamon woman. He winked at her. Her response was to put a hand up to smooth her hair.

Then the man pointed out several other pastries, insisting that she try them. "On the house. It is my shop to do as I please." And then he came around the counter, extended his hand and introduced himself as Gérard, who, it turned out, knew English so well because his father had been American. "I am a widower, *madame*. Please take pity on me and have your rolls and coffee at my table."

How could she say no to such a delightful flirt?

Within minutes, Vella was sitting across from Gérard at a small table within a peaceful courtyard at the rear of the bakery. There were lovely flowers and a grand view of the town cascading down the hillside. A woman brought them coffee, and over the sweet rolls, the two of them chatted. Gérard went into detail about how he made his pastries. He was a man in love with his craft. And with life, Vella thought, watching him with envy.

They talked on, sharing the particulars of their lives and families, and each brought out pictures. His wife, dead for many years, had been a real beauty. He had eight children. He was kind to say that Vella's daughters had the faces of angels. At this, she gave both of her daughters' photographs a second look.

When she noticed the time, that she had been at the bakery for nearly two hours, she got quite flustered. "Oh, my goodness! I must find my friend and the tour."

"Here…here, take these with you." Gérard pressed a bag of his sweet delicacies into her hand. "You are an angel to spend time with me today…talking of our families. Thank you." He kissed her cheek.

She put her hand up to where his lips had been and gazed at him for an uncertain moment. Then she quickly kissed his cheek, turned and hurried away up the sidewalk. Curiosity caused her to look back over her shoulder. Gérard was there, gazing after her. She waved, then headed on at as close to a run as she could manage and not look silly.

Suddenly tears blurred her vision. She did not understand it at all, but she felt a lot less homesick. In fact, she quite suddenly took note of the beautiful blue sky above, and thought that halfway around the world in Valentine, her dear daughter and friends would look up and see the same sky. All along her way back to the tour bus, she was aware of the familiar: people nodding and smiling in greeting, the warmth of the sun, the shade of trees.

When she reached the bus, she found that it sat at the curb of a small park with carefully mowed grass that she had not noticed when they drove up. The other members of the tour were sitting around on benches and on the grass. Vella threw herself on the grass and looked around, wondering what other things she had been missing.

It turned out the bus had broken down, and they got to sit

there some time, talking with one another, without the distraction of sightseeing and schedules. Vella was delighted.

Valentine, Oklahoma, U.S.A.

When they returned home after the *Wake Up* show, delicious breakfast aromas greeted the four of them—Papa Tate, Mr. Winston and Willie Lee and Munro.

"Looks like Rosalba is havin' a cookin' day," said Mr. Winston, casting Willie Lee an eager grin.

Papa Tate headed upstairs, two at a time with his long legs, to speak to Willie Lee's mother, who called down over the banister, while Mr. Winston and Willie Lee went on to the kitchen.

Rosalba had made sausage and warm cinnamon rolls. She asked if Willie Lee and Mr. Winston wanted eggs. Mr. Winston said, "Does the sun shine?" and Willie Lee said simply, "Yes, ma'am." He carefully washed his hands at the sink and then scooted onto his chair at the table. His feet still did not touch the ground. Munro lay just beneath them.

Willie Lee gazed at the pan of cinnamon rolls atop the stove. He loved cinnamon rolls.

I want one.

Willie Lee looked downward to see Munro's brown button eyes regarding him intently.

Okay. He petted the dog's head.

His mother and Papa Tate approached through the dining room, their voices coming on ahead of them.

"It is a good thing John Cole made it to the hospital," said his mother as she came through the door. "I'll bet Emma is beside herself."

"Everything is in his favor. He's a young man, and he wasn't even passed out or anything. He was drivin' himself to the hospital," responded Papa Tate, using his best reasonable voice, as Corrine labeled it.

His mother and Papa Tate were talking about Mr. Berry's heart attack. Papa Tate had heard about it that morning and told Mr. Winston on the way home. Willie Lee knew it did not mean the heart had attacked Mr. Berry, but that his heart had failed…but not like a test. It was failing to work correctly, thought Willie Lee, as he observed his parents. He could practically see the worry swirling in his mother's head. Corrine said worrying was something at which his mother excelled naturally. Papa Tate was being more jovial than usual, attempting to joke her out of it, as he always did.

"'Keep on the sunny side…always on the sunny side,'" he sang to her, making a silly face.

As if not hearing him, she said, "I'll call Belinda in a minute and get the details." Then she frowned at the table, where Rosalba was setting out plates of food. "Well, here's a heart attack waitin' to happen."

Uh-oh, said Munro, and he crawled a couple more inches from view beneath the table.

Then, as Rosalba set the pan of cinnamon rolls on the table, right in front of Willie Lee, his mother instantly snatched them up again. One minute they were there, and the next they went flying up into the air, where they hovered, while his mother said something about the fat content clogging up Papa Tate's arteries and carb grams laying Winston flat out with his diabetes. "You have already had one heart attack, Winston— do you want to lose your feet?"

Willie Lee wondered at the statement as he gazed at the cinnamon rolls hovering in the air.

Mr. Winston said, "Might as well, since no one lets me drive anymore."

The pan of cinnamon rolls had made it to the counter. Mr. Winston reached out and took it up and returned it to the table, where it landed with a thud in front of Willie Lee again.

Papa Tate was saying, "We hear your point, Marilee, but we have the breakfast now. Let us just eat it and not waste. Rosalba has gone to a lot of work, and there are people all over the world who are starvin'."

"Why should that mean you kill yourself?" asked his mother.

While his parents threw this argument back and forth, Willie Lee reached out and succeeded in getting a thick, gooey cinnamon roll. Across the table, his mother snatched up the plate of eggs that Rosalba had brought Mr. Winston.

"Winston does not need three eggs—one is plenty." She scraped two of Mr. Winston's eggs onto Willie Lee's plate, then returned Mr. Winston's single egg to him. Mr. Winston gazed at the plate as if he wasn't certain what had happened. "And don't make Mr. Holloway any at all. He can have two pieces of the sausage."

I want eggs. Munro came up off the floor, nose high and sniffing hopefully.

Willie Lee passed the rest of his cinnamon roll down to the dog and reached for another one from the pan, fearing that his mother might snatch them away at any moment.

"And this is all you expect me to eat?" said Papa Tate, gazing at the two small links of sausage in front of him.

"Well…" His mother eyed the table, and Willie Lee's fear for the fate of the cinnamon rolls escalated.

"I'll make you some oatmeal," said his mother in a voice

echoing with triumph. "And whole-wheat toast, and I still have a jar of my homemade strawberry jam."

At the mention of the strawberry jam, Willie Lee looked at Papa Tate, who looked at Winston. No one had ever wanted to tell his mother that her jam was like rubber.

While his mother flew to the pantry, Rosalba, who was always wise and never entered controversy in the home, put down her cooking utensils, pulled a package of cigarettes from her skirt pocket and stepped out the rear screen door.

Winston said, "Now, look here, Marilee…how long do you want me to live, anyway?"

"Forever, if I have anything to say about it." She spoke as if she thought she did have say.

"Well, here is the thing." Mr. Winston threw his napkin on the table and got to his feet. "I am tired of bein' treated like a da—dadgum baby. I may be old, but I am still a man, and I'll eat my meat and eggs, thank you."

As Mr. Winston spoke, he rolled half a dozen links of sausage onto his plate, took up Willie Lee's plate and retrieved one of the eggs and secured a cinnamon roll from the pan, plopping it on top of everything. Then he took up the plate and left the room, at which time Papa Tate also threw down his napkin and got to his feet.

"I do a lot of things for you, Marilee, but I'm not eatin' oatmeal. No, sir."

He stalked out of the room, with Willie Lee's mother following after him, saying, "Tate…I'll put raisins in the oatmeal…and slivered almonds…."

Papa Tate responded, "If you add all that crap, I might as well eat eggs and cinnamon rolls."

Their voices trailed off as the two went into Papa Tate's study and the door closed.

A pleasant morning breeze came in the back screen door, bringing a faint scent of Rosalba's cigarette smoke mixed with warming earth.

Willie Lee happily ate a cinnamon roll, breaking off pieces to share with Munro. He gave Munro a piece of sausage, too.

Gooood breakfast. Munro's pink tongue licked his mouth.

Yes, it is.

His mother returned to the kitchen, and Munro lay down all the way under the table again. Although his mother did not even seem to remember him, or Willie Lee. Being what Corrine called preoccupied with matters of life and death, she went to the cabinet and got out her tin of powdered mocha and mixed herself a cup. His mother was a chocoholic. She said so herself, and this was not bad. It made her sweet, Papa Tate said.

Then, holding her mug in both hands, she turned, saw him there and said, "Honey, eat your sausage and egg, too." She brought her mocha to the table. "You're a growin' boy. You don't have to worry about things like cholesterol and fat and carbohydrates. You need all those things for growing." Content to have patched up her instructions, she lapsed again into thought as she drank deeply from her mug.

Willie Lee ate part of the egg, but seeing that his mother was preoccupied, he reached for yet another cinnamon roll. She did not notice. He ate and continued to share with Munro, who kept putting his chin onto Willie Lee's knee.

Just then Willie Lee noticed his mother gazing at him. He hoped she was not about to scold him for eating so many cinnamon rolls.

She said, "How is Winston, Willie Lee? He has looked so…
Well, is he…?" She raised an eyebrow.

He licked his fingers. "He is o-ld and ti-red, but he will not
have a heart at-tack to-day. He will not have a heart at-tack…"
He thought. "For a while."

"Well…that's good. Thank you." His mother relaxed slightly.
Then, leaning forward and speaking in a low tone, "What
about your Papa Tate? Is his heart okay?"

"Yes, it is."

She breathed deeply and relaxed in her chair. "Well, that's
all we can ask, isn't it?"

"Yes, ma'am."

She tilted her head, gazing thoughtfully at him. He could
practically see thoughts nesting in her hair, but then she seemed
to really see him and asked with a little alarm, "How many
cinnamon rolls have you had?"

"Two. Mun-ro ate one," he lied. He used to not lie, but he
was growing, as she said, and lying more.

"Well, honey, that's enough." She frowned at the remaining
cinnamon rolls, looked at Willie Lee, then moved the pan of
rolls and offered Willie Lee a banana, which he declined. He
was feeling a little sick from all the cinnamon rolls. Or maybe
from the lying.

Gabby came on her bicycle, all giggles and curly hair flying.
Hopping off her bike, Gabby threw herself at Willie Lee and
hugged his neck. That was always the first thing she did with
him, or most anyone. Willie Lee liked the hug, and the sweet
way Gabby smelled, and the way her hair was so curly and
shiny. He also liked that she was small for her age, like he was,
and not yet taller than him. Corrine said that since Gabby was

small at her age, it was quite possible that she might always stay small.

One time Willie Lee had said to her, "I hope you stay smaller than me."

Gabby had asked, "Why is that?"

And Willie Lee had said shyly, "Be-cause I am re-tard-ed and you are not, so-o I would like you to not be big-ger."

And Gabby promptly, her hand to her hip, said, "You are not retarded—you are *special*. And now I don't want to get bigger, either, so I will ask God to not let me get taller than you." Her curls had bounced as she jutted her chin for emphasis.

Willie Lee had thought this over for some time. He had asked God to make him be like other boys, and that had not happened. He kept watching Gabby, thinking that she would grow up and leave him behind, as all his other friends had done. But so far she had not only not gone away, she had not grown taller than him. He had discussed this matter with Mr. Winston, and Mr. Winston said some prayers were answered as expected, and some were answered in a different way, but always just right. When Willie Lee confided that he had prayed to be made smart like other boys, Mr. Winston had said, "Son, we need you just the way you are. You don't see me tryin' to be like anybody else, do you?"

This was true and clear. Papa Tate was always saying that Mr. Winston was not like anybody else.

"And if you were smart like other boys," said Mr. Winston, "your intellect would only get in the way of your wider knowledge."

Mr. Winston often spoke of Willie Lee's wider knowledge, something that Willie Lee was not quite clear on.

"And Gabby gal might not like you as much, would she?" continued Mr. Winston. "Do you really think she could like you any more than she does?"

"Well...I guess not."

"There you go.... And who would be here to be my friend and help me like you do? Or take care of Munro, and give Munro somebody to take care of? And what about your mother and Corrine? And all those pets and birds and rabbits you keep savin'? Nope, buddy, we all need and love you just like you are. God has special work for you. Be proud...stand up straight. There you go...work on bein' proud. I think you gained an inch right there."

Willie Lee and Gabby were petting the new three-week-old kittens that lived with their mother under the back steps when Mr. Winston and Papa Tate came out the back door.

All of a sudden Willie Lee remembered that it was time for Mr. Winston's *Home Folks* show. Since Mr. Winston had started the midmorning radio program, Willie Lee had accompanied him on the days that he did not have school or managed to skip out. Right that moment, Munro padded away toward the car, where Papa Tate was already getting into the driver's seat.

Willie Lee looked from Gabby to Mr. Winston.

"You have fun with Gabby this time, buddy," said Mr. Winston, casting him a wink. "You can come with me next time."

The old man's eyes rested on Willie Lee's for several seconds.

Willie Lee said, "Yes, sir."

Gabby looked up from the kitten in her arms and noticed Willie Lee gazing after Mr. Winston as the older man made his way to the car. "Do you want to go with him?" Gabby's eyes were deep blue. "It's okay. I can go with you…or just wait here. I don't mind."

"No. I am with you today."

Munro returned and sat, letting the kittens pull at his fur, while Papa Tate and Mr. Winston drove away.

Willie Lee, still standing, saw Mr. Winston put a hand out the window in a wave. He waved back.

It was the first time that he could remember that he chose something other than accompanying Mr. Winston.

After the kittens, they played with Corrine's mare in the corral; the horse did everything Willie Lee told her to do. Sometimes he spoke to her, and other times he simply thought the instruction. She would look at him, blink her large dark eyes and willingly do whatever he wanted. She let Willie Lee and Gabby climb all over her, and finally she lay down in the scattered hay, with Willie Lee and Gabby lying against her warm, gurgling belly, and Munro lying against Willie Lee. Gabby said the mare smelled like "hay and sunshine." All four of them drowsed.

Then Corrine came out on her way to work in the drug-store and paid them each five dollars to clean the mare's stall. Willie Lee liked that he was strong and could push the wheel-barrow full of manure and bring back the bags of sawdust. He liked to see the muscles on his arms bulge.

He noticed, too, although he did not say anything, that Gabby was getting a girl figure, like Corrine.

Afterward, Willie Lee asked his mother if he and Gabby could go to the drugstore for a sundae. He showed her the money he had made. His mother said okay. "But now be careful and watch both ways for cars…and don't talk to strangers," she added in her worried way of loving, which he knew was a little elevated because of Mr. Berry's heart attack.

He and Gabby and Munro headed for Main Street along the sidewalk. The scent of summer heat and dust came up off the concrete, where trees did not shade it. There was a big oak tree in front of the Ellsworths' house whose large knobby roots grew into the sidewalk and cracked it. The city had one time come out to cut down the tree, but Mrs. Ellsworth had tied herself to the tree to save it. Gabby talked about this as she and Willie Lee walked around the tree on the rough roots. Willie Lee leaned against the tree, listening to the trunk that did not so much speak as smile.

A car slid up to the curb. It was Miss Belinda, who gave them a ride to the drugstore. She also gave them free sundaes. Miss Belinda was being nicer to him than she ever had. She kept giving him a secret wink, too. There was a question in her eyes. Willie Lee did his best to think reassurance to her, and she seemed to relax.

He and Gabby sat at the counter and ate their ice cream, while they got to watch Corrine wait on people, and Miss Belinda tell everyone who came in and asked her about Mr. Berry that he might be in for open-heart surgery. Gabby talked to everyone, too, almost like a grown-up, while Willie Lee, sitting on the very end stool, did not say anything, as usual. No one took any notice of him, either, as if he was not there at all, which was also usual. But he could hear their thoughts, just the same.

The women were worried about their own husbands having heart attacks. Some said this, others did not.

Willie Lee watched Miz Inez move from foot to foot as she talked about Mr. Berry's heart attack and said that she really hoped he did not smoke cigarettes. Miz Inez never could be still. She had dark birds flying in and out of her hair. Only

Willie Lee could see them, of course, although he noticed that Miss Belinda seemed to look up over Miz Inez's head a couple of times with a puzzled frown. Before she left, Miz Inez bought a packet of aspirin for her terrible headache.

The men who came in and asked about Mr. Berry would nod at what Belinda said, then take their orders and leave with fast steps.

Jaydee Mayhall sat on a counter stool and kept looking in the mirror and smoothing his hair, while Miss Belinda made him a latte and they talked about Mr. Berry. Jaydee Mayhall said maybe he would go see Mr. Berry that evening, but Willie Lee knew that he was thinking of excuses not to go.

Miss Fayrene came in, with her latest heartthrob, as Willie Lee's mother called him. Andy was his name. Miss Fayrene was a happy-sad woman, but Willie Lee thought her nice, and she was the only one to say hello directly to him. She asked Miss Belinda about Mr. Berry, then turned and went to the card rack. Right away Mr. Oran appeared to help her pick out a card. Mr. Oran was also a happy-sad person, and he stood so close to Miss Fayrene that it seemed like they were happy-sad together.

Miss Fayrene's latest heartthrob, Andy, sat on a stool beside Gabby and talked to her for a minute. His eyes kept moving all around, though, as if on lookout. Once they shifted to Willie Lee for a long minute.

Miss Fayrene filled out her card for Mr. Berry and added it to the stack of others—Willie Lee had counted nine—that lay on the counter, where people kept leaving them for Miss Belinda to deliver.

Miss Belinda said she would have to thank Mr. Berry for giving her a good trade in get-well cards.

"I ought to charge for delivery service," she said.

★ ★ ★

Shade came over the side yard in the late afternoon, and Willie Lee and Gabby went there and lay down in the grass, with the tops of their heads touching. The sky was very blue above, and the grass cool and fragrant beneath them. Papa Tate had mowed just the previous day. Willie Lee's mother sometimes said that Papa Tate loved the yard almost more than he loved her. He was always fertilizing it and mowing it.

"It's a guy thing," Corrine had told Willie Lee. "Guys like to fertilize and kill weeds and mow."

"Will e-ven *I* do that when I grow up?" Willie Lee had asked his cousin, with some hope that maybe he could grow up to do one normal thing like other boys.

"Oh, yeah, I imagine so. I don't think you can escape it. It seems to start at about the age of thirty, from what I can tell," Corrine had replied very seriously.

Willie Lee was lying there thinking of this, when Gabby said in a dreamy voice, "The sky is bluer than blue."

"Why?" asked Willie Lee.

"Well…because of the sun. The sun is a powerful source of light, and it is lighting up the *whole* sky…and it scatters the atoms, and sends all the other colors— Oh, look!"

Willie Lee had already seen. It was two angels who came around the big cedar tree and headed across the yard, chattering about which direction they needed to take first. Both looked over and waved at Gabby and Willie Lee, who sat up and waved back.

The angels disappeared, and Gabby turned her eyes on Willie Lee. They were sad. "Willie Lee…I don't see them very often anymore. Do you?"

"Yes." He felt a little bad to tell her this, but he did not lie to Gabby.

He watched her rest her chin on her knee and thought how Gabby was the only one who had ever seen angels with him. He had known for some time that he was still seeing them but Gabby did not so much anymore. He did also tell his mother, but his mother had never seen the angels, and she told him, "Willie Lee, don't go tellin' people about those things—seein' angels and how you can hear people think and make animals better. Just don't do it."

Gabby lifted her chin. "Willie Lee, I am goin' to stay with you forever. We are goin' to get married when we grow up, and you can see the angels for me, and I will take care of you."

"Okay," he said happily. "And I will cut the grass."

CHAPTER 14

Heart Attack

MORNING SICKNESS.

Upon first opening her eyes, it came sudden, hard and fast, causing her to jump out of bed.

Belinda had not really considered her morning sickness as a great problem. She had been too caught up with the dreadful possibilities of miscarriage, high blood pressure, diabetes, birth defects. Now that she thought of it, she could not recall one thing on all the Internet pages of doom and gloom for pregnant women over thirty-five addressing the possibility of dying from morning sickness. And she was pretty certain she had just thrown up her stomach.

Tying her robe around her, she walked barefoot and very slowly, so as not to jar either her belly or her head, into the kitchen to find, hopefully, some ginger ale. Absently, she switched on the radio.

"…GET UP, YOU SLEE-PY-HEAD. GET UP AND GET YOUR BOD-Y FED!"

"Oh, Winston, I'm tryin'."

There was no ginger ale.

Reba McEntire sang out from the radio about being a survivor.

Not being too certain in that moment that *she* would survive, Belinda switched off the radio. She made a cup of weak tea and sat sipping it while wondering at all she had heard about morning sickness fading. Hers was getting worse. She had actually lost five pounds in recent weeks.

Hearing Lyle drive up, she put a bright smile on her face.

"Hi, sugar. You're home a little early."

"Yeah, Giff said he'd take over. He's got insomnia." He put his gun atop the refrigerator and loosened his shirt. "What are you doin' up, beautiful?" He bent to give her a quick kiss.

"Oh, I'm goin' to pick up Emma, take her to the hospital."

"I guess she's anxious to get there early."

"Well, I didn't want to rush."

"Uh-huh. You want some breakfast?" He pulled broccoli and an apple from the refrigerator.

"No…I'm not hungry."

She sipped her tea and watched Lyle's back. She needed to tell him. She needed to face what might happen and get it over with.

"Lyle, sugar, could we talk?"

"Sure, honey. Uh…just a minute for me to finish up here."

The blender whirred. Belinda watched Lyle's back, saw him reach for the bag of ground flaxseeds. The blender's whirring went higher. Then it shut off. Lyle got a glass and poured his concoction into it.

Belinda found herself looking at a glass of bile-colored liquid.

"Okay, honey…" He lifted the glass and turned toward her.

"Oh! I don't want to forget my earrings," was the first thing she could think to say as she hopped to her feet and hurried away to the bathroom.

A little later Lyle knocked on the door. "Honey, I'm gonna hit the bed. Did you want to tell me whatever it was first?"

"No, sugar, I'll tell you later. It's not important right this minute."

Emma was normally a quiet, retiring sort of person. She was one to think a lot. There had been times when she and Belinda would drive somewhere, and Emma would not say more than three sentences in an hour.

Today Emma talked the entire thirty-minute drive to the hospital.

"Charles and Joella are comin' over. That's John Cole's oldest brother and his wife…oh, that's right, you've met them. I think that is the kindest thing for them to come. They have the store and all, you know. His other brother, Lloyd, may come, but his sister, Peggy, is gonna handle the store. Peggy and John Cole never have been close. I told Joella they did not need to come. There isn't anything that they can do, but Joella insisted. I may be sorry…but it is still nice of her. The doctor showed us yesterday how the operation— It was after you left that second time, really late in the evenin'. I sure hope the doctor got home and got a good night's sleep. Did I tell you they moved John Cole into a room on the heart floor? They all call John Cole a young man. His daddy isn't up to comin'. He's in a wheelchair now, did I tell you that? Joella said when they take Pop away from the house these days, he sometimes gets all confused about where he is. John Cole and I were supposed to go over there in two weeks. I have not called Mama. I don't want to interrupt her vacation. There isn't anything she can do. I wish I had brought a bottle of water... had it right out on the counter. I can get one at the hospital.... Maybe I should call Mama, and she could be prayin'."

Belinda did her best to nod and say, "Uh-huh," at the right moments. She simply had to be present for her friend. Either from her determination of will or by the grace of God, but the morning sickness passed.

Emma talked all the way from the parking lot into the hospital shop and up the elevator to the third floor, then down the hall to John Cole's room.

Upon opening the door, she suddenly stopped both her speech and her steps so abruptly that Belinda ran into her. Looking over Emma's shoulder, she saw the room crowded with people.

"Oh, Emma, honey!" A woman with pale blond hair came slipping past people to throw herself on Emma. "You come on in here...I have saved you a chair."

The room was divided with John Cole's family on one side, along the window, and his work colleagues—half a dozen people—on the other, standing against the bathroom and entry doors. John Cole was smack in the middle, sitting up in the bed, acting more as a host than a man with three clogged arteries who was scheduled for open-heart surgery in a few short hours.

Emma sat in a chair next to him, with her hand in his, a smile plastered on her face. Her sister-in-law, Joella, stood next to her, and her husband, John Cole's eldest brother, Charles, leaned against the windowsill. At the end of the bed, John Cole's other brother, Lloyd, sat in the only other chair in the room. He had his right leg in a full cast. Lloyd was a rodeo bronc rider. Even if Belinda had not already known this, she would have known it instantly by one look at him.

Belinda considered fleeing to the hall, where there was more air to breathe, but both her concern for Emma and her high curiosity had her take a place on the family side. She went so far as to perch on the arm of Lloyd Berry's chair. In fact, he scooted over, giving her both room and a welcoming look, as if glad their side had increased.

Among the work colleagues, Belinda recognized Shelley Dilks, John Cole's secretary. The woman and man standing closest to Shelley were apparently managers at two of the Berry Quick Stops. Two young men in the corporation's red shirts were assistant managers, evidenced by the name tags above their pockets. A large, boisterous man was a fuel supplier or something of that sort, and shortly they were all joined by a stylish professional woman, who was apparently the personal banker for the corporation. She brought a box of candy. John Cole had Shelley open it and pass it around the room.

John Cole and the Berry Corp side chatted all about work. John Cole kept thinking of instructions, and the employees kept thinking of questions. There were about a thousand of these, although only a dozen were spoken. The rest seemed strung in the air, like a strong cord.

The Berry family was totally silent. They all stood there staring at those across the room, as if trying to figure out who they were and why they were there. Belinda, being on the family side, tried to think of something to say. Amazingly, she found her mind blank. Finally Joella spoke up. She posed questions to the Berry employees, like, "Are you married?" "Do you have children?" "How long have you worked for Berry Corp?" Belinda, not to be nosy, found it all fascinating.

Johnny and Gracie arrived, and people parted to let them through. They took the only available space, which was sitting on the foot of John Cole's bed. Johnny, interestingly enough, sat on the Berry Corp side and Gracie on the family side.

Tate Holloway, and Pastor Smith and his wife, Naomi, arrived. Belinda heard Tate's voice from the hallway and saw the top of his head as he pushed through, bringing the much milder-mannered pastor and Naomi with him.

It was at this point, much to Belinda's relief, that the boisterous fuel distributor and stylish banker took their leave. Belinda had begun to feel as if there was not enough air in the room. She had gone into a hot flash. She had not known that she could have a hot flash and be pregnant, but apparently it was so. Glancing over to the windowsill, she saw a brochure. A hospital guide. She snatched it up and began fanning herself.

After a brief chat, in which Emma actually spoke, Pastor Stanley offered a prayer. Belinda saw Naomi put her hand over on John Cole's foot covered by the sheet. Naomi believed strongly in laying on hands. Belinda wanted to support her but could not reach John Cole's foot. She took hold of Naomi's other hand. *Such as I am, Father.*

Tate and Pastor Stanley and Naomi bade everyone goodbye. Belinda saw John Cole's eyes follow Tate.

The Berry Corp people stayed and kept chatting, while the Berry family continued to hold their silence. Joella went out and returned with another bottle of water for Emma, who had drunk the one she had gotten when they arrived at the hospital.

Charles Berry moved from foot to foot, and Lloyd Berry squirmed to ease his leg.

A nurse came in. She looked surprised at everyone and said, "So, there's a party."

Belinda expected the nurse to tell people to leave, but the woman simply did her checking of John Cole and the equipment, and left.

Next came two large orderlies, who said they were there to prepare John Cole for surgery. They checked his vitals and hookup to the monitor, instructed him about what to expect when they came again, then left.

Emma slipped out of the chair and crawled up into the bed with John Cole.

No one left. Chatting resumed about all manner of business at the Berry Corporation. Belinda saw it suddenly: their need of and care for him were that great.

Finally she could no longer stand it. "Well, I think we all need to get out of here and give John Cole and Emma some time alone." She got to her feet.

"Yes...that is a good idea," Joella said instantly and began to move, too.

Johnny started to rise, and Belinda put a hand on his shoulder, pushing him back down on the bed, while Joella instructed, "Not you, Johnny—you stay. Come on, Charles... Lloyd, here's your crutches. Come on, ever'body, let's go...."

Having been moved into action, the woman gestured at the Berry Corporation people, who reluctantly offered John Cole good wishes and trickled out the door, with Joella more or less sweeping them along from behind. She cast a glance over her shoulder at Belinda, instructing with a nod, *You get that last straggler.*

The last straggler was Shelley Dilks, who lingered, putting her hand on John Cole's arm and saying she would see him later. The look of panic and need on the woman's face struck Belinda deeply. She waited for Shelley to go ahead of her out of the room, cast a wave and kiss to Emma and John Cole, then closed the door after her.

Fear gripped her, too. Not just for John Cole but for all of them.

"Belinda…honey, we're goin' on to the waitin' room. You're gonna wait with us, aren't you?" asked Joella in a sort of panic.

"Yes. I'll be there in a minute. I'm just goin' in here for some…gum."

She went into the gift shop. There was a cushioned bench. She sank down upon it and breathed deeply. She relaxed her neck muscles, and then on down her body. Her spinning head settled.

She looked over and saw there was a pharmacy in the back, and there, near the pharmacy window, was one of those chairs with a blood pressure cuff.

Glancing around furtively, she slipped over to the chair and put her arm through the cuff, pushed the button.

One eighty-eight over ninety-nine. *Oh, dear.*

She sat gazing at the red digital numbers, followed by an exclamation point. That really was not helpful to lowering blood pressure.

Her imagination pictured John Cole in the operating room, the doctors over him.

She blinked and told herself to calm down. Breathe deeply. It would really be bad if she collapsed right during John Cole's surgery. That would be the most embarrassing thing, and no help to Emma at all.

Just stop it, she said to her body.

She sat there, suddenly wishing for her mother and quite absurdly about to cry.

Then she telephoned Lyle and woke him up. "Sugar, could you drive up here to the hospital. I'd just like you here."

"Honey, I'll be there soon as I can," said Lyle, who was amazed and thrilled that Belinda had asked something that he could give.

All the Berry Corp people went back to work when John Cole went into surgery, except Shelley Dilks. Joella took charge of the woman, sitting beside her and chatting nonstop. A lot of what Belinda overheard was a sort of grilling, consisting of the same questions: "How long have you worked for John Cole?" "How long have you been married?" "What does your husband do?" "Do you have children?" "How old?"

The men gathered around the television. Pastor Smith joined them when he returned. Naomi, who came with him, sat beside Emma and offered both her sense of calm and tips on recovery after the surgery. Belinda—and Emma, too—had forgotten that Pastor Smith had undergone the same surgery a number of years before. When Naomi spoke of this, Emma tore her eyes from the double doors of the operating rooms, looked at Pastor Smith, and then at Naomi. Emma's entire face relaxed, and she leaned toward the pastor's wife as if to say, *Tell me everything that you can.*

Glancing over at Gracie, Belinda saw the younger woman having much the same reaction. In all truth, and no matter that Belinda had been somewhat jealous of the girl, it was no secret how much Gracie adored her in-laws. Now she leaned forward to listen carefully to Naomi, who had a gentle voice with a

Southern accent that Belinda loved to listen to, but which could sometimes be hard to hear.

"I think you will find this somethin' of a gift time," said Naomi, looking into Emma's eyes. "This is yours and John Cole's time. You are goin' through this surgery, too, honey. You both will need a lot of time to process it and to recover. A lot more time than it would seem. Time alone, just the two of you.

"And you will need to make this clear to John Cole's employees. They rely on him, and they will miss him terribly. The same for some friends. I had people callin', wantin' to talk to Stanley about the silliest things. One of his cousins who always cut firewood with him wanted to talk all about firewood."

"I'll tell Johnny," said Gracie, touching Emma's hand. "He will handle it. He'll tell everyone to report to him first."

"And, Gracie…I even told my children that they needed to keep their visits short. I instituted visiting hours."

Naomi had such a gracious way of speaking that she could tell someone to eat boogers, and they would not take offense.

"We will only visit a short while in the evenings, Mom," said Gracie earnestly, adding to Naomi that she and Johnny would take good care of Papa John Cole and Emma.

Belinda was surprised to find tears in her eyes. Blinking them away, she looked over at Lyle. Suddenly the picture of herself and Lyle in Emma and John Cole's situation flashed across her mind. Although it would likely be her in the surgery. Putting her hand to her belly, she wondered if Willie Lee was truly correct and she carried a daughter. She hoped so, and felt pity on the child at the same time. She also felt a sense of inadequacy as a daughter. She did not feel she had been much of a help to her mother when her father had been sick.

★ ★ ★

"It looks like John Cole's gonna do just fine, honey. I'm goin' to go on to work." Lyle put an arm around her shoulders. "If you're okay."

"Yes…I'm fine."

"I'll call you tonight, probably come by, if you are home."

She waved at him as the elevator doors began to close.

Then he was gone.

She had so wanted to say more, to say how much she appreciated his coming when she called. That she felt closer to him than she ever had, and how she had not known things could be this way for them.

But she had not been able to say any of it.

The visiting hours waned, and the hospital got much quieter. Belinda, Emma and Gracie were the only ones left in the ICU waiting room.

Looking over at the other two women, Belinda knew she was no longer needed. She gathered her purse and bid them goodbye. She hugged each one. Gracie held tight a few seconds longer, whispering, "Thank you for being here, Miss Belinda. I'll call you, keep you informed."

The two women gazed at each other. A new sort of bond had been born. It was odd how these things worked out. It so often took a crisis to bring people together.

Belinda went down through the quiet hospital and out into the soft night. The concrete was still warm. She breathed deeply, again awash with profound gratitude of the sort that comes when a crisis has passed, leaving one's emotions raw.

Just then she saw Shelley Dilks standing down near a bus stop.

After a moment's hesitation, she changed direction and walked toward the woman, who looked up and saw her coming.

"Are you waitin' for a bus? I can give you a ride," said Belinda.

"Oh, no…I was just standin' here to use this ash can," she said, putting her cigarette out in the sand. "My car's right over there."

"Ah."

Belinda gazed at the woman, who gazed back.

Then Shelley Dilks said, "I thought I'd go back up, just to check and make sure John Cole's restin' okay. They said they were gonna take the breathin' tube out about now."

"They did. He's out of the critical time now and restin' comfortably." She repeated the nurse's words.

"Oh…well, good." The woman made no move toward her car.

Belinda said, "Gracie is up there with Emma. They may stay the night."

"Oh."

"I know that you are close with John Cole…that you've been his secretary for some time."

"I am manager of the Berry Corp offices and John Cole's friend for over sixteen years." Hand on her hip, she jutted her head slightly.

"I know this must be a horrible time for you. It sure has scared me. But right now is their private family time. You can help John Cole best by keeping the office runnin' smoothly. When he goes back to work, you will then have your place with him again. For right now, he needs his wife."

Shelley Dilks's eyes regarded her for long seconds, while Belinda placidly looked back. Then the woman turned and walked away to her car, got in it and drove off.

Belinda watched the taillights of the woman's car, until it turned onto the boulevard. Then she started her own car and headed for home.

As she drove along the dark highway, she peered into the black night beyond the lights, mindful of the unexpected—a stalled car, someone walking at the edge of the road, a stray dog or loose cow. In the distance she could see the glow of Valentine, where she was heading.

Life, she thought, was a lot like that. One could see only what was immediately ahead. The glow of future ideas and dreams kept one heading on with hope, but in between was the vast dark unknown where anything could happen.

Impulsively, she lowered the windows. The summer breeze blew inside, bringing the pungent scents of soil and grasses, and, as she came into Valentine, the scent of dust and concrete and fertilizer from MacCoy's Feed and Grain.

Only two cars were parked on Main Street, and a single truck, far down, was turning the corner. An energetic soul worked over his car at the car wash, and several people talked in the parking lot of the IGA, which was turning out its lights.

The Berry Quick Stop was still open. Belinda pulled in to get gas. Paris Miller worked the cash register and asked eagerly after John Cole.

"Mr. Johnny called earlier and said that Mr. Berry's operation went well. Is he still okay?"

"Very well, with an excellent prognosis. The doctors expect a full recovery, with little or no heart damage."

"Oh, good!" The girl's intense expression relaxed, but then there were tears in her eyes.

Belinda reached across the counter to squeeze the girl's arm. "He's gonna be okay, sugar."

On the drive home, faces and scenes from the day flitted across her mind: John Cole and Emma in the hospital bed together, and Johnny and Gracie, the brothers and sister-in-law. Joella was, well, unforgettable, and Belinda found herself smiling. She thought of Lyle, Pastor Stanley, the Berry Corporation people.

It was the hard times that really brought people together. Through John Cole's suffering, Belinda had been brought back to her friendship with Emma, and to more understanding that relationships ebbed and flowed as people changed and grew. Both Gracie and Johnny were brought closer to their parents— Gracie, the daughter that Emma had always wanted. She had that now, and Belinda was glad for her.

John Cole's bond with Shelley Dilks and the others of the Berry Corporation came from all the hard struggles to build that corporation. Now they were a little lost without him, a little frightened in not knowing a way to help, yet in the struggle to cope, they were all brought closer together, too.

Her thoughts traveled back to when she had been a young woman caught in her mistake, in believing in a romance that had never really been, and alone and pregnant. How different it might have been had she chosen to go to her mother and father. Perhaps if she had been able to open up and let them help her, they all might have been brought closer.

But she had been too frightened of rejection. Too doubtful of being loved and lovable.

And perhaps she still was.

CHAPTER 15

Heard It on the Radio

FOURTEEN WEEKS.

She marked the little calendar that she kept in her purse. She and her baby had made it through the first trimester. With wonder, hope, fear, she put a hand to her belly.

At least a dozen times in the past week, she had started to tell Lyle. Ever since John Cole's heart attack, she had felt close to Lyle in a manner that she had not before experienced.

Yet, for reasons she really could not understand, whenever she opened her mouth to speak to him not only about the baby but about the emotions in her heart, no words would come out. Each day she got more in a pickle, more stressed, more anxious.

Stopping at the message board in the kitchen, she wrote: *Honey, let's go for dinner up at Logan's and drive out to the lake on the way home so we can be alone. Love you.*

She went out through the back door, closing it softly behind her. Halfway along the walkway, she turned and went back into the kitchen and over to the message board.

She erased what she had written, took up the marker and stood gazing at the blank board for long seconds.

Taking a deep breath, she wrote: *Honey, we are pregnant.*

There. She might not be able to say it, but she could write it.

She turned and walked out of the house, got into her car and headed for Main Street.

Have you lost your mind? Telling him on a blackboard? And then, *Will you tell him the entire truth? Will you tell him about what you did?*

I don't know.

She could write it all on the message board, but it would be long.

When she paused at the stop sign at the corner, she almost turned back to go wipe off the message, but she put her foot hard on the accelerator, sending the car forward.

She was quite scattered all day. She mixed up orders, called customers that she had known all her life by the wrong name, and then, right in front of Arlo, she was in tears at a news report of a mother giving birth to quadruplets.

"You okay, Belinda?" Arlo asked. He had never seen his cousin cry.

"Of course I am. It was just touching. They gave them ten thousand dollars and a Caravan." She gestured. "You act like you have never seen a woman get emotional."

"Well, I never saw you do it."

"You talk like I am hard-hearted Hannah."

"I didn't say that. I just meant that—"

"I don't care what you meant. I can get upset just like anyone else!"

Arlo retreated to the storage room with a comic book.

★ ★ ★

Belinda slipped back to the restroom with a blood pressure monitor.

Of course it was up! She was going on four months pregnant and had informed her husband by a note on a message board.

Not only that, but her body was no longer her own. She felt taken over by an alien. The term *morning sickness* was definitely misleading. Hers could strike at any time, day or night, and usually when she felt the least upset. Her tastes were unreliable, too. The idea of coffee had become sickening, but she accepted rich latte. Anything fattening and artery clogging was what her pregnant body craved.

And then there was her emotional state. She had never been one to cry. She could watch the most heartbreaking news, like whole families made homeless in storms, and be told about car wrecks, sickness or death, and she took it as the inevitability of life and death, but now, when she saw a stray dog, she got all teary. This was not helped by her energy level dipping in the afternoons. She had fallen asleep over the drugstore accounts. And she could not remember things, had clean forgotten to pay the Visa bill, and was absolutely horrified. She had never been a forgetful person, most especially when it came to money.

Marilee's voice came over the phone. "Corrine has been accepted into the Oklahoma School of Science and Mathematics." Her tone wavered between pride and despair. "We didn't say anything before, because we were not certain about her actually going—it's so far away. But she has decided to go, so please mention about her being accepted on the *About Town* spot today."

"Today? Is it…well, of course it is." Belinda was embarrassed for Marilee to know she had forgotten her own radio spot.

Marilee appeared not to have noticed. She said, "You know, the school is all the way up in Oklahoma City. Corrine will have to stay in a dormitory durin' the week and only come home on the weekends." Marilee's voice cracked. "But the school only accepts about seventy high-school sophomores each year, so it is a real honor. Say that her family is very proud of her."

"Of course you are."

"It'll just be so hard with her away." Marilee's voice broke.

And Belinda surprised herself by blurting, "It sure *will!*" Her vision blurred as she noted for *About Town*: *Corrine Pendley accepted by prestigious school up in Oklahoma City.*

After hanging up the phone, she went to get herself a latte. She filled the cup half-full and resisted adding whipped cream. She was attempting to balance calories and stress. Food did calm her, and calmness was an important factor. No matter what experts said, grabbing an apple simply did not have the same comfort effect.

Thinking of this gave her the idea to put Saint-John's-wort, valerian root and fish oil as that week's Blaine's Drugstore specials. She would throw in the basic blood pressure machine, too, at ten percent off. There had been a higher interest in the blood pressure machines since John Cole's heart attack. People generally skipped over the cheaper model for the more expensive one once they got into the store.

She was making the sale tags when Oran Lackey came hurrying through the door, and instead of going to the pharmacy, he came straight over to the soda fountain counter.

"Winston just had an accident."

"What happened? How bad is it?" Belinda reached for her purse.

"He was drivin' his lawn mower again and ran into the sheriff's car. Right into it." Oran smacked his hands for illustration.

"Did they take him to the hospital? How bad is he?" She dug for her keys.

"Oh, no. He's okay. He hung on to that mower, never came off. He was a little jarred, but he seemed okay. Just mad. I drove him on home."

"Oh...well, good." Relief mingled with annoyance that Oran had not said that in the first place. She actually felt a little faint and reached for the counter to steady herself.

A few minutes, and more latte, later, she thought to ask how fast the sheriff had been driving.

"Oh, the sheriff's car was parked," Oran told her. "Right around on Church Street toward the rear of the station. Winston said he swerved to miss a squirrel. The mower is out of commission, the front wheels are all out of whack. Sheriff's real glad."

"Oh."

"I witnessed the whole thing," said Oran. "I'm not sayin' there was no squirrel. I'm just sayin' I did not see one."

Belinda gazed at Oran, then bent her head to make a note for the *About Town* spot: *Winston had an accident, but he is fine.*

She checked the clock for the twentieth time. It was still too early for Lyle to be awake yet.

She headed down to the post office, where she ran into Emma and received a full report on John Cole's progress.

"The first couple of nights he was home were rough, but we're doin' better now," Emma reported to both Belinda and Julia

Jenkins-Tinsley, stationed behind the counter. "He still has to sleep in his big chair in the family room—it hurts him to lie down—but he is sleepin'. It's still real painful for him to cough. He has to hold this pillow against his chest—it's just awful to watch."

"Well, I saw my daddy after that same surgery," said Julia, "and if I ever have to have it, just let me die. They pry your ribs right open."

Watching the postmistress illustrate with her hands, Belinda swallowed.

Emma said, "John Cole has been so brave through it all. Never a word of complaint. And he's already walked out to his shop a couple of times. I watched him from the window."

They all agreed that modern heart surgery was a miracle.

Belinda jotted: *John Cole Berry, a very good patient, recovering nicely at home in the loving arms of his grateful wife and family.* Goodness, she was teary when sad; she was teary when happy.

Julia said, "If people would just do aerobic exercise and eat right, they wouldn't have to go through such an operation."

"Bingo Yardell had a heart attack, and he's skinny and plays tennis," Belinda said, tears gone and ready to smack Julia with her own mail.

Emma jumped in. "John Cole is not overweight, Julia, and heaven knows he was on the go." Then, with a lowered voice, "I did find out that he was still sneakin' cigarettes from friends around him."

For once Julia did not comment. Belinda was glad Inez was not around.

"I do believe that the key is to relax more and often," said Emma with conviction. "He is just doin' so well bein' relaxed about everything. You learn what is really important." She turned to Belinda. "Honey, would you please tell it on *About Town* today—that we so appreciate all the cards and good wishes John Cole has received. He has learned that he has so many friends. And say that he is doin' real well. But he is not up for visitors or telephone calls the rest of this week."

"Will do." She noted: *Good recovery, good friends, no visitors this week,* and underlined the last part.

"And Naomi was just so right," Emma said, before going out the door. "This time is a real gift, bringin' me and John Cole closer together like we never have been before. You just don't know what you have until you almost lose it."

She smiled brightly and waved. Both Belinda and Julia smiled and waved back.

As Emma disappeared from sight, Julia said, "Seems like she's pleased that John Cole had the heart attack."

Belinda opened her mouth to respond, then shut it. Might as well save her breath.

Julia weighed the packages Belinda had brought—exchanges to QVC and HSN—and said, "I'll tell you somethin' else that can bring a couple together."

"What's that?" Belinda placed her wallet back into her purse and checked to see if she had any chewing gum.

"Separatin'."

"Uhmm?"

"Separating. Havin' some space between you. That's what Juice and I are doin'."

"You and Juice are separating?" Belinda's head snapped up.

"Uh-huh. We are gonna stay married separately. The Long-acres next door to us are sellin' their house. They're movin' down to Ardmore—she's inherited her mother's home. Big thing from what she says."

"I know. I told it last week on *About Town*."

"Yes, and that's when I had the idea. I'm goin' to buy their house and move over there. I always loved her kitchen—it has the nicest nook."

"Ah-huh." Belinda stared at Julia.

"Juice is just too sloppy for me, and he eats the junkiest stuff and snores the roof off. He just annoys the fire out of me, and I don't want to live with him anymore. But I do not want to divorce him. He's a great Chinese checker and Scribbage player…and we do like to take road trips together."

"Ah-huh."

"So we're stayin' married but livin' in different houses."

"Ah-huh."

"You know where I got the idea? Quote by Katharine Hepburn. Hepburn said men and women would do best to live next door and visit now and then. Juice thinks it is a good idea, too. This way we can each live just how we want to. And we're gonna share Pixie, our little dog. Juice is puttin' a little doggie door in the fence. He's just real good at stuff like that. Why would I want to divorce him?"

"Ah-huh."

"I want you to tell everyone on your radio spot today. I don't want a lot of gossip. We'll just lay the facts out there. We are doin' this to bring us closer all the way around. You can note that down." Julia motioned.

"Ah-huh." Belinda brought out her small note card and jotted on it.

"Oh, here's the weekly postcard from your mother. She says the same ol' thing."

"Ah-huh."

"I'll be listenin' today." The postmistress smiled quite happily.

To each his own, thought Belinda.

Stepping briskly, she walked the short distance on the sunny sidewalk to the bank. At the double doors, Iris MacCoy and Norman Cooper were coming out. Iris gave her always-friendly hello, and Norman his shy one. Norman kept his head down as he held the door for Belinda. Suddenly the door banged into her elbow. Rubbing it, she saw with annoyance that Norman had taken off to catch up with Iris at the curb. He all but had his tongue hanging out after her like a dog after a bone. Or a big sugary cake. Iris was an Amazon-size woman, a full head taller than slight Norman, Belinda thought, with some amusement at her own comparison.

The teller, Maggie Lou Blades, leaned forward. "Did you see Norman Cooper and Iris MacCoy?"

Belinda looked at the woman's avid expression. "No, I didn't." She passed over the drugstore deposit.

Maggie Lou said, "Well, I saw you pass them on your way in." She counted the bills in the swift manner of all tellers who could talk and count at the same time.

"Really? I didn't notice."

"He was about fallin' all over her when he met up with her in here. He's at that age, you know."

Belinda looked at her. "And what age is that?"

"Well…when men start wantin' to stray around."

"How old are you?" Belinda asked.

"I'm…twenty-nine. Why?" She slid the receipt across the counter.

"I'll mention that on *About Town* today. I guess that is the age for turnin' into a gossip."

"Why…Belinda, what is wrong with you today?"

"Thank you for the service, Maggie Lou. I'll mention on

About Town today that the bank customers can come in here and see you and hear about everyone's business."

She turned and left with Maggie Lou calling after her, "I did not say anything of the sort. Don't you say that on the radio."

She supposed she had reacted a little crazy to Maggie Lou. She never had pretended to like the woman, but she supposed it was that mention about age that caused her to be irrational. And the idea of gossiping, although why gossip would bother her now, after all these years, she had no idea.

Because she was pregnant and a bundle of hormones and emotions, and waiting for her husband to find out he was going to be a father by a message on the refrigerator. What had she been *thinking?*

She was not thinking, obviously.

She craved a vanilla shake. Surely it would be okay. She had been very good with food. A treat was surely in order, and she would get it from the Burger Barn before her radio spot.

With the car windows down and the summer breeze blowing through, she sat beneath the shade of the parking overhang and drank her sweet treat. It was like a mini vacation. After sucking up every bit with the straw, she sighed, set the cup aside and repaired her lipstick in the visor mirror.

Catching a movement in the mirror, she peered closer. She saw a lanky figure at the pay phone at the edge of the Burger Barn lot.

Yes, it was Andy Smith there, talking on the phone.

The pay phone was the only one left in town anymore. Everyone had cell phones these days.

One would think Andy would have a cell phone. Or use the phone at the café or Woody's house, where he was reportedly living.

She watched him finish talking and hang up the phone. He hung it up very gently and stood there as a person does in thought. Then he walked over to the order window of the Burger Barn.

Belinda got out of her car and went over to him. "Hi, Andy."

He glanced over, eyebrows going up. "Hello."

"I'm Belinda Blaine…from Blaine's Drugstore. We met a few weeks ago at the café—maybe you remember?"

"Uh…yes. Good day." The server appeared at the window with two drinks for him. Andy paid, took the drinks and stepped away from the window. "Would you like to order something now?" He gestured at the window.

"No. I had a milk shake earlier. I just saw you and thought I would say hello…and ask you how you are doin' in town."

His eyebrows went up, and then with something of a crooked grin, he dropped his gaze downward for a long second. Then, "I'm enjoying it quite a lot. It's a nice place, Valentine, and I like working for Fayrene." His eyes came up, and he smiled.

"So you've decided to stay?"

"Guess so. Well, thanks for the chat, but I need to get back to helping Woody with his flower bed…take him his drink. It's pretty hot out here." He cast her a smile as he started away, but his eyes were hard.

She called after him, "It sure is hot, but we're all used to it. Is it this hot where you come from?"

"Sometimes." He did not look back or break stride.

Belinda felt foolish. And hot. Turning from watching him cross the road, she got back in the car that had been sitting in the shade, started it and turned the air-conditioning up high.

As she drove away, she thought of the people she had spoken to, and about, that day. Life just continuing to happen, as it normally did, which for some reason at the moment seemed strange and quite annoying.

She checked her cell phone, wondering if Lyle had called while she was out talking with Andy. That would be just like life to have it happen that way.

There had been a call, but it was listed as an unavailable number. Most likely her mother calling from France. Disappointed, Belinda closed her phone.

Catching sight of Larry Joe Darnell and Monica Huggins in front of the Texaco garage—Monica straightening Larry Joe's collar—she thought that it was a lot easier to pay attention to the lives of other people than to her own. She could get everyone else straightened out and taken care of in five minutes, if they would just listen to her.

Her own life was much more difficult.

She ran into him coming out the back door of the drugstore.

"Lyle!"

"Hi, honey." He bent to give her a quick kiss. He was holding two to-go cups of coffee, putting her in mind of Andy earlier.

"You're on duty?" She ran her eyes over his uniform, as if she might be mistaken.

"Yeah, but just workin' a few hours this afternoon, that's all. Sheriff had to go to court, and Dorothy Jean already had the afternoon off. Another doctor appointment. She may be pregnant, but don't mention it to anyone, because if she is, the sheriff is gonna be mad," he confided in a lowered tone. "I'm gonna help Giff cover, but I told them I needed off by seven. Mason's gonna come in then. We can still go to dinner."

"Go to dinner?"

"Yeah. You said last night that you kinda wanted to go out to eat tonight."

"I said that?"

"I thought you did." He gave his usual uncertain expression, then, "Over at the café Woody has made fresh peach pie from the first peaches off his tree. You always like that. Guess I do, too." He grinned his charming grin.

"Oh."

Down the alley behind the sheriff's office, Giff pulled in and beeped the horn of the patrol car.

"Lyle, didn't you see the message on the refrigerator?"

He looked guilty. "Ah, honey, no, I'm sorry. I didn't think to look. I was hurryin' to get here. What was it?"

"Uh…nothin'. I'll tell you later."

"Okay." He lifted the cups to her and gave a loving wink, then headed away with his long-legged stride.

She thought to go home and erase the message. That would be best. But she had her radio spot first. She hurried into the drugstore, where the air conditioner above the rear door dripped on her head. She called for Arlo to bring her some cold sweet tea as she went to her little office. She threw her purse on the desk and dug for the bits of notes she had been making all day.

Of course he had not read the note. Whatever had possessed her to think that he would? Did he ever read the notes on the message board? No. He would get in the refrigerator and never see them. Half the time he couldn't find the ketchup in the refrigerator right in front of his face.

And she well knew all that, so why had she written the note in the first place? Because she just found talking so darn hard. People talked to her all the time, but she did not talk to them, unless she was telling them what to do in their lives. She did not talk about her own life.

Arlo brought the cold tea. "You sure look hot."

"Now why would I be hot on a ninety-degree day?" she said, and his head instantly disappeared back around the partition.

She drank deeply of the sweet, cold liquid, then rubbed her head. *May be pregnant, but don't mention it to anyone, because if she is, the sheriff is gonna be mad…*

She felt dizzy. Her brain was too full of knowledge of people's lives, things she was to tell and things she was not.

The phone rang. Belinda answered, heard Jim say, "Thirty seconds," and then listened to the Blaine's Drugstore jingle play.

"Hello, ever'body. My goodness it is hot today, and that leads to a lot of stress. Over here at Blaine's Drugstore, we've got a few helpful stress remedies on special…." As always when on the radio, her words just flowed out. She even sat up straighter.

She told of Corrine's achievement and prospect of going far away to school. She relayed the news about Winston's accident, and that everyone was grateful he was unhurt, and that anyone can make a mistake. She told about John Cole's splendid recovery and loving the attention of family and friends, and about Julia and Juice's clever marriage solution, and thanked Maggie Lou Blades, who was twenty-nine, for excellent service at the Community Bank, and welcomed Andy Smith to town and invited people to stop by to meet him at the Main Street Café.

She had never given such a cheery, positive spin to her reporting. A number of people in her audience picked up something in her tone and turned puzzled faces to their radios.

And then, as she wrapped one arm around herself, she said, "There is also news of a special nature close to home. We have a pregnant woman in our midst...."

There was a pause, and out of her mouth tumbled, "Belinda Blaine of Blaine's Drugstore...me...I am going to have a baby.

"That's all for now. See you next week on *About Town and Beyond*."

She clicked off the phone and carefully returned the receiver to its cradle.

Out in the front of the drugstore, Arlo, looking a little stunned, said, "Well, who would have thought?"

Corrine replied, "It makes sense." She was rarely surprised by anything, and realized some part of her had seen this coming. She had a lot of experience with her aunt Marilee. She was also getting a lot of experience with life, period, she thought.

Jaydee Mayhall at the counter sat with his coffee cup halfway to his lips. Oran Lackey came out from the pharmacy, scratching his head.

Down at the post office, Julia Jenkins-Tinsley said aloud to the radio, "Well, dang, Belinda, do you have to go that far to upstage me?"

Across the street, Fayrene whipped her car to a stop in her parking place behind the café, grabbed up the sacks of onions and summer squash she had just bought at the IGA and hurried inside to tell everyone what she had heard on the radio. The girls thought she was kidding, but Woody grinned and said, "I don't know why anythin' like that should su'prise y'all."

"Her condition has mellowed her," Fayrene pronounced. "She gave the café free publicity, mentionin' it and welcomin' you to town, Andy."

"Welcoming me? What did she say?"

Fayrene noticed he looked oddly alarmed. "She was really nice," she reassured him. "She said a welcome to Andy Smith, who likes our town, and for people to stop over at the café to meet you." Fayrene remembered to enunciate her words a little better. Andy seemed to talk well and was so sophisticated; she did not want to sound like a hick around him.

Down at the bank, Maggie Lou Blades was still at her teller station and, in fact, preparing to wait on Inez Cooper, who had just come in. Maggie Lou was forming a way to mention about Norman Cooper's earlier visit, when her boss called her over, told her about Belinda's complimentary mention on the radio and said that, as a result, Maggie Lou was named employee of the week and was possibly up for a promotion to loan officer.

Still sitting at her desk, now with her arms around herself, Belinda might have been quite surprised to know that many people were thrilled for her. Rosalba Garcia, who had secret reason to be indebted to Belinda, excitedly told her employer, Marilee Holloway, who said, "Oh, finally somethin' I can help Belinda with!" John Cole Berry, bored and having caught the announcement on the coffee-machine radio, told Emma, who instantly started planning a baby shower to end all baby showers. And Winston, who was playing dominoes at the senior center, excused himself and, in a very rare move, went to Grace Florist and had a dozen red roses sent to Belinda.

As he stepped back out onto the bright sidewalk, he looked up and down Main Street and said, "Well, Lord, another young one to carry on."

The sound of an approaching siren brought Belinda out of her thoughts. She was still sitting at her desk, hiding, as it were. She had heard some whispering on the other side of the panel, but no one had appeared, thank heaven.

She listened to the siren grow louder and louder, until it was right outside. Then silence. A car door slammed, and the rear door of the drugstore opened and closed.

Belinda's eyes went to the corner of the partition.

Lyle's tall frame in his tan uniform appeared.

"I was over at the Texaco, pumpin' gas…. I didn't hear it, but Giff had the radio on and he says…" His dark eyes ran over her face as he spoke. "Did you say…?"

She was already bobbing her head up and down.

He came around her desk, and she rose up to meet him. He pulled her into his arms and lifted her clean off the ground and spun her around.

"Lyle…I can't breathe."

When she continued to gasp for breath even after he sat her down, he panicked and called for Oran, who had her breathe into a paper bag.

Lyle grabbed cigars from the case near the soda fountain and passed them to everyone in the drugstore, and by that time quite a number of people had come in to congratulate Belinda. She hung back, but Lyle was all out there, until Giff dragged him away to deputy duty. Even then he kept having Giff stop— at the Texaco, at MacCoy's Feed and Grain, out at the Ford dealership—and he kept handing out cigars.

It was not until that evening when he came home that he finally asked Belinda when the baby was due to be born. All afternoon she had managed to evade answering that question for anyone else.

Now she told Lyle, "November 29 is the due date the doctor has set…but you know that is just an estimate."

"November 29?" Lyle frowned in thought and cocked his head to the side.

Belinda turned away to the refrigerator. "Honey, would you like a Coke?" She brought one forth.

Lyle said, "You are four months pregnant?"

She gazed at him. "A little shy of that."

"How long have you known? You mean you've seen a doctor and gone all these months and didn't tell me?"

"Honey, I have been afraid I might lose the baby. I am thirty-eight, and miscarriage rates go up for older mothers. I didn't want to tell you and then lose the baby."

"My mother had me at forty-three."

"I know, honey, but she had children before you. This is my first one…to be delivered."

He turned and gazed out the window.

Belinda realized she still stood with a bottle of Coca-Cola in her hand and the refrigerator door open. She closed the door.

Lyle remained silent for long seconds, before looking at her again with an expression that took her breath. "So you were just goin' to maybe lose the baby and never tell me you had even gotten pregnant?"

"No, honey. I would have told you. It's just that I wanted to make sure."

"I'm the father, Belinda. And I'm your husband. I have a right to be in this with you all the way. Good times and hard times."

He shook his head, looking away again with as pained an expression as she had ever seen on him. "You just shut me out all the time. You still, after all these years, keep me shut out. It ain't supposed to be like that."

They went to a late supper at the café, where Fayrene gave them the peach pie on the house as a celebration of their parenthood. Fayrene made a big deal about the pregnancy, as did a number of their friends and neighbors who came into the café while they were there.

"Now, when is this baby due?"

"End of November."

"What? I'm sorry, I didn't hear you."

Belinda cleared her throat. "I said the end of November." She saw Lyle look down at his plate.

"Well, that is comin' on fast.... She said end of November," Fayrene told the Peele sisters several booths over.

"You and Lyle can sure keep a secret," said Luwanna, who came to refill their cold tea.

It seemed throughout their entire meal people kept congratulating them and telling them how now their lives were going to change. Lyle was very jovial, as always, and Belinda remained her normal down-to-earth self. She was overwhelmed by everyone's good wishes. She really had not thought so many people would care about her life. She found all the attention horribly uncomfortable.

On the way home, she and Lyle said not a word to each other, other than Belinda having to say, "I just have to turn up this air-conditioning. I can't breathe."

Usually Lyle was the one to make an effort to cover such silences, but that night he didn't try at all. Every time he looked at Belinda, his eyes were pained.

Later, in their bed, he turned from her. She lay there thinking of how to tell him all the things that kept running through her mind.

Each time she tried to speak, she could not bring forth words. They jammed up inside her, and she felt as if she was going to crack right apart.

Belinda lay on the exam table, while the woman technician and doctor hovered on either side, and Lyle at her head.

"Okay…it looks like a girl," said the doctor and technician together.

The next instant the two women jumped to grab Lyle and get him to a chair, leaving Belinda totally forgotten.

Belinda watched Lyle being fawned over and put her hand to her belly, silently telling her daughter, *I will be here for you, always. That's what I can do.*

Lyle drove them home. In town, they passed Willie Lee walking along in front of the IGA with Gabby Smith.

"Pull over. I need to tell Willie Lee," Belinda instructed. She lowered the window. "Willie Lee, it *is* a girl."

He squinted at her from beneath his ball cap. "Yes," he said, and gave a crooked grin.

Lyle said, "So Willie Lee even knew before me?"

Belinda breathed deeply and sat there, looking out the windshield, her spirit doing a nosedive. Then it came to her. "Willie Lee even knew before me. He knows everything before everyone."

"Oh. Yeah," Lyle said.

When they reached home, Lyle said, "I'm goin' to call my sister and tell her."

He seemed to hesitate as he took up the cordless phone and dialed. When his sister came on the line, he walked away to his workout room, out of Belinda's hearing. He had never before deliberately done that.

PART THREE

Between Birth and Heaven

CHAPTER 16

1550 on the Radio Dial
Winston Is in the Building

HE OPENED HIS EYES, AND THERE WAS WILLIE Lee's face staring at him, blue eyes blinking slowly, curiously, behind his thick glasses.

"Good morn-ing," Willie Lee said. "We are late."

Winston felt disoriented. Then he saw the numerals on the clock. They read 5:50. Coming to the present, he threw back the quilt with a curse. "Why didn't you wake me earlier?" He saw that Willie Lee was dressed, and Munro waited by the door.

"Be-cause Cor-rine is not here to w-ake us," said Willie Lee, frowning. He was not happy about his cousin having gone away to school.

Winston did not bother to do more than splash water on his face and rinse with mouthwash.

"Why didn't you hooligans wake me up?" he demanded of

Marilee and Tate, who came when they heard him pounding stiff-legged down the stairs, carrying his boots, his shirttail half into his pants, unshaven but with his hat on. "Didn't you miss me?"

"I am busy, in case you have not noticed," said Marilee, with one child holding to her leg and the other crying in her arms. "And I thought you needed sleep."

"You were afraid to find out I had died," he accused. "Well, I'm not dead yet! Come on, Tate, get a move on."

Tate and Marilee shared a glance, and then Tate hotfooted it after the older man. It was a relief to see Winston moving faster than he had in some time.

Earlier that morning, when Tate had come down to the kitchen and found the coffeepot empty and unused, his first thought was that Winston had already gotten up and gone before anyone else. He had raced out to the garage to see if Winston had managed to get the keys and use the car. But the car was there, as was the bunged-up and unusable riding lawn mower. When he had peeked into Winston's room, the old man appeared to be still asleep, so Tate had gone to awaken Marilee and ask her what to do. She, too, had felt compelled to look into Winston's room.

"He needs his sleep. Don't go in." And she shut the door quietly.

But what Winston had said was closer to the truth, which was that they had been a little worried that he might have expired, and neither wanted to be the one to find him dead in his bed.

Obvious to all was the bitter reality that Winston had begun to fail, as the saying went. No one could face it. No one mentioned it to anyone else, and everyone went on as they always had, which was with the idea that Winston had always been there and always would be. Winston was one of those people everyone expected to live forever.

For his part, Winston knew better than anyone else that he was failing. He was also aware, painfully so, that no one around him could face the fact. Except perhaps Willie Lee, who, Winston noticed, had begun to stick close. Everyone else seemed to look away.

"Get on outta my chair!"

At Winston's holler, Everett hopped up as though he had been stuck with a cattle prod. He stumbled to his own smaller chair, while shouting into the microphone, "He's arrived, folks! *Winston is in the building!*"

Those were the first strong words Everett had been able to get out since opening the show without Winston. The *Wake Up* show was Winston's show, no matter how hard Everett had fought against it. People expected Winston's cutting up. Everett was the straight man. Without Winston, Everett couldn't be straight; he just sort of fell over flat. When time had come to open the show and Winston was not there, the best Everett could do was come out with a croaking, "Gooood mornin', folks! Welcome to the *Wake Up* show. Er…this is Everett— Winston and Willie Lee have not yet arrived. Let's get started…uh, here's the weather…."

He had stumbled through fifteen minutes of the show, while calls began to come in, people asking where Winston was. Everett thought to announce that Winston had taken a day off, and after he said that, he had to blow his nose in his handkerchief and drink hot coffee to get his voice back.

Now, Winston took over once again, "I overslept and no one woke me up…so I guess I need to say this again. Wake up,

WAKE UP, you SLEE-PY-HEAD…this is Winston, and he AIN'T YET DEAD!"

Everett breathed deeply. He took hold of the microphone and said, "We thank you for that notification, Winston. I'll make sure I alert the newspapers. Now, may I give the school lunch menu?"

Everything was all right in the world again.

During the rest of the program, Everett played straight man to Winston's jokes in a contented manner he had not before known. He was flying high on being the straight man, on giving Winston the majority of the airtime until just thirty seconds before the ending reveille, when he remembered his own coming show.

He got control of the microphone. "Stay tuned for the *Everett in the Morning* show. We've got big news. A complete carousel has been found and purchased. We're going to talk with Mr. John Cole Berry, who will be calling from Chicago, where he found the carousel. We'll also be talking to Mrs. Vella Blaine, who will be dedicating the laying of the foundation of the carousel building this afternoon. We'll see you right here at 1550 on the radio dial…*Everett in the Morning*."

He had learned from Winston to repeat his name, and he was getting good at it.

While commercials and public announcements played, Everett sat back, wiped his face with a handkerchief and looked over at Winston.

Winston looked very old.

"I missed you this morning, Winston," Everett blurted. "I don't think I could do the show without you."

Winston lazily looked at him. "Oh, I know it'll be hard, but you've been watchin' me for all this time. You'll get it done."

This reply was more disconcerting than reassuring. Everett

wanted Winston to say that he was going to be there to do the show forever. And Winston's mildness was aggravating.

Then Winston said, "I'm mighty proud to share the airwaves with you, Ev."

"Well…well, likewise." Everett ducked his head and pretended to read the papers he assembled for his upcoming program.

Passing behind Everett as he left, Winston squeezed the other man's shoulder. Everett swallowed hard.

Jim Rainwater called over, "Everett, you got five seconds."

It turned out that Winston had not actually left the station building. All he had done was get a cup of coffee. As Everett got John Cole Berry on the phone and introduced him to the audience—"Mr. Berry and I have been working together on the carousel committee"—Winston stepped over to the microphone to say, "Hey, there, John Cole, how you doin' up there in Chicago?"

And darned if Winston didn't manage to end up dominating Everett's interview of John Cole, even from Everett's smaller chair, which Winston slipped into.

"Describe this carousel you've found, J.C. We'd like some details."

"Well, it's all wooden horses. We didn't open all the crates, but we're pretty sure it is all horses, anyway. The figures need some work—"

"You said the carousel seems to need mostly painting," Everett interjected, attempting to get back into the conversation.

"Yes. It is being shipped today to the restorer in California."

Winston said, "Tell us about this restorer. Is it a company that does only carousels? Didn't know there was such."

"Yes, sir. They specialize in building and restoring carousels. They have done…"

Winston leaned forward, both arms on the table. Everett looked at him, and then sat back and let Winston and John Cole talk.

When Vella Blaine arrived at the studio for her interview, she looked around with a puzzled expression. "Where's Winston? I thought he was doin' your show today."

"He was," said Everett. "He's gone now, but don't expect it to be for good."

Willie Lee found his mother dressing his two little sisters in their room. His eyes widened a little at the sight of her—her hair was on end, and she had on a red sweatshirt and Papa Tate's pajama bottoms. She was having a very hard time coping with Corrine having gone away to school. That was what she would say to Papa Tate: "I'm havin' such a hard time copin' with Corrine gone."

Although every time Corrine called, and especially during her first weekend home, his mother made a point to be all happy and pleasant. But when Corrine was gone, his mother cried into Papa Tate's shirt.

Several times Corrine had called and asked Willie Lee, "How is Aunt Marilee really doin'…? How are you all gettin' on?"

Willie Lee replied, "We are do-ing good. Mo-ther is cop-ing."

Gabby had helped him with the statement. She had said it would be kind, and he was getting much better at lying. He wanted Corrine to be happy, but he knew she was not. He could hear her unhappiness over the phone line, but she would only say, "I'm doin' real good at school. This is a great opportunity."

He did not know how something could be a good thing when so many people were not happy about it.

He knew his mother was not going to be happy when he told her, "Mo-ther, I am not go-ing to scho-ol."

"What? Of course you are. We've been through this, Willie Lee. I know you don't like school…I know it is hard, but you need to go because it will help you to grow up. You've only been going a few weeks this year—it will get better, I know it will."

He had rehearsed with Gabby all of what he needed to say. "May-be that is true, but now I am go-ing to be with Mr. Winston. That is what I need to do now."

His mother looked over from pulling up Victoria's pants. She regarded him, and he regarded her, each speaking without words in the way of certain mothers and sons, and each knowing they were stepping into a new place.

"All right," Marilee said. "We'll try it for a bit."

Her son gave a rare wide smile that touched Marilee to her core. He came and hugged her, and she hugged him, letting him go by only the strongest effort. Her son had his own life to live. She watched him race away, listened to his footsteps pound and him call out, "Pa-pa Tate…Mis-ter Win-ston! Wait for meee!"

"Safe in the arms of God," she whispered.

Leaving her little girls' room, she paused to look into Winston's bedroom. It was like looking back seventy-five years. There was not even a television. She made up the covers on the old spool bed. Then she paused to look over the pictures on the aged oak veneer dresser—his family in frames a hundred years old. Glancing around the room again, she rubbed her shoulders, feeling as if there were voices and emotions from the past all around her. People who had lived and loved and left their mark forever, as everyone did, one way or another.

Later Marilee went to the telephone and called the school to say that Willie Lee would not be there. "We are goin' t' home-school Willie Lee for a while," she said. She had not expected a problem, and there was none. The school officials had long ago given up trying to make Willie Lee be a normal boy and were relieved to have any sort of a break from the attempt.

Willie Lee again became Winston's shadow. He could be seen pushing the old man in the wheelchair or simply walking along beside him, and always a little dog following at their heels. As the days passed, the old man was seen more and more leaning on the boy. Every once in a while, after school and on weekends, they were joined by a small curly haired girl.

CHAPTER 17

Second Chances

BELINDA STRAIGHTENED THE MAGAZINES AND stacks of newspapers on the far side of the magazine rack. Eye falling to the *Valentine Voice,* she took up a copy. Her mother, stylishly dressed but wearing a hard hat, smiled out from the front page. She had been formally initiating the start of construction on the carousel building, which was well under way. Not shown were a small dozer and cement truck, and the crew of eight who had paused out of the way of the camera.

Just then voices floated over from the soda fountain—her mother, Jaydee and Winston. Winston was reading the newspaper article aloud and offering his comments, as he liked to do, to which her mother would throw in a *c'est la vie* or a *oui* now and again.

Since her return, her mother kept peppering her speech

with French. She would say, "*Bon-jour,* sugar," and "*Par-don,* honey." "Well, *merci beaucoup,* darlin'," and *"à tout à l'heure!"*

Intent to always secure his position with her, Jaydee had learned a few phrases. The one he seemed to remember best was, "Darlin', *je t'aime à la folie!"*

Winston, being quite jealous of Vella and Jaydee's relationship, got so annoyed at that moment that he came out with, "Here's a French word for you—*idiots!* Stop it or I'm gonna have t' slap you silly."

Belinda looked around the end of the magazine rack and saw her mother put her hand to her hip in the habit she had, replying, *"Désolée...excusez-moi!"*

Belinda came around the long magazine rack, saying to no one in particular, "And this is from whom I come." She crossed the soda fountain area and entered the back room and her partitioned office, where she dropped gently into her chair and propped her feet on a small milk crate.

Absently stroking her burgeoning belly, she gazed at the rusted and filmy window high on the wall, hearing her mother's voice far in the front of the store, and frowning as jumbled thoughts on being a mother, courtesy of her own mother, tumbled across her mind.

After some minutes, she realized that the tiny girl moved within her, seemingly in rhythm to her mother's voice.

Wasn't that the way for all women? Belinda thought. *Before we are even born, we begin moving to the voices of our mothers, our grandmothers and all those women who came before.*

"Yes, I will marry you," Vella Blaine said at last. It had been coming for some time. She inclined her head and cast Jaydee

Mayhall a sultry smile while fanning her face with a delicate scented handkerchief.

The two sat in the glider on Vella's rear flagstone patio in the cooling evening twilight.

Jaydee was so thrilled that he could hardly think straight. His eyes moved to the beautiful night coming in the eastern sky. A faint late-summer moon was rising. He pointed it out to Vella, and, sitting there gazing at the sky with her, a humbleness came over him. He felt the mercy of God. Heaven knew he had been a womanizer and generally rowdy man until age had begun to catch up with him. He had done nothing to deserve Vella, but she was going to marry him, and he would not have to be old alone. He was going to have a good, strong woman to help him.

"We will need a prenuptial agreement," said Vella, whose thoughts were quite straight, and mostly on her grandchild. It had been Vella's experience that men came and went, but this grandchild would be around the rest of Vella's life.

Jaydee nodded and said, "Good idea." Jaydee was a secure man about money.

They chatted easily about the matter of their union. Vella would take Jaydee's name, a practical decision all the way around, as she saw it. They would live together in Vella's house. Jaydee would sell his, even though his was modern and large and with every convenience. He would keep the Mayhall family farm and old farmhouse; that could be his retreat. Vella wanted to do some traveling, sometimes alone, sometimes she would want Jaydee's company. He agreed. He wanted her to join him in some horse activities, and she wanted him to help with her rose garden. Friday night would be date night, a commitment, and there would be candlelight and wine often.

They would each keep their own finances but work out an equitable sharing of the utility bills. They would give time and money to church as a couple.

Vella sighed with contentment. "It's all so much easier now, at this time of life."

Jaydee agreed with a smile.

Vella thought him the most good-natured man, especially for an attorney, that she had ever known. She supposed all the young hot girls with whom he had been involved the first half of his life had worn him out.

Then Vella had a thought. "Let me speak to Belinda before we announce our marriage."

Jaydee's eyebrows went up. "What if she doesn't like it?" It was no secret that Belinda had never much liked him.

"Oh, I'm not askin' her permission. It's just that I want to include her." Vella bit her bottom lip, then her eyes lit up. "Belinda can be my matron of honor. She might like that. It will mean a new dress and shoes, and I'm buyin'."

When Jaydee suggested spending the night, Vella told him, "No…we are goin' to be grandparents. We must set a good example."

She watched him take that in with a startled blink. Leading him to the front door, she kissed him with a passion that she knew surprised him. At her age, it was often expected for passion to have passed.

"You're gonna love bein' Papa, *mon cher,*" she said into his ear.

He went away looking a little dazed, as she had intended.

Sitting at her dressing table, Vella unscrewed the cap of a crystal jar while gazing into the mirror.

There was a rumor going around town that she had undergone cosmetic surgery while she was in France. She looked that much improved. She admitted to discovering a line of Swiss facial products that she promised to carry in the drugstore.

Belinda had advertised the products on the *About Town* radio spot, saying, "I do not know if my mother had a face-lift. Please stop askin' me. Ask Lillian Jennings."

Lillian Jennings told everyone, "I was not with Vella for days on end. For all I know she had everything lifted."

It was true that Vella looked rejuvenated. That was what months away from the rigors of everyday life, doing nothing a person did not want to do—not counting having to listen to Lillian talking about history or money—did for a person.

A long time ago Vella's grandmother had told her that life was made up of time, dirt and money. Her grandmother had said, "Too much or not enough of any of those is the constant sorrow of the heart and wears on the body."

The dirt that Vella thought of now as she creamed her face was that of the failings and disappointments, and downright sins, accumulated as one went through life. One's soul became as tarnished as the cabinet door where the hand constantly reached for the everyday dishes. No matter how hard a person tried to keep things clean, dirt seeped in, like grit through windows in the Oklahoma wind.

The lengthy months in France, away from her everyday life, had turned out to provide exactly what Vella had needed to cleanse her body and soul. The trip had given her the distance she needed to see herself and her life clearly.

Brushing her hair briskly, she thought, *I'm older, yes, but so very wiser.*

And her failures—she leaned close into the mirror, studying the lines on her face. She had earned every line, and they were precious. Just so the failures, which had helped to make her who she was.

Perhaps it was the promise of the grandchild that had as much to do with her renewed liveliness. What a surprise it had been to find out about Belinda's pregnancy! She had thought she would never be a grandmother, and now here it was, a second chance to get things right. To make up for her past as a poorly attentive mother, about which she had no illusions.

Now, with the coming grandchild, Vella was certain that she could be a grand dame of a grandmother as she never had been a mother. And maybe, just maybe, her granddaughter would be a bridge to a new relationship with Belinda. Maybe it was not too late for Vella to be an attentive mother to her adult daughter in a way that she had not been able to be in Belinda's childhood.

Maybe, Vella thought as she took up a magnifying mirror to pluck her eyebrows, she had finally grown up enough to equal Belinda.

Setting aside the mirror, she reached for the phone and dialed. "Belinda?"

"Yes, Mother. Who else would answer my phone at nine o'clock at night?"

Vella ignored the comment and launched in with, "Sugar, I just had an idea. I want to be called Big Mama instead of Gramma or Granny, or any of those other names. You'll be Mama, and I'll be Big Mama."

"Ah-huh," said Belinda after a few seconds of silence. "Big Mama is for great-grandmothers."

"Well, honey, I'm not goin' to live *that* long. You've gotten too late a start."

★ ★ ★

Two days passed, and she still did not tell Belinda about her marriage plans. It was the most surprising thing, and silly, too, but she found herself a little afraid to tell Belinda. It was the prospect of doing one more thing to disappoint her daughter.

Second chances appeared to carry with them the lessons from the first.

"Are you goin' to tell her this afternoon?" Jaydee asked.

They had just come back from observing the work on the carousel park, which was progressing at an astoundingly good rate.

"I could." Vella's gaze slid to the drugstore window, where sunlight fell on the display of lotions and creams, and the two fine perfumes Vella had brought from France. "It should be a good time—slow, before the kids get out of school." She spoke absently, her thoughts picturing Belinda.

"Do you think she will object?"

Her gaze came round to see his eyes intent upon her. "Not really…it's just that, well, she's pregnant and a little grumpy."

"Belinda has always been a little grumpy."

"Oh, honey, you do not understand the combustion of pregnancy, hormones and emotions." Jaydee had little experience with a pregnant woman. "Yesterday she smacked Larry Joe Darnell with a newspaper."

"What for?"

"Oh, he was wearin' some knit shirt with a collar that Belinda took exception to. Preppy, she called him. Basically, she does not approve of his new close haircut, nor the woman to whom he is engaged."

"She has strong opinions…like her mother." Jaydee grinned.

Vella adored that Jaydee had such lovely white teeth, especially for a man his age. She said, "Well, I'm not askin' her opinion about our marriage. I am simply goin' to tell her and ask her to join us as my matron of honor." She put a hand to his chest. "You don't need to come in. I want to speak to her alone. I'll call you after. And don't you say a word to anyone until I call you."

Jaydee saluted smartly.

The bell rang out as she entered the dim and much cooler store. Blinking, Vella heard familiar voices. It was Marilee with Belinda over at the soda fountain counter. Marilee, it turned out, was reading a letter from Corrine—six pages front and back.

"She is quite a writer," said Marilee proudly, when Vella commented on the length. "And she didn't come home last weekend. She had to write all about goin' to a friend's, who has horses not far out of the city. Corrine's goin' to work at a ranch for handicapped children up there…. Here, I'll start over for you to hear the whole thing. Look, she even drew pictures."

Marilee flashed the papers at Vella. There were clever little drawings all around the edges of the writing.

Adjusting her new reading glasses, Marilee launched into the letter as if she found it another *War and Peace,* which maybe it sort of was. Corrine had a flair for observing characters' foibles. She told of the romantic triangle of three students, and, in detail, the story of one of the professors who admitted to mistaking a large dried dropping of bird poo for preserves and taking a bite. The professor said it was salty.

As often happens in these cases, while Marilee was in the midst of the second reading, Paris Miller arrived, slipped up on a stool and ordered a cherry Coke. "Two cherries, please, like Corrine made 'em." Marilee offered to begin reading Corrine's letter again for the girl's benefit. She had gotten to page two, when Larry Joe Darnell came in for three barbecue sandwiches and drinks to take back to his crew at the Texaco. He made his order politely to Belinda, taking care to stand two steps back from the counter, presumably out of range of her newspaper.

Marilee started Corrine's letter over once more for Larry Joe's benefit. While she read, Larry Joe edged near to look over her shoulder. He kept interrupting by pointing out different illustrations on the edges of the paper. Paris stared down into her cold drink, quietly swirling the straw.

Vella, sitting on her stool, watched all of this, her eye running from face to face, as her thoughts revolved around telling Belinda her news. Telling everyone her news. In fact, it came to her that telling Belinda with people present might be a good idea. She determined to speak at the first opening. Very casually, say something like, *I have news….*

When Marilee finished reading, Larry Joe said, "So Corrine's gonna work up at that ranch for special kids?"

"Yes." Marilee carefully folded the letter, running her fingers over the folds.

The next instant she smacked Larry Joe with the folded letter. Once, twice, three whacks at the back of his neck. "And it's all your fault…you…you mo-ron!" She smacked him again, made a frustrated noise and stalked from the drugstore.

Larry Joe, wide-eyed, looked at Vella and Belinda and Paris. "What'd I do?"

"You are a *mo*-ron," said Paris, and walked from the drugstore.

Belinda then said, "What did you do? You made the stupid choice to get engaged to a selfish piece of fluff who wants to make you over, instead of waitin' for a solid young woman who loves you just like you are. Here's your order. Pay Mama."

Then Belinda stalked away.

Vella felt a little like the only tree left standing in a wood. Deciding not to enter into the fray, she calmly took Larry Joe's money without comment. If he wanted to ask her anything, he didn't do it. He didn't wait for change, either, but snatched up his bags of food and disappeared out the door.

Giving a deep sigh, Vella wiped a wet cloth over the counter. She glanced at the clock, thinking it a good idea to give Belinda ten minutes or so to settle her feathers.

Unfortunately, it was during this settling time that Inez Cooper came in, ordered a cold tea and went back to speak to Belinda. Vella found this behavior curious. She was actually a little jealous. Inez and Belinda had never been great friends. It seemed that a number of people who used to come to Vella for consultation had, during her time in France, changed their allegiance to Belinda.

She started toward the rear, not really to eavesdrop but just to listen a little, and after all, her own desk was there.

Before she reached the doorway, however, Belinda's voice floated forward.

"Inez, I do not have another remedy for you to try on Norman, but I do have one for you to try on yourself. Stop all your houndin'. If it isn't workin', don't keep doin' it. Quit tryin' to fix Norman and do some fixin' on yourself. I suggest you go get your hair done, buy some sexy nightgowns and maybe read up on how to relate to a man. The bookstores are filled with that sort of help."

"Well!" said Inez.

In two strides Vella was back at the soda fountain counter, feeling silly for running.

Inez came flying past. She got halfway across the store,

turned and stalked back to the counter, swept up her cold drink at the same time tossing down two dollars. She then strode away hard enough to hurt her feet.

Vella thought that she was making a great profit on everyone leaving their change, which she put into her own pocket this time.

Jaydee had spilled it all to Winston, of course. "He wormed it out of me."

"Well, I'm old but I'm not blind," said Winston.

The two men and Willie Lee came into the drugstore the following day, during the lunch rush. They took their place at their customary table. Vella brought the men cold tea and barbecue sandwiches, and a chicken salad for Willie Lee and Munro, who hid among the human feet under the table. She returned a minute later with a tall latte for herself.

"Did you tell Belinda?" asked Jaydee.

Vella answered a little testily. "Not yet…there hasn't been a moment."

Winston reached out and took her hand, then pressed it to his lips. Their eyes met, and then skittered away from each other and then back again, as they shared faint smiles. In that instant the past and what might have been fell around them like a spray of sweet perfume. Vella was struck sharply by her position, smack in the middle between the two men.

"There's Belinda," said Jaydee.

"I know, sugar. Belinda has been here all afternoon. It's just that there hasn't been time…. We've been busy, and—"

"Belinda?" Winston called out, interrupting.

"Yes, Winston?"

Vella, who had experienced a prick of concern at Winston's

action, was distracted from this as she watched Belinda saunter toward them. Her daughter really looked unusually pretty in her pregnancy.

"How are you feelin', darlin'?"

"Well, I'm fat and my back hurts, and I threw up my lunch, and right now I have a bit of a headache. How are you and everyone else?" Laying a hand on Winston's shoulder, Belinda took them all in with her gaze.

"Doin' pretty well, thanks," said Jaydee.

And Winston said, easy as could be, "Jaydee and your mother are gonna get married."

Vella was caught with her cup of latte halfway to her mouth. She had suspected Winston was going to do this, and she had been undecided as to wanting him to do the job and not wanting him to. Now she tipped over to wishing he had not. She looked at Belinda to gauge her daughter's response and try to marshal words to deal with it.

But Belinda said quite blandly, "A blind person could have seen it comin'."

"That's exactly what I said," Winston said.

Belinda's eyes met Vella's. "Congratulations, Mama. When are you doin' it?"

"Thank you, sugar. We aren't certain yet. Only a few weeks, though."

"Uh-huh. Well, I guess you can tell me more later, but *excusez-moi* for right now, y'all. I'm off to the bank, then home." Belinda patted Winston's shoulder as she left.

Vella, with both her thoughts and her gaze following her daughter, noted that Belinda was starting to waddle. She was going to be quite large as a matron of honor.

The next instant, right before Vella's eyes, Belinda went down, just like a piece of cloth fluttering to the floor.

For the first time in her life, Vella was so struck that she could not move.

CHAPTER 18

What We Do Not Know

"SO, WHAT'S THIS ABOUT YOU FAINTIN' YESTERDAY?"

Dr. Zwolle's blue eyes shifted from Belinda to Lyle, who sat beside her.

Lyle had insisted on attending each consultation since he had learned about the baby. He brought his small notebook, where he jotted all manner of notes, as he did when doing an investigation. Then he would come home and look up things on the Internet. As he was not very experienced with using the computer and Internet, Belinda often had to help him. This caused her to read a number of things she found unhelpful to her frame of mind, as well as her blood pressure. She developed a method of looking at the computer screen with a squint.

"It was just a little spell," Belinda clarified, finding herself squinting now. "I sort of went down, but I came back immediately."

"I see. And what preceded this little spell?"

"Well, I hadn't felt good all day, threw up my lunch, and I was hungry…and a little dizzy. But immediately after, I was back to myself. The baby was movin' and kickin' a-plenty, and Oran—that's our pharmacist, and he was a paramedic in the army—he said I was okay, and all my vitals were okay."

Really, it had been Willie Lee's pronouncement of her overall health and that of the baby that had been enough to reassure Belinda and cause Winston to support her decision to simply go home and rest. All three—her mother, Winston and Jaydee—had insisted on driving her home, where her mother had prepared a can of chicken noodle soup and insisted on helping her get to bed. It had been a strange experience. She could not recall her mother ever tending her with chicken soup or putting her to bed.

Lyle cleared his throat and read from his notebook. "Her blood pressure was at one eighty-nine over one ten."

"Ah-huh." The doctor nodded, her gaze returning to Belinda's chart. "It's milder today, one thirty-five over ninety," she said for Lyle's benefit, watching him write. Then the doctor smiled in a reassuring manner. "This is not terribly unusual or anything to panic about. I think we do need to get a check on your sugar levels, though."

"She's havin' nightmares," Lyle said.

"Oh?" The doctor's eyes shifted to Belinda.

"Sometimes I do that. I've done that since I was a kid…."

"I don't remember you doin' that."

"You were not with me when I was a kid, Lyle. But you might remember that I did go through a time of nightmares right after we bought the house." Back to the doctor: "The baby's gettin' heavier, and it's just a little more difficult to sleep.

My body is under a lot of stress. And I'm kind of anxious about bein' a first-time mother."

"And her mother told her yesterday that she's gettin' married."

"It was not a surprise, Lyle."

The doctor's eyes moved back and forth between them. "I understand. It's a busy, stressful time." Then to Belinda, "Are you worried about losin' the baby?"

Belinda swallowed. "I guess I am. I mean, everyone keeps askin' me how I am doin', and then there's all those cautions for a woman over thirty-five, and I keep throwin' up, and I can't have hardly anything sweet and have to walk, and I hate to walk…and people seem to think I'm gonna be upset about things that I am not. It is amazin' the top of my head isn't comin' off."

She closed her mouth, suddenly realizing how she was running on.

The doctor nodded. "You sound pretty normal, given your situation."

Belinda held her breath, wondering if the situation the doctor was thinking of was having had an abortion. *Oh, God, don't let her say anything….*

The doctor said, "We have to get you to relax."

Dr. Zwolle outlined a plan for daily walking in the morning and rest each afternoon. "Feet elevated, at least an hour and a half…alone and quiet," she instructed in a firm tone.

The doctor even gave Belinda the name of a meditation CD she wanted her to get from the bookstore.

"I'll get it," said Lyle, writing like crazy in his notebook.

A breeze gently moved the sheers at the bedroom window. There came the scent of fall, even though the air was yet warm.

Belinda stretched on her back in bed, her head resting on two down feather pillows covered in crisp cotton cases and her feet propped on two thick foam throw pillows. She felt like a watermelon in a patch, her arms and legs vines.

Dropping her head back onto the feather pillows, she donned a silk lavender-scented eye mask and clicked on the stereo using the remote. Ethereal flute music floated forth, followed by a voice that told her to inhale deeply. "One…two…that's it…three, four. Now let it out to the count of six. One…feel it…"

Belinda found that she was paying more attention to what to do than doing it. She felt lacking in not being able to keep up.

Pointing the remote again, she clicked the button. The stereo whirred, another CD started. Instrumental music, pleasant guitar sound.

Breathing deeply, she told her body to relax. *Yes, you, too, legs. There.*

The baby kicked. The little one was not relaxing. "Mama loves you," she whispered, and stroked her belly. Tears sprang to her eyes beneath the mask. She lay there feeling the life within. Marveling at it.

This went on for some time, and then there was a sound. Someone in the room?

Belinda lifted her mask to peek.

"Mama! How long have you been standin' there?"

"A couple of minutes. I thought you were asleep, and then I saw you rubbin' your belly. What did the doctor say?" her mother asked as she crossed the room and threw herself in the overstuffed chair.

So much for resting alone, Belinda thought.

"I am fine. I just have to walk every mornin' and rest every afternoon. You can ask Lyle for details."

"Was that Lyle I heard in the garage?"

"I hope so." Belinda punched the pillows behind her head. The doctor had said an hour and a half with feet up, minimum. Lyle had shown her in his notes. She just never was good at being told what to do, and forced rest seemed to defeat the purpose.

"I heard what sounded like a power saw. I didn't know he could use a saw."

Belinda looked at her mother. "I guess he can." She really hadn't known, either. Now she felt a little worried.

"What's he doing?"

"He's makin' somethin'. It is a surprise. Somethin' with wood. I'm goin' to put this mask on again—I'm supposed to relax." The CD still played.

"Go ahead. I do not want to interrupt you. I just came for a minute to see how you were."

Why was it that people never thought of "just a minute" as anything other than an interruption?

"Sugar…I have been thinkin' that Jaydee and I might wait until after the baby comes to get married. I know this is a stressful time for you. I don't want to make it more so."

There was that tone. It said: *Tell me what to do. Make me feel better.*

Belinda lifted one side of the mask and peered out.

"I do not want to be the cause of any upset at this time," said her mother.

Belinda pulled the mask off. "Mother, I have a body with a trillion cells taking part in this. It is not all about *you*."

They gazed long at each other.

"You and Jaydee go ahead and get married." She felt guilty for her impatient attitude. She wished she could quit feeling guilty.

"Well, we could do it quickly, so as not to be crowdin' your due date, and so we can be married by the time my grand-daughter arrives."

"Good idea."

"I hope you will be my matron of honor." With that statement, her mother brought forth three pieces of fabric and waved them in the air. "What do you think of these colors? This one is mine, and this is for you, and this one for Marilee. She's gonna be bridesmaid. Margaret Wyatt already has this fabric from Jean Lundy's canceled wedding. Winston is goin' to give me away, and…"

While her mother elaborated on plans for a wedding to take place in the astonishingly short time of two weeks, the relaxation music played in the background.

Belinda noticed that her right foot kept twitching and the baby was rollicking in her belly.

Maybe this was as relaxed as either of them was meant to get.

Nurse Betty's clipped tone came over the telephone line. "I have the results of your blood tests yesterday."

"Oh, yes." A sliver of cold passed up her spine.

"Your iron is good, but your sugar level indicates the beginning of gestational diabetes…."

Well, for heaven's sake. Belinda sank down into the kitchen chair.

When she hung up after Nurse Betty's brief instructions, she felt both relieved and dismayed. Relieved because she had thought the woman might be going to say something much worse, and dismayed as she got up and looked in the refrigerator.

Then she sat back down and rubbed her forehead. Never

mind being a mother, she wasn't certain she had what it took to get through the pregnancy.

"God, if You will, please help me." A whisper.

Only believe.

Oh, she wanted to!

She peered out the window over the kitchen sink into the darkness. Light flowing from the garage window made a patch on the ground. She could faintly hear the music from the old radio that Lyle listened to.

He would not tell her what he was working on. For the baby, surely. Likely a cradle. He had told her to choose whatever crib and other things that she wanted, but not to get a cradle. Why didn't he just tell her what he was making?

Belinda was, as her mother had been, a little mystified about Lyle using a power saw. She had not even known he owned one, nor that he had the notion or ability to make something. He did have a workbench, but in all the years they had been together the only thing she had ever seen him use it for was to assemble weight-lifting equipment.

It was amazing what two people who lived together, shared a bed together and made a baby together did not know about each other. It was thought provoking that really knowing each other had absolutely nothing to do with those three things.

What did it have to do with? she wondered.

Emma called while Belinda was in the tub, soaking in bubbles. "I'm givin' you a baby shower—me and Gracie and Marilee. They wanted it to be a surprise, but I said we could never keep it from you, and besides, I know you hate surprises."

"Thank you for tellin' me. And for givin' me a shower," she added, feeling shy. She was in totally unfamiliar territory. She stared at the shiny bath tile. In all her life, no one had ever given her a party. This seemed inconceivable, and not something she could tell anyone.

Emma was saying, "Well, honey, of course I'm givin' you a baby shower! And I've designed these really cool invitations. I know you will want to market them. They—and the entire party theme—are goin' to be your color pink!"

Belinda thought how Emma knew things about her. Things like how she did not like surprises, and did like the challenge of marketing and a particular shade of pink. Things that likely Lyle, whom she had pledged to love and cherish until death did them part, and with whom she had sex and had gotten pregnant, did not know.

Emma, the quintessential Southern lady, elaborated on her shower party plans. It would be held at Emma's lovely house, with only those people Belinda really would want to attend, and lots of pink decorations, and chicken salad and a salmon dip—both from Paula Deen's magazine—a light punch, sugar cookies with pink sprinkles and an apricot aspic.

Emma said, "Apricot was as close as I could get to pink. It will be so pretty."

When Emma was about to hang up, Belinda could not resist asking, "How do you know so much about me?"

"Like what?"

"That I wouldn't want a surprise party, and just who I would not want to come…and my favorite color pink."

"Well…I don't know. I guess because you've told me."

Belinda thought about that answer as she got out of the now-cold tub and wrapped herself in her robe.

Lyle's words came back to her: *You don't let me in.*

Understanding came in that sudden fashion: she kept him out by not telling him the things that let him see into her heart.

And the same with her mother, she thought, jerking tight the belt of her robe.

Lyle had breakfast waiting for her. Two boiled eggs (she ate just the yolks, high in cholesterol but easy on her stomach), a banana and a cup of vanilla yogurt. Breakfast was no longer an inviting proposition. But she smiled as she sat down, because he was watching her with a worried air.

"Are you gonna start pickin' things out for the nursery?" Lyle asked hesitantly.

Belinda dug out the yolks. "Yes…I've been lookin'."

"Well, I thought I'd paint the wall this weekend, since it is my off weekend. You'll need to pick up the paint."

She watched him spread strawberry jam thick on an English muffin.

"Are you really gonna paint?" She decided she could risk just a tiny bit of strawberry jam on a rice cake and got up to get it from the cabinet.

"Yeah." Pointedly said. "The walls really need it."

"Oh." Then, "Have you ever painted? We could hire someone. That's what I thought we would do."

"I've painted." He was emphatic. "I painted the rooms of my mom's house, and my sister's, back before I moved up here. It isn't somethin' you forget. And Giff's gonna help me."

"Okay. I'll get it at MacCoy's today."

On her way to the bedroom to dress, she veered on down the hall and opened the door to the room Lyle had emptied of his weight equipment.

Sunlight poured through the window. Running her gaze over the room, Belinda also ran her hand over her belly.

She and her daughter had made it well past six months now. The most serious chance of miscarriage was behind them.

"I can do this, sugar, if you can," Belinda whispered.

Moving quickly, she went to her bedroom, where she retrieved two magazines from her night chest drawer. She drew them out in a manner similar to someone hiding illicit pornography. Carrying the magazines to the empty room, she looked at the colorful pages of nursery decorating ideas and then around the room. Her mind bloomed with images.

Pink. A bright shade. Her pink, Emma called it. Accented with white and lime green. Old-fashioned dotted Swiss at the window. Crib and dresser of natural oak. She could stencil butterflies all over this one wall. Easy, the article said. Belinda had never done such a thing.

And—no question about it—a door cut in the wall to connect it with the master. Maybe a French glass door. Or none at all. She was such a heavy sleeper—what if she did not hear her baby cry? The prospect caused her to press the magazine to her heart.

"Oh, here you are." Lyle stood in the doorway. "I'm headin' out."

"I want a door there." She pointed. "I want to be able to hear the baby and get in here quick."

"Okay." He grinned.

Then she burst into tears and hid her face in her hands.

"Honey, what is it?" He pulled her against him.

She held the magazine page up to him, saying, "I—I want to stencil these…but-terflies…but I have-n't ever done anything like that. Will…will you help me?"

"Sure I will, honey!"

He was rewarded by her smile.

★ ★ ★

Her feet had expanded. She got new walking shoes to help encourage her. Bright pink.

"You aren't likely to get run over wearin' those," her mother had commented when she saw them.

Belinda sat at her desk chair and tied on the shoes. Then she slipped her cell phone into the pocket of her dress. She had grown out of her walking suit. She felt like a ripe giant peach, with bright pink feet. There truly was no way anyone was likely to run her over.

Yet someone did in the next moment, just as she headed for the front of the store. She was looking down at her pink shoes, and apparently Andy Smith was not looking where he was going, either. He came barreling through the doorway and smacked into her so hard that he about knocked her over. She would have fallen had he not grabbed hold of her.

"I'm sorry. Are you okay?"

"Yeah…I'm fine. Really." She was mostly stunned to see him, and so close. And he was sort of dancing her around as he moved into the back room.

"Uh, I was just…on my way to the restroom."

"Uh-huh. It's right through there."

"Thanks."

She wondered at him being in the drugstore, and that maybe he had a bladder control problem. Then, rubbing her belly as if to reassure her little girl, she thought that, no matter her size, she needed to keep a lookout.

Her mother was taking care of the soda fountain, which was all but empty except for Winston at a table reading the paper and a man at the counter whom Belinda did not recognize. Judging from his appearance (he had carefully styled longish hair and wore a sport coat), he was a stranger passing through. Her mother was serving him a large latte and engaging him in conversation. He was middle-aged, which put him twenty years younger than her mother but still within flirting range, apparently.

"Mama, I'm off for my walk. I'll be back in about half an hour." Continuing toward the front door, she paused in an uncharacteristic manner to kiss the top of Winston's head as she passed.

He looked up with some surprise.

She had surprised herself, too, but she only smiled. It was rather nice being pregnant. One could do things and not be thought of as strange. It was all put down to hormones. She wondered if she could get away with shooting a few people.

Sticking on sunglasses, she turned toward Church Street and walked with determination.

Just then she saw the surprising sight of Andy Smith at the corner. He stepped off the sidewalk and headed with his long-legged lope across the street. He must have gone out the rear door of the drugstore and come around. The man was a puzzle.

The weather was staying sweetly pleasant longer into the day. This made walking easier for her. The short distance east on Main, turn up Church at the corner by the sheriff's office, puff a little as the sidewalk headed uphill, but then she turned back west on Porter. Such a lovely street, with tall trees and deep yards. Then down First to Main again, and one full loop around Main, if she could get herself to do it.

"Here." Julia Jenkins-Tinsley jumped out the door of the post office, startling her, as she thrust forward a small contraption. "It's an iPod."

"I know. I've seen them." And had deliberately avoided them. She drew the line at a cell phone.

Julia said, "I have this one all fixed with music that's good to walk to. All you have to do is press this and you're set. I know you don't especially like walkin'. Maybe this will help."

"Uh, thank you." Belinda was touched by Julia's generosity and tender expression.

"Use it as long as you want. I got a new one. I'd walk with you and keep you company, if you didn't walk midmornin'."

Belinda stuck the earpieces in her ears and waved as she headed away. She did not want to give Julia any chance to figure out a way to walk with her.

At that moment Reba McEntire's voice rang in her ear. "Walk on…"

Julia *was* a clever sort of person.

Day after day, she continued her routine, although her strides became slower and slower as her belly grew and she had to manage to balance it. The orange tabby cat that lived somewhere in the alley or a house right behind took to joining her. He would walk along beside her like a dog, his tail a flag flying. She named him Bubba.

Belinda would admire Sybil Lund's chrysanthemums and exchange greetings with Leon Purvis, who had in his retirement taken up making his yard look like the cover of *Home and Garden*. In a manner that she had never before experienced, she would gaze with fascination at the five little children playing in the fenced yard of the house where Connie Barco ran a day care.

During the middle of the day, she worked at the drugstore, and in the early afternoon it was back home for her rest, where she discovered that Agatha Christie audiobooks worked better than meditation CDs. Very often she fell asleep before the end, because she had a mind to figure out the plot. When she would arise, she would take her blood pressure, and it would be the lowest of all day.

She began to actually like to walk, and to rest. Her careful diet, however, was another matter. She got very tired of carrot and celery sticks. Sugar-free cookies were a help, as was a good cup of tea sweetened with agave, which she allowed herself each day. Yet any of that fell far short when fears or overpowering aggravation assailed her.

It was bound to happen, of course. She went into the Quick Stop at the end of her walk, telling herself she was simply going to get a bottle of cold water, which she definitely needed. Upon passing the display of Little Debbie snack cakes, however, her hand reached out of its own accord and grabbed a package of chocolate cupcakes. Right in front of Paris Miller at the checkout counter, she tore open the package and took an enormous bite of the sweet cupcake.

Oh, my goodness. She closed her eyes as her tongue delighted in the ecstasy of rich flavor and melting texture.

Then she opened her eyes to see Paris snatch the second cupcake and begin wolfing it down. Gazing at each other, they continued to eat.

Belinda, finished and, breathing deeply, said, "Well, I feel better. Thank you for helpin' me out."

"You're welcome," said Paris, still chewing.

Belinda was lying on the couch reading, when, much to her surprise, Fayrene appeared in the dining room entry.

"You don't have to get up," said Fayrene. "I didn't mean to interrupt."

"It's okay." Belinda had succeeded in getting herself into a sitting position.

"I just wanted you to know that I brought your supper. I put it in the refrigerator."

"Uh…thank you."

"Well, Lyle came by and said you're havin' a little trouble with your appetite. I know you like Woody's chicken salad." Fayrene came slipping into the room and down onto the edge of a chair, while casting curious glances around. Her gaze returned to Belinda. "Lyle, he's crazy about you, you know."

Belinda couldn't find anything to say to that.

"We left off the pie—in your supper—but Woody sent a small piece of his corn bread…and a jar of his split-pea-and-ham soup that was on the lunch menu today. He says it'll keep for a couple of days. None of us could remember if you like that."

"Yes, I do. Thank you. That's really nice of you."

"Oh, I was on my way to the laundry, anyway. So, how are you doin'?" Fayrene's eyes scanned Belinda.

Belinda looked down at herself. Could people not see she was growing enormous, tired and bloated?

"Fine," she said. It was easiest, and she did not want to whine. "Catchin' up on my readin'." She lifted the paperback book in her hand—*The Complete Guide to Parenting*—and gestured at the four other books lying around her legs, three more books on parenting and one Agatha Christie novel.

Fayrene looked at the books, nodding. "That's good." She took up one of the parenting books and glanced over it. "I always wanted a baby. Guess that sounds silly, but I did."

"It doesn't sound silly," said Belinda. Improbable, but not silly.

"Well, things never worked out, and I guess that's for the best. I'm happy for you. I really am. You'll be a great mother."

"Why do you say that?" asked Belinda, startled. The entire visit was a surprise.

"You just will. You mother everyone."

Fayrene left moments later. Belinda listened to the back door close. Then she managed to get herself up off the couch. She went to the kitchen, where she brought the foam container of chicken salad from the refrigerator. The food was all arranged in a pretty fashion.

As she sat at the table and ate, she thought of what Fayrene had said. Maybe it was true that she did mother people.

CHAPTER 19

Vella Blaine Gets Married

CORRINE PENDLEY CAME HOME THE WEEKEND of Aunt Vella's wedding. She came with a new red dress and high-heeled shoes to match for the occasion, a new haircut and six weeks of living away on her own under her belt.

As she drove Aunt Marilee's car around town, drinking in the familiar sights with a thirsty soul, Corrine suddenly thought she might cry. *Home.* The word swelled her heart and made a lump in her throat.

Yet she saw things that she had not seen before. How small the town seemed. How shabby and old-fashioned much of it looked. She was different, she thought. More mature. She sat up straighter. In the few weeks she had been away, the girl she had been had rather disappeared. She felt very much a young woman now.

She cruised to the school. After the metropolitan campus of the School of Science and Mathematics, the old school looked minuscule, and it was funny to see the little ones playing in the field. A yearning touched her to be with her friends inside, yet something told her that she no longer fit. It was quite a confused feeling. She never had really fit very well with others of her own age. She had always felt so much older.

Then, "Hi, Mr. Grace!" She waved out the window at the florist, who was arranging a display of yellow, orange and crimson chrysanthemums in front of his shop.

Maybe that girl was still there inside, after all, she thought, laughing.

At the stoplight at First and Main, she looked in the mirror to make sure of her hair and her lipstick, and the bit of mascara she wore these days. Then she turned down First and drove to the Texaco, pulling smoothly to a stop in front of the pumps.

The next instant, here came Jojo out the station door. The girl flung herself into the passenger seat with a wide grin. "So look who's home! Like the haircut."

"What are you doin' out of school? Oh, Jojo!" Corrine bent over to hug her younger friend.

"How ya' doin', Corrine?"

Larry Joe was at her window.

"Oh, fine…glad to be home."

He smiled at her, like he always did, and she smiled back.

"Aunt Marilee said to fill it up and charge her."

Larry Joe went about putting fuel into the car, and Jojo explained that she was out of school that morning because of an early-morning dentist appointment and had to return after lunch. Corrine barely heard a word. She was busy looking in the side-view mirror, watching Larry Joe.

Jojo leaned over and whispered something that Corrine did not fully hear.

"What?" Corrine leaned toward Jojo.

"He broke up with Miss Huggins," whispered Jojo.

Corrine's eyes widened, and Jojo nodded.

Then Larry Joe appeared, washing the windshield. He looked in at Corrine through the glass, and she looked back at him, until she did the silliest thing. She jerked her gaze from Larry Joe, turned to Jojo and said, of all things, "Want to go get a Bama Pie at the Quick Stop?" in a childishly high-pitched tone. She could have died.

When Larry Joe handed her the receipt, she lowered her tone to a woman's voice as she thanked him. She headed the car out onto the street with her foot heavy on the accelerator, like a woman who knew what she was doing.

All the way to the Quick Stop, she quizzed Jojo about the facts of the breakup, but all Jojo repeated was, "I don't know."

Finally Jojo said, "I really don't know anything but that they broke up. I don't know when, I don't know why. I don't even know if they won't make up…but Mama doesn't think so. That's what she said when she told me and Mason this mornin' at breakfast.

Corrine bit her lip and focused on her driving. Having an accident because she was distracted over Larry Joe Darnell would be highly embarrassing, and not at all mature.

It turned out that Paris Miller was working the cash register at the Quick Stop. She hugged Corrine in her cool manner, explaining, "Half the class is off at a pep rally, and I'm failin' algebra, anyway. I like your hair."

"Thanks." Corrine put a hand to her hair. She had always been somewhat awed by Paris, but just then she realized that view had faded. She noted changes in her friend. Paris had always been both lean and gloomy, but now she seemed gaunt and totally without spark. And as Paris turned away to return behind the checkout counter, Corrine saw a large bruise on her friend's neck.

Corrine and Jojo got their Bama Pies and cold fountain drinks, and stood there eating and chatting with Paris. Corrine surreptitiously searched her friend's face. She would need to talk to her privately. In her newfound maturity—even if she was munching on a Bama Pie the same as when she had been ten—she felt she must do something to help Paris.

Just then Belinda Blaine came blowing in the glass door. "Hey, y'all." She wore both a sun visor and sunglasses.

Corrine's gaze dropped to Miss Belinda's belly, which the woman seemed to stick out ahead of her in an effort at balance as she made a beeline for the coolers.

Paris came hurrying out from behind the counter, ran over and planted herself in front of a shelf, with legs wide and arms splayed.

Miss Belinda, now returning from the cooler with a moist bottle of water, said, "Thank you, sugar."

"You bet, Miss Belinda."

"Bye, y'all." The woman, arms pumping, pushed her belly out the door.

Corrine said to Paris, who was returning behind the counter, "What were you doin'?"

"Protectin' Miss Belinda from the Little Debbies."

The wedding day dawned in a great deluge of fall rain that came straight down in sheets, poured on rooftops, flowed down drain spouts and filled drainage ditches and creeks.

Paris Miller was awakened by water dripping on her face. Over at the Valentine home, Willie Lee saw water pooling around the house and went hurrying out beneath the back porch to get the kittens, who were now full grown but new in the ways of such a flood. At his pleading, his mother said he could put them up on the porch. Julia Jenkins-Tinsley battled water running under the rear door of the post office by throwing down wads of paper towels. The only one to really be happy was the fire chief; the threat of a summer-drought grass fire was gone.

"Dear Lord, please let it stop rainin' and clear for Vella Blaine's weddin'," prayed Inez Cooper. Having recognized an uncharitable attitude toward Vella, she prayed for some ten minutes. Ever since her blowup with Belinda, she had been seeing things about herself. She wanted to be a nicer person. She also had a surprise planned for her Norman and everyone else, at the wedding reception, and wanted all to go well.

Vella Blaine, used to running her own life, did not really think of praying. She looked out her living room window at the rain and thought, Into every life a little rain must fall. When the rain had not let up by ten o'clock, she called all the women of her wedding party and told them to bring their dresses to the church. "We'll all get dressed at the church and keep dry."

She called Jaydee to have him order an awning for the church's front steps.

"Already on it, sweetheart," he said proudly.

Vella could see that Jaydee was not going to be a man who needed much direction. She had finally chosen well.

Although not officially taking part in the ceremony, Corrine went along with her aunt Marilee to be of help where she could, just like always. She had shown her aunt the new dress she had bought for the occasion, but she was relieved that her aunt would not see her *in* it until they were at the church and surrounded by a lot of other people. She had been very careful when she bought the dress. It was perfectly proper; however, Aunt Marilee had higher standards than most.

At the church, Corrine ran through the rain to help Aunt Vella and Miss Belinda bring in their things from their cars. Afterward she had to towel dry her dripping hair. Then she took the bows Aunt Marilee had made and fastened them to the ends of the pews along the center aisle. She arranged the flowers according to Miss Belinda's direction, and lit each of the twelve candles on the single candelabra to make certain they would burn at the correct time.

Aunt Vella, Miss Belinda and Aunt Marilee viewed it all and pronounced it perfect. "Understated elegance," said Aunt Marilee. Understated elegance was equal to righteousness in her book.

In the large dressing room in the rear of the church, Corrine, fetching and helping, watched them, these women of her family. Dampened and askew from hurry and rain, breathless and flush with excitement, they worked hair dryers and curling irons, and even had an ironing board and iron. They called back and forth to each other, and laughed and made risqué comments of a private nature they never would have spoken to others outside themselves.

Miss Belinda and her mother were amazingly cordial to each other, until Aunt Vella lit up one of her cigarillos. Miss Belinda threw a hissy about tobacco smoke in her and the baby's vicinity. Usually Aunt Vella never took correction well, but this time, she said, "Ohmygosh, what was I thinkin'?" and raced to open the window and blow out the smoke she held in her mouth. She started to throw the cigarillo out the window, but then she decided that since she had it, she might as well take comfort in a few puffs, so, dressed in a bra, panties and slip, she leaned halfway out the window and smoked. Aunt

Marilee, deep into carefully making up her face, remembered the camera that she had stuffed into her purse and had Corrine take it out and start snapping shots.

Then the three women were dressed and admiring one another. It was agreed that Aunt Vella was handsome and Aunt Marilee beautiful. Corrine said Miss Belinda was lovely, but Belinda looked at herself and said, "*Enormously striking* may be the better description."

Aunt Vella produced a picnic basket—"a light repast to see us through," she said in her flamboyant manner—and dispatched Aunt Marilee to the church kitchen to bring back a pot of hot tea to go with cheese and crackers and strawberries and chocolate sauce.

Corrine went behind the dressing screen and slipped into her dress and shoes. "Miss Belinda, will you zip me up?"

At the moment that Miss Belinda zipped, Aunt Marilee came through the door with a tray bearing the pot of tea and cups.

Miss Belinda said, "My goodness, you're a knockout, sugar."

Corrine glanced to see her image in the mirror and then at Aunt Marilee, who stood as if frozen, staring at her. Corrine turned in a slow circle, displaying herself.

At last Aunt Marilee smiled. "You are beautiful," she said, blinking rapidly. And then, "And what else would we expect? The apple doesn't fall far from the tree!"

When Winston checked himself in the men's room mirror, he saw Coweta's image right behind his shoulder.

"We are finally gonna see Vella settled happily," she said with a bright smile.

"Yep, we are."

"Well, I thought you might take up with her, but you passed on that."

"Wasn't a good idea," Winston said, with some regret. "I'm too old."

"Yes, you are," Coweta agreed more readily than he would have wished. "Straighten your tie, Winston."

"What's wrong with my tie?" Even so, he did as she said. He was proud to still have the knack of tying a bow tie, even if his hands shook quite a bit.

"You look quite debonair," Coweta said.

"I do, don't I?" Winston smiled as he surveyed himself. "What do you think of this suit?"

Just then the men's room door opened. It was his grandson, Larry Joe, along with Willie Lee and Munro.

He looked around for Coweta, but she was gone.

"Mis-ter May-hall and Pa-pa Tate said to find you," said Willie Lee, taking his hand.

"Well, I'm not lost."

"They need help with Jaydee's bow tie." Larry Joe came close on the other side, taking his arm.

Winston shook them off. "Not yet, boys. I can still walk on my own."

He straightened himself for proof, leaning only lightly on his cane as the three of them stepped out into the hallway.

Just then the door several yards farther along—the door to the bride's dressing room—opened, and a beautiful young woman appeared. He liked a woman in deep red. *Good mercy almighty!* It was Corrine. It was hard to reconcile this young woman with the girl who had been plain faced and in her bathrobe that morning in his kitchen.

She came toward them, and Larry Joe stopped in his tracks.

His eyes went wide. Winston watched his grandson and this young woman whom he loved as a granddaughter. So taken up with each other, the two young people no longer saw anyone else.

"You look awfully pretty," Larry Joe said in a sort of choking voice.

"Thank you…you look nice, too." She momentarily shifted her eyes to Winston and Willie Lee, saying, "All of you look handsome," but then her gaze returned to Larry Joe.

The two young people stood staring at each other in a foolish manner. Light bloomed from the glass front doors, silhouetting the couple. Winston's eyes squinted and watered.

Winston turned and started along the corridor. Willie Lee joined him, and a moment later Larry Joe caught up with them. He took Winston's elbow, and this time Winston did not shake him off.

At the door of the pastor's study, Winston looked at his grandson. "Larry Joe."

"Yes, sir?"

"You wait for Corrine. She's the one for you. You don't get distracted again." It was time to say things straight.

"Yes, sir," Larry Joe said solemnly.

Winston entered the pastor's office, where he found best man Tate Holloway wrestling with Jaydee's bow tie, with Pastor Smith giving instruction. Winston took over to do the job.

"Just hold still," said Winston, wrestling the silk tie with his gnarled and shaking fingers.

Jaydee kept swallowing, and his Adam's apple bobbed. Winston had not before noticed that Jaydee had such a sizable Adam's apple.

"The ring. I can't remember what I did with the ring," said Jaydee.

Tate produced it.

Winston finished with the tie, and Jaydee checked himself in the mirror on the wall behind the door. The man, usually quite self-satisfied, was a picture of doubt.

"This deal is for good with Vella," he said, his Adam's apple bobbing again. "We did a prenuptial, but it pretty much slammed the door on divorce. Vella might kill me, but she isn't likely to give me a divorce." His baleful gaze passed over the other men.

"Well, I do think you might have thought of that before now," said Winston. Then he put his arm around the younger man's shoulders. "Listen, buddy, let me share my secret to dealin' with Vella Blaine. Just say with regularity, 'I think you're probably right,' to anything she says, no matter what you really think."

Jaydee's thoughts passed across his face in a studied frown. "Well, I don't know…"

"Now don't let your pride get in the way. What you are choosin' is to be happy instead of right. It's takin' the higher ground." He patted Jaydee on the back. "I'm countin' on you to take good care of her. I know you are the man for the job."

Jaydee nodded as a promise. He suddenly had developed a lump thick in his throat and thought that he could not talk.

The sun came out just as Vella and Winston walked through the side door into the sanctuary, her arm through his. Light falling through the stained glass high up behind Pastor Smith gave the room a rosy glow and seemed to fall like a benediction on the bride.

In that moment Belinda saw her mother's face and thought that she had never seen her mother so happy. Her mother's expression, and her baby picking that moment to shove a foot into her bladder, took Belinda's breath and brought tears to her eyes.

When Pastor Smith said, "Who gives this woman to this man?" Winston moved Vella's hand from his arm to Jaydee's and said, "I do!" so loudly that a few in the congregation were momentarily confused and wondered if Winston was marrying her.

Vella frowned, annoyed that she had overlooked how such a phrase would sound. She was not property to be given by any man. But then she guessed that Winston really was giving up once and for all what might have been. And she was, too.

Her gaze lingered for a moment on Winston, knowing that she had moved on in her life. Then she became aware of how hard Jaydee was shaking. She hoped he did not die of a heart attack and leave her a widow before she was fully married.

Pastor Smith was speaking, and she had to catch up. When he indicated it was her part, she instantly jumped in, saying rapidly, "In the name of God, I, Vella, take you, Jaydee, to be my husband…."

Belinda shifted her flowers into her right hand and pressed her left hand into the side of her belly, attempting to move the baby. The ceremony seemed to go on forever, with Jaydee saying his part, then Pastor Smith going into this long spiel.

Lyle, who was in the front row right beside Winston and Willie Lee, saw Belinda seeming to list to one side. A little alarmed, he edged to the end of the pew.

Naomi Smith stepped up beside the organ and belted out "There Is Love."

The congregation joined in. All four verses, and holding long on "…there…is…love." People began crying and sniffing and passing around tissues.

Belinda crossed her legs and said her own prayer not to wet her pants.

The song ended, and Pastor Smith lifted his hand in a motion of blessing. "God bless and keep you in love..." Some faint sound caused him to glance in Belinda's direction. As a man whose wife had born six children, he said, "Go-and-serve-God-together-amen."

Lila Hicks hit the keys on the organ, Jaydee grabbed Vella and bent her backward in a dramatic kiss that had the congregation on their feet with applause and Belinda, unnoticed by everyone but Lyle, hurried through the side door to the corridor and the ladies' room.

After the bride and groom had their pictures taken, everyone piled into their cars and took off through the wet streets bright with sunshine for the reception, held on the opposite end of town at the just-finished carousel building. Vella and Jaydee, being very much business people and active members of the chamber of commerce, saw their wedding as an opportunity to promote the progress of the carousel park built mainly by the two of them.

Because of the earlier heavy rain and there being as yet no landscaping, people had to cross the muddy ground to the carousel building over two-by-six boards. Women balanced precariously in high heels, and at least two lost both their balance and a shoe stuck in the mud. Vella took off her heels and raced across the board at a speed calculated to prove her vigor for the years of marriage ahead. Emma Berry started to do the same, but then John Cole swept her up in his arms and, to much applause, carried her across, proving he had fully healed from his heart operation. Seeing this, Larry Joe Darnell astounded Corrine by doing the same, proving the direction of his affections. Julia Jenkins-Tinsley looked at G. Juice, who shook his head and waved her gallantly ahead of him. Winston said to her, "Come on, darlin', we'll take hands."

Refreshments were served, the bride and groom made speeches, friends made speeches, and toasts were given for a happy life. Jim Rainwater, wearing a vintage coat and hat, set "Stompin' at the Savoy" playing from his portable DJ equipment, and Vella and Jaydee took to the dance floor.

People clapped around them and then joined in. Inez Cooper surprised her husband, Norman, as well as everyone else, when she went to dancing in movements that sent her fluid rayon skirt swirling high enough to show her pale thighs. Norman stood there stunned. He had not known that his wife could possibly move like that anymore.

It had been noticed over the past couple of weeks that Inez had gotten a modern, sassy haircut and was using hair gel, brighter makeup and wearing new stylish clothing. She had of late surprised a number of her neighbors by going out of her way with pleasant greetings. Julia Jenkins-Tinsley had seen a padded envelope come through the P.O., with a return address of the Positive Thinkers Club and addressed to Inez. Norman had faintly noticed that his wife had been disappearing several afternoons a week for the past three weeks, and he had caught her a couple of times doing yoga with the television. When Inez had come downstairs that afternoon, ready for the wedding, he had been startled to see that she wore a dress that showed a curvy shape that he had not known she had. He had been so struck by this difference in his wife that he had peered up the stairs with the foolish urge to go check and make certain his real wife was not lying up there on the bed like something out of *The Twilight Zone.* Now he watched his wife as she did the close-in and swing-out steps of the boogie-woogie.

The next instant, Norman came to life. When Inez closed in, he took hold of her, brought her hard against him, then spun her out. While his steps were heavy and rusty, his memory quickly returned.

Norman and Inez had been the 1982 Oklahoma Ballroom Swing champion couple. They had loved to dance, and had traveled as far as California and New Jersey for ballroom dancing events. It had been the happiest, most romantic time of their married life. For two weeks now, Inez had secretly taken Lindy Hop lessons in the deep hope of rekindling the romance of that time with her husband.

That evening Inez realized her hope. The couple was the hit of the dance floor. People were flabbergasted to believe this was the same Inez and Norman they had known for years.

Inez felt pretty flabbergasted, too, but Norman, once over his surprise, said, "Honey, you've always been hot."

All during the reception, Inez looked for Belinda to tell her thank-you for the hard truth that Belinda had told her that day, when she had said that Inez needed to work on herself.

But Inez never did find Belinda.

This was because while Inez did the Lindy, Belinda lay in the emergency room attached to a fetal monitor and other contraptions in an effort to stop premature labor.

CHAPTER 20

Bed Rest

"WE ARE GOING TO BRING THIS BABY GIRL healthy into the world. You are going to do just as I say." Dr. Zwolle shook her finger at Belinda.

And what the doctor said was that Belinda was to be in bed for the next week. Not on the couch or in a recliner, but in bed. She could get up to go to the bathroom and to get something from the kitchen. She was allowed to take a bath and encouraged to relax for those minutes, but warm water, not hot.

"Lyle, you could draw the bath and light candles around for her," said the doctor.

Lyle diligently scribbled every word into his little notebook.

Each morning and afternoon Belinda was to do specific mild exercises and take a ten-minute leisurely stroll outside. She was to peruse the fall colors and other calming things, and if she was having a good time, she could extend the stroll to fifteen minutes. In inclement weather, she was to stroll around inside the house and only look at pretty things.

She was to do absolutely no work of any kind, and no reading the paper or watching the news, no horror or thriller movies or books. Nothing that might possibly raise her blood pressure.

"What about visitors?" asked Belinda.

"I think visitors might…" The doctor's eyes came round to meet Belinda's. "On second thought, limit your visitors. Just tell everyone 'doctor's orders' for this first week. Lyle, you take charge of that."

Lyle, scribbling, nodded and set himself to see that Belinda followed every word of the doctor's orders.

He need not have worried. If the doctor had told Belinda to walk five miles a day and never have another Little Debbie snack cake ever in her life in order to bring the baby healthy into the world, Belinda was ready to do it.

"We'll have to postpone our honeymoon," Vella told Jaydee. "I'm the only one Belinda will feel comfortable having in charge of the drugstore."

"You are right as rain," Jaydee instantly agreed. He was a quick study, and also occupied with moving all his things into Vella's house at last. He didn't want to go anywhere else.

Instructed by Lyle as to the doctor's orders, Vella called only after the first day to tell in glowing detail how wonderfully the store was doing and all the money it was making. She thought this would reassure Belinda, but then Jaydee pointed out that Belinda might be hurt to think the store could do without her, so Vella called the next day to ask her daughter's advice on a few matters. Then she worried about upsetting Belinda. Vella got into an unusual twist over it all, with the result that she ended up on blood pressure medication for the first time in her life, a circumstance that she went around telling everyone and then cautioning them not to tell Belinda.

Emma Berry and Naomi Smith came without notice. Emma brought a tossed salad and chicken pot pie and a Lindt dark chocolate bar, with a note that read: *In case of emergency.* Naomi sat at Belinda's feet, put her hands on them and prayed in her soft, deep voice. "Dear Father God, it is written that where two or more are gathered in prayer, You hear. We here at this time hold Belinda and her dear sweet baby up to You, askin' for Your special care. We trust that all is well and all will be well, in Jesus' name, amen."

"Thank you…thank you both," Belinda said, the sound of her words stilted as she willed herself to perfect composure.

If they only knew, a voice whispered deep inside.

The women's visit lasted no more than five minutes. A half an hour later, Lyle discovered a note taped to the back door: *Patient resting. Do not disturb.*

Curious, he went to the front door. A note of the same sort was taped there, too. He left them.

"Maybe we can get someone to come help," said Lyle. "Maybe Marilee could spare Rosalba."

The idea of some stranger in the private sanctuary of her house made Belinda's eyes go wide. "No! I only want you."

"Well, honey, you got me."

Lyle was thrilled. His wife really needed him. He took the week off work to wait on her hand and foot.

Their days were idyllic. Mornings began with Belinda waking earlier than normal and listening to the *Wake Up* radio program, while Lyle made breakfast and brought it in on a tray. They breakfasted together in bed, and then Lyle got busy on the nursery. The hole had been cut in the wall for the door, and Belinda and Lyle could wave back and forth at each other. A dozen times a day, he asked her, "You need anything, honey?"

Sometimes on her walk to the bathroom or outside, she would pause and look into the nursery and say with a smile through tears, "She's goin' to love it…and I love you."

Lyle put together the crib and brought in the dresser with changing top. He brought home the rocker Belinda had chosen and let her direct the placement, again and again.

"Ummm, two inches right…back a little…no, forward. There."

He hung the curtains three times, due to Belinda wanting to get them just right. And then he brought in what he had been building in the garage: an oak cradle with spindles, and carving at the head and foot.

Belinda cried over the cradle in such a way as to worry Lyle. Finally she seemed to calm down a little. He put the cradle where she could touch it from the bed. Time and again, as she listened to her meditation CD or an Agatha Christie mystery, she would reach out and set the cradle to rocking. "Practicing," she told him.

Cards of encouragement poured in. Soon they covered all the surfaces around the room, all seeming to smile at her. Many were from customers who wrote, *You may not remember me, but you helped me….* They told of things that Belinda for the most part did not recall doing. A card bearing a shiny photograph of red roses was signed *James Thomas Bartholemew*, written in a very lovely hand, and below that was the explanation: *I am the fellow you have fed out the back door.*

Belinda cried against Lyle's chest again. He was growing used to it, and he liked it, although he began to think that maybe he should limit her reading the cards.

No one she would rather see! Emma, Winston, Willie Lee and Munro.

"I ran into Lyle," Emma said, rolling up her sleeves. "He said the doctor ordered a second week of bed rest. He looked a little worried about havin' to leave you, and I thought maybe you could use a hand around here. We won't tire you."

Willie Lee said in his normal factual manner, "We came to see you and make you feel bet-ter."

"I brought your mother's sweet tea and some lemon," said Winston, easing himself down into the nearby wingback chair.

Belinda, with unaccustomed eagerness, invited Willie Lee and Munro onto the satin covers of the bed. Emma brought them glasses of the sweet tea, then returned to clean the kitchen, leaving Winston and Willie Lee to fill Belinda in on everything happening around town.

While Willie Lee told about dancing with Gabby at the wedding reception, Winston fell asleep. The quickness of it startled Belinda.

"He is on-ly sleep-ing," Willie Lee assured her. "He will wake up soo-n."

"Ah." Belinda's gaze lingered on Winston's dear old face, and then she looked at Willie Lee and asked in a hushed voice, "How is my little girl?"

He put a gentle hand on her belly, tilted his head as if listening, then said, "She says she is well."

"Oh, good." Belinda brightened with anticipation of getting out of bed and doing many things.

But Willie Lee added, "I think may-be you sh-ould still stay in bed, thou-gh."

"Oh. Really?"

"Yes. Miss Des-i-rée Jane is a lit-tle tir-ed."

"Oh. Is that her name?"

Willie Lee nodded. "Yes. That is the na-me she wants."

"It is a beautiful name," Belinda said, smiling softly as she thought of the two women who were an enormous help to bringing her baby into the world: Dr. Desirée Zwolle and Agatha Christie's famous fictional Miss Jane Marple.

"Yes."

When, at the next visit, Dr. Zwolle told her bed rest for the remaining weeks of her pregnancy, Belinda said, "Yes, I know. I'm ready."

Dishes perpetually filled the sink, washing piled up in the laundry room and the house generally went to disarray, and so did Lyle, trying as he was to work and take care of his wife.

"This isn't nothin'," his fellow deputy and father of two, Giff, told him. "You wait until the baby comes. You might as well get used to bein' sleepy and messy and hungry for the next five years."

When the audio book ended, she heard sirens.

Sounded like fire engine sirens.

It really was aggravating to be so out of things. But she did not need to know everything, she told herself, and decided to attack the crochet baby blanket again. Learning to crochet at this particular time might not have been a good idea.

Sirens again. She tilted her head, listening. Ten minutes later, curiosity overcame her, and she picked up the phone to call Lyle.

He sounded breathless. "It's Joe Miller's house. He burned it down."

"Oh, my…are they okay? Was Paris there…was she…"

"Paris is okay. She got a few burns, but she's okay. Joe got smoke inhalation, but looks like he's gonna be okay, too. Look, I got to go. You just keep relaxed. Paris and Joe are bein' taken care of. You stay off the phone, and I'll call you back soon as I can."

"Okay." Belinda laid the phone beside her in the bed.

Stroking her belly, she considered getting in the car and driving over to see for herself. What exactly did a few burns mean? Hands? Face? *Eyes?*

In the next five minutes, the phone rang twice. First it was her mother, and Belinda answered before she thought. Her mother told her that she was on her way to the Millers', and that two more houses had caught on fire from sparks from the original fire, but, "Don't even think of comin'. The firemen have it under control, and the paramedics, too. And Jaydee and I are right here."

"Mama…get that burn remedy. The one with aloe and grapeseed oil." The idea seemed important in that minute.

The second call was Julia Jenkins-Tinsley, and seeing the name on the caller ID, Belinda had the presence of mind not to answer and tie up the line. Then she changed her mind and answered, but Julia had hung up.

She got out of bed and padded to the bathroom to use the toilet, and since she was up, she thought she might as well get dressed, and perhaps drive over and see for herself. Paris might need her. Surely a drive over could not raise her blood pressure any more than it already was, which really did not seem all that much. She felt fine, with the exception of carrying around a thirty-pound watermelon belly that had begun kicking and tumbling.

The phone rang. Dang it—she had left it on the bed. Holding her heavy belly, she moved as fast as she could.

Emma Berry, read the caller ID.

"Hello? Emma?"

"Yes. Honey, I've got Paris."

Belinda could hear noise in the background. "Lyle called earlier and told me about the fire. How is she? Is she badly burned?"

"No…no, she got some burns and some scrapes, but she's okay." Then, Emma's tone dropping low, "Oh, Belinda…she had just gotten home and saw the smoke. She ran in to save her granddad. He was passed out…you know. She pulled him out just in time."

"Oh, Lord." It was a prayer, eyes closing.

"Belinda…she wants to come to you."

"You said I could call you," Paris said, the poor girl shivering and babbling. "That day you brought me home. I just—"

"You come in here…. Shush…don't talk. Just come on in. I've got a hot bath ready for you."

The girl had a bandage on her forehead, and several more were revealed when she peeled away the blanket in which she was wrapped.

Belinda cautioned the girl to leave the bandages on and not get them wet. She was loathe to leave her alone, but the girl obviously was waiting for her to do so. Belinda understood the deep need for privacy. "You holler if you need anything. I'll just be in my room across the hall."

Emma told all in a low voice. "It looks like Joe may have passed out with a lit cigarette. The house was just a tinderbox, anyway. He was still incoherent when the paramedics worked on him. Newley Dodd said he thinks Joe is malnourished due

to alcoholism, and could be he's lost his mind. I can't believe
Paris went in there and had to drag him out. Lucky he doesn't
weigh too much, skinny as he's gotten. The roofs on the houses
on either side caught fire, but the firemen saved them.

"They're takin' Joe to the VA hospital. The sheriff is pretty
sure they will keep him on the psych ward for a while, at least.
He called DHS, and someone from their office should show
up here soon. He said that was policy. I told him—and Paris—
that she was welcome to come to stay with us, but she wanted
to come here."

"Well, of course she can stay here," Belinda said instantly.
"I told her a number of months ago to call me if she needed
me."

Emma touched her arm. "Just don't you overdo it, honey."

They sat in silence for a long minute, and then Belinda ex-
pressed what they were both thinking. "We should all be
ashamed for not doin' somethin' about the situation before it
came to this."

Paris let Miss Belinda tuck her into bed like a baby. It was
in Miss Belinda's guest bedroom, with a private bathroom and
everything, including the prettiest bed Paris had ever in her life
slept in, with the softest sheets and fluffiest pillow. Still, even
wearing Miss Belinda's pajamas—silky soft and by Ralph
Lauren—and under the blanket and comforter, she could not
quit shaking.

Miss Belinda appeared again. "Here, sugar. These will help
you."

"These" were two hot water bottles that Miss Belinda
tucked around her; then she adjusted the covers again around
her chin.

"Did anyone call about my granddaddy?"

"Not yet, but you rest assured he is bein' taken care of. You know that the sheriff and Lyle will see to it. You got him out, sugar—you saved his life. You were so brave…and that is all you possibly can do. Now, you get some sleep…and you are on complete bed rest for the next three days, you hear me? I'm the doctor, and those are the orders. Believe me, I know about bed rest, and it cures a multitude of conditions, at least for about three days."

The entire time Miss Belinda talked, she straightened the covers and stroked Paris's forehead, until Paris's eyes closed all on their own.

Miss Belinda smelled good, she thought…everything in the room smelled good. Her shaking was stopping.

The lamp went out, and there was a soft sound of Miss Belinda leaving, whispers in the hallway. Miss Emma. She sure hoped that Miss Emma was not mad at her for not going to her house. She would not want to offend Miss Emma, who had been so nice to her for so long.

But Paris had been thinking about coming here since the day Miss Belinda had said to call her. She was so ashamed about how glad she was to be here, away from her grandfather and all that life.

Her last thought was, *I'm glad our house burned down.*

The next day, Miss Belinda repeated what she had said about bed rest. She said she would order lunch delivered from the Main Street Café, and Lyle would be home to cook supper. At lunch they sat together at the kitchen table, and Miss Belinda said that Paris was welcome to live with them until she went to college, or as long as she wanted.

"We'll fix the bedroom up any way you like…and Emma Berry and I think it would be good for you to take at least two weeks off work to rest."

Miss Belinda seemed to have her life pretty well mapped out, and Paris was relieved. She could hardly think, and those things she did seem to think, she did not want anyone to know.

That evening she finally was able to ask again about her grandfather. She was told that he had been taken to the VA hospital, and that it looked as if he was going to be there for some time.

"Honey, he is too weak to leave, and his mind…well, he is suffering dementia now. He wouldn't be able to talk to you on the phone."

Paris's head dropped as she began to cry. She was so embarrassed for anyone to see her cry, so embarrassed over her entire life. All she could think of was how she had failed her grandfather, and now everyone knew how bad it was.

Then Miss Belinda was there beside her, enveloping her.

What made Paris quit crying was the baby kicking her in the face. She pulled back and looked at Miss Belinda's belly in surprise, and then upward at the woman's face. They broke into laughter.

She had a thought then. "I can help you around here."

The house really was messy. Beautiful and awesome, but messy.

"You sure can," said Miss Belinda, smiling.

Paris was surprised to see that Miss Belinda had tears running down her face, too.

CHAPTER 21

1550 on the Radio Dial
Stay Tuned for Further Developments

"IN THE HEADLINES THIS MORNIN'—THE VALENTINE school district just signed a new head principal, who will be takin' over first of December. Fine fella by the name of Josh Tillman, and with that name, I imagine he has some Chickasaw in him. We may even be related. Seems like my wife had some Tillman in her...what? Oh, yes, movin' on—the Valentine area received six inches of rain yesterday, and the Church Street extension is closed, you'll have to use First Street. And—here's the biggie—the carousel for Valentine's Carousel Park has been lost in transit.

"Everett, I'm turnin' the microphone over to you to tell about this situation."

"I, uh..."

Taken by surprise, Everett stared at the microphone. *Winston turning it over to him?* "Yes, we have a situation here." Realizing his high tone, he lowered it, reaching for Walter Cronkite level. "John Cole Berry, who has been handling the logistics of the carousel, was told last night that the carousel is missing in transit. It was supposed to show up to Oklahoma City yesterday, and it didn't. The authorities have been notified, and an all-points bulletin has gone out for it…for the carousel."

Everett shifted uncomfortably. He might have misspoken with that term "all-points bulletin." Hope he didn't sound silly.

Winston was saying, "Well, now, Everett, the Valentine hundredth anniversary party is comin' up here in a couple of weeks. Can you give us the details on just what…"

For the next ten minutes, not only did Winston interview Everett, but people called in with questions, and Winston let Everett do all the talking.

Everett found himself the star of the *Wake Up* show.

Early that morning, after a fitful night of sleep and being awakened by a riotous cat fight in the alley, Fayrene got dressed and came down to her small office at the back of the café, and was surprised to find Andy there and on the telephone. The question of why she should be surprised fluttered across her mind and was quickly taken over by embarrassment because of the way Andy looked surprised and sort of ducked his head, lowering his voice and saying into the phone, "Okay…I have to go, but you can tell—"

"Oh…you go ahead and talk! I'm just gettin' this menu." And she scurried from the room.

The last thing she wanted to do was make Andy feel unwelcome in her office or anywhere else. After all, she had given the office over to him for doing the café accounts. That had been a good decision, no matter what anyone else (she thought of Belinda) said. Andy did a better job by far than she ever had, and he had taught her a lot, too. Business accounting was just not her strong point. Lots of people wondered how she ever ran the café, and when it came to accounting, she wondered that, too.

She sat on a stool at the counter and hurriedly worked on the week's menu changes in the ten minutes before the café opened. On the other side of the pass-through, Woody sang along with the radio as he made biscuits. "A-a-amen, alle-lu-yahh…"

Just because she had never seen Andy use the phone, that did not mean he did not use it. He was in the office all the time and likely used the phone plenty. He had looked so surprised…sneaky…at seeing her. Of course, she had been extra early.

Who do you suppose Andy had been talking to? *Well, likely some woman.*

Heaven knew that she had a whole potful of experience with men leaving her for other women.

Not that Andy was actually *with* her, she guessed. They… dated. Yes, they did, even if they did not really go anywhere besides the café or Woody's house. Twice up to Lawton. He worked in her café, ate there, and in a million ways acted as if he was with her. And she was in love with him…*and the men she loved had always left her.*

"Did you hear about that, Miss Fayrene?" said Woody.

"What?" She had been lost in thought. Shoot, she hadn't even gotten the menu changes done, and the clock read two minutes to opening.

"Mr. Everett tellin' about the carousel. It's been lost in shipment."

"It has?" She leaned over to catch what was on the radio, but all she heard was Winston saying, "…developments," and then the Bellamy Brothers started singing.

Woody said, "They were just talkin' about that the carousel's gone missin'. I doubt it's a joke. Mr. Winston was foolin' like he sometimes does, sayin' stay tuned for further developments, but you could tell Mr. Everett is full upset."

"How can somebody lose a carousel?"

"Well, Miss Fayrene, there is such a thing as cargo theft."

He looked at her in a way that caused her to gaze back at him with a puzzled frown.

There came a rapping on the glass door, drawing her head around. Sheriff Neville peered in and rattled the door.

"Okay. Keep your shirt on." Fayrene hurried to open. Since his marriage had broken up, Sheriff Neville had formed the habit of getting his coffee first thing from the café, and like most middle-aged men, he liked his habits.

John Cole Berry was with the sheriff. The two men took stools at the counter, and Fayrene came immediately with the first pot of the day.

"Emma is limitin' my coffee," John Cole said to the sheriff.

Fayrene rather pulled the pot back, and John Cole gave her the eye. "That's why I'm here," he said firmly.

She filled his cup with some trepidation, remembering his heart attack. He looked really good, though. John Cole Berry was a handsome man, Fayrene thought with a mental sigh, as she passed the men's order ticket through to Woody. What did women like Emma Berry, married for years and years, know that she did not? Maybe that she should have caught her man early and stuck.

Andy came out and joined them, and Woody leaned forward in the pass-through as the talk turned to the loss of the carousel.

"The driver's missin', too," John Cole told them. "The feds have been called in, and hopefully they can find the thing before it's too late."

"How can someone hide a carousel?" asked Fayrene, still skeptical. "I mean, there just can't be too many people linin' up to buy a carousel."

"Ship it overseas, lots of buyers," said the sheriff, his eyes fastened on his plate, heaped with over-easy eggs, biscuits and gravy, which Fayrene plunked in front of him.

"They hide and dispose of whole shipments of computers and plasma TVs. I think they can manage a carousel," said John Cole.

Fayrene noticed him eyeing the plate of scrambled eggs and a single biscuit, and the fruit bowl, which she had placed in front of him. His eyes shifted to look at the sheriff's plate, then back to his own, then up at her.

"I ordered the same as the sheriff."

"And I gave you the heart-healthy special," said Fayrene. "I want to be able to look Emma in the face if she comes in later today."

Such was a small town, thought John Cole.

People asked Winston about it everywhere he went, and he would drawl, "Yes, it's true, sad to say. You'd best get the details from Everett. He's head of the carousel committee." Only a few people noticed that he would then turn the conversation and say, "Ain't this a pretty day for fall? This rain'll pass—why I remember back in…"

Everett was thrilled with people calling and coming up to him, asking him about the situation. He was flooded with calls on his *Everett in the Morning* program, and stopped three times on the street just trying to go to the post office and then to pay his water bill at city hall. At home, the phone rang so many times that his wife, Doris, got aggravated.

"I am head of the committee," Everett told her, "and we have a situation here. Everything is set—the governor and Reba McEntire are coming." He jutted his head toward her. "It's my civic responsibility to be available, and keep people informed and get this *straightened out.*"

To this, Doris said, "I married somebody who never got involved in stuff like this and preferred quiet to a lot of talk. All those years I could not even get you in a good conversation or to go to the PTA."

After several seconds of looking at her, Everett replied, "Doris, I am older and different. And I've got more time now."

Just then the phone rang. He turned instantly to answer.

Doris regarded him for a moment, then left the room, returning ten minutes later with her jacket and lipstick on, and a purse in her hand.

"I'm going shopping."

With Tate Holloway talking in his ear, Everett simply nodded.

That evening he was somewhat flabbergasted when Doris returned. She handed him a batch of receipts and said, "Will you help me unload?"

He had to make three trips to the car for an electronic convection oven, an enormous artificial flower arrangement and four large shopping bags. Standing in the kitchen, he looked over the receipts, and his eyes widened. He had never known her to buy so much at one time.

When he mentioned this, Doris said, "I'm older and different, too. You have more time, and I have more money."

The next morning, Everett came hurrying in late to the radio station. Even though he was late, Winston was still in the act of getting his coffee and bringing it slowly to the booth, wishing Everett a good morning even as Jim Rainwater called, "One minute."

Everett said, "Car wouldn't start. Had to get Doris… I got a statement from the carousel committee about the celebration." He spoke quickly, as if by doing so, he could hurry Winston along to his seat. He was made even more on edge to see Willie Lee coming behind Winston and positioning himself beside his chair.

"I'll read this at the end of the news," said Everett, waving a typewritten paper.

Winston nodded and fumbled with his headphones.

Knowing that no matter the time, Jim Rainwater would not start until Winston was ready, Everett dropped his gaze to his statement and began rereading.

"GET UP, GET UP, YOU SLEE-PY-HEAD. GET UP AND GET YOUR BOD-Y FED!"

Everett jumped. Winston always shouted the call, rather than use the recording, just when Everett least expected it.

"This is 1550 on the radio dial—the *Wake Up* show with Brother Winston."

"And Wil-lie Lee and Mun-ro." The dog barked.

"And Everett," Everett said quickly, frowning at the dog. He came after a boy and a *dog*.

Again he returned his attention to the statement, wanting to commit it to memory, while Winston went into his usual chatty opening, giving the weather, the school lunch menu and the news headlines with his comments, which of late had consisted of a lot of retelling things that had happened in the past.

After a couple of minutes, Everett became aware that Winston had gone from talking about the rainy weather to telling about a tornado that had taken place back in 1945, and how it had torn up a German prisoner-of-war camp and sailed Winston's wife's chickens a quarter of a mile to her cousin's yard. "I'm not makin' that up. You can ask Coweta."

Everett waved and pointed at his watch.

Winston frowned and gave him a puzzled look.

"I need to make the announcement." Everett waved the paper.

"Oh, okay, folks…here's an announcement." Winston sat back.

Everett looked at him with raised eyebrows, then quickly took over the microphone. "This is Everett, with an announcement from the Carousel Park Committee. As most of you probably know, the carousel has been lost in transit. Authorities are working hard on tracing the shipment and expect to find it quickly." (He wanted to present everything in the best light.) "However, there is a chance it may not be present in time for the Valentine Carousel Park Centennial Celebration festivities, which are already planned.

"The centennial celebration *will* take place. I repeat—Valentine's hundredth anniversary event will take place as planned. We have both the Honorable Governor *and* Reba McEntire scheduled to join us. The carousel building is in full operation and the landscaping directly around it almost finished. There will be free refreshments, a chili cook-off, a car show sponsored by the Flatlanders Street Rod Club and a PRCA sanctioned rodeo sponsored by the Valentine Roundup Club at the rodeo grounds, which adjoin Carousel Park. A parade will kick it all off in the morning, and you won't want to miss any of…it."

A sound drew his head around. While he had been making the announcement, Winston and the boy had left the sound booth. Everett now saw Winston in the doorway, coffee cup tilting from one hand, while his other reached out for the frame as he sort of melted downward.

Everett stared at Winston's crumpled form on the floor. At the boy kneeling by Winston's head.

Music suddenly played into Everett's ears. Jim Rainwater lunged from his chair toward Winston, shouting something at Everett that he had trouble hearing. Then the young man's lips and voice came together. "Call 9-1-1!"

"You carry on, Everett," was the last thing that Winston Valentine said.

"I will," Everett said, but Winston's eyes had already closed.

Willie Lee, with Mr. Winston's head on his knees, saw Mr. Winston's pale spirit rise. He felt a warm breeze across his cheeks and a certain pressure on his shoulder, Mr. Winston saying goodbye.

Mr. Winston's face relaxed. He was gone.

A quiet seemed to sweep the whole town, as listeners tilted their ears to the radio and held their breath, waiting for Winston's voice, while song after song played and the half hour passed without the signature reveille. Many along Main Street heard the siren and went to the window to see the emergency squad pass. Eyes met questioning eyes. Winston's name was mentioned, but in a whisper that was quickly hushed. "Don't talk like that!" As if by not speaking of it, it might not be true.

At the café, Woody took two sacks of garbage out to the bin in the alley, and he looked up at the sky, saw the clouds clearing, the rising sun shining golden. And he noted that there was not a bird singing. Just an eerie silence.

Woody came back in and said, "I imagine Mr. Winston has done passed on."

"Oh, don't say that, Woody!" said Fayrene, tearing off her apron and running across the street to the drugstore, more than usually heedless of automobiles.

Later, Woody was to mention the phenomenon of the sky clearing and no birds singing that happened at the time of Winston's death, and lots of people eagerly agreed that they had noticed the same, in the way people like to do with those stories.

When Winston's son, Freddie, came to town and heard the tale, he privately, with a mixture of sadness and awe, told his wife, "All my life Daddy managed to make himself larger than life. There was just no way to match him."

CHAPTER 22

Dearly Departed, But Not Gone

WHILE BIRDS COULD BE HEARD SINGING AS MUCH as usual—plenty of people stopped frequently to check—and the sun shone and a light breeze blew, a definite pall swept over the town. Losing both the carousel and their beloved leading citizen within two days was a blow that left the town stunned.

"Death comes in threes," Julia Jenkins-Tinsley said, with a raised eyebrow. This idea was picked up and repeated, with speculation as to who would be next. A number of wives shouted it at their husbands at opportune times.

"The carousel ain't dead," someone pointed out. "It's just stolen."

"Near enough. It's gone," was the dour reply.

The passing of Winston Valentine has left a wide hole in our town, in our hearts and, dare I say, in the world, wrote editor Tate

Holloway late that night as he composed his editorial for the *Valentine Voice*.

The editorial would go on to be a eulogy that took up half of the front page and then the second and third with photographs of major events from Winston's life entwined with the town.

There would also end up being a photograph of the long funeral procession, led by the antique black-and-gilded hearse pulled by two white furry-footed draft horses in show livery, with Winston's grandchildren on horseback, followed by three long black limousines of family and close friends, and nearly a mile of cars and trucks. The procession snaked slowly down Main Street, a street, Tate Holloway sentimentally pointed out, that Winston had helped build and had walked nearly every day of his long life.

The funeral was the largest Clara Chisum could ever recall at the Chisum Funeral Home. Claire Ford reported that her Goodnight Motel was booked to capacity, and she allowed three RVs to camp in the motel lot, and hook up to electricity and water. A number who attended the funeral had never personally met Winston but had been listening to him on the radio so long that they felt as though he was their kin.

The president of Blue Boy Dog Food, which Winston had advertised, flew in by helicopter, bringing two retired congressmen. Three country-music stars that had passed the height of popularity but were still recognizable showed up in dark cars and dark glasses. It was reported that at least three elderly people out at the nursing home got out of their beds and arranged for a generous orderly to drive them over. One man, who caught Winston's program on a skipping radio signal, came all the way from Kansas.

The day of the funeral was bright and sunny and warm for

fall, as had been every day since the morning of Winston's death. Even with all the people gathered and talking, there was a sense of quiet. Barely a breeze ruffled the turning leaves in the large elms towering over the graveside service, and while birds sang, there were precious few.

Winston viewed the scene from above. He wasn't flying. He just seemed to be suspended there, and Coweta beside him.

She said, "There's our children…oh, honey-bunnies, don't be too sad."

"Helen ain't," said Winston.

At that moment, his son's wife was leaning forward and frowning as she watched chairs being brought for Vella and Belinda to sit at the end of the family line.

"They're not family," Helen said to Freddie. Her voice traveled to Winston clearly above the other murmuring. It was like a movie film, where the microphone zoomed in.

Freddie did not respond, just kept staring at the flag-and-flower-draped coffin in front of him. He did actually look sad, thought Winston, who stretched forward an unseen hand that could not touch.

Helen poked Freddie with her elbow. "They aren't family, Freddie. They need to sit behind."

"Someone ought to poke *her* in the behind," Winston said.

A second later a bird dropping splatted on Helen's shoulder. Winston looked at it, then looked upward, but he didn't see a bird. He didn't see clouds or actual sky, just all around him a sort of glow. He looked over at Coweta, who grinned at him.

"Who did that? I didn't…did I?" The idea was both disturbing and enticing.

"No. I don't know who did it, but that's how these things generally work."

Winston was a little disappointed.

He ran his gaze over the faces, people he had known much of his life—some he could recall when they had been born— remembering the tragedies and triumphs they had gone through.

There were each of his children. Funny how he did not know them so much anymore. He never had known Freddie, didn't think anyone did, especially not Freddie.

"Oh, honey, look, there's our grands." Coweta pointed as the children were lined up on the other side. Five, because Rainey had two children now. Willie Lee and Corrine joined them. Corrine slipped her hand into Larry Joe's.

Vella pulled a tissue out from her bosom and pressed it to her nose. She kept her back straight, but her lips trembled. She and Belinda held hands. Winston never thought he would live to see the day that happened, and come to think of it, he hadn't.

He realized that he seemed to be able to move around as he thought, because when he wondered what Pastor Smith was going to say, he found himself looking over the pastor's shoulder and saw the notes. "Aw, just speak from your heart, Stanley."

A moment later, three five-by-six note cards went flying into the hole in the ground. The pastor looked down. Everyone looked down.

Winston raised an eyebrow at Coweta right beside him. She gave him an amused look he couldn't quite read.

Then Pastor Smith cleared his throat and began in a stilted manner. "I've known Winston Valentine probably a far shorter time than any of you here, but since I first arrived, he provided me with wise guidance and unfailing encouragement, always in his pithy manner."

Swallowing, he looked at the surrounding faces. "What can I say? Winston Valentine was a man beyond my words. Our sorrow is great, but Winston had a good life, and I know he is with our Heavenly Father, and that he is havin', as he always did, a bang-up time. And he would tell us to get over our grievin' quickly. Winston wasn't a grievin' man. He was a man of amazin' faith and everlasting joy, and this is the legacy he left. Winston Valentine has departed this earth, but he will never be gone from our hearts."

Seconds passed, and everyone looked at the pastor, startled to realize he had quit speaking and in fact seemed finished.

The pastor seemed a little surprised himself.

Just then Felton Ballard began to sing "I'm Going Home." His wife joined in with him.

Winston said to Coweta beside him, "Do you see that? They're givin' me a grand send-off."

"I see, Winston."

He pulled a handkerchief out of his back pocket to blow his nose, and after doing so, he looked at his handkerchief, then down at his clothes, all familiar. "How come I have a hand-kerchief…and all this…up here?"

"Why wouldn't you?"

"I don't know. Just unexpected to have normal things from earth." Although feeling foolish, he had rather expected a gown and wings. Then a horrible thought… "I did make it to heaven, didn't I?"

"Yes, honey." Coweta chuckled.

"Well, I just don't seem to be…so gone. I'm still here." He held his hands out, looking at the cuffs of his shirt.

"Yes, sugar. And you always will be here, just like Stanley said, in all the good you've left behind."

"What about the bad?" Winston knew he had done some of that.

"God's grace is greater than your bad, honey."

Coweta's laughter rang like sweet bells as she seemed to move off into the glowing air, her voice floating back to him. "Just as life on earth was mostly unexpected, so it is in heaven, too. Nothing about that changes."

"I can't believe he's gone," Marilee told Tate that evening in the kitchen. "I swear, when I looked into the living room, I thought I saw his old rocker rockin'."

This sentiment was repeated again and again all over town. And as is normal after the loss of a loved one, in the following days Winston's family and friends, both close and casual, experienced a sense of his presence.

That first night after Winston's funeral, his daughter Charlene sat right up in bed, scaring her husband. "I dreamed of Daddy," she told him, breaking into tears. "He told me he wanted me to know he loved me, that he felt he had not paid me enough attention." Charlene had always felt her father did not pay her attention, that her sister had been the favored one, and her brother, by virtue of being the boy, got more attention still.

Feeling very much loved, she went to her kitchen to get a cup of tea and found her sister, Rainey, who was staying the night, there ahead of her. "I dreamed of Daddy, too," said Rainey, and the two sisters talked long into the early hours, as they had not in years.

The morning following the funeral, over at the Valentine-

Holloway house, Rosalba came downstairs and told her employer, "I'm not gettin' the sheets off Mr. Winston's bed. I felt him in there, and I could smell him."

"Of course you can smell him in his bedroom," replied Marilee. "He always used all that aftershave." She went up to get the sheets off the bed, and she caught the scent so strongly that she had to check the aftershave bottle to make certain the lid was on tight. Then she sat in the rocker by the window and reflected on how much the old man had given them, and how much more of a woman she had become in these years in this house.

Vella called Belinda and told her, "I saw the glow in Winston's yard again, by Coweta's rosebushes. You know that happened a lot for a long time after Coweta died."

Belinda said to this, "Mama, I'm glad for you—Winston loved you," in such an unusually caring manner that Vella started to cry.

Later that morning, when Vella went to Winston's big Victorian house to attend the reading of the will, she sat in Winston's old rocker-recliner, rubbing her palms down the leather arms that were worn soft from the years of Winston's own hands. She felt him all around her, and she reminisced aloud of their years together, which caused Rosalba to look in on her once.

As others began arriving, Vella stayed solidly in Winston's chair, even when Winston's grown children arrived.

"I think you should let Freddie sit there," Freddie's wife, Helen, told her. "He is Winston's son and eldest," the woman prodded.

To which Vella snorted, then replied, "Where has Freddie been all these years? We thought he'd died." And she rocked on.

★ ★ ★

That afternoon Corrine and Larry Joe went downtown in Larry Joe's big truck. They thought to get away from all the talk going on in the house following the reading of the will. Willie Lee and Munro jumped up from the porch and went with them.

On the sidewalk, they ran into Paris coming out of the drugstore. "I came down to get Miss Belinda some essential oils for her relaxation aromatherapy."

"Her what?" asked Larry Joe.

"Don't ask," Paris and Corrine said as one, in the tone employed when women know fully something a man will not understand.

Then Corrine looked at the drugstore. "I don't want to go in there. Not yet. It'll be so odd without Mr. Winston."

"Everywhere is odd without Mr. Winston," said Paris. "Did you hear Everett on the *Wake Up* program this mornin'?"

"No," said Larry Joe shortly, and Corrine said she had slept in.

"Well, Belinda called him and told him he had better stop the effort on the *Wake Up* call."

There was a moment of silence, and then Willie Lee interjected, "The caf-é has rai-sin pie now, Cor-rine." Although he did not like the café as much, because Munro had to wait outside. But he wanted to be helpful, and he felt the need to visit the café.

Corrine's spirits rose. Faced with returning to school far from home, she desperately needed something precious and familiar, and the pie was just that. She led the way, crossing the street in the middle of the block.

"Jaydee was in a bit ago and told us all about the will. He was still sweatin' from the effort of the reading like it was July, and ordered the roast beef and potatoes and gravy plate to re-juvenate himself." Fayrene opened her pad. "So…what'll you all—"

"I want raisin pie," said Corrine, who was eager to get things moving in the direction of comfort.

After Fayrene had taken their orders and walked away, Paris said, "Miss Vella came over to Miss Belinda's after and told us everything. She said a paintin' fell off the wall and hit your uncle Freddie's wife in the head." She looked at Larry Joe, adding, "She said she thought it was Mr. Winston."

"Maybe it was," Larry Joe said. "Mom said Helen has groused over that paintin' for years, claimin' that Grandma gave it to her a long time ago. She's takin' it home with her," he added.

"How is it workin' out, stayin' at Miss Belinda's?" Corrine asked Paris, changing the worn-out subject that depressed her, even though she had also been named in Winston's will (which had added to Helen Valentine's hissy fit).

Paris seemed to have changed dramatically in only a little more than a week of living with Belinda. Her face was lighter. Aunt Marilee said it was not so heavy because Paris no longer wore three layers of makeup and all that hardware. The earrings were gone from her eyebrows and her nose. Only one large and one small remained in each earlobe. The finger rings and wrist chains were also gone. She had definitely been toned down and softened.

"Okay," Paris said with a shrug. "She says I can stay with her and Lyle for as long as I want. And I can help her right now, you know, with her supposed to be on bed rest, and when the baby comes. I run her errands and help her with the cooking when I'm there." She paused, then said, shyly averting her gaze, "She's been real generous."

With a bit of eagerness, she told of shopping online for clothes. She and Corrine discussed the various clothing Web sites and what they liked.

Paris said, "Belinda's pretty strict about what she lets me buy, but it's all nice stuff." Remembering suddenly Belinda's admonishment about posture, she adjusted her spine and squared her shoulders.

Corrine asked gently about Paris's grandfather.

"So far he still don—doesn't know where he is. I don't know." She pressed her lips together and gazed at the table.

No one knew what to say in the face of that. Luckily, a few seconds later Fayrene brought their orders, slices of raisin pie for Corrine and Willie Lee, hamburgers for Paris and Larry Joe.

Corrine gazed at her pie for long seconds, then dug into it. The taste brought back so many memories of her hometown and family. After two bites and feeling teary, she said, "I've been thinkin', and I don't think I'll go back to school in OKC. I think I'll just come home and finish out here in Valentine, and then use the money Mr. Winston left me to go to junior college and live at home."

"Oh, no, you don't," Larry Joe said instantly. "You're gonna finish the year out up there, at least. It's a great opportunity, and after that you'll go to OU, at least. Granddad would have my tail if I let you come home. You get your schoolin', and I'll use my inheritance to build up the station and garage, and then we can get married."

Corrine's eyes flashed. "You cannot *let* me do anything. I know what I need and want, and it's all right here. Ambition is highly overrated," she added, just then remembering Miss Belinda's words.

Paris's gaze went back and forth between the two. "Look,

kids…" she said with an air of the worldly wise. "Corrine, you know it probably would be a good idea for you to finish what you started up there at school. That's far enough to know for now. And you guys cannot block out your entire future this minute. It's a really bad time…after what's happened." She could not speak directly of Mr. Winston's death.

Corrine and Larry Joe nodded, although Corrine added, "I am not waitin' ten years to get married."

Larry Joe grinned, winked at her, then leaned over and kissed her stubbornly held cheek.

The same thought passed through Corrine's and Paris's minds, which was: *he looks just like his grandfather.*

Paris hung her head as the image of her own dissipated grandfather rose up in her mind. The knowledge that people lived on in what they passed on to their children and grand-children welled up in her chest. What about her? Would her life always be tainted by her mother and grandfather, and the pain they had passed on to her?

"Can I get anybody anything?" It was Fayrene's man, Andy, which was how each of them thought of him, having heard it from the older women in all their lives. He was passing by with a pot of coffee in hand.

Willie Lee, whom everyone had more or less forgotten like usual, said, "Yes. I wo-uld like the car-ou-sel found."

They all looked surprised.

"Well, the best I can do, boy-o, is get you another piece of pie," Andy said.

Winston's recorded *Wake Up* call was retired to the archives, as was all his recorded advertising. The old man in the wheel-chair accompanied by the boy and the dog was no longer seen on the streets. His customary seats at the café and the drug-store and the bench beneath the tree on Main Street remained empty.

Once, at the drugstore, Vella started to correct a stranger who came in and sat in Winston's chair.

"Yes?" said the gentleman, his bottom hovering over the chair and his eyes wide with alarm.

"Oh, I'm sorry." Vella covered by waving him downward with a towel. "Please sit—it's just that I realized I need to wipe that table. There now. That's better." She smiled more, but the gentleman looked nervous and did not stay long.

Postmistress Julia Jenkins-Tinsley, who had witnessed the scene, said, "It is just darn weird without Winston. He was here all my life."

To which Inez Cooper, who was getting a sweet tea, said, "Well, he's not now," and sighed deeply.

Rosalba Garcia no longer woke her husband and sons by banging pots and pans. She lost the heart for it. Her menfolk were actually disappointed.

Paris found herself a little disoriented, awakening each morning to such quiet, and in fine sheets and a bright room. One time she thought she was in her car again and the sun was coming up. So used to worrying about something, she twice ran in to make certain that Miss Belinda was all right.

Up at the Oklahoma School of Science and Mathematics, Corrine almost missed her first class three mornings in a row because of soothing herself by talking to Larry Joe and wanting him to tell her everything that went on in Valentine.

He said, "Honey, you've only been gone a couple of days. Not that much happens here. And nobody else has died," he thought to add, hoping to help settle her.

John Cole filled his morning coffee cup in a leisurely manner, knowing that Everett's milder voice coming over the coffeemaker-radio was not about to disturb Emma. Winston's death had pointed up his own close call and gift of life and health; he determined to relax and enjoy it. While still rising early, John Cole now sat for long peaceful moments on the rear sunporch in the cool early mornings, watching the world awaken and often feeding the birds.

Tate Holloway had his coffee alone and sometimes found himself talking to Winston. Once Marilee caught him at it.

"Are you talkin' to Winston?"

"Yep," said Tate. "Why not? Willie Lee does."

"Ah-huh," said Marilee with a nod and a sigh, realizing some things simply *were*.

Jaydee thought much the same thing. It was a fact that he had married Vella, but it also seemed a fact that a part of Vella's heart still belonged to Winston, a man dead but not, to all intents and purposes, gone. Rather than be jealous, he accepted that and comforted himself that he was the one to have married Vella and would have her with him as he faced his own aging years.

Everett never would have talked to Winston, but he thought of him often.

"The *Wake Up* show is *my* show now," he told Doris, when she suggested he go back to doing his original show at seven. "Winston was right about it, too. A lot of people listen on the way to work—people that have no chance to listen any other time."

What Everett did not say was that he liked the man that he had become in the months of hosting the *Wake Up* program. He was fighting to hold on to that and not go back to what he had been: a retired old man who did not care about much of anything.

However, he was finding it hard going. From the first morning as the single host of the *Wake Up with Everett* show, he fell flat. He could not do the *Wake Up* reveille call; that was obvious.

He tried opening the program with the ringing of a cowbell, only to have it slip out of his hands and fly across the room, hit a piece of equipment and break off a knob. Then he brought up the subject of Carousel Park, reporting on the upcoming celebration even without a carousel. He got so tangled with that, he wasn't certain what he finally said. He received only two phone calls, one wanting a repeat of the school lunch menu and another from some drunk fool who wanted to hear Winston's *Wake Up* call for old times' sake.

"No way, Jo-sé," Everett said instantly, which at least got a chuckle out of Jim Rainwater.

That evening, Everett went over to ask Willie Lee to return to the morning program. "People have asked me about you, Willie Lee. You are part of the show, and I'd really love to have you…and Munro. I need you."

He was very surprised when Willie Lee shook his head.

"No, than-k you, sir. I have oth-er things to do."

The next morning, when Willie Lee's mother had found out about the exchange and asked him what things he had to do, Willie Lee thought for a moment and then replied, "Things…and I think I will go back to scho-ol." He said this with an eye on the cinnamon rolls Rosalba had made that morning.

As he hoped, his mother got all excited about the mention of school and did not see that he and Papa Tate, and Munro, ate all the cinnamon rolls.

★ ★ ★

That afternoon, Willie Lee went down to the Main Street Café. He told Munro to wait outside, and the dog lay down obediently beside the entry, while Willie Lee went in, climbed up on a stool and ordered a piece of raisin pie from Andy behind the counter.

Willie Lee ate the pie, then sat looking at Andy, who was busy writing something on a tablet.

Andy looked up and saw the boy gazing at him. "Do you want something else?"

"I wo-uld like the car-rou-sel," said Willie Lee.

Fayrene, coming up at that moment, said, "Well, honey, we would all like that," and stroked Willie Lee's head, then picked up his money from the counter and stuffed it back in his hand. "Pie is on the house, hon. You want a soda?"

"No, thank you." He climbed down, went out the door and across the street, where he and Munro sat on the bench they used to sit on with Winston.

"Willie Lee is so lonesome for Winston." Fayrene gazed out the plate-glass window. "I guess he comes in here because he and Winston mostly used to be at the drugstore. It's probably painful for him over there." She didn't mean to be delighted to have Willie Lee coming to the café, but she was.

Andy looked over her shoulder and saw the boy, who appeared to be gazing at the café. "That kid is strange."

"Not really, it's just that he…" She bit her lip and looked away.

"He what?"

She moved to the cash register. "He's mentally handicapped. I thought you knew."

"Oh, yeah. I heard something about that."

Fayrene watched Andy go back to the office and stared for

some minutes after he had disappeared. Only a few of them in town knew, but never told, the truth of Willie Lee.

The following afternoon, Andy looked up from the computer to see the boy in the office doorway, gazing at him. Andy did not say anything, and neither did the boy. Then the boy turned and left.

Five minutes later, when Andy came out of the office, the boy was at the counter eating another piece of raisin pie and talking with Fayrene. As Andy slipped behind Fayrene on his way to get a cup of coffee, he caught the boy saying, "Mr. Winston says the carousel…"

Coming back past the two, he heard Fayrene saying, "…ask him if I'm ever gonna get married."

"What are you two talking about?" Andy asked.

"Uh…oh, we're just rememberin' Winston," Fayrene said.

The boy blinked at Andy behind his thick eyeglasses. There was something unnerving about the look.

"Uh-huh," Andy said, and quickly headed back to the office.

CHAPTER 23

Welcome to Your World, Sweetie Pie

BELINDA FELT THE FIRST CONTRACTIONS WHEN she was telling Everett on the *Wake Up* show that she thought the Valentine Carousel Park should be renamed Winston Valentine Park.

"We need a town monument to Winston."

Belinda had taken the death of Winston harder than anyone had ever seen her take anything, even her own father's death.

She told Lyle through the tears that seemed to come all the time these days, "You know, I loved Daddy, but even when Daddy was there, most of the time he wasn't there. But Winston was always there, even when he wasn't there. And now he is not here and never will be again."

Lyle could think of nothing to say to that. He bought her flowers, sugar-free candy and the entire *PBS Masterpiece Miss Marple Mystery Series I and II* on DVD.

Seeing Belinda heartbroken as she was rattled Paris badly, yet brought out the sense of purpose to fix the situation that she had not enjoyed since her grandfather had been taken away. Paris played chess with Belinda in the evenings, and phoned several times a day between classes and her job. She also brought home packages of Little Debbie chocolate snack cakes, which she rationed to Belinda, giving her one and taking one for herself.

The third day that she did this, Belinda looked at the cupcake, then shook her head and said, "I'm swearin' off of them. I gotta take care of my little girl."

Watching Belinda stroke her belly, Paris suspected then that so much of Belinda's melancholy was tied up with worry over something possibly happening to her baby.

Now Everett said through the phone, "That's a good idea for taking a poll! Let's have some call-ins and discuss this matter— who wants to change the name of Carousel Park to Winston Valentine Park? There are a lot of things to consider on this—"

Belinda cut in. "Nothing else really matters but what is right. Winston had the idea for the carousel. It is his. Everyone who wants to name the park Winston Valentine Park, call in and say so. Everyone who does not, just keep quiet."

"Well, that's not really a poll," said Everett, back to his annoying voice. "And there are some considerations…and maybe suggestions on what else we might name the park."

"Do not confuse the issue with a lot of talk. Everyone who wants to name the park Winston Valentine Park, phone in quick. Jim, are you listenin'? Play some sort of sound and get it started."

Jim Rainwater instantly complied. The ring of a bell and a man saying, "They're off!" sounded.

This helped propel Belinda to throw her legs off the bed and push herself and her belly upward. At the same time, a pain around her middle surprised her.

"Belinda? Belinda, are you still there?" Everett's voice from out of the phone.

"Yes…honey," she said a little breathlessly.

"I appreciate you calling in yesterday and today and helping me get the ball rolling again on Carousel Park. We've got to get interest kindled again. We've got the celebration coming up in ten days." His voice went up in pitch. "And we already have the park sign. It's gonna cost to change that. I don't know…"

Belinda pressed a hand into her side. "Honey, excuse me, but I have to get to the bathroom." *She sure hoped she was not on the air.*

"You call back anytime," said Everett earnestly.

She kissed Lyle goodbye, and waved a ten–dollar bill at Paris on her way out to school. "Here, you get a good lunch."

"I don't need ten dollars for lunch."

"Well, you may need it for somethin'."

"You don't have to keep givin' me—"

Belinda waved the bill. "Sugar, when anyone gives you money, take it. Now go on and be smart and don't do anything foolish."

Paris took the bill but tossed over her shoulder, "I don't think a person should take money from any stranger, though." A minute later there came the sound of the back door closing, and seconds later the roar of Paris's old car starting and going away down the driveway.

Alone at last.

Belinda got out of bed and went to the bathroom to look

in the full–length mirror. She turned first right, then left, then back to her front again. Her belly looked very odd. The lump was moving downward.

Definitely dropping.

Well, she was not telling anyone until she was sure. She did not want to be embarrassed by false runs to the hospital.

She got back in bed and searched through two of the pregnancy books to read about the signs of being in labor. Apparently she could have already been in labor a half-dozen times. It was such a general thing.

"They come and they go," Belinda explained to Nurse Betty on the phone.

"Where are they now?"

"Well…I don't have one now." Belinda could feel her blood pressure rising, as it perpetually did when speaking to the woman.

Nurse Betty cleared her throat in a pointed manner. "I mean, are you having pains at regular intervals?"

"I had one about twenty minutes ago, I think. Only they aren't pains. They are just more…discomforts."

"No bleeding?"

"No." Belinda's eyes widened with the idea.

"Uh-huh…you know, being pregnant, you are goin' to have all kinds of aches and pains."

Thank you, thought Belinda, and bit her bottom lip.

Nurse Betty said, "You are not quite thirty-seven weeks. It could be gas pains. Your appointment is in two days. I think you can just wait and see the doctor then. Don't worry—you'll know when you are in labor."

"How am I gonna *know?*" Belinda said, making a face at the phone as she hung up.

She read from the book again, but it was no more helpful. She could be having those false labor contractions. She did not quite feel as she had months earlier in preterm labor.

"Hi, sugar. How are you feelin' today?" Her mother appeared through the bedroom doorway.

"Fine, Mama." Belinda pressed her side and considered for a brief second asking her mother how to tell if she were in labor.

"Well…" Her mother moved a pile of clothes so she could sit in the chair. "I brought you a few grilled chicken breasts and some coleslaw and a can of cranberry sauce, and Inez sent a bowl of her ambrosia. I put it all in the refrigerator."

"I appreciate that, Mama…."

"I asked Inez if she had added any sugar to her ambrosia, and she said she didn't."

"Uh-huh. Listen, have you heard the *Wake Up* show with Everett?"

"No, honey…I haven't listened since the day Winston died. I just can't."

"Well, that's the problem with everyone. *Nobody* is listenin' to the show. Nobody is payin' attention to the park and the carousel. And Winston started it all. We can't just let it go— we need to get the name of the park changed to Winston Valentine Park. I can't stand it if his name just disappears."

She plucked at a pillow, realizing she sounded upset, especially when her mother answered with a soothing voice.

"Sugar, people are payin' attention to the park. Just this mornin' it was set for Jaydee and I to meet Reba McEntire and escort her for the centennial celebration and park dedication. I know it isn't quite the same without a carousel and Winston, but we'll get a carousel, and…well, we'll always have Winston in our hearts."

"That is not the same! The park needs to be *Winston Valentine Park*."

Her mother gazed at her as if taking her temperature. Whatever she saw prompted her to say smartly, "You are right. We do need to name the park after Winston. We should have done that from the beginning."

"Well, I started the ball rolling on the *Wake Up* show this mornin'. I think it would be a big help if you called around and asked people to tune in to the show tomorrow, and to call in and vote for the name change. And maybe get a conversation started about why can't we find that carousel. Lyle does not know anything. He says it is in the hands of the CBI and the FBI, and—"

"What's the CBI?" her mother interrupted with a puzzled frown.

"California Bureau of Investigation. The carousel was shipped from California, so they're in charge out there—them and the FBI. Lyle says that the FBI has a lot more important things to work on than a single shipment of a carousel. But Winston would not have stood for this, Mama…just waitin' around."

Her throat felt thick again.

"Well, there's no tellin' what Winston might have done," her mother said. "Are these clothes clean?"

"No. I think you should go to Tate Holloway and see what he knows, and if he has any ideas of what can be done."

"All right. I guess if anyone would know, it would be Tate." Her mother seemed to be drifting off in thought.

"Go today, Mama."

"I will, sugar." Her mother's gaze came back to her. "And I'll have Jaydee make a few calls. He knows people. Between all of us, we'll get things movin' along. Now you just calm down, sugar, and get some rest."

"Mama, I don't know how I can rest any more than I am. I'm in bed day and night!"

"I know, sugar, but it'll be over soon. I'll just take these clothes to your laundry room." Her mother wisely beat a retreat, calling brightly from the back door, "I enjoyed visitin'. I'll call you later."

Hearing the door close, Belinda gave a large sigh, looked around the room of which she was sorely tired and listened to the silence. She picked at the bed covers while staring into space.

The silence grew, and so did the emotions inside. She needed to speak to someone, to talk about how she felt about the abortion. She wanted more than anything in that moment to talk to Winston about it. If only she had talked to him when he had been alive….

Little Desirée Jane moved, seeming to do a flip. Belinda felt the tightness go all the way around her middle.

It did feel like gas.

Get up, get up, you slee-py-head!
Oh, Winston, hush.

She did not want to wake up. She was tired.

But the next instant a baby's crying brought her eyes opening wide.

Her baby's crying.

She jumped out of bed in a panic and raced around looking for the crying baby. The crib and cradle were empty! She searched frantically through all the rooms of the house, which was dark. She kept flipping on light switches, but they did not work.

She had lost her baby! How could she have done that?

Because she was not a very good mother, that's how.

Oh, God, let me find her and I'll be better. I'll be the best mother in the world.

Then suddenly there was her baby, in Winston's arms, as he sat in a white wicker rocker on the front porch of her mother's house.

"I've been looking for her everywhere!" Belinda told him with aggravation.

Then, noting Winston smiling down tenderly at her baby, who slept peacefully, she felt great relief. And joy. Here was not only her baby, but Winston!

She slipped into an adjacent rocker. Her mother had the porch fixed up so lovely these days, with jade plants and potted herbs, all so green against everything else painted white.

She gazed at Winston with the baby. She told him how glad she was that he got to see her sweet Desirée Jane.

"I'm so afraid, Winston. I don't think I'm goin' to make a very good mother. I'm so afraid I'm goin' to make a mistake and hurt her...or that...God will punish me by takin' my baby."

Belinda told him then, all about having the abortion years ago. Further, it was as if every bad thing she had ever done poured out of her mouth. As she spoke, she felt heavier and heavier with grief, and everything got very dim. And then, quite surprisingly, a flock of guinea hens came clucking and pecking right across the porch. Belinda had not known her mother had gotten hens.

Winston began to talk about his mistakes, saying he had made some doozies. And then, very clearly, "God knows all we've ever done and are ever gonna do. We aren't any surprise to Him."

Then he was smiling at her and tucking the baby into her arms. "You'll be a fine mother."

"Oh, don't go, Winston." She reached out to grab him, but she missed.

He smiled and said something.

The porch had become very bright again, and the guinea hens were chattering so that she could not quite catch what else Winston was saying. It was something important, though.

"What?"

He paused and smiled at her, and she heard very clearly: "…already forgiven. PS 30, 5. Pass it on."

Quite suddenly, right as she was running after Winston, she came awake.

She had been dreaming. So real that she glanced around, looking for Winston and the baby, and the guinea hens.

The dream lingered. *Doozies. No surprise to God. PS 30, 5.*

What was that? A flight number?

Just then something popped inside her belly. The baby moving, her body moving. A contraction came, hard enough to cause her eyes to open wide.

She checked the clock, picked up her tablet and pen, and noted the time. She got out of the bed and went to the bathroom, and decided to take a quick shower. While she was about this, another contraction came. She peeked from the shower at the clock. Eight minutes.

Out of the shower, she dressed and decided to also put on her makeup. She intended to set a good example for little Desirée Jane right from the beginning. She did not want her daughter to ever be ashamed of her. She also donned the earrings that went so well with her turquoise outfit, pausing to note the time of the next contraction. Nine minutes apart. There was time to tidy up the bathroom.

Just as she took a final check in the mirror, a hard contraction hit her. She looked down with wide eyes to see her belly ripple. Then she checked the clock.

Oh…mercy! Five minutes apart.

Don't panic.

She was ready. She got her purse and was getting her hospital bag when something happened inside her. Water gushed from between her legs.

She looked at the mess for a moment, then grabbed a towel from the laundry and threw it on the puddle. She must be crazy, she thought, yet she simply had to clean up the mess, at the same time grabbing the phone to call Lyle, trying to ignore the voice that wanted to change clothes.

As she listened to the ringing over the line, she stepped out of her wet panties.

Lyle did not answer, and she could not find any panties in the basket of clean laundry.

Taking up her hospital bag in one hand and her purse in the other, she went out the door, waddling to her car in the driveway.

At the moment Lyle's cell phone rang, he and Giff had just seen Andy Smith come running from the alley behind the *Valentine Voice* and take off up Church Street, north past the Cut & Curl.

"Now, that's a runnin' *from,* not *to,* wouldn't you say?" said Giff.

"Yep…yep, I would," said Lyle, forgetting his phone in his observation of the man. He accelerated until he caught up with Andy.

Andy saw the patrol car, and rather than run away from it, he waved and headed toward it, jumping into the backseat even before Lyle got fully braked.

"Don't shoot! I don't have anythin'. Honest." He held up both his hands.

Giff and Lyle looked at each other with puzzled expressions. Neither had touched his gun nor even thought of doing so.

"What's up?" Giff asked Andy.

"Ah…could you guys drive around to the sheriff's office? I'm turnin' myself in. I've got somebody after me, and I'd rather he didn't catch me."

Lyle and Giff looked at each other again.

Lyle said, "You want to see what's goin' on? Belinda just called. I got to call her back."

While he pulled the car to the curb and dialed Belinda, Giff questioned Andy. Lyle halfway listened to the men while he waited for Belinda to answer. Suddenly he realized that Andy did not have his Australian accent.

He looked around at the man, but then heard the voice mail pick up. Belinda had not answered.

"Belinda didn't answer the phone," he said to Giff, with some agitation. "Got to try her cell."

"Uh, fellas…could we move along?" said Andy from the backseat.

Lyle heard Belinda's voice with some relief. "Hey, honey. I'm sorry I missed your call, but we just picked up An—"

"Sugar…listen. I am okay, but—now don't panic—I'm in labor."

"You are?"

"Yes. I'm not talkin' just to hear myself talk. My water broke, Lyle!"

"Okay, honey. Now just stay calm. I'm on my way. You be out front, and I'll pick you up in the squad car." He found himself yelling into the phone as he reached his hand across to shift into gear.

Belinda yelled, "Lyle? Lyle!"

"Yeah?" He was getting all confused, holding the phone and trying to put the car into gear.

"This just happened so fast. I am already headin' for the hospital."

"You are *what?* Wait! I'm comin'…you…*wait!*" he ordered, pointing at the air.

"Well, Lyle, I cannot tell this baby to wait. She is comin', and I am *not* gonna have her in this car! If you want to join me at the hospital, you come on there!"

Belinda snapped the phone closed and threw it on the seat beside her as another contraction swept her.

Gripping the wheel with both hands, she remembered to pant and attempt to relax, as she had been learning in her birthing classes. As the contraction eased, she whispered, "Don't you worry, sweetheart. I'm gettin' you to the hospital. Mama is takin' care of you."

She punched the gas pedal.

Belinda had driven the highway all her life and knew every inch of it, where to slow down and where to go like the wind. Her Chrysler 300 easily passed a large John Deere towing a cotton wagon, and two oil-field pickup trucks in a row.

Just then she heard a siren. In the rearview mirror, she saw a patrol car's lights flashing. Lyle's car, with Lyle at the wheel and all but pushing her bumper.

Her cell phone rang. She managed to answer, hearing, "Lyle says pull over."

It was Giff's voice.

"I do not have any time to waste. Y'all just come soooonnn!" Another contraction. She watched the clock and saw they were barely a minute apart now. There had not been anything about such a rapid progression in any of the information she had read. What she should have paid more attention to was how to slow it all down.

Lyle stayed right on her tail. He was afraid to pass her and end up in a race.

Three cars ahead of Belinda heard the siren and pulled off the road to let them pass. When she reached the edge of town, a city squad car appeared ahead of her, leading the way. They had to increase speed to keep ahead of Belinda.

At the hospital emergency entrance a number of people hanging about turned at the sound of the sirens. They watched a police car, a Chrysler 300 and another police car come racing up. Both squad cars' doors flew open, and policemen hopped out and hurried toward a woman who struggled out of the Chrysler. The onlookers wondered what she might have done, and at least one ducked behind a pillar, in case the woman had a gun.

Lyle reached her first, and Belinda took hold of him. She was then amazed to see Andy Smith right behind Lyle's shoulder.

"What are you…?" But a wave of pain sent her bending over.

Lyle swept Belinda up into his arms. Leaving the other men gaping at him, he strode easily to the double doors. Two men in white coats hurrying through the doors met him with a rolling bed.

★ ★ ★

A bare ten minutes later, with a lot of yelling by almost everyone, little Desirée Jane entered the world, in the hospital, just as her mother had determined.

Her father, unfortunately, saw it all and promptly fainted.

Dr. Zwolle appeared around the curtain.

Belinda sat up in the bed, lipstick refreshed, holding her precious bundle of joy, with Lyle leaning close.

"So I hear you have a fine, healthy baby girl." The doctor, smiling as big as if she were responsible, came forward to admire the baby that Belinda held toward her.

The doctor took the baby carefully and talked to her as foolishly as all adults. Then she handed her back to Belinda. "You had this one easy as pie. You need to have a couple more."

"Maybe so," Lyle said, grinning broadly at Belinda.

Belinda quickly looked down into the face of her angel, running her eyes over her in an intensive search to catch anything wrong that the doctors might have missed.

That evening Belinda was reminded of when John Cole had been in the hospital. At one point, there were fourteen people crowded into her room. Jaydee sat on one side of the end of her bed and Naomi Smith on the other. A short woman with her hair in a braided crown squeezed in, presented Belinda with a lovely wrapped gift and joined in the conversation. Belinda kept trying to recall who the woman might be. After some ten minutes, it was discovered that the woman was really the aunt of the woman in the next room. Vella returned her present before she left.

It soon became apparent that one reason for the crowd in

her room was the curiosity of everyone wanting to talk to Lyle about the bigger story of Andy Smith. Lyle was both a new father and a hero who had helped capture Andy Smith, or saved him, depending on the slant of the story and who was telling it, *and* effected the return of the carousel.

Andy Smith, whose name was really, of all things, Ansel Sullivan, was also heralded as something of a hero, depending on the slant of the story. It turned out that Andy had been part of a gang of nationwide cargo thieves. The FBI had been watching him, until he went into hiding in Valentine. Working with the sheriff and John Cole in secret, Andy had made some calls that located the carousel but had also revealed where he was hiding out, and then the thieves had come after him.

"We didn't capture him," said Lyle. "He about run us down to turn himself in."

"Well, he didn't have any choice but to do that. If you'd had those fellas after you, you would have done the same," said Jaydee. "They saw him and took off after him, and Munro grabbed one by the ankle and Willie Lee grabbed his other leg. Fayrene had just poured my coffee, and she screamed and poured coffee everywhere. Got it on my new shirt." He pointed to his chest. "Then there was all this poundin' from the kitchen. Andy had shut the back door, and Woody hit one of those fellas with a pan."

Everybody started chuckling and putting in remarks. Marilee said she came into the café right in the middle of the whole thing, and Julia said she heard it from next door, where she was delivering a package.

"The sheriff and John Cole knew about Andy a number of days ago," put in Emma. "John Cole can keep a secret."

"I talked to the FBI man a few weeks ago," Vella said. "He

came in the drugstore and just chatted. I knew he was somethin' in the government."

"His ex-wife really wanted him," Tate said. "She was the actual one in charge down t' Dallas, and she sent those two fellas. They were not playin' around."

"So Andy told where the carousel was? Is it…?"

"Well, he only thought…"

"I don't think he…"

"Poor Fayrene. Has anyone talked…?"

No one noticed that Belinda did not say anything. As people talked, she would look up at the faces around her and catch snatches of conversation, but then her gaze and total attention would return to her newborn daughter.

She kept studying the tiny fresh-born face, the delicate curve of her cheek and her velvet-soft skin, the tiny eyebrows, the fringe of imperceptible eyelashes. All the happenings of the previous hours, the mad dash to the hospital and all the excitement of discovering the truth about Andy and the carousel, none of that mattered one whit in the face of the reality of being a mother holding her child.

Several times the nurses came to take the child to the nursery for testing. Belinda had all but gotten up and gone with them. She was the mother, and she was ready to slap people silly at the sound of her baby's cry, which she was certain she could pick out above the others floating the short distance down the hall.

Just then, she carefully laid her Desirée Jane between her legs and loosened the cotton blankets. She got hold of one of the tiny hands, marveling at how small and perfect it was.

The tiny eyes came open, and Belinda gazed into them.

"Look…her eyes are open," someone said.

"Hey, there…"

"Are they blue?"

"Only because she's new…too early to tell for certain."

"Look at all that hair."

"She looks like Belinda."

"I think she favors Lyle."

Belinda looked around to see heads crowding around her own, adults making all manner of foolish faces and noises.

Then her mother's head came pushing up next to Belinda's. "You need to wrap her up—babies like to be swaddled."

Her mother's hands were suddenly there, taking hold of the blankets.

Belinda pushed her mother's hands away and cuddled the baby up close to her neck.

Conversation began again around her.

She could feel her mother's eyes as she rocked Sweetie Pie back and forth.

"I really think you should wrap her up," said her mother. "Here's a new blanket I bought her."

Belinda took the blanket and, with the voices twirling all around her, whispered to her daughter, "Welcome to your world, Sweetie Pie."

They were alone at last. The lights in the hospital room were low. Lyle, sitting on the chair, leaned on the bed, and Belinda bent near, with Sweetie Pie, as they now called her, sleeping peacefully between them. They kept gazing at her, then foolishly grinning at each other.

Belinda said in a low but firm voice, "I have something to tell you."

Lyle's eyebrows went up. His dear face regarded her expectantly.

She took a deep breath and launched in. "I spoke with

Winston. It was a dream, but it really was him. I know. And now I want to tell you…about something. I wish I had been able to tell you a long time ago…."

She told him then. Everything. All about her heartbreak over the abortion, and how ashamed and fearful she had been all the months of carrying Desirée Jane, and on to what she had learned in the dream. When she finished, both she and Lyle were crying.

He reached for her. "I love you, Belinda. There is nothing you can do to change that. I love you and always will."

And Belinda knew clearly in that moment that Lyle was one of the rare ones capable of such unconditional love, and that she was truly blessed by God. She was a woman loved, and more, she was at last a woman who knew how to let herself love.

EPILOGUE

From the Beginning,
We're All Looking for a Happy Ending

THE DAY OF VALENTINE'S CENTENNIAL CELEBRATION arrived. Everyone marveled at the weather—high of seventy-two, faint breeze and a satin-blue cloudless sky.

All over town, those people who had attended several celebration committee meetings six months previously and remembered the arguing that had gone on about changing the date to late spring, said, in so many words, "Winston was right. November is lots better than if we'd waited until next June or July. We would have sweltered."

Belinda dressed her sleeping nine-day-old daughter in a pink outfit with frills and a cap, wrapped her in a pink blanket and put her in her pink-print car seat.

"Looks like an explosion of pink," said Vella, who had come to accompany Belinda and the baby to the park. Lyle had been gone since early morning, preparing for security and crowd control.

"Oh…let me get some pictures. And of you, too." Vella positioned Belinda. "I want to send some to my friend Gérard over in France."

Belinda smiled proudly for quite a few flashes. Then, "Okay, come on. I want to get there before Sweetie Pie wakes up and needs feedin'. Mama, you bring the stroller."

"I am *Big Mama,*" said her mother pointedly.

When Belinda headed toward Main Street, instead of the park, Vella asked her where she was going.

"To see if I can get Fayrene to come to the celebration," Belinda said. "Woody said he could not get her to go."

"Uh-huh. And why should you be able to do it?"

"I don't know, Mama."

Belinda parked in front of the café. There were only three other cars parked on the street, although there was quite a bit of traffic going in the direction of the park. Leaving her mother in the car with the baby, Belinda hurried into the café.

The café was empty of customers. Carlos and Luwanna sat at the counter, chatting.

"Fayrene's upstairs," Luwanna told her, pointing with a curious expression.

Belinda mounted the stairs. She had only been up to Fayrene's apartment one time, and that long ago. She called out, "Fayrene…it's Belinda."

Fayrene met Belinda in what appeared to be a small living room decorated so as to make Belinda feel she was stepping back in time to the seventies. No wonder Fayrene wore that awful blue eye shadow.

"What is it?" asked Fayrene. Her skinny body was all

tight, and her eyes were red, and she had a wadded tissue in her hand.

"I want you to come join us at the centennial celebration."

Fayrene's eyes widened, and then she turned her back. "That's very nice of you, but I'm busy today. I have a café to run." She sat and started putting on shoes.

"Oh, come on, Fayrene. Luwanna and Carlos can handle it for a few hours. It isn't like there's any customers downstairs. Why should people come in, when they can get free barbecue and Coca-Cola out at the park? We've closed the drugstore for the whole afternoon."

"I don't want to go…and with the drugstore closed, the café definitely needs to stay open." She jerked her shoelaces.

Belinda looked down on the top of Fayrene's head, seeing the outgrowth of gray hair at the crown.

"Are you gonna stay holed up in this café for the rest of your life? So, you made a little mistake about Andy. Things could have been a lot worse. Let it go and get on with your life."

"I feel like such a fool. Everybody is sayin', 'Fayrene lost another one.' 'She falls for everything in pants.' You think I don't know how you and everyone else has made fun of me forever? You just wouldn't know how it feels to always make mistakes with men. You're just always so certain about everything."

Fayrene finished tying her shoes and stood. Belinda found she had to look up at her.

"Just 'cause I know how to appear not to make mistakes doesn't mean I don't make them," Belinda returned in a similar bitter tone.

Seconds of tense silence ticked by.

Then, grabbing patience, "Oh, Fayrene, every woman alive

has made mistakes with men, and every man with women. Every one of us makes all sorts of amazingly foolish mistakes. But that's just how life is. And I say again, things could have been worse. You could have lost all your money and the café."

"I know, and it terrifies me. *It's all I've got.*"

Fayrene's voice dropped so low with the last that Belinda only faintly heard the words. But she heard clearly the pain, and it unnerved her so much that she said the silliest thing.

"All you lost was a bit of pride, Fayrene. But you gained so much more. You did get your books all caught up-to-date."

Fayrene shook her head.

Belinda thought hard. "Sugar, when you think about it, Andy took refuge here. That says somethin' good about you. You did a good thing. You pretty much showed him a better way of life, and saved him until he was willin' to give himself up to witness protection. By what you did, you also probably saved our carousel. It really was all part of a larger plan."

Belinda was surprised at this idea popping into her mind. It was a very good argument.

Fayrene glanced up with a sigh. "Well, good ol' Fayrene. She gives men a place to rest and hide. I've been doin' that all my life."

Then, frowning, she asked, "And what do *you* care, anyway?"

"Lord a'mercy, I don't know, but I *do*. We've known each other for as long as I can remember. And what would Lyle and I do without the café's steaks and raisin pie? Who else in the world ever even heard of raisin pie? You think this café is all you have? Look, you and this café together are a part of this town, Fayrene. You have lots of friends who care about you—people depending on you to keep a halfway balanced state of mind. Now, go fix your makeup and come on with me and let them prove it."

Fayrene pressed her lips together.

"Come on, Fayrene. You can sit with me and Oran…. Oran could use some cheerin' up. You are not the only one with problems, you know."

Fayrene took a breath, then headed toward the bathroom. "What's wrong with Oran?"

"Oh, you know, he gets those blue moods. It's his war stuff actin' up. We all got to cheer him up."

As she watched Fayrene touch up her face, she thought that her next project was going to be to get Fayrene to lay off the blue eye shadow.

The stone-and-steel arch over the entry said Centennial Park and would for the next hundred years. To change the sign to read Winston Valentine Centennial Park would have required a brand-new purchase, and everyone agreed this was a foolish expenditure.

"I don't know what they are goin' to call the park after a hundred years," said Belinda, who became disgruntled all over again about the matter as she drove beneath the sign, following a string of vehicles ahead of her.

Larry Joe Darnell was on parking duty. He waved her to a stop. "There's a parkin' space saved for y'all up by the carousel building. Got your name posted." While bending to look in the window, he remained several feet from the car; likely he would never forget Belinda hitting him with a newspaper.

In an effort to make up, Belinda blew him a kiss. Turning the wheel, she cut away from the line of traffic and took the curve toward the carousel building. Some distance down from the building, but at the curb, an empty space between the mayor's and Jaydee's cars appeared with a post and a sign reading: Blaine. Fayrene jumped out to move the sign, and Belinda pulled in to park.

The women piled out of the car and began gathering the baby and all the necessary paraphernalia. Belinda loaded Fayrene down with lawn chairs and a picnic box. Just then Oran appeared.

"Let me help you ladies."

Oran and Fayrene went on ahead, leaving Belinda getting Sweetie Pie and her car seat attached to the stroller, with her mother offering safety tips, as if Belinda had not already done it half a dozen times.

Belinda started the stroller along the sidewalk toward the large blue awning with the Blaine's Drugstore banner.

Suddenly, as she passed two large cedar trees, the carousel building came into full view.

It was the first time she laid eyes on the totally completed building, which now had a large sign curved over the front opening. Colorful and ornate, it read: The Winston Valentine Centennial Carousel.

Belinda stopped and stared. "Mama…"

"Surprise," said Vella brightly.

Belinda's gaze traced over the sign again, then downward to see the doors fully opened, revealing the carousel, with children climbing over a single wild wooden horse.

"All the carousel people had time to put on the carousel was that one horse," said Vella, linking her arm through Belinda's. "Come see the rest."

The rest were photographs of Valentine down through the years, all from Winston's and Vella's collections, adorning the inner walls of the curved building.

And then a bronze plaque that read:

This building given by Vella and Belinda Blaine,
in honor of their neighbor, friend and originator of
the Centennial Carousel, Winston Valentine.

His motto: Psalm 30:5
For His anger is but for a moment, His favor is for life;
Weeping may endure for a night, but a shout of *joy*
comes in the morning.

A shiver passed over Belinda as she read the plaque. "Oh, Mama, it is *wonderful*."

"It is, isn't it?" said Vella in a highly satisfied tone. "Charlene was talkin' the other day about how she had ordered Winston's headstone with Psalm Thirty, verse five printed on it, so I decided to note it here. I think Winston would like it—you know he said that verse a lot." Then, "We got to talkin' about it the other day in the store. You know why he said that?"

Belinda shook her head as she wiped away tears.

"A long time ago, couple of years after the war, Winston was thirty-eight or -nine, he ran over George Showalter's little girl. Killed her. Right in the Showalters' driveway, as he was backin' out."

"Oh my God." A hard shiver ran through Belinda, and she clutched the baby's stroller tight.

Vella nodded. "It was an awful time. He and George were runnin' moonshine—Oklahoma was still a dry state then, you know, clear into the fifties, and Winston, and a whole lot of people, made a lot of money runnin' booze in from Texas. He and George had both been out all night, drinkin' and carryin' on, and not payin' attention. Winston was so broken up over what happened that he carried on even more for years. He told me one day that Psalm 30 had helped him, that his life had been like that."

Taking hold of Belinda's arm, Vella directed them along the sidewalk toward the large awning. "We got a tent all set up—a comfort station for mothers of young children, lots of complimentary products from the store…."

"Mama…I dreamed of Winston the day Sweetie Pie was born." Belinda squinted and stuck on her sunglasses. She had to wipe away more tears that seemed to keep coming.

"You did?"

"Uh-huh. And I don't think it was just a dream."

"Ah-huh."

"I think Winston was really there, talkin' to me. He said, 'PS 30, 5,' and I thought he was maybe mentionin' a schedule or a date. But I see now it was the Psalm, and I guess I need to read it. I think he was tellin' me to forgive myself."

"What for, sugar?"

"Oh, I'll tell you the whole thing later," Belinda said as she saw Jaydee approaching with long strides.

"Hey, Belinda…hey, darlin'," said Jaydee, taking Vella by the hand. "Come on over here. Reba is askin' for you."

"Oh! All right! Sugar…you and the baby check out the mothers' comfort station," Vella threw over her shoulder as she raced off with Jaydee.

Belinda pushed the stroller leisurely along the sidewalk. At the drugstore awning, she found Oran and Fayrene sitting next to each other, and talking about the various photographs of the town and citizens that hung front and back on partitions. Belinda chatted with them and others who stopped in to get a look at the new baby, and to reminisce about old times.

Then Lyle joined them, and together they pushed Sweetie Pie, viewed photographs set up in other awnings and tents and visited with their neighbors—and strangers, too—talking about years past and years still to come.

"Valentine is a good place to raise a family," Lyle said so many times to so many strangers that Belinda finally told him to stop it.

"Sugar, if all those people you have been invitin' to move here actually do, Valentine will not be a nice little town anymore."

The *Valentine Voice* Sunday edition carried full coverage of the centennial celebration in photographs. The entire run of papers for that week sold out, with everyone sticking the copies away to have for the next hundred years' celebration.

A week later, Fayrene Gardner and Oran Lackey got married. Belinda and Lyle stood up with them. Sometime later the couple bought the house across the street from Belinda. In later years, Sweetie Pie took up saying, "Mamaw Fayrene and Poppy Oran." It was twenty years before Belinda got Fayrene to give up the blue eye shadow.

Within the following month, Jim Rainwater joined Everett as cohost of the *Wake Up* show. Everyone was surprised at how clever and funny he could be. Within eighteen months, Jim had been lured away by a Dallas rock station, but the lifestyle and pressure so unnerved him that he was back home in six months.

Paris Miller lived with Belinda and Lyle for the next seven years, all the way through the hard struggle of college, which had been extended because she decided to get a degree in business law. By the time she came home to Valentine to take a top position in the Berry Corporation, she had become an ultra-conservative, wearing her amazingly beautiful brown hair in a soft blunt cut, only one pair of stud earrings in each ear and Ann Taylor suits. She bought her own home and did not marry until she was thirty-five. Her husband, an Air Force pilot, died while on a secret mission in Afghanistan. She never remarried, although one day she caught a boy trying to steal her car. She smacked him, took him home, made him take the earrings out of his ears and gave him a home until he graduated from law school, paid for by Paris.

Julia Jenkins-Tinsley and her husband, Juice, lived happily in their side-by-side houses for another twenty-five years, until Julia's death while jogging. Julia's house then sold to a widow, whom Juice married.

Inez and Norman Cooper joined a dance club and took trophies in competitions from Oklahoma to Atlanta. When Inez modernized their house, they added on a studio and ran a dance school. Several of their young students went on to appear and win on the *So You Think You Can Dance* television show. Norman continued to secretly smoke cigarettes and Inez continued to pretend she did not know.

John Cole Berry served on the Valentine city council, and was mayor twice. Emma Berry became a volunteer at the hospital. She made encouraging get-well and comfort cards, and advised many an anxious woman waiting with a husband having bypass surgery. Eventually, in collaboration with Naomi

Smith, Emma wrote and illustrated a small booklet of tips for families of patients undergoing surgeries, and had it published and distributed throughout the hospitals of several counties.

Little Gabby Smith went away to Rice University and became a much respected and quoted anthropologist, although in physical stature she remained petite, a half inch shorter than Willie Lee's adult height of five foot four inches. She and Willie Lee married, and the two of them traveled extensively in connection with Gabby's research, speaking and teaching. Everywhere they went, even on airplanes, they were accompanied by Munro. The story was told that the dog was with Willie Lee until the day he died an old man, then disappeared.

Corrine Pendley married Larry Joe Darnell the day after her high-school graduation, when barely eighteen years old. At the age of thirty-five, Corrine returned to school to earn a degree in special education; she taught in the Valentine schools for twenty-five years. She and Larry Joe bought one of the large, graceful houses at the edge of town, about halfway between the Holloway home and Larry Joe's parents' ranch. It had a wide expanse of lawn always filled with happy children. Often she and her aunt Marilee and her mother-in-law, Charlene, sat on the front porch with glasses of cold sweet tea. Other women would drive by, see them and stop in.

Corrine and Larry Joe were married for sixty-five years, had four children, eleven grandchildren and eight great-grandchildren. Corrine only spent two nights away from Larry Joe during her entire married life, and except for one trip to Baton Rouge, for her mother's funeral, she never went farther than thirty miles from Valentine. Corrine was as content as she had known she would be.

Vella Blaine became an Oklahoma congresswoman. Jaydee threw himself into being "the congresswoman's husband." After fifteen years together, Jaydee died, very unexpectedly but happily in Vella's arms. She had caught him as he had hoped.

While cleaning out his belongings, Vella found a journal that Jaydee had kept for decades, recording secrets of people's lives that he had learned as an attorney and then in their years in politics. She set out to write the story of Valentine, and ended up writing a book about half the state.

Belinda, who had never thought she would be a mother, found deep fulfillment in the role. She and Lyle had two more children after Sweetie Pie, a boy and then a girl. In addition to these, after Paris moved out, they took in three foster children over the years.

And between motherhood and running the drugstore, and having more and more people come to her for advice than to her aging mother, Belinda better appreciated what her own mother had gone through in the early years. And she became very close to her mother.

Belinda and Lyle's son grew up and joined the Army and had a twenty-year career in the military police, eventually retiring and joining the Valentine sheriff's department, under his father, who became sheriff.

Belinda's daughters came to work in the drugstore. Very often, the three generations of women were gathered, hollering back and fourth over the shelves and partitions. Belinda found herself saying to her daughters, and to the audience of her *About Town and Beyond* radio program, many of the same things that her mother had said to her.

She thought of this and laughed some nights, when, after the death of her mother, she told the girls good-night at the drugstore and drove home alone through the twilight.

Often on pleasant late afternoons, she would detour to Centennial Park and past the Winston Valentine Centennial Carousel. As she watched mothers and children ride the carousel, she would remember how for many years she had brought her own children to ride it, and then her grandchildren, and how she told them all again and again the stories of the carousel's beginners.

Sometimes as she aged, Belinda would ride the carousel alone.

Without fail she would note children and grandchildren and even great-grandchildren of people she knew.

"Oh, Winston," she would say, "I hope you know what you left behind behind."

Over the years, strangers would come to town, often in the early hours of the morning, either walking or driving in from the west highway. These strangers either kept on going, or took jobs and stayed awhile. Each had his own story; many did not tell it. At least two spoke privately to Fayrene, one saying Anton in Chicago said to ask her for a job, and another saying it was a man named Arthur in Las Vegas. If Fayrene could not give them a job, she sent them to the drugstore or the newspaper or the feed and grain.

More than one of these strangers over the years reported having thought they saw, from a distance down the highway, in the early dark hour before dawn, the carousel going with lights and music. When each man got up close to the park, however, dawn would be about to break, and the carousel building was dark, silent and locked. This strange and delicious tale was told and retold. Kids very often snuck out of bedrooms after dark and tried to stay awake all night to see the carousel go on its own. Some kids swore they saw it. Quite a few fell asleep under trees and bushes trying.

Everyone was teasing, of course, but it made for a good tale to say that, in the early hours, Winston Valentine liked to ride his carousel. That was one old story that never died, a hundred years after he was gone.

USA TODAY BESTSELLING AUTHOR

Curtiss Ann Matlock

Chin Up, Honey

It takes a lot of work to plan a wedding—and even more to save a marriage. But in Valentine, Oklahoma, there's always someone to help you keep your chin up.

Emma Cole's son is getting married, and she's determined to make everything perfect—even if that means asking her estranged husband to come home and pretend they're still together. Now he wants a second chance.

As the wedding approaches, the many meanings of love, commitment and happiness capture the hearts of folks in town. And, surrounded by the warmth and spirit of her neighbors, Emma starts to see new beginnings instead of endings.

Available wherever books are sold.

MIRA®

www.MIRABooks.com

MCAM2558TR